William Roscoe

The Life of Lorenzo De' Medici - the Magnificent

Volume II

William Roscoe

The Life of Lorenzo De' Medici - the Magnificent
Volume II

ISBN/EAN: 9783742895240

Manufactured in Europe, USA, Canada, Australia, Japa

Cover: Foto ©Raphael Reischuk / pixelio.de

Manufactured and distributed by brebook publishing software
(www.brebook.com)

William Roscoe

The Life of Lorenzo De' Medici - the Magnificent

THE

LIFE

OF

LORENZO DE' MEDICI,

CALLED

THE MAGNIFICENT.

BY WILLIAM ROSCOE.

VOL. II.

BASIL:

Printed and ſold by J. J. TOURNEISEN.

MDCCXCIX.

CHAP. VI.

LORENZO endeavours to secure the peace of Italy—Rise of the modern idea of the balance of power—Conspiracy of Frescobaldi—Expulsion of the Turks from Otranto—The Venetians and the pope attack the duke of Ferrara—Lorenzo undertakes his defence—The Florentines and Neapolitans ravage the papal territories—The duke of Calabria defeated by Roberto Malatesta—Progress of the Venetian arms—Sixtus deserts and excommunicates his allies—Congress of Cremona—Death of Sixtus IV.—Succeeded by Giambattista Cibò, who assumes the name of Innocent VIII.—Lorenzo gains the confidence of the new pope—The Florentines attempt to recover the town of Sarzana—Capture of Pietra-Santa—Lorenzo retires to the baths of S. Filippo—The pope forms the design of possessing himself of the kingdom of Naples—Lorenzo supports the king—Prevails upon the Florentines to take a decided part—Effects a reconciliation between the king and the pope—Suppresses the insurrection at Osimo—Capture of Sarzana—Lorenzo protects the smaller states of Italy—The king of Naples infringes his treaty with the pope—Peace again restored—Review of the government of Florence—Regulations introduced by Lorenzo—Prosperity of the Florentine state—High reputation of Lorenzo—General tranquillity of Italy.

SOON after the termination of hostilities between Sixtus IV. and the republic of Florence, Lorenzo began to unfold those comprehensive plans for ſecuring the peace of Italy on a permanent foundation, which confer the higheſt honor on his political life. Of the extenſive authority which he had obtained by his late conduct, every day afforded additional proof; and it appears to have been his intention to employ it for the wiſeſt and moſt ſalutary purpoſes. By whatever motives he was led to this great attempt, he purſued it with deep policy and unceaſing aſſiduity; and finally experienced a degree of ſucceſs equal to his warmeſt expectations.

The ſituation of Italy at this period afforded an ample field for the exerciſe of political talents. The number of independent ſtates of which it was compoſed, the inequality of their ſtrength, the ambitious views of ſome, and the ever active fears of others, kept the whole country in continual agitation and alarm. The vicinity of theſe ſtates to each other, and the narrow bounds of their reſpective dominions, required a promptitude of deciſion in caſes of diſagreement, unexampled in any ſubſequent period of modern hiſtory. Where the event of open war ſeemed doubtful, private treachery was without ſcruple reſorted to; and where that failed of ſucceſs, an appeal was again made to arms. The pontifical ſee had itſelf ſet the example of a mode of conduct that burſt aſunder all the bonds of ſociety, and operated as a convincing proof that nothing was thought unlawful which appeared to be expedient. To counterpoiſe all the jarring intereſts of theſe different governments, to reſtrain the powerful, to ſuccour the weak, and to unite the whole in one firm body, so as to enable them, on the one hand, successfully to oppose the formidable power of the Turks, and, on the other, to repel the incursions of the French and the Germans, both of whom were objects of terror to the less warlike inhabitants of Italy, were the important ends which Lorenzo proposed to accomplish. The effectual defence of the Florentine dominions against the encroachments of their more powerful neighbours, though perhaps his chief inducement for engaging in so extensive a project, appeared in the execution of it, rather as a necessary part of his system, than as the principal object which he had in view. In these transactions we may trace the first decisive instance of that political arrangement, which was more fully developed and more widely extended in the succeeding century, and which has since been denominated the balance of power. Casual alliances, arising from consanguinity, from personal attachment, from vicinity, or from interest, had indeed frequently subsisted among the Italian states; but these were only partial and temporary engagements, and rather tended to divide the country into two or more powerful parties, than to counterpoise the interests of individual governments, so as to produce in the result the general tranquillity(*a*).

(*a*) It is commonly understood that the idea of a systematic arrangement, for securing to states, within the same sphere of political action, the possession of their respective territories, and the continuance of existing rights, is of modern origin, having arisen among the Italian states in the fifteenth century. *Robertson's Hist. of Cha.* V, v. i. *sec.* 2.

But before Lorenzo engaged in these momentous undertakings, he had further personal dangers to encounter. The moderation of his conduct could neither extinguish nor allay the insatiable spirit of

But Mr. Hume has attempted to show that this system, if not theoretically understood, was at least practically adopted by the ancient states of Greece and the neighbouring governments. *Essays*, *v.* i. *part.* ii. *Essay* 7. In adjusting the extent to which these opinions may be adopted, there is no great difficulty. Wherever mankind have formed themselves into societies, (and history affords no instance of their being found in any other state,) the conduct of a tribe, or a nation, has been marked by a general will; and states, like individuals, have had their antipathies and predilections, their jealousies, and their fears. The powerful have endeavoured to oppress the weak, and the weak have sought refuge from the powerful in their mutual union. Notwithstanding the great degree of civilization that obtained among the Grecian states, their political conduct seems to have been directed upon no higher principle; conquests were pursued as opportunity offered, and precautions for safety were delayed till the hour of danger arrived. The preponderating mass of the Roman republic attracted into its vortex whatever was opposed to its influence; and the violent commotions of the middle ages, by which that immense body was again broken into new forms, and impelled in vague and eccentric directions, postponed to a late period the possibility of regulated action. The transactions in Italy, during the fourteenth and fifteenth centuries, bear indeed a strong resemblance to those which took place among the Grecian states; but it was not till nearly the close of the latter century, that a system of general security and pacification was clearly developed, and precautions taken for insuring its continuance. Simple as this idea may now appear, yet it must be considered, that, before the adoption of it, the minds of men, and consequently the maxims of states, must have undergone an important change: views of aggrandizement were to be repressed; war was to be prosecuted, not for the purpose of conquest, but of security; and above all, an eye was to be found that could discern, and a mind that could comprehend so extended an object.

revenge that burnt in the breaſt of Girolamo Riario. Defeated in his ambitious projects by the ſuperior talents of Lorenzo, he once more had recourſe to his treacherous practices; and, by an intercourſe with ſome of the Florentine exiles, again found, even in Florence, the inſtruments of his purpoſe. By their inſtigation Battiſta Freſcobaldi, with only two aſſiſtants, undertook to aſſaſſinate Lorenzo in the church of the Carmeli, on the day of Aſcenſion, being the laſt day of may, 1481. This attempt was not conducted with the ſame ſecrecy as that which we have before ralated. The friends of Lorenzo were watchful for his ſafety. Freſcobaldi was ſeized, and having upon his examination diſcloſed his accomplices, was executed with them on the 6th day of the following month (a) The treachery of Freſcobaldi occaſioned at Florence general ſurpriſe, and was almoſt regarded as an inſtance of inſanity. He had been the conſul of the Florentine republic at Pera, and it was at his inſtance that Bandini, the murderer of Giuliano, had been delivered up by Mahomet II. Yet neither the atrociouſneſs of the crime, nor the dread of the example, deterred him from a ſimilar enterpriſe. From this circumſtance Lorenzo perceived the neceſſity of being more diligently on his guard againſt the attempts of his profligate antagoniſts; and whilſt he lamented the depravity of the times, that rendered ſuch a precaution neceſſary, he was generally ſurrounded, when he appeared in public,

(a) The other conſpirators were Filippo Balducci, and Amoretto, the illegitimate ſon of Guido Baldovinetti. *v. Ammir. lib.* 25.

by a number of tried friends and adherents. In this respect he has not however escaped censure, although from a quarter where it should have been silenced by the sense of decency, if not by the feelings of gratitude. The kindness shown by him to Raffaello Maffei the brother of Antonio, who, in the conspiracy of the Pazzi, had undertaken to be the immediate instrument of his destruction, has before been noticed (*a*). In return for such unmerited attention, this historian has availed himself of a measure which was rendered necessary by repeated instances of treachery, to represent Lorenzo as a gloomy tyrant, who supported his authority, and secured his safety in Florence, by the aid of a band of ruffians, and who found in music alone a solace from his anxiety (*b*). The reputation of Lorenzo is not however likely to suffer more from the pen of one brother, than his person did from the dagger of the other.

On the conclusion of the contest with the papal see, the first object not only of Lorenzo, but of all the Italian potentates, was the expulsion of the Turks from Otranto. For this purpose a league was concluded, to which the Venetians only refused to

(*a*) *Vol.* i. *p.* 212.

(*b*) "Post hæc Laurentius defunctus periculo, resipiscere paulatim, "majoreque postmodum apud suos cives esse auctoritate, ac Tyranno "propius agitare; cum sicariis incedere, excubiis ac nunciis diligen-"tius invigilare, denique amissas in bello facultates undecunque "recuperare cœpit. Vir aspectu tristi, ore truculento, sermone "ingratus, animo factiosus, in curis agitans continuo præter unum "musicæ solatium." *Raph. Volt. Com. Urb. p.* 153.

accede. Suspicions had already been entertained that Mahomet II. had been incited to his enterprise by the representations of that state; and these suspicions were strengthened by the indifference which the Venetians manifested on so alarming an occasion. It is however probable, that they kept aloof from the contest, merely for the purpose of availing themselves of any opportunity of aggrandizement, which the exhausted situation of the neighbouring states might afford. With the powers of Italy, the kings of Aragon, of Portugal, and of Hungary united their arms. The city of Otranto was attacked by a formidable army under the command of the duke of Calabria; whilst the united fleets of the king of Naples, the pope, and the Genoese were stationed to prevent the arrival of further aid to the besieged. The place was however defended with great courage, and the event yet remained doubtful, when intelligence was received of the death of the emperor Mahomet II. who had established the seat of the Turkish empire at Constantinople, and been the scourge of Christendom for nearly half a century. Upon his death, a disagreement arose between his two sons Bajazet and Zizim; in consequence of which, the Turkish troops destined to the relief of Otranto were recalled, and the place was left to its fate. A capitulation was concluded on the tenth day of September 1481, by which the Turks stipulated for a free return to their native country; but the duke of Calabria, on the surrender of the city, found a pretext for eluding the treaty, and retained as prisoners about fifteen hundred Turks, whom he afterwards employed in the different wars in which he was engaged (*a*).

Whilſt the other ſtates of Italy were thus engaged in the common cauſe, the Venetians had been deviſing means for poſſeſſing themſelves of the dominions of Ercole d'Eſte, duke of Ferrara, and by the aſſiſtance of Girolamo Riario, had prevailed upon the pope to countenance their pretenſions. The duke had married the daughter of Ferdinand, king of Naples; an alliance, which as it contributed to his credit and independence, had given great diſſatisfaction to the Venetians. The firſt aggreſſion was the erection of a fortreſs by thoſe haughty republicans, on a part of the territory of Ferrara, which they pretended was within the limits of their own dominions. An embaſſy was immediately diſpatched by the duke to Venice, to avert, if poſſible, the hoſtile intentions of the ſenate, and to conciliate their good-will by the faireſt repreſentations, and the fulleſt profeſſions of amity. Finding his efforts ineffectual, the duke reſorted for ſuccour to the pope; but Sixtus was already apprized of the part he had to act, and whilſt he heard his ſolicitations with apparent indifference, was ſecretly preparing to join in his ruin. The motives by which Sixtus was actuated are not difficult to be diſcovered. If the family of Eſte could be deprived of their dominions, many circumſtances concurred to juſtify the pretenſions of the papal ſee to the ſovereignty of Ferrara. That city was itſelf ranked among thoſe over which the

(*a*) *Murat. Ann.* v. ix. *p.* 537.

pontiffs asserted a signorial claim, which lay dormant, or was revived, as circumstances required; and although Sixtus could not singly contend with the Venetians in the division of the spoil, yet he well knew that the rest of Italy would interpose, to prevent their possessing themselves of a territory which would add so considerably to their power. In the contest therefore which he supposed must necessarily take place, Sixtus was not without hopes of vesting the government of Ferrara in his own family, in the person of Girolamo Riario, who was indefatigable in preparing for the approaching war.

In this exigency, the duke of Ferrara had two powerful resources. One of these was in the support which he derived from his father-in-law the king of Naples; and the other in the claims which he had upon the known justice of Lorenzo de' Medici. Neither of these disappointed his hopes. By the interference of Lorenzo, the duke of Milan joined in the league; and the marquis of Mantua, and Giovanni Bentivoglio, also became auxiliaries in the cause. The command of the allied army was intrusted to Federigo, duke of Urbino; but the preparation and direction of the war chiefly rested on Lorenzo de' Medici, on whose activity and prudence the allied powers had the most perfect reliance (*a*).

The first object of the allies was to discover the

(*a*) Fabroni has preserved a letter from the duke of Urbino to Lorenzo de' Medici, which sufficiently shows the confidence that was reposed in him by the allies, and the active part which he took in preparing for the contest. *v. App. No.* XLIII.

intentions of the pope. No ſooner had the Venetians commenced their attack on the territory of Ferrara, than a formal requeſt was made to Sixtus, to permit the duke of Calabria, with a body of Neapolitan troops, to paſs through his dominions. His refuſal ſufficiently diſcovered the motives by which he was actuated. The duke immediately entered in a hoſtile manner the territories of the church, and having poſſeſſed himſelf of Terracina, Trevi, and other places, proceeded without interruption till he arrived within forty miles of Rome. At the ſame time the Florentine troops attacked and captured Caſtello, which was reſtored to Nicolo Vitelli, its former lord. By theſe unexpected and vigorous meaſures, Sixtus, inſtead of joining the Venetians, was compelled to ſolicit their aſſiſtance for his own protection. The duke had approached ſo near to Rome, that his advanced parties daily committed hoſtilities at the very gates of the city. In this emergency, the pope had the good fortune to prevail upon Roberto Malateſta, lord of Rimini, to take upon him the command of his army. This celebrated leader, who was then in the pay of the Venetians, on obtaining their permiſſion to aſſiſt their ally, proceeded to Rome. Having there made the neceſſary arrangements, Roberto led out the papal troops, which were ſufficiently numerous, and were only in need of an able general effectually to oppoſe their enemies. The duke of Calabria, being in daily expectation of a reinforcement under the command of his brother Federigo, would gladly have avoided an engagement, but his adverſary preſſed him ſo vigorouſly, that he was compelled either to riſque the event of a battle, or to incur the ſtill greater danger of a diſorderly retreat. This engagement, we are aſſured by Machiavelli, was the moſt obſtinate and bloody that had occurred in Italy during the ſpace of fifty years (*a*). After a ſtruggle of ſix hours, the conteſt terminated in the total defeat of the duke, who owed his liberty or his life, to the fidelity and courage of his Turkiſh followers. Having thus delivered the pope from the eminent danger that threatened him, Roberto returned to Rome to enjoy the honors of his victory; but his triumph was of ſhort duration, for a few days after his arrival he ſuddenly died, not without giving riſe to a ſuſpicion, that poiſon had been adminiſtered to him by the intervention of Girolamo Riario (*b*). This ſuſpicion received confirmation in the public opinion, by the ſubſequent conduct of Sixtus and his kinſman. No ſooner was Roberto dead, than the pope erected an equeſtrian ſtatue to his memory; and Riario proceeded with the army which Roberto had lately led to victory, to diſpoſſeſs his illegitimate

(*a*) " E ſu queſta giornata combattuta con più virtù, che alcun " altra che fuſſe ſtata fatta in cinquanta anni in Italia; perchè vi morì " tra l'una parte e l'altra più che mille uomini." *Mac. Hiſt. lib.* 8.

(*b*) Gli ſcrittori dicono che fu ſoſpetto che egli foſſe morto di veleno, & io nelle notizie private di Malateſti ritrovo, che l'autore di tanta ſceleratezza fu creduto eſſere ſtato il conte Girolamo, nipote del papa, o per invidia, o pure con ſperanza di poter metter le mani a quello ſtato, non laſciando Ruberto figliuoli leggitimi.

Ammir, lib. 25.

fon Pandolfo, to whom he had bequeathed his poffeffions, of the city of Rimini (*a*). In this attempt the ecclefiaftical plunderers would probably have been fuccefsful, had not the vigorous interference of Lorenzo de' Medici, to whom Pandolfo reforted for fuccour, and who fent a body of Florentine troops to his fpeedy relief, fruftrated their profligate purpofe. Riario then turned his arms towards Caftello, which was courageoufly defended by Vitelli, till the Florentines once more gave him effectual aid. A fimilar attack, and with fimilar fuccefs, was about the fame time made by Sixtus on the city of Pefaro, the dominion of Conftantino Sforza; who having firft engaged in the league againft the Venetians, afterwards deferted his allies, and entered into their fervice, and was fuppofed to have died of grief becaufe they had defrauded him of his ftipulated pay (*b*).

Whilft Sixtus was thus employed in defending his own dominions, or in attempting to feize upon thofe of his neighbours, the duke of Urbino had oppofed himfelf to the Venetian army; but not with fufficient effect to prevent its making an alarming progrefs, and capturing feveral towns in the territory of Ferrara. The death of that general (*c*),

(*a*) *Mac. Hift. lib.* 8.

(*b*) " Conftantinus Sforzia Pifauri princeps fidus antea Florentinis, " durante adhuc ftipendio, defecit ad Venetos. Neque multos poft " dies, tertiana febri correptus, mœroré ut creditur violatæ fidei, & " a Venetis pacti non foluti ftipendii V. Kal. Sextilis interiit. ".

Fontius in Annal. ap. Fabr. ii. *p.* 235.

(*c*) The duke of Urbino and Roberto Malatefta died on the fame day; one at Bologna, the other at Rome; each of them, although at

and the ſickneſs of the duke of Ferrara, which rendered him incapable of attending with vigor to the defence of his dominions, opened to the Venetians the fulleſt proſpect of ſucceſs. This ſudden progreſs of the republican arms was not however agreeable to the pope; who, having given no aid in the conteſt, began to be apprehenſive that he could claim no ſhare in the ſpoil, whilſt ſo conſiderable an acceſſion of power to the Venetians might ſcarcely be conſiſtent with his own ſafety. At the ſame time he perceived a ſtorm gathering againſt him from another quarter. The emperor had threatened to call together a general council of the church; a meaſure either originating with or promoted by Lorenzo de' Medici; and for the effecting of which he had diſpatched Baccio Ugolino to Baſil (*a*). Induced by theſe various conſiderations, Sixtus was at length prevailed upon to detach himſelf

the head of adverſe armies, having recommended to the other the protection of his poſſeſſions and ſurviving family: "A di 12 di "Settembre, 1482, ci fu nuove ch'il Magnifico Roberto de Rimini era "morto a Roma di fluſſo. Stimaſi ſia ſtato avvelenato. El duca "d'Urbino era morto in Bologna, che era andato al ſoccorſo di "Ferrara. Morirono in un di, e ciaſcuno di loro mandava a rac- "comandare all' altro il ſuo ſtato, e l'uno non ſeppe la morte dell' "altro." *Ex Diario Allegretti ap. Fabr. v.* ii. *p.* 245.

(*a*) Ugolino tranſmitted to Lorenzo, from time to time, a full account of his proceedings in ſeveral letters which are publiſhed by Fabroni, *in vitâ Laur. v.* ii. 227. From which it appears, that he was not without hopes of accompliſhing his important object. "Non "& non domandate," ſays he, "come queſti dottori della Univerſità "leggano con fervore le ſcripture che io ho pubblicate qui in Conſilio. "Che più? Il papa è più inviſo qui che coſtì, & ſe l'Imperatore non "ce la macchia, non ſum ſine ſpe di far qualcoſa."

from the Venetians, and to liſten to propoſitions for a ſeparate peace. Under the ſanction of the imperial ambaſſador, a league was concluded at Rome for five years, between the pope, the king of Naples, the duke of Milan, and the Florentines, for the defence of the duke of Ferrara. Sixtus, having engaged in the common cauſe, was not inactive. Having firſt warned the Venetians to deſiſt from the further progreſs of the war, and finding his remonſtrances diſregarded, he ſolemnly excommunicated his late allies (*a*). The Venetians however perſiſted in their purpoſe, regardleſs of his denunciations, and having captured the town of Ficarola, laid ſiege to the city of Ferrara itſelf.

At this important juncture a congreſs was held at Cremona, for the purpoſe of conſidering on the moſt effectual means of repreſſing the growing power of the Venetians, and of ſecuring the reſt of Italy from the effects of their ambition. The perſons who aſſembled on this occaſion were Alfonzo duke of Calabria, Lodovico Sforza, Lorenzo de' Medici, Lodovico Gonzaga marquis of Mantua, the duke of Ferrara; and on the part of the pope, Girolamo Riario, and the Cardinal of Mantua, with others of inferior note. The king of France, aware of the character of Riario, adviſed Lorenzo by letter not to truſt himſelf to this interview (*b*); but the important

(*a*) *Fabr. in vitâ Laur. adnot. & monum.* ii. 234.

(*b*) Thus he addreſſes Lorenzo in a letter dated xiii. Kal. Febr. 1482, *Fabr. adnot. & mon. v.* ii. *p.* 243. "Alla Giornata di Ferrara "dove dite avere promeſſo andare, vi avrei conſigliato non andaſte "punto, ma che guardaſte bene tener ſicura voſtra perſona; perchè

consequences

consequences expected from it induced him to disregard the precaution. Among other arrangements it was determined that the Milanese should endeavour to form a diversion by an attack on the Venetian territory, and that the duke of Calabria should repair with a powerful body of troops to the relief of the duke of Ferrara. By these decisive measures, a speedy and effectual stop was put to the further progress of the Venetian arms, whilst the allied troops over-ran the territories of Bergamo, of Brescia, and of Verona. Finding their attempt to subjugate the city of Ferrara frustrated, and solicitous for the safety of their own dominions, the Venetians had recourse to negotiation, and had sufficient influence with Lodovico Sforza to prevail upon him to desert the common cause. His dereliction induced the allies to accede to propositions for peace, which, though sufficiently favorable to the Venetians, secured the duke of Ferrara from the ambition of his powerful neighbours, and repressed that spirit of encroachment which the Venetians had manifested, as well on this as on former occasions.

As soon as the affairs of Italy were so adjusted as to give the first indications of permanent tranquillity, Sixtus died. The coincidence of these events gave rise to an opinion which was rendered in some degree credible by the knowledge of his

" non conosco nè i personaggi nè il luogo, dove v'habbiate a trovare, " e v'avrei mandato uno imbasciatore di quà in vostra excusatione; " nientedimanco, poichè l'avete promesso, me ne reporto a voi; & " alla buona hora sia, & a Dio. Luis."

restless disposition, that his death was occasioned by vexation at the prospect of a general peace (*a*). Of the character of this successor of St. Peter, we have already had sufficient proof. It must indeed be acknowledged, that no age has exhibited such flagrant instances of the depravity of the Roman see, as the close of the fifteenth century, when the profligacy of Sixtus IV. led the way, at a short interval, to the still more outrageous and unnatural crimes of Alexander VI. The avarice of Sixtus was equal to his ambition. He was the first Roman pontiff who openly exposed to sale the principal offices of the church; but not satisfied with the disposal of such as became vacant, he instituted new ones, for the avowed purpose of selling them, and thereby contrived to obtain a certain emolument from the uncertain tenure by which he held his see. To Sixtus IV. posterity are also indebted for the institution of inquisitors of the press, without whose licence no work was suffered to be printed. In this indeed he gave an instance of his prudence; it being extremely consistent, that those who are conscious of their own misconduct should endeavour to stifle the voice that publishes and perpetuates it. Even Muratori acknowledges, that this pontiff had a heavy account to make up at the tribunal of God (*b*).

(*a*) He died on the 12th of August 1484, being the fifth day after peace was proclaimed at Rome. *Murat. Ann. v.* ix. *p.* 546. 549. "O perchè fusse il termine di sua vita venuto, o perchè il dolore "della pace fatta, come nemica a quella l'ammazzasse."

(*a*) "Di grossi conti avrà avuto questo pontefice nel tribunale di "Dio." *Annal. v.* ix. *p.* 538.

The death of Sixtus IV. who for the ſpace of thirteen years had embroiled the ſtates of Italy in conſtant diſſenſions, was a favorable omen of the continuance of tranquillity; and the choice made by the conclave of his ſucceſſor ſeemed ſtill further to ſecure ſo deſirable an object. Giambattiſta Cibò, who obtained on this occaſion the ſuffrages of the ſacred college, was a Genoeſe by birth, though of Greek extraction. The urbanity and mildneſs of his manners formed a ſtriking contraſt to the inflexible character of his predeceſſor. From his envoys at Rome, Lorenzo became early acquainted with the diſpoſition of the new pope, who aſſumed the name of Innocent VIII. At the time of his elevation to the ſupremacy, he was about fifty-five years of age, and had ſeveral natural children. Veſpucci, the correſpondent of Lorenzo, repreſents him as a weak but well-diſpoſed man, rather formed to be directed himſelf than capable of directing others (*a*).

Lorenzo had perceived the diſadvantages under which he labored in his political tranſactions, on account of his diſſenſions with the papal ſee; and he therefore learnt with great ſatisfaction that the pope, ſoon after his elevation, had expreſſed a very favorable opinion of him, and had even avowed an intention of conſulting him on all important occurrences. The power of the other Italian potentates was bounded by the limits of their reſpective dominions; but Lorenzo was well aware that the Roman

(*a*) Many particulars reſpecting this pontiff may be found in the letter from Veſpucci to Lorenzo, extracted from the documents of Fabroni. *App. No.* XLIV.

pontiff, independent of his temporal possessions, maintained an influence that extended throughout all Christendom, and which might be found of the utmost importance to the promotion of his views. He therefore sedulously improved the occasion which the favorable opinion of Innocent afforded him; and in a short time obtained his confidence to such a degree, as to be intrusted with his most secret transactions and most important concerns (*a*). This fortunate event also first opened to the Medici the dignities and emoluments of the church, and thereby led the way to that eminent degree of splendor and prosperity which the family afterwards experienced.

To the carrying into effect the pacific intentions of Lorenzo, several obstacles yet remained. During the commotions in Italy, consequent on the conspiracy of the Pazzi, the town of Sarzana, situated near the boundaries of the Genoese and Florentine dominions, and which the Florentines had purchased from Lodovico Fregoso, had been forcibly wrested from them by Agostino, one of his sons. The important contests in which the Florentines were engaged had for some time prevented them from attempting the recovery of a place, to which,

(*a*) "Assettate che saranno queste vostre cose co' Genovesi Lorenzo "conoscerà che non fu mai Pontefice, che amassi tanto la casa sua "quanto io. Et avendo visto per esperienza, quanta sia la fede, "integrità & prudentia sua, io farò tosto governarmi secondo i ricordi "& pareri sui." Such was the language in which Innocent addressed himself to Pier Filippo Pandolfini, the Florentine ambassador, *Fabroni in vità, v. ii. p. 263.*

according to the established custom of the times, they had undoubted pretensions; but no sooner were they relieved from the anxiety and expense of external war, than they bent their whole attention to this object. In order to secure himself against the expected attack, Agostino had made a formal surrender of the town to the republic of Genoa, under which he professed to exercise the government. Lorenzo therefore entertained hopes, that, by the mediation of the new pope, his countrymen the Genoese might be induced to resign their pretensions; but his interference having proved ineffectual, the Florentines prepared to establish their right by arms. The approach to Sarzana necessarily lay by the town of Pietra-Santa, the inhabitants of which were expected to remain neuter during the contest; but a detachment of Florentine troops, escorting a quantity of provisions and ammunition, passing near that place, were attacked and plundered by the garrison (*a*). So unequivocal a demonstration

(*a*) Machiavelli, pleased in relating instances of that crooked policy in which he is supposed to have been himself an adept, informs us, that the Florentines, wanting a pretext for a rupture with the inhabitants of Pietra-Santa, directed a part of their baggage to pass near that place, for the purpose of inducing the garrison to make an attack upon it. *Hist. lib.* 8. And Fabroni, on what authority it is not easy to discover, expressly attributes this artifice to Lorenzo de' Medici, *in vità Laur. v.* i. *p.* 127. But Ammirato, whose veracity is undoubted, asserts that this incident took place without any premeditated design on the part of the Florentines, introducing his narrative with a direct censure of the relation of Machiavelli: "Hor "volle più tosto il caso, che artificio alcuno, il quale và il Machi-"avelli accattando, &c." *Ist. Fior. lib.* 25.

of hostility rendered it necessary for the Florentines, before they proceeded to the attack of Sarzana, to possess themselves of Pietra-Santa. It was accordingly invested, and such artillery as was then in use was employed to reduce the inhabitants to submission. The Genoese however found means to reinforce the garrison, whilst the sickness of some of the Florentine leaders, and the inactivity of others, contributed to protract the siege. Dispirited by resistance, the count of Pitigliano, one of the Florentine generals, ventured even to recommend to the magistrates of Florence the relinquishment of the enterprise as impracticable, at least, for that season. These representations, instead of altering the purpose of Lorenzo, only excited him to more vigorous exertion; by his recommendation, the command of the Florentine troops was given to Bernardo del Nero, and soon afterwards Lorenzo joined the army in person. His presence and exhortations had the most powerful effect on his countrymen. Within the space of a few days after his arrival, the besiegers reduced the place to such extremity, that proposals were made for a capitulation, which were acceded to by Lorenzo; and the town was received into the protection of the Florentine republic, without further molestation to the inhabitants (*a*).

From Pietra-Santa it was the intention of Lorenzo, notwithstanding the advanced season of the year, to have proceeded immediately to the attack of Sarzana, but the long and unhealthy

(*a*) *Ammir. Ist. Fior. lib.* 25.

ſervice in which the army had been engaged, rendered a temporary ceſſation of hoſtilities indiſpenſible. Several of the principal commanders together with Antonio Pucci, one of the Florentine commiſſioners to the army, had fallen victims to the fatigues of the war; and Lorenzo, who labored under a chronic, and perhaps an hereditary complaint, was ſoon afterwards obliged to reſort to the baths of S. Filippo for relief. Before he recovered his health, his attention was called towards a different quarter, in which all his exertions became neceſſary to preſerve his pacific ſyſtem from total deſtruction.

This commotion originated in the turbulent deſigns of Sixtus IV. who had ſown the ſeeds of it in his lifetime, although they did not ſpring up till after his death. The Neapolitan nobility, exaſperated with the princes of the houſe of Aragon, who had endeavoured to abridge their power and independence, were prepared, whenever occaſion offered, to attempt the recovery of their rights. In reſtraining the exorbitant power of the nobles, which was equally formidable to the king and oppreſſive to the people, Ferdinand might have been juſtified by the expediency of the meaſure, and protected by the affections of his ſubjects; but, in relieving them from the exactions of others, he began to oppreſs them himſelf, and thus incautiouſly incurred that odium, which had before been excluſively beſtowed upon his nobility. The ſpirit of diſaffection that ſoon became apparent was not unobſerved by Sixtus, who, in addition to the ambitious motives by which he was generally actuated, felt no small degree of resentment against Ferdinand, for having, without his concurrence, concluded a peace with the Florentines. A secret intercouse was carried on between the pope and the Neapolitan barons, whose resentment was ready to burst out in an open flame when Sixtus died. This event retarded, but did not defeat the execution of their purpose. No sooner was Innocent seated in the chair, than they began to renew with him the intercourse which they had carried on with his predecessor. They reminded him that the kingdom of Naples was itself a fief of the Roman see; they represented the exhausted state of the king's finances, and the aversion which he had incurred from his subjects, as well by his own severity, as by the cruelties exercised in his name by the duke of Calabria; and exhorted him to engage in an attempt, the success of which was evident, and would crown his pontificate with glory (a) The pacific temper of Innocent was dazzled with the splendor of such an acquisition. He encouraged the nobility to proceed in their designs, he raised a considerable army, the command of which he gave to Roberto Sanseverino; several of the principal cities of Naples openly revolted, and the standard of the pope was erected at Salerno. On the first indication of hostilities, the king had sent his son John, who had obtained the dignity of a cardinal, to Rome, for the purpose of inducing the pope to relinquish his attempt; but the death

(a) *Valor. in vitâ Laur. p.* 51.

of the cardinal blasted the hopes, and added to the distresses of his father (*a*). Attacked at the same time by foreign and domestic enemies, Ferdinand saw no shelter from the storm, but in the authority and assistance of Lorenzo. The attachment that subsisted between him and the pope was indeed known to Ferdinand; but he had himself some claims upon his kindness, and had reason to believe that he could not regard with indifference, an attempt which, if successful, would effect a total change in the political state of Italy. Lorenzo did not hesitate on the part it became him to act. No sooner was he apprized of the dangerous situation of Ferdinand, than he left the baths of S. Filippo and hastened to Florence, where, on his first interview with the envoy of the king, he gave him the most unequivocal assurances of active interference and support. Lorenzo however saw the necessity of applying an effectual remedy to the increasing evil, and with a degree of freedom which the urgency of the occasion required, entreated the king to relax in his severity towards his subjects. " It grieves me to the soul," thus he writes to Albino the Neapolitan envoy, " that the
" duke of Calabria should have acquired, even
" undeservedly, the imputation of cruelty. At all
" events he ought to endeavour to remove every
" pretext for the accusation, by the most cautious

(*a*) His death was attributed to poison, given to him by Antonello Sanseverino, prince of Salerno. *Murat. Ann.* v. ix. *p.* 542. The frequency of these imputations, though perhaps not always founded on fact, strongly mark the character of the age.

" regard to his conduct. If the people be displeased " with the late impositions, it would be advisable " to abolish them, and to require only the usual " payments; for one *carlino* obtained with good-" will and affection, is better than ten accom-" panied with dissatisfaction and resentment." He afterwards remonstrates with the king, through the same channel, on his harsh and imprudent conduct to some merchants, who it appears had been dismissed from Naples, for having demanded from him the monies which they had advanced for his use." " If the king satisfy them not," says he, " by paying their demands, he ought at least to " appease them by good words; to the end that " he may not afford them an opportunity of treating " his name with disrespect, and of gaining credit " at the same time to what is, and to what is " not true." The reply of Ferdinand to Albino is sufficiently expressive of the respect which he paid to these admonitions (*a*); but unfortunately, the precepts which he approved in theory, he forgot to adopt in his practice; and to the neglect of these counsels, rather than to the courage or the conduct of Charles VIII. the subsequent expulsion of his family from the kingdom of Naples is unquestionably to be referred.

The authority of Lorenzo de' Medici in Florence

(*a*) In reference to this letter of Lorenzo, which may be found in the Appendix, No. XLV. The king replies to Albino, " Lo con-" siglio de detto Mag. Lorenzo, che abbiamo li occhi ad tutto, e " mostramo in alcuna cosa non intendere, &c. ci è stato gratissimo, " per essere prudentissimo e sapientissimo."

was not the authority of deſpotiſm, but that of reaſon; and it therefore became neceſſary, that the meaſures which he might adopt ſhould meet with the approbation of the citizens at large. He accordingly, without delay, called together the principal inhabitants, but had the mortification to find that the propoſition which he laid before them, to afford aſſiſtance to the king, was received by his hearers with general diſapprobation; ſome exclaiming againſt him, as being too precipitate in involving the republic in dangerous and expenſive wars; whilſt others condemned the freedom with which he oppoſed the Roman pontiff, and ſubjected himſelf and his fellow-citizens to thoſe eccleſiaſtical cenſures, the ill effects of which they had ſo recently experienced. On this occaſion, Lorenzo was reminded, that the Venetians would probably unite with the pope in ſubjugating the kingdom of Naples; in which caſe, the intervention of the Florentines would only involve them in the ſame ruin that threatened the Neapolitan ſtate. The ſolicitations and remonſtrances of his fellow-citizens ſhook not the purpoſe of Lorenzo. Through the thick miſt of popular fears and prejudices, he diſtinctly ſaw the beacon of the public welfare; and the arguments of his adverſaries had already been anticipated and refuted in his own mind. That eloquence which he poſſeſſed in ſo eminent a degree was never more ſucceſsfully exerted; and the reaſons that had determined his own judgment were laid before his audience in a manner ſo impreſſive, as to overpower all oppoſition, and induce them unanimoufly to concur in his opinion. "This oration," fays Valori, "as committted to "writing by fome of his hearers, I have myfelf "perufed; and it is not poffible to conceive any "compofition more copious, more elegant, or "more convincing (*a*)."

The fituation of Ferdinand became every day more critical. A general defection of his nobility took place. The two brothers of the family of the Coppula, one of whom was his prime counfellor, and the other the treafurer of the kingdom, held a treacherous correfpondence with his enemies; and the duke of Calabria, who had advanced towards Rome to prevent a junction of the pontifical troops with thofe of the infurgents, was totally defeated by Sanfeverino, and obliged to fly for protection into the territories of Florence. It was matter of gratification to fome, and of furprife to all, that the very man, who, by his fanguinary and tyrannical difpofition, had a fhort time before fpread terror through the whole extent of Tufcany, fhould now appear as a fugitive at Montepulciano, imploring the affiftance of the Florentines, and waiting the arrival of Lorenzo de' Medici; who, being prevented by ficknefs from complying with his expectations, difpatched two of the principal citizens to affure the duke of the attachment of the Florentines to the houfe of Aragon, and of their determination to exert themfelves to the utmoft in its defence.

(*a*) *Valor. in vitâ Laur. p.* 53.

The military force of the republic, which seldom exceeded five thousand men, would have rendered small service in the contest, and it therefore became necessary to resort to other expedients. By the pecuniary assistance of the Florentines, the duke of Calabria was again enabled to take the field, and at their instance several eminent leaders of Italy engaged in the service of the king. The influence that Lorenzo possessed with Lodovico Sforza was successfully exerted to engage the states of Milan in the same cause. The powerful Roman family of the Orsini was induced not only to discountenance the enterprise of the pope, but to appear openly in arms against him; and Innocent began to dread that the conflagration which he had excited, or encouraged, in the kingdom of Naples, might extend to his own dominions. At the same time Lorenzo de' Medici, having still maintained an uninterrupted intercourse with the pope, assailed him with those arguments which he knew were best calculated to produce their effect. He represented the evils and disgrace that must arise to all Christendom, from the frequent example set by the head of the church, of appealing on all occasions to the sword. He pointed out the improbability that the northern powers of Italy would permit the Roman see to annex to its dominions, either directly or indirectly, so extensive a territory as the kingdom of Naples; and earnestly exhorted the pope not to waste his resources, disturb his tranquillity, and endanger his safety, in a conflict which, at best, could only terminate in substituting to the house of Aragon some of those fortunate adventurers who had led the armies employed in its expulsion. Whether the appearances of hostility operated on the fears, or the reasoning of Lorenzo on the judgment of the pope, may remain in doubt; but the ardor with which he engaged in the conflict gradually abated, and Sanseverino was left to avail himself of his own courage, and that of the troops under his command, without receiving either orders to retire, or supplies to enable him to proceed. The languor that became apparent between the contending sovereigns seemed to have communicated itself to their armies; which having met on the eighth day of May 1486, an encounter took place, in which Ammirato not only acknowledges; that not a soldier was slain, but that he had found no memorial that even one of the combatants was wounded, though the contest continued for many hours, and only terminated with the day (*a*). In this harmless trial of muscular strength, Sanseverino and his followers were however forced off the field, and the consequences were as decisive as if the contest had been of the most sanguinary kind; for the king, availing himself of this circumstance, and apprized by Lorenzo of the favorable alteration in the temper of the pope, lost no time in laying before him such propositions for the accommodation of their dispute, as afforded him an opportunity of declining it with

(*a*) Ecco che nel volersi movere, si venne l'ottavo giorno di maggio al fatto d'arme; se merita di fatto d'arme haver nome una giornata, nella quale non che fosse alcun morto, ma non si fa memoria, che fosse alcun ferito. *Ammir. Ist. Fior. lib. 25. p. 174.*

credit to himſelf, and apparent ſafety to his Neapolitan confederates. By the conditions of this treaty, the king acknowledged the juriſdiction of the apoſtolic ſee, and agreed to pay to the pope a ſtipulated ſubſidy. Beſides which, he engaged to pardon, freely and unconditionally, the nobles who had revolted againſt him.

The oppreſſive conduct of the Italian ſovereigns, or the reſtleſs diſpoſition of their ſubjects, ſeldom admitted of a long continuance of tranquillity; and as Lorenzo had acquired a reputation for impartiality and moderation, the diſſenſions that occaſionally aroſe were generally ſubmitted to his deciſion. The political contentions in which the pope was engaged, diſplayed indeed an ample field for the exerciſe of his talents. Important as the favor of the Roman ſee might be to the ſucceſs of his labors, it was not preſerved without an unremitting attention to its intereſts, In the year 1486, Buccolino Guzzoni, a citizen of Oſimo, a part of the papal territories, incited the inhabitants to revolt. The cardinal Giuliano della Rovere, afterwards Julius II. was diſpatched by the pope to reduce the place to obedience; but threats and entreaties were alike ineffectual, and the inhabitants avowed their reſolution to ſurrender the city to the Turks, rather than again ſubmit to the authority of the pope. From the ſucceſs of the inſurgents, the example began to ſpread through the adjoining diſtricts; when Lorenzo diſpatched Gentile, biſhop of Arezzo, with inſtructions to treat with Buccolino for a reconciliation. What the obſtinacy of Buccolino had refused to the representations of the pope, was conceded to those of Lorenzo, under whose sanction the terms of the treaty were speedily concluded, and Buccolino accompanied the ambassador of Lorenzo to Florence. Muratori informs us, that the artifice by which Lorenzo extricated the pope from his turbulent adversary, was the timely application of some thousands of golden ducats; and this he accompanies with an insinuation, which, if justly founded, would degrade the magnanimous character of Lorenzo to a level with that of his sanguinary and treacherous contemporaries. "Having invited Buccolino to Florence," says that "author, Lorenzo, with great address, prevailed "upon him, for his further security, to repair to "Milan; but the security that he there found was "a halter from the hands of Lodovico Sforza (a)." If, however, the death of Buccolino, when the contention was over, was of such importance as to induce Lorenzo to the commission of so atrocious a crime, it is scarcely probable that he would have afforded his victim so favorable an opportunity of escaping the blow; but without having recourse to conjecture, a refutation of this calumny may be found in an author, who, not being considered as partial to the Medici, may on this occasion be admitted as an authentic witness. "After the "surrender of Osimo," says Machiavelli, "Buccolino "resided a considerable time at Florence, under "the safeguad of Lorenzo, honored and respected. "He afterwards went to Milan, where he did not

(a) *Murat. Ann. v. ix. p. 554. cit. Raynal. Annal. Eccles.*

"experience

" experience the ſame fidelity, having been " treacherouſly put to death there by Lodovico " Sforza (*a*)."

The remonſtrances of the Florentines to the Genoeſe to relinquiſh the dominion of Sarzana, being yet diſregarded, and the peaceable intervention of the pope and the duke of Milan appearing to be ineffectual, Lorenzo prepared for a powerful attack; and not only engaged the lords of Piombino, Faenza, Pitigliano, and Bologna in his cauſe, but applied to the king of Naples for ſuch aſſiſtance as he could afford. In his anſwer to this requiſition, Ferdinand confeſſes high obligations to Lorenzo, and after lamenting his inability to repay them in a manner adequate to their importance, promiſes to furniſh a ſupply of ſhips againſt the Genoeſe, and to give ſuch other aid as the embarraſſed ſtate of his affairs would permit (*b*). The command of the army, deſtined to the attack of Sarzana, was given to Jacopo Guicciardini, and Pietro Vittorio, who, having defeated a body of the Genoeſe that oppoſed their progreſs, began the ſiege of the place. The reſiſtance which they met with was however more obſtinate than might have been expected. Impatient of the delay, Lorenzo reſolved to join the army, and endeavour by his preſence to promote the exertions of the commanders, and excite the ardor of the ſoldiery. His exhortations, addreſſed perſonally to every rank and denomination, produced an inſtantaneous effect: a vigorous attack was made;

(*a*) *Mac. lib.* 8.

(*b*) *v. App. No.* XLVI.

and the citizens, perceiving no profpect of further fuccour from the Genoefe, furrendered at the difcretion of the conquerors. It is not improbable, that the remembrance of the difafter which took place on the furrender of Volterra, had operated as an additional motive with Lorenzo to be prefent at the capture of Sarzana; however this may be, his conduct was marked with the greateft clemency to the inhabitants, and the city was received into the protection of the Florentine ftate, to which it was only defirable, as oppofing a barrier to the incurfions of the Genoefe. Elated with conqueft, the Florentine commanders wifhed to carry the war into the ftates of Genoa; but Lorenzo oppofed himfelf to this defign; juftly conceiving it to be inconfiftent with the interefts of his country and his own character to deftroy that general equilibrium of the Italian ftates, which his utmoft endeavours were conftantly exerted to maintain. The apprehenfions entertained by the Genoefe were productive however of confequences as unfavorable to their liberties, as any which they could have experienced from a hoftile invafion. To fecure themfelves from the expected attack, they furrendered their ftates to the duke of Milan, probably with the intention of again afferting their independence as foon as they had an opportunity; an artifice to which they had frequently reforted on former occafions (*a*).

In the conduct of Lorenzo towards the fmaller governments in the vicinity of Florence, he gave

(*a*) *Murat. Annal.* v. ix. p. 555.

a ſtriking inſtance of prudence and moderation. Inſtead of ſeeking for pretences to ſubjugate them, he, upon all occaſions, afforded them the moſt effectual aid in reſiſting every effort to deprive them of their independence. In his eſtimation, theſe were the true barriers of the Tuſcan territory. By the conſtant intercourſe which he maintained with the ſubordinate ſovereigns, and the chief nobility of Italy, he was enabled to perceive the firſt indications of diſagreement, and to extinguiſh the ſparks before they had kindled into a flame. The city of Perugia was held by the Baglioni, Caſtello by the Vitelli, Bologna by the Bentivoli, and Faenza by the Manfredi; all of whom reſorted to him as the umpire of their frequent diſſenſions, and their protector from the reſentment, or the rapacity, of their more powerful neighbours. Innumerable occaſions preſented themſelves, in which the Florentines might have extended the limits of their dominions, but it was uniformly the policy of Lorenzo, rather to ſecure what the ſtate already poſſeſſed, than, by aiming at more extenſive territory, to endanger the whole; and ſo fully did he accompliſh his purpoſe, that the acute, but profligate Lodovico Sforza, was accuſtomed to ſay, "*That Lorenzo had converted into iron what he* "*found fabricated of glaſs* (a)." The views of Lorenzo were not however limited by the boundaries that divide Italy from the reſt of Europe. The influence of other ſtates upon the politics of that country was daily increaſing. He had therefore,

(a) *Fabr. in vitâ Laur. vol. I. p.* 181.

at almost every court, envoys and correspondents, on whose talents and integrity he had the greatest reliance; and who gave him minute and early information of every circumstance that might affect the general tranquillity. By these men, he heard, he saw, he felt, every motion and every change of the political machine, and was often enabled to give it an impulse where it was supposed to be far beyond the limits of his power. In conducting a negotiation, all circumstances seemed to concur in rendering him successful; but these were not the effects of chance, but of deep and premeditated arrangement. Knowing the route he had to take, the obstacles that might have obstructed his progress were cautiously removed, before his opponents were apprized of his intentions. Hence, as one of the Florentine annalists expresses it (*a*), he became the balance point of the Italian potentates, whose affairs he kept in such just equilibrium as to prevent the preponderancy of any particular state. Surrounded as he was by ambitious despots, who knew no restraint except that of compulsion, or by restless communities constantly springing up with elastic

(*a*) " Era venuto Lorenzo in tanta riputazione e autorità appresso
" gli altri principi d'Italia, &c, che tutti gli Scrittori di que' tempi,
" e le memorie ancora degli uomini, che vivono, e che sono vivuti
" a tempi nostri unitamente s'accordano, che, mentre ch'egli visse
" fu sempre l'ago della bilancia tra' principi predetti, che mantenne
" bilanciati gli stati loro, e di tal maniera gli tenne uniti, e ciascuno
" di essi ristretti dentro a' termini de' loro confini, che si potette dipoi,
" dopo la sua morte, vedere questa verità detta di sopra," &c.
Filip. de' Nerli, Comment. de' Fatti civili di Fir. lib. 3. Ed. Ven. 1728.

vigor againſt the hand that preſſed them; it was only by unwearied attention that he could curb the overbearing, relieve the oppreſſed, allay their mutual jealouſy, and preſerve them from perpetual contention. By inducing them to graſp at unſubſtantial advantages, he placed in their hands real bleſſings; and by alarming them with imaginary terrors, averted their ſteps from impending deſtruction.

We have already ſeen, that by the terms of the treaty between the pope and the king of Naples, Ferdinand was to pay an annual ſubſidy to the Roman ſee, and was alſo to grant an unconditional pardon to his refractory nobles. The latter of theſe conditions he immediately broke, and the other he only adhered to as long as he conceived that the pope was able to compel its performance. The cruelty and perfidy ſhown by Ferdinand in his treatment of the Neapolitan nobility, fixes an indelible ſtain upon his character; but the operations of the moral world are not leſs certain than thoſe of the natural, and the treachery of Ferdinand brought forth in due time its fruits of bitterneſs. It is true indeed, as Muratori well obſerves, "God "does not always repay in this world, nor are his "judgments laid open to us; but if we may on "any occaſion be allowed to interpret them, it is "when they ſeem to be the retribution of cruelty. "In fact, the calamities of Ferdinand were not "long poſtponed. The lapſe of a few years de"prived him of life, and his poſterity of the "kingdom of Naples. Surely, he can never be

" worthy to rule over a people, who knows not " how to forgive (*a*)."

The refusal of Ferdinand to comply with his engagements, again roused the resentment of the pope the inadequacy of whose temporal arms to enforce his pretensions, was supplied by the spiritual terrors of excommunication. On this occasion, the intervention of Lorenzo de' Medici again became necessary. A long negotiation ensued, in the progress of which he availed himself of every opportunity afforded him by the circumstances of the times, the temper of the parties, and his own credit and authority, to prevent the disagreement from proceeding to an open rupture. Of his letters written in the course of these transactions, some are yet preserved, which, whilst they display the refined policy and deep discernment of their author, demonstrate how assiduously he labored to avert the calamities of war. "It appears to me," says he writing to Lanfredini his confidential envoy at Rome, who was to lay these representations before the pope, " that his holiness must propose to himself " one of these three things; either to compel the " king by force to comply with his requisition; " or to compromise matters with him on the most " advantageous terms that can be obtained; or, " lastly to temporize till something better may be " effected." He then enters into a full discussion of the difficulties and dangers that seem likely to

(*a*) " Certo non sarà giammai degno di reggere popoli, chi non sa mai perdonare," *Murat. Ann. v. ix. p.* 556.

attend the making an hostile attack on the kingdom of Naples. He lays before the pope the situation not only of the other states of Italy, but of Europe; and shows the indespensible necessity of entering into treaties for assistance, or neutrality, before he engages in so hazardous an attempt. Having thus endeavoured to deter the pope from adopting any violent and unadvised measures, he adverts to the probability of terminating their differences by negotiation; the opportunity for which, however, he thinks as yet crude and immature, and as likely to be still further delayed by any severe or incautious proceedings. "With respect to temporizing," says he, "this is undoubtedly the only course to be "pursued, because it is better beyond comparison "to let matters remain in their present state, with "reputation to his holiness, than to risk a war; "especially as the king has it in his power to do "him essential injury." He concludes with a a recapitulation of his former opinions. "If the "pope can accommodate matters with the king, "consistently with his own honor, it seems to me "that a tolerable compromise is better than a "successful war. But as difficulties present them-"selves to an immediate agreement, I would "endeavour to protract the discussion as long as "it might be done with safety and propriety; all "that I have advanced is however upon the idea "that the pope is not prepared to carry his point "by force, for if that were the case, the king would "soon submit; but I fear he is too well apprized "how far he is liable to be injured, and on this

" account will be more obſtinate (*a*)." By repreſentations of this nature, founded on inconteſtable facts, and inforced by unanſwerable arguments, Lorenzo at length ſo far mitigated the anger, or abated the confidence of the pope, as to diſpoſe him to liſten to propoſitions of accommodation; whilſt, through the medium of his ambaſſador at Naples, he prevailed on the king to aſſent to the payment of the ſame ſubſidy which his predeceſſors had paid to the holy ſee. It is not eaſy to ſay to which of the contending parties the conduct of Lorenzo was moſt acceptable; the pope omitted no ſubſequent opportunity of conferring on him and his family the moſt important favors; whilſt Ferdinand unequivocally acknowledged, that to his friendſhip and fidelity, he and his family were indebted, not only for the rank they held, but even for their continuance in the kingdom of Naples (*b*).

The external concerns of the republic being happily adjuſted, and the tranquillity of Italy ſecured, Lorenzo applied himſelf to the regulation of the internal diſcipline of the Florentine ſtate. The government of this city was founded on the broadeſt baſis of democratic equality. By its

(*a*) For this letter, *v. App. No.* XLVII.

(*b*) Ferdinand thus addreſſed himſelf to Antonio della Valle, one of the agents of Lorenzo at Naples: " Lorenzo ha provato, che " veramente ho amato lui & quella città; ed io ho avuto a provare, " che ha amato me, e i miei figliuoli, che ſenza lui, nè io nè loro " ſaremmo in queſto regno, il quale beneficio noi nè i noſtri diſ- " cendenti mai ſi hanno a ſcordare." *Pet. Lutetii Ep. ad Laur. Fab. v.* ii. *p.* 369. Theſe obligations are alſo warmly acknowledged by Ferdinand in a letter to Lorenzo himſelf. *v. App. No.* XLVIII

fundamental principles, every person who contributed by his industry to the support or aggrandizement of the state, had a right to share in the direction of it; either by delegating his power to others, or in exercising a portion of the supreme control, under the suffrages of his fellow-citizens. Inactivity was the only circumstance that incapacitated him from the enjoyment of political rights. The Florentines, as early as the year 1282, had classed themselves into distinct bodies, or municipal companies, according to their various professions; and in order to place their government on a truly popular foundation, had determined, that no person should be eligible to a public office, unless he were either actually, or professedly, a member of one or other of these companies. By this regulation, the nobility were either excluded from the offices of the state, or, in order to obtain them, were obliged to degrade the honors of their rank, by the humiliating appellation of artisan (*a*). From these associated bodies, a certain number of members were deputed to exercise the supreme government, in conjunction with an officer, whom we have frequently mentioned by the name of

(*a*) Et sopra tutto parve, che si havesse havuto riguardo à fondar uno stato affatto popolare, non volendo che fussono ricevute al governo persone, che non fussero comprese sotto il nome, e insegna d'alcuna arte; eziandio che quelle arti non esercitassero, perciocchè si come non stimavano cosa conveniente il levar in tutto il governo di mano de' nobili, così giudicavano esser necessario, che almeno col nome che prendevano, deponessero parte dell' alterigia che porgea loro quella boriosa voce della nobiltà. *Ammir. Ist. lib.* iii. *v.* i. *p.* 160.

Gonfaloniere, whoſe authority was however ſubordinate to that of the delegated mechanics, or *Priori delle arti*, who continued in office only two months, and from three in number, had increaſed, at various intervals, to ſix, to eight, and laſtly to ten (*a*). This inſtitution had, in the time of Lorenzó de' Medici, ſubſiſted nearly two hundred years, during which the office of Gonfaloniere had been filled by a regular ſucceſſion of twelve hundred citizens, who had preſerved the dignity and independence of the republic, and ſecured to their countrymen the exerciſe of their rights. With this laudable jealouſy of their own liberties, the Florentines did not, like the Romans, from whom they derived their origin, exert their power to deſtroy the liberties

(*a*) The jealous temper of the Florentines in providing for the ſecurity of their liberties, is exquiſitely ſatirized by their firſt poet:

Or ti fa lieta, che tu hai ben onde,
Tu ricca, tu con pace, tu con ſenno;
S'i' dico 'l ver, l' effetto nol naſconde
Atene, e Lacedemona, che fenno
L'antiche leggi, e furon sì civili,
Fecero al viver bene un picciol ſenno
Verſo di te, che fai tanto ſottili
Provvedimenti, ch'a mezzo Novembre
Non giunge quel, che tu d'Ottobre fili.
Quante volte del tempo, che rimembre
Legge, moneta, uficio, e coſtume,
Ha' tu mutato, e rinnovato membre?
E ſe ben ti ricorda, e vedi lume,
Vedrai te ſimigliante a quell' inferma,
Che, non può trovar poſa in ſulle piume
Ma con dar volta ſuo dolore ſcherma.

Dante. Purg. Cant. vi.

of others. They wisely repressed the dangerous desire of subjecting to their dominion surrounding states, nor aspired to the invidious honor of sparing the subservient, and overturning the proud; and, though a community of freemen, were content to be the first in those accomplishments, which the flatterer of Augustus affected to despise (*a*).

There is however reason to conjecture, that the Florentine government, although sufficiently vigorous for internal regulation, was inadequate to the exertions of external warfare. The hand that may steer a vessel through the tranquil ocean, may be unable to direct the helm amidst the fury of the storm. It may indeed well be conceived, that the delegated magistrates, being so extremely limited, as well with respect to their number, as to the duration of their power, would reluctantly determine on, and cautiously engage in measures, which involved the welfare, and perhaps the existence of the community. Accordingly it appears that on important occasions it was customary for the magistrates to assemble the most respectable citizens, from whose advice they might derive assistance, and by whose countenance they might

(*a*) Excudent alii spirantia mollius æra,
Credo equidem, vivos ducent de marmore vultus,
Orabunt caussas melius, cœlique meatus,
Describent radio & surgentia sidera dicent:
Tu regere imperio populos, Romane, memento,
(Hæ tibi erunt artes,) pacique imponere morem,
Parcere subjectis, & debellare superbos.

Æn. lib. vi.

fecure themfelves from cenfure. During the late dangerous conteft, this meafure had been frequently reforted to, and with fuch manifeft advantage, that Lorenzo, after the reftoration of the public tranquillity, recommended, and obtained the eftablifhment of a body of feventy citizens, who, in the nature of a fenate, were to deliberate and to decide on all the tranfactions of government, as well in the affairs of peace, as of war. This inftitution, for which he might have pleaded the example of the Spartan legiflator, was probably intended, not only to give a greater degree of ftability and energy to the government, but to counteract the democratic fpirit, which was fuppofed to have rifen to a dangerous excefs (*a*), and to operate as a fafeguard againft an abufe which was the deftruction of all the free ftates of antiquity—the exercife of the powers of government by the immediate interference of the citizens at large.

At this period, the city of Florence was at its higheft degree of profperity. The vigilance of Lorenzo had fecured it from all apprehenfions of external attack; and his acknowledged difintereftednefs and moderation had almoft exftinguifhed that fpirit of diffenfion for which it had been fo long remarkable. The Florentines gloried in their

(*a*) "All free governments," fays Hume, very decifively, "muft "confift of two councils, a leffer and greater; or, in other words, "of a fenate and people." "The people" as Harrington obferves, "would want wifdom without the fenate; the fenate, without the "people, would want honefty." *Idea of a perfect Commonwealth.*

illustrious citizen, and were gratified in numbering in their body, a man who wielded in his hands the fate of nations, and attracted the respect and admiration of all Europe. Though much inferior in population, extent of dominion, and military character, to several of the other states of Italy, Florence stood at this time in the first degree of respectability. The active spirit of its inhabitants, no longer engaged in hostile contentions, displayed itself in the pursuits of commerce, and the improvement of their manufactures. Equally enterprising and acute, wherever there appeared a possibility of profit, or of fame, they were the first to avail themselves of it; and a Florentine adventurer, though with doubtful pretensions, has erected to himself a monument which the proudest conqueror might envy, and impressed his name upon a new world in characters that are now indelible (*a*). The

(*a*) Amerigo Vespucci, who has contended with Columbus for the honor of the discovery of America, was born at Florence in the year 1451, of a respectable family, of which several individuals had enjoyed the chief offices of the republic. The name of Amerigo was at Florence a common name of baptism. For an account of the controversy that has taken place respecting the pretensions of these eminent navigators, I must refer to Dr. Robertson's History of America, *book* ii. *note* 22. without however approving the severity of his animadversions on the respectable Canonico Bandini, who has endeavoured, from original and almost contemporary documents, to support the claims of his countryman. *Band. vita di Amerigo Vesp. Flor.* 1745. However this may be, it is certain, that about the year 1507, Vespucci resided at Seville, with the title of master pilot, and with authority to examine all other pilots; for which he had a salary assigned him; an employment, as Tiraboschi well observes, suitable to a skilful navigator, but far below the pretensions of a man who had first

ſilk and linen fabrics manufactured by the Florentines, were in a great degree wrought from their native productions; but their wool was imported from England and from Spain, whoſe inhabitants indolently reſigned their natural advantages, and purchaſed again at an extravagant price their own commodities. In almoſt every part to which the Florentines extended their trade, they were favored with peculiar privileges, which enabled them to avail themſelves of the riches they had already acquired; and the ſuperſtitious prohibitions of the clergy againſt uſury were of little avail againſt a traffic in which the rich found employment for their wealth, and the powerful relief in their neceſſities. The conſequence of theſe induſtrious exertions was, a ſudden increaſe of population in Florence; inſomuch that Lorenzo was under the neceſſity of applying to the pope, for his permiſſion to build in the gardens of the monaſteries within the walls of the city. By his attention, the police was alſo effectually reformed. A contemporary author aſſures us, that there was no part of Italy where the people were more regular in their conduct, or

diſcovered the new continent. This employment, however, afforded Veſpucci an opportunity of rendering his name immortal. As he deſigned the charts for navigation, he uniformly denominated that continent by the name of AMERICA, which being adopted by other mariners and navigators, ſoon became general. *Tirab. Storia della Let. Ital. v. 6. par. i. p.* 192. The memory of Veſpucci is therefore now ſecured by a memorial,

> Quod non imber edax nec aquilo impotens,
> Poſſit diruere, aut innumerabilis
> Annorum ſeries, & fuga temporum.

where atrocious crimes were leſs frequent (*a*). "We have here," ſays he, "no robberies, no "nocturnal commotions, no aſſaſſinations. By night "or by day every perſon may tranſact his concerns "in perfect ſafety. Spies and informers are here "unknown. The accuſation of one is not ſuffered "to affect the ſafety of the many; for it is a maxim "with Lorenzo, *that it is better to confide in all than* "*in a few.*" From the ſame authority we learn, that the due adminiſtration of juſtice engaged his conſtant attention, and that he carefully avoided giving riſe to an idea, that he was himſelf above the control of the law. Where compulſory regulations loſt their effect, the aſſiduity and example of Lorenzo produced the moſt ſalutary conſequences, and baniſhed that diſſipation which enervates, and that indolence which palſies ſociety. By forming inſtitutions for the cultivation of the ancient languages, or the diſcuſſion of philoſophical truths, by promoting the ſciences, and encouraging the uſeful and ornamental arts, he ſtimulated talents into action, and excited an emulation which called forth all the powers of the mind. Even the public ſpectacles, intended for the gratification of the multitude, partook of the poliſhed character of the inhabitants, and were conceived with ingenuity, and enlivened with wit. The proſperity and happineſs which the citizens thus enjoyed were attributed to their true ſource, and Lorenzo received

(*a*) *Philippus Reddiſus Exhort. ad Pet. Med. Laur. fil. inter opuſc. Joan. Lamii. Delic. Erudit. Flor.* 1742.

the beſt reward of his labors in the gratitude of his country.

Beyond the limits of Tuſcany, the character of this illuſtrious Florentine was more eminently conſpicuous. The glory of the republic appeared at a diſtance to be concentered in himſelf. To him, individually, ambaſſadors were frequently diſpatched by the firſt monarchs of Europe; who, as their concerns required, alternately courted his aſſiſtance or ſolicited his advice (*a*). In the year 1489, when the emperor Frederick III. ſent an embaſſy to Rome, he directed them to paſs through Florence to obtain the patronage of Lorenzo; being, as he ſaid, convinced of his importance in directing the affairs of Italy. An interchange of kind offices ſubſiſted between this eminent citizen and John II. king of Portugal, who was deſervedly dignified with the appellation of great, and was deſirous that the tranſactions of his life ſhould be recorded by the pen of Politiano (*b*). From Matteo Corvino whoſe virtues had raiſed him to the throne of Hungary, many letters addreſſed to Lorenzo are yet extant, which demonſtrate not only the warm

(*a*) C'étoit une choſe auſſi admirable qu'éloignée de nos mœurs, de voir ce citoyen, qui faiſait toujours le commerce, vendre d'une main les denrées du Levant, & ſoutenir de l'autre le fardeau de la république; entretenir des facteurs, & recevoir des ambaſſadeurs; réſiſter au pape, faire la guerre & la paix, être l'oracle des princes, cultiver les belles-lettres, donner des ſpectacles au peuple, & accueillir tous les ſçavans Grecs de Conſtantinople. Il égala le grand *Coſme* par ſes bienſaits, & le ſurpaſſa par ſa magnificence.

Volt. Eſſai, v. ii. *p.* 284.

(*a*) *Pol. Epiſt. lib.* x. *Ep.* 1, 2.

attachment

attachment of that monarch to the cauſe of ſcience and the arts, but his eſteem and veneration for the man whom he conſidered as their moſt zealous protector (*a*). As the reputation of Lorenzo increaſed, the aſſiduities of Louis XI. of France became more conſpicuous; and in exchange for profeſſions of eſteem, which from ſuch a quarter could confer no honor, we find him ſoliciting from Lorenzo ſubſtantial favors (*b*). The commercial intercourſe between Florence and Egypt, by means of which the Florentines carried on their lucrative traffic in the productions of the eaſt, was extended and improved by Lorenzo; and ſuch was the eſtimation in which he was held by the ſultan, that, in the year 1487, an ambaſſador arrived at Florence, bringing with him, as a mark of his maſter's eſteem, many ſingular preſents of rare animals and valuable commodities; amongſt the former of which, a camelopardalis principally attracted the curioſity of the populace (*c*).

This epoch forms one of thoſe ſcanty portions in the hiſtory of mankind, on which we may dwell without weeping over the calamities, or bluſhing for the crimes of our ſpecies. Accordingly, the fancy of the poet, expanding in the gleam of

(*a*) Theſe letters are preſerved in the *Palazzo Vecchio*, at Florence. *Filz.* xlvii.

(*b*) A letter from Louis XI. to Lorenzo, moſt earneſtly entreating his aſſiſtance in promoting the intereſts of the king's favorites in a propoſed nomination of cardinals by Innocent VIII. is preſerved in the *Palazzo Vecchio. Filz.* lix.

(*c*) Of theſe articles Pietro da Bibbiena, the ſecretary of Lorenzo, gives an inventory to Clarice his wife, *v. App. No.* XLIX. *Fabr.* ii. 337.

proſperity, has celebrated theſe times as realizing the beautiful fiction of the golden age (*a*). This ſeaſon of tranquillity is the interval to which Guicciardini ſo ſtrikingly adverts, in the commencement of his hiſtory, as being "proſperous beyond any "other that Italy had experienced, during the "long courſe of a thouſand years. When the "whole extent of that fertile and beautiful country "was cultivated, not only throughout its wide "plains and fruitful vallies, but even amidſt its "moſt ſterile and mountainous regions; and under "no control but that of its native nobility and "rulers, exulted, not only in the number and "riches of its inhabitants, but in the magnificence "of its princes, in the ſplendor of many ſuperb "and noble cities, and in the reſidence and majeſty "of religion itſelf. Abounding with men eminent "in the adminiſtration of public affairs, ſkilled in "every honorable ſcience and every uſeful art, "it ſtood high in the eſtimation of foreign nations. "Which extraordinary felicity, acquired at many "different opportunities, ſeveral circumſtances "contributed to preſerve, but among the reſt, no "ſmall ſhare of it was, by general conſent, aſcribed "to the induſtry and the virtue of Lorenzo "de' Medici; a citizen, who roſe ſo far beyond "the mediocrity of a private ſtation, that he regu-"lated by his counſels the affairs of Florence, then

(*a*) From the numerous pieces which allude to this period, I ſhall ſelect the poem of Aurelius (or Lippo) Brandolini, *De laudibus Laurentii Medicis*, as it is given in the *Carmina illuſt. Poet. Ital.* v. ii. p. 439. A collection now very rarely met with. *v. App. No.* I.

" more important by its ſituation, by the genius " of its inhabitants, and the promptitude of its " reſources, than by the extent of its dominions; " and who having obtained the implicit confidence " of the Roman pontiff, Innocent VIII. rendered " his name great, and his authority important in " the affairs of Italy. Convinced of the perils " that might ariſe, both to the Florentine republic " and to himſelf, if any of the more powerful " ſtates ſhould be allowed to extend their domini- " ons, he uſed every exertion that the affairs of " Italy might be ſo balanced, that there ſhould be " no inclination in favor of any particular ſtate; " a circumſtance which could not take place " without the permanent eſtabliſhment of peace, " and the minuteſt attention to every event, how- " ever trivial it might appear." Such are the repreſentations of this celebrated hiſtorian. It is only to be regretted that theſe proſperous days were of ſuch ſhort duration. Like a momentary calm that precedes the ravages of the tempeſt, they were ſcarcely enjoyed before they were paſt. The fabric of the public happineſs, erected by the vigilance, and preſerved by the conſtant care of Lorenzo, remained indeed firm and compact during the ſhort remainder of his days; but at his death it diſſolved like the work of enchantment, and overwhelmed for a time in its ruins even the deſcendants of its founder.

CHAP. VII.

DIFFERENT progreſs of Italian and claſſical literature —Latin writings of Dante, Petrarca, and Boccaccio —Effects produced by them—Emanuel Chryſoloras—Conſequences of improvement—Progreſs of the Laurentian Library—Introduction of printing in Florence —Early editions of the claſſic authors—Politiano corrects the Pandects of Juſtinian—Miſcellanea of Politiano—His controverſy with Merula—Eſtabliſhment of the Greek academy at Florence—Joannes Argyropylus—Demetrius Chalcondyles—Engliſh ſcholars at Florence—Political importance obtained by men of learning — Florentine ſecretaries — Bartolommeo Scala—His controverſy with Politiano—Learned ſtateſmen in other governments of Italy — Men of rank devote themſelves to ſtudy—Pico of Mirandula —Learned women — Aleſſandra Scala — Caſſandra Fidelis — Reſult of the attention ſhown to claſſical learning — Tranſlations — Italian writers of Latin poetry — Landino — Ugolino and Michael Verini — Other Latin poets of the fifteenth century—Character of the Latin poetry of Politiano — General idea of the ſtate of literature in Florence in the latter part of the fifteenth century.

OF the improvement that took place in the Italian language in the fourteenth century, of its rapid and unexpected decline in that which ſucceeded and of its reſtoration under the auſpices of Lorenzo de'

Medici, ſome account has already been given; but in tracing the hiſtory of the revival and progreſs of the ancient languages, we ſhall find, that as they were influenced by other cauſes, they neither flouriſhed nor declined with the ſtudy of the national tongue. On the contrary, a daily proficiency was made in claſſical literature, at the very time that the Italian language was again ſinking into barbariſm and neglect; and the former advanced, by a gradual but certain progreſs, towards that perfection which the latter ſuddenly and unexpectedly attained, from the cauſes to which we have before adverted.

In aſſigning the reaſon for this remarkable diſtinction, we muſt again recur to the times of Dante, of Petrarca, and of Boccaccio; and obſerve the effects produced by the exertions of thoſe great men, whoſe talents throw a luſtre over a period which would otherwiſe be involved in total darkneſs. In eſtimating their labors, we ſhall find that their various attempts to reduce into form their native language, and to revive the ſtudy of the ancient tongues, were not only attended with different degrees of ſucceſs, but were followed by conſequences preciſely the reverſe of thoſe which might have been expected. With whatever juſtice Petrarca and Boccaccio might, in their own days, have boaſted of their voluminous productions in the Latin tongue, the increaſing applauſe beſtowed on their Italian writings ſoon obſcured their fame as Latin authors; and they are indebted for their preſent celebrity to works which they almoſt bluſhed to own, and were ashamed to communicate to each other (*a*). The different merits of their Latin and their Italian compositions were however soon appreciated; and whilst the latter were daily rising in the estimation of the world, the former lost a great share of their reputation before the close of the succeeding century. " It is not to be denied (*b*)," says a very judicious critic of that period, " that " both Dante and Petrarca were warm admirers " of the ancients; but the Latin writings of Dante, " like a picture that has lost its color, exhibit little " more than an outline. Happy indeed had it " been, had this author been enabled to convey " his sentiments in Latin, as advantageously as he " has done in his native tongue. The numerous " works of Petrarca, the offspring of that solitude " in which he delighted, are lasting monuments " of his industry and his talents. Yet his style is " harsh, and scarcely bears the character of Latinity. " His writings are indeed full of thought, but de- " fective in expression, and display the marks of " labor without the polish of elegance; but as we " sometimes take a potion, not for the sake of

(*a*) The Decamerone of Boccaccio was not communicated to Petrarca till many years after it was written (*Manni, Illust. del Boccaccio, p.* 629.); and Petrarca himself confesses, that the reception of his Italian writings was far more favorable than he expected.

S'io avessi pensato che si care,
 Fossin le voci de' sospir miei in rima,
 Fatte l'avrei dal sospirar mio prima,
 In numero più spesse, in stil più rare.

Son. 253.

(*a*) *Paulus Cortesius, De Hominibus doctis, p.* 7. *Ed. Flor,* 1734.

« gratification, but of health, fo from thefe writings « we muft expect to derive utility rather than « amufement. Rude as they are, they poffefs how- « ever fome fecret charm which renders them « engaging. The diftinguifhed talents of Boccaccio « funk under the preffure of the general malady. « Licentious and inaccurate in his diction, he has « no idea of felection. All his Latin writings are « hafty, crude, and uninformed. He labors with « thought, and ftruggles to give it utterance; but « his fentiments find no adequate vehicle, and the « luftre of his native talents is obfcured by the « depraved tafte of the times." Whilft fuch was the fate of the Latin productions of thefe authors, their Italian writings were the objects rather of adoration than applaufe. No longer confined to the perufal of the clofet, and the gratification of an individual, the poems of Dante and of Petrarca were read in public affemblies of the inhabitants of Florence, and their beauties pointed out, or their obfcurities illuftrated, by the moft eminent fcholars of the time. No fooner was the art of printing difcovered, than copies of them were multiplied with an avidity which demonftrates the high efteem in which they were held. Even the prolix annotations with which thefe early editions were generally accompanied, if they do not for the moft part difplay the talents of the critic, are a proof of the celebrity of the author. This obfervation is not however applicable to the commentary of Dante by Landino, who, with a laudable perfeverance, has preferved the remembrance of many historical facts, and related many circumstances indispensibly necessary to the explanation of the *Divina Commedia.* His industry in the execution of a task so grateful to his countrymen, was rewarded by the donation of a villa, or residence, on the hill of Casentino, in the vicinity of Florence, which he enjoyed under the sanction of a public decree. Whilst the annotator was thus compensated, the exiled poet was, upwards of a century after his death, restored to his family honors, with the same formalities as if he had been still living; his descendants were permitted to enjoy the possessions of their illustrious ancestor, and his bust, crowned with laurels, was raised at the public expense.

It might then have been expected, that the successful efforts of these authors to improve their native tongue, would have been more effectual than the weak, though laudable attempts made by them to revive the study of the ancient languages; but it must be remembered, that they were all of them men of genius, and genius assimilates not with the character of the age. Homer and Shakspeare have no imitators, and are no models. The example of such talents is perhaps upon the whole unfavorable to the general progress of improvement; and the superlative abilities of a few, have more than once damped the ardor of a nation (*a*). But if the

(*a*) Dopo la morte di Cicerone e di Vergilio due chiarissimi specchi della lingua Latina, cominciò il modo dello scrivere Romanamente, cosi in versi come in prosa, a mutarsi & variare da se medesimo, e andò tanto di mano in mano peggiorando, che non era quasi più quel desso. Il medesimo nè più nè meno avvenne nella

great Italian authors were inimitable in the productions of their native language, in their Latin writings they appeared in a ſubordinate character. Of the labors of the ancients, enough had been diſcovered to mark the decided difference between their merits and thoſe of their modern imitators; and the applauſes beſtowed upon the latter, were only in proportion to the degree in which they approached the models of ancient eloquence. This competition was therefore eagerly entered into; nor had the ſucceſs of the firſt revivers of theſe ſtudies deprived their followers of the hope of ſurpaſſing them (*a*). Even the early part of the fifteenth century produced ſcholars as much ſuperior to Petrarca, and his coadjutors, as they were to the monkiſh compilers, and ſcholaſtic diſputants, who immediately preceded them; and the labors of Leonardo Aretino, Gianozzo Manetti, Guarino Veroneſe, and Poggio Bracciolini, prepared the way for the ſtill more correct and claſſical productions of Politiano, Sannazaro, Pontano, and Augurelli. The declining ſtate of Italian literature,

lingua fiorentina; perchè ſpenti Dante, il Petrarca, e'l Boccaccio, cominciò a variare e mutarſi il modo e la guiſa del favellare, e dello ſcrivere fiorentinamente, e tanto andò di male in peggio che quaſi non ſi riconoſceva più, &c.

Varchi L'Ercolano, vol. i. p. 63. *Ed. Padova,* 1744.

(*a*) Difficilis in perfecto mora eſt; naturaliterque quod procedere non poteſt, recedit. Et, ut primo ad conſequendos, quos priores ducimus, accendimur; ita ubi aut præteriri aut æquari eos poſſe deſperavimus, ſtudium cum ſpe ſeneſcit; & quod adſequi non poteſt, ſequi deſinit: præteritoque eo in quo eminere non poſſimus, aliquid in quo nitamur conquirimus. *Velleius Paterc. lib. i. cap.* 17.

ſo far then from being inconſiſtent with, was rather a conſequence of the proficiency made in other purſuits, which, whilſt they were diſtinguiſhed by a greater degree of celebrity, demanded a more continued attention, and an almoſt abſolute devotion both of talents and of time.

Whatever may have been the opinion in more modern times, the Italian ſcholars of the fifteenth century did not attribute to the exertions of their own countrymen the reſtoration of ancient learning. That they had ſhown a decided predilection for thoſe ſtudies, and had excited an ardent thirſt of further knowledge, is univerſally allowed; but the ſource from which that thirſt was allayed, was found in Emanuel Chryſoloras, who, after his return to his native country from his important embaſſies, was prevailed upon by the Florentines to pay a ſecond viſit to Italy, and to fix his reſidence among them. The obligations due to Chryſoloras, are acknowledged in various parts of their works, by thoſe who availed themſelves of his inſtructions; and the gratitude of his immediate hearers was transfuſed into a new race of ſcholars, who by their eulogies on their literary patriarch, but much more by their own talents, contributed to honor his memory (*a*). On his arrival in Italy

(*a*) Chryſoloras died at Conſtance, when the council was held there in 1415. A volume, conſiſting of eulogies upon him, lately exiſted in the monaſtery at *Camaldoli*. (*Zeno. Diſſ. Voſſ. v.* i. *p.* 214.) Poggio and Æneas Sylvius (Pius II.) each of them honored him with an epitaph. In the latter, the merit of having been the reviver of both Greek and Latin literature, is explicitly attributed to him.

in the character of an instructor, he was accompanied by Demetrius Cydonius, another learned Greek. The ardor with which they were received by the Italian scholars, may be conjectured from a letter of Coluccio Salutati to Demetrius, on his landing at Venice (*a*). "I rejoice not so much," says he, "in the honor I receive from your notice, as for "the interests of literature. At a time when the "study of the Greek language is nearly lost, and "the minds of men are wholly engrossed by am-"bition, voluptuousness, or avarice, you appear "as the messengers of the Divinity, bearing the "torch of knowledge into the midst of our darkness. "Happy indeed shall I esteem myself, (if this life "can afford any happiness to a man to whom

Ille ego, qui Latium priscas imitarier artes,
Explosis docui sermonum ambagibus, & qui,
Eloquium magni DEMOSTHENIS & CICERONIS
In lucem retuli, CHRYSOLORAS nomine notus,
Hic situs emoriens, peregrina sede quiesco, &c.

Hod. de Græc. illust. p. 24.

Janus Pannonius, a scholar of Guarino Veronese, (for whose history and unhappy fate, *v. Valerianus De infelicitate Literatorum,*) in an elegant Latin panegyric on his preceptor, also pays a tribute of respect to the Greek scholar:

Vir fuit hic patrio CHRYSOLORAS nomine dictus,
Candida Mercurio quem Calliopæa crearat,
Nutrierat Pallas: nec solis ille parentum
Clarus erat studiis, sed rerum protinus omnem
Naturam, magna complexus mente tenebat.

Jani Pannonii Quinqueeclesiensis Episc. Paneg. ad Guar. Ver. preceptorem suum ap. Frobenium. Basil. 1518. *p.* 11.

(*a*) *Mehus, in vitâ Amb. Trav. p.* 356. This early visitor has escaped the researches of Dr. Hody. *De Græc. Illust.*

" to-morrow will bring the close of his sixty-fifth " year,) if I should by your assistance imbibe those " principles, from which all the knowledge which " this country possesses is wholly derived. Perhaps, " even yet, the example of Cato may stimulate me " to devote to this study the little that remains of " life, and I may yet add to my other acquirements, " a knowledge of the Grecian tongue."

If we advert to the night of thick darkness in which the world had been long enveloped, we may easily conceive the sensations that took place in the minds of men when the gloom began to disperse, and the spectres of false science, by turns fantastic and terrific, gave way to the distinct and accurate forms of nature and of truth. The Greeks who visited Italy in the early part of the fifteenth century, if they did not diffuse a thorough knowledge of their language, and of those sciences which they exclusively possessed, at least prepared a safe asylum for the muses and the arts, who had long trembled at the approach, and at length fled before the fierce aspect of Mahomet II. From that period a new order of things took place in Italy; the construction of language was investigated on philosophical principles; the maxims of sound criticism began to supplant the scholastic subtilties which had perverted for ages the powers of the human mind; and men descended from their fancied eminence among the regions of speculation and hypothesis, to tread the earth with a firm foot, and to gain the temple of fame by a legitimate, though laborious path.

The eſtabliſhment of public libraries in different parts of Italy, whilſt it was one of the firſt conſequences of this ſtriking predilection for the works of the ancients, became in its turn the active cauſe of further improvement. To no deſcription of individuals is the world more indebted, than to thoſe who have been inſtrumental in preſerving the wiſdom of paſt ages, for the uſe of thoſe to come, and thereby giving, as it were, a general ſenſorium to the human race. In this reſpect great obligations are due to the venerable Coſmo (*a*). From the intercourſe that in his time ſubſiſted between Florence and Conſtantinople, and the long viſits made by the Greek prelates and ſcholars to Italy, he had the beſt opportunity of obtaining the choiceſt treaſures of ancient learning; and the deſtruction of Conſtantinople may be ſaid to have transferred to Italy all that remained of eaſtern ſcience (*b*). After the death of Coſmo, his ſon Piero purſued with ſteady perſeverance the ſame object, and made important additions to the various

(*a*) *Bandini, Lettera ſopra i principj, &c. della Biblioteca Laurenziana. Fir.* 1773.

(*b*) The library of S. Marco, which, as we have before related, was founded by Coſmo, with the books collected by Niccolo Niccoli, and augmented at his own expenſe, was, in the year 1454, almoſt buried in ruins by an earthquake, that continued at intervals for nearly forty days, during which ſeveral perſons loſt their lives. Coſmo however not only reſtored the building to its former ſtate, but raiſed the ceiling, ſo as to admit of a more extenſive collection. At the ſame time a new arrangement of the manuſcripts took place, and the Greek and Oriental works were formed into a claſs diſtinct from the Latin. *Mehus in vitâ Amb. Trav. p.* 66. 73.

collections which Cosmo had begun, particularly to that of his own family (*a*). But although the ancestors of Lorenzo laid the foundation of the immense collection of manuscripts, since denominated the Laurentian Library, he may himself claim the honor of having raised the superstructure. If there was any pursuit in which he engaged more ardently, and persevered more diligently than the rest, it was that of enlarging his collection of books and antiquities. " We need not wonder," says Niccolo Leoniceno, writing to Politiano (*b*), " at " your eloquence and your acquirements, when " we consider the advantages which you derive " from the favor of Lorenzo de' Medici, the great " patron of learning in this age; whose messengers " are dispersed throughout every part of the earth,

(*a*) The manuscripts acquired by Piero de' Medici are for the most part highly ornamented with miniatures, gilding, and other decorations, and are distinguished by the *fleurs de lys*. Those collected by Lorenzo are marked not only with the Mediceean arms, but with a laurel branch in allusion to his name, and the motto SEMPER. When we advert to the immense prices which were given for these works, and the labor afterwards employed on them, they may be considered as the most expensive articles of luxury. A taste for the exterior decoration of books has lately arisen in this country, in the gratification of which no small share of ingenuity has been displayed; but if we are to judge of the present predilection for learning by the degree of expense thus incurred, we must consider it as greatly inferior either to that of the Romans, during the times of the first emperors, or of the Italians in the fifteenth century. And yet it is perhaps difficult to discover, why a favorite book should not be as proper an object of elegant ornament, as the head of a cane, the hilt of a sword, or the latchet of a shoe.

(*b*) *Polit. Epist. lib. ii, Ep.* 7.

"for the purpose of collecting books on every "science, and who has spared no expense in "procuring for your use, and that of others who "may devote themselves to similar studies, the "materials necessary for your purpose. I well "remember the glorious expression of Lorenzo, "which you repeated to me, that he wished the "diligence of Pico and yourself, would afford him "such opportunities of purchasing books, that "his fortune proving insufficient, he might pledge "even his furniture to possess them." Acting under the influence of such impressions, we cannot wonder at the progress made by Lorenzo, in which he derived great assistance from Hieronymo Donato, Ermolao Barbaro, and Paolo Cortesi; but his principal coadjutor was Politiano, to whom he committed the care and arrangement of his collection, and who made excursions at intervals through Italy, to discover and purchase such remains of antiquity, as suited the purposes of his patron (*a*). Two journies, undertaken at the instance of Lorenzo into the east, by Giovanni Lascar produced a great number of rare and valuable works. On his return from his second expedition, he brought with him about two hundred copies, many of which he had procured from a monastery at Mount Athos; but

(*b*) Of the vigilance of Politiano in these pursuits, we have the most explicit evidence, in a letter from him to Lorenzo, first published by Fabroni, which may justify the forcible remark of that author on the literary agents of Lorenzo. " Porro ipsos venaticos canes dixisses, " ita odorabantur omnia & pervestigabant, ut ubi quidque rarum " esset, aliqua ratione invenirent atque compararent."

Fabr. in vitâ Laur. v. i. p. 153. App. No. LI.

this treafure did not arrive till after the death of Lorenzo, who in his laft moments expreffed to Politiano and Pico, his regret that he could not live to complete the collection which he was forming for their accommodation (*a*). Stimulated by the example of Lorenzo, other eminent patrons of learning engaged in the fame purfuit. Thofe who particularly diftinguifhed themfelves were Matteo Corvino king of Hungary, and Federigo duke of Urbino (*b*), to both of whom Lorenzo gave permiffion to copy fuch of his manufcripts as they wifhed to poffefs; nothing being more confonant to his intentions than to diffufe the fpirit of literature as extenfively as poffible.

The newly difcovered art of printing, contributed alfo in an eminent degree, to accelerate the progrefs of claffical literature. This art was practifed very early in Florence, and fome of the Florentine authors have even been defirous of conferring on one of their countrymen, the merit of its invention (*c*); but this acute people have too many well-founded claims on the gratitude of pofterity, to render it neceffary for them to rely on doubtful commendation. It is however certain that whilft Venice folicited the affiftance of Nicolas Jenfen, a native of France, and Rome began to practife the

(*a*) Non nihil etiam tunc quoque jocatus nobifcum, quin utrofque intuens nos; Vellem ait diftuliffet me faltem mors hæc ad eum diem quo veftram plane bibliothecam abfoluiffem. *Pol. Ep. lib.* iv. *Ep.* 2.

(*b*) *Pol. Ep. lib.* iii. *Ep.* 6. *Fabr. in vitâ Laur. v.* i. *p.* 154.

(*c*) *Manni, della prima promulgazione de' Libri in Firenze. Fir.* 1761.

art

art under the guidance of the two German printers, Sweynheym and Pannartz, Florence found amongst her own citizens, an artist equal to the task. Taking for his example the inscriptions on the ancient Roman seals (*a*), or more probably stimulated by the success of his contemporaries, Bernardo Cennini, a Florentine goldsmith, formed the *matrices* of his letters in steel; by means of which, with the assistance of his two sons, Domenico and Piero, he began in the year 1471, to print the works of Virgil, with the commentary of Servius, which he published at Florence in the following year (*b*).

Lorenzo de' Medici saw the importance of a discovery, which had been wanting to the completion of the generous views of his ancestors, and availed himself of it with a degree of earnestness which sufficiently shows the motives by which he was actuated. At his instigation, several of the Italian scholars were induced to bestow their attention, in collating and correcting the manuscripts

(*a*) *Manni, della prima promulgazione de' Libri in Firenze. p.* 3.

(*b*) At the close of the Bucolics in this edition, is the following inscription:

AD LECTOREM
Florentiæ vii. *Idus Novembres*
MCCCCLXXI.

Bernardus Cenninus Aurifex omnium judicio præstantissimus & Dominicus ejus F. egregiæ indolis adolescens: expressis ante calibe characteribus, ac deinde fusis literis, volumen hoc primum impresserunt. Petrus Cenninus Bernardi ejusdem F. quanta potuit cura & diligentia emendavit, ut cernis. *Florentinis ingeniis nil ardui est.* And at the close of the volume is another inscription, with the date of October 1472.

of the ancient authors, in order that they might be ſubmitted to the preſs with the greateſt poſſible accuracy. In the dialogues of Landino, publiſhed by him under the name of *Diſputationes Camaldulenſes*, to which we have had occaſion to refer (*a*), that author has devoted his third and fourth books to a critical diſſertation on the works of Virgil, particularly with a view of explaining ſuch parts as are ſuppoſed to contain an allegorical ſenſe; but he ſoon afterwards performed a much more grateful office to the admirers of the Roman poet, by correcting the errors with which his works abounded, and endeavouring to reſtore them to their original purity. In the proeme to this work, which he has inſcribed to Piero de' Medici, the ſon of Lorenzo, he recapitulates the favors which the anceſtors of his patron have beſtowed on men of learning, and particularly recommends to his imitation, in this reſpect, the example of his father. He adverts to the aſſaſſination of Giuliano de' Medici, and attributes the preſervation of Lorenzo at that critical juncture to his own courage and magnanimity (*b*). Returning to his immediate ſubject, he thus proceeds: "In my dialogues of Camaldoli, I have given

(*a*) *Vol.* i. *p.* 103.

(*b*) Dabis, ſuaviſſime Petre, hoc in loco roganti mihi veniam, ſi barbaricam illam, & omnium ſceleratiſſimam ac ſine exemplo conjurationem ſilentio præterierim: qua in templo marmoreo inter ſacra ſolemnia & Julianus frater ſæviſſime trucidatus, & ipſe Laurentius, inter ſtrictos, & undique eum petentes gladios jam jam caſurus, ita elapſus eſt, ut non humano, ſed divino auxilio, & ſua animi præſtantia, quæ audaciſſimum quemque terrere poterat, de manu inimicorum ereptus videatur. *Band. Spec. Lit. Flor. v.* i. *p.* 223.

"a philosophical comment on the works of Virgil. "I now mean to perform the office of a grammarian and critic on this author. In my former "attempt, as the subject is of more dignity, I "have introduced your father as one of the disputants; but these observations, which are intended to inculcate a knowledge of the Latin language, "I consider as more properly addressed to a young "man of your promising talents and cultivated "understanding (*a*)." In the year 1482, Landino published also an edition of the works of Horace, with numerous corrections and remarks, which he inscribed to Guido da Feltri, the son of Federigo, duke of Urbino (*b*), to whom he had dedicated, in terms of the highest commendation and respect, his *Disputationes Camaldulenses.* Landino was one of the first scholars who, after the revival of letters, devoted himself to the important task of restoring and elucidating these favorite authors, and his labors were received with unbounded applause. Of his observations on Horace considerable use has been made by many subsequent editors. On their publication, Politiano accompanied them with the following ode, not unworthy of the poet whose praises it is intended to celebrate (*c*):

(*a*) *Band. Spec. Lit. Flor. v.* i. *p.* 225.

(*b*) *Impressum per Antonium Miscominum, Florentiæ, anno Salutis* MCCCCLXXXII. *nonis Augusti.* These commentaries were republished at Venice, *per Joannem de Forlivio & Socios,* in the following year, and several subsequent editions have taken place.

(*c*) This ode is not printed in the works of Politiano, and is very inaccurately given by Bandini. *Spec. Lit. Flor.* It is here republished from the edition of Horace by Landino, *Ven.* MCCCCLXXXIII.

E 2

AD HORATIUM FLACCUM.

Vates Threicio blandior Orpheo,
  Seu malis fidibus ſiſtere lubricos
  Amnes, ſeu tremulo ducere pollice
  Ipſis cum latebris feras;
Vates Aeolii pectinis arbiter,
  Qui princeps Latiam ſollicitas chelyn,
  Nec ſegnis titulos addere noxiis
  Nigro carmine frontibus;
Quis te a barbarica compede vindicat?
  Quis frontis nebulam diſpulit, & ſitu
  Deterſo, levibus reſtituit choris,
  Curata juvenem cute?
O quam nuper eras nubilus, & malo
  Obductus ſenio, quam nitidos ades
  Nunc vultus referens, docta fragrantibus
  Cinctus tempora floribus!
Talem purpureis reddere ſolibus
  Laetum pube nova poſt gelidas nives
  Serpentem, poſitis exuviis, ſolet
  Verni temperies poli.
Talem te choreis reddidit & Lyrae,
  Landinus, veterum laudibus æmulus,
  Qualis tu ſolitus Tibur ad uvidum
  Blandam tendere barbiton.
Nunc te deliciis, nunc decet & levi
  Laſcivire joco, nunc puerilibus
  Inſertum thyaſis, aut fide garrula,
  Inter ludere virgines.

Poet, than whom the bard of Thrace
  Ne'er knew to touch a ſweeter ſtring;

O whether from their deep receſs
  The tenants of the wilds thou bring,
With all their ſhades; whether thy ſtrain
  Bid liſtening rivers ceaſe to flow;
Whether with magic verſe thou ſtain
  A laſting blot on vice's brow;
Poet! who firſt the Latian lyre
  To ſweet Æolian numbers ſtrung!
When late repreſſed thy native fire,
  When late impervious glooms o'erhung
Thy front, O ſay what hand divine
  Thy rude barbaric chains unbound,
And bade thee in new luſtre ſhine,
  Thy locks with vernal roſes crown'd?
As when in ſpring's reviving gleam
  The ſerpent quits his ſcaly ſlough,
Once more beneath the ſunny beam,
  In renovated youth to glow;
To thy lov'd lyre, and choral throng,
  LANDINO thus their poet brings;
Such as thy TIBUR heard thy ſong,
  Midſt her cool ſhades and guſhing ſprings.
Again with tales of whiſpered love,
  With ſprightly wit of happieſt vein,
Through bands of vine-crown'd youths to rove,
  Or ſport amidſt the virgin train.

It is greatly to the credit of Politiano that theſe verſes were addreſſed to the perſon who was his moſt formidable rival in thoſe ſtudies to which he had particularly devoted his talents. In reſtoring to their original purity the ancient authors, he was himſelf indefatigable; and if to the munificence of Lorenzo de' Medici we are to attribute the preſervation of many of theſe works, Politiano is perhaps entitled to our equal acknowledgments for his elucidations and corrections of the text, which, from a variety of cauſes, was frequently unintelligible, illegible, or corrupt. In the exerciſe of his critical talents he did not confine himſelf to any preciſe method, but adopted ſuch as he conceived beſt ſuited his purpoſe; on ſome occaſions only comparing different copies, diligently marking the variations, rejecting ſpurious readings, and ſubſtituting the true. In other caſes he proceeded further, and added Scholia and notes illuſtrative of the text, either from his own conjectures, or the authority of other authors (*a*). Beſides the advantages which he derived from various copies of the ſame work, which enabled him to collate them ſo as to aſcertain the true reading, he obtained

(*a*) In the edition of Cato, Varro, and Columella, publiſhed at Paris, *ex off. Rob. Stephani,* 1543, with the corrections of Pet. Victorius, that excellent critic thus adverts to the labors of Politiano: "Non exemplar ipſum ſemper conſului, ſed habui excuſos formis "libros, quos cum antiquis illis *Angelus Politianus* ſtudioſe olim "contulerat, eoſque, quantum mihi commodum fuit, pertractavi; illi "enim quoque publici ſunt. Eruditiſſimi igitur viri labor, magno "me labore levavit; qui quidem, ut erat diligens, & accuratus, hac "librorum collatione mirifice delectabatur: & ita poſſe bonos auctores "multis maculis purgari, vere exiſtimabat. Quæcumque igitur in "priſcis exemplaribus inveniebat, in impreſſis ſedulo adnotabat. "Quod ſi diutius ille vixiſſet, & quæ mente deſtinaverat perficere "potuiſſet, opera ſedulitaſque ipſius magnos ſtudioſis litterarum fructus "attuliſſet, multoſque qui poſtea huic muneri corrigendorum librorum "neceſſario incubuerunt, magna prorſus moleſtia liberaſſet."

great aſſiſtance from the collection of antiques formed by Lorenzo and his anceſtors; and amongſt his coins, inſcriptions on marble, and other authentic documents, frequently elucidated and determined what might otherwiſe have remained in darkneſs or in doubt (*a*). At the cloſe of his remarks on Catullus, a memorial appears in his own handwriting, in which he indulges himſelf in an exultation of youthful vanity, in the idea of having ſurpaſſed all his contemporaries in the diligence which he has ſhown in correcting the ancient authors. This memorial, which bears the date of 1473, at which time he was only eighteen years of age, is ſubſcribed *Angelus Baſſus Politianus.* Before, however, we accuſe our youthful critic of an oſtentatious diſplay of learning, or an improper confidence in his own abilities, we ought to advert to another entry made two years afterwards at the cloſe of the works of Propertius in the ſame volume, by which he confeſſes, that many of his previous obſervations do not approve themſelves to his riper judgment, and requeſts the reader not to form an opinion of his talents, his leaning, or his induſtry, from ſuch a ſpecimen. There being many things

Me quoque, qui ſcripſi, judice digna lini.

Which I, their author, well might wiſh to blot (*b*).

(*a*) *Menck. in vitâ Pol. p.* 237.

(*b*) The reader may conſult theſe memoranda in the Appendix, No. LII.

In this subsequent entry he denominates himself *Angelus Politianus*, which sufficiently marks the period when he chose to discontinue the appellation of *Bassus* (*a*); but what is of more importance, it serves to convince us, that with the errors of his judgment Politiano corrected also those of his temper, and that his proficiency in learning was accompanied by an equal improvement in modesty and candor. Among the ancient authors which he has thus illustrated are Ovid (*b*), Suetonius (*c*), Statius (*d*), The younger Pliny (*e*), The Scriptores Historiæ Augustæ (*f*), and Quintilian (*g*); some of which have been published with his emendations, while his valuable remarks on others are yet confined to the limits of the Italian libraries. The example of Politiano was followed by many other celebrated scholars, who regarded Lorenzo de' Medici as the patron of their studies, and inscribed their labors with his name. Thus Domitio Calderino undertook to regulate the text of Martial (*h*), Bartolommeo Fontio employed his talents on

(*a*) On this point, which has been so much contested, I find the opinion of Bandini before cited in this work, *v.* i. *p.* 144, is confirmed by that of Laur. Mehus, *Vita Amb. Traversarii, p.* 87.

(*b*) In the Bibliotheca Marciana.

(*c*) In the Laurentian Library. *Plut.* LXIV. *cod.* 1.

(*d*) In the Corsini Library at Rome.

(*e*) In the Laurentian Library. *Plut.* LXVII. *cod.* 7.

(*f*) Ib. *Plut.* XLIV. *cod.* 1.

(*g*) Ib. *Plut.* XLVI. *cod.* 5.

(*h*) Printed at Rome per Joannem Gensberg, 1474, *v. De Bure*, No. 2818.

Perſius (*a*), and Lancelotto on Columella (*b*). Nor were the Greek authors neglected. In the year 1488, Demetrins Chalcondyles and Demetrius Cretenſis publiſhed at Florence the firſt edition of the works of Homer, which is inſcribed to Piero de' Medici, the ſon of Lorenzo (*c*).

The ſyſtem of juriſprudence which in the fifteenth century prevailed throughout the greateſt part of Europe, was that of the Roman or civil law, which was principally founded on the pandects or conſtitutions of Juſtinian. Hence the correction and explication of the ſubſiſting copies of this work became of high importance to the community. This taſk was reſerved for the indefatigable induſtry of Politiano, whoſe labors in this department entitle him to rank not only with the earlieſt, but with the moſt learned modern profeſſors of this ſcience. In his letters he has himſelf given ſome account of his progreſs in this laborious work. Much additional information may be found in the narrative of his life by Menckenius; and Bandini, who has lately had the good fortune to recover the commentary of Politiano and reſtore it to its former ſtation in the Laurentian Library, has

(*a*) Publiſhed in 1481. *Band. Cat. Bibl. Laur. v.* ii. *p.* 679.

(*b*) *Band. Cat. v.* ii. *p.* 564. In the preface to this author, the editor thus addreſſes Lorenzo: "Ab incunte etenim ætate, ſplendidiſ-"ſima nominis tui fama, ad tuam benevolentiam captandam ita me "compulit, ut cunctis potius honoris tui ſtudioſum oſtendere hoc ævo "malim, quam in decorem meum reticere."

(*c*) Florentiæ imp. *Typis Bernardi & Nerii Tanaidis Nerlii Florentinorum. Nono menſis Decembris Anno* 1488. 2 vol. fo. For an account of this magnificent work, *v. De Bure, No.* 2493.

publiſhed an hiſtorical narrative expreſſly on this ſubject (*a*). In the accompliſhment of this taſk, which he was induced to undertake at the inſtance of Lorenzo de' Medici, Politiano had ſingular advantages. An ancient and authentic copy found at Piſa, and ſuppoſed to have been depoſited there by the orders of Juſtinian himſelf, had on the capture of that place been transferred to Florence (*b*), and was afterwards intruſted by Lorenzo de' Medici to the ſole cuſtody of Politiano (*c*). By this he was enabled to correct the numerous errors, and to ſupply the defects of the more recent manuſcripts, as well as of two editions which had before iſſued from the preſs (*d*). The

(*a*) *Raggionamento Iſtorico ſopra le collazioni delle Fiorentine Pandette, fatta da Angelo Poliziano, ſotto gli auſpicij del Mag. Lorenzo de' Medici, &c. Livorno* 1762.

(*b*) "Principio igitur ſcire te illud opinor, Imperatorem Juſtinia-"num poſteaquam jus civile perpurgavit, in ordinemque redegit, "caviſſe illud in primis, ut in omnibus civitatibus quæ dignitate "aliqua præcellerant, exemplaria legum quam emendatiſſima publice "aſſervarentur — ſed nullum ex his clarius tamen aut celebratius, "quam quod ad uſque urbis ejus captivitatem, Piſis, magna religione "ſit cuſtoditum." *Pol. Ep. lib.* 10.

(*c*) "Hoc ergo mihi inſpicere per otium licuit, rimarique omnia, "& olfacere, quæque vellem excerpere diligenter, & cum vulgatis "exemplaribus comparare. Tribuit nam hoc mihi uni *Laurentius* "*ille Medices*, vir optimus ac ſapientiſſimus; fore illud aliquando "arbitratus, ut opera; labore induſtriaque noſtra, magna inde omnino "utilitas eliceretur." *Ib.*

(*d*) Mr. Gibbon gives Politiano the appellation of an enthuſiaſt, for ſuppoſing this manuſcript to be the "authentic ſtandard of Juſtinian "himſelf." "This paradox," ſays he, "is refuted by the abbrevia-"tions of the Florentine manuſcript, and the Latin characters betray

civilians of the ensuing century have freely confessed their obligations to a commentator who first with the true spirit of research, applied himself to the elucidation of a science in itself sufficiently complex and obscure, but which was rendered still more so, by the imperfect state of those authorities to which its professors were constantly obliged to refer.

Of the critical talents of Politiano, and of the variety and extent of his erudition, his *Miscellanea* alone afford a sufficient testimony (*a*). For the publication of this work, which consists principally of observations on the writings of the ancient

" the hand of a Greek scribe." *Hist. of the Decline and Fall of the Roman Empire, lib.* 44. But Politiano had duly considered all the peculiarities of the manuscript, of which he was a complete judge, and was fully of opinion that it was the production of a Latin scribe, and not of a Greek. " Est autem," says he in an epistle to Lod. Bolognese (lib. xi.), " liber characteribus majusculis, sine ullis com-" pendiariis notis, sine ullis distinctionibus; nec *Graecus*, sed *Latinus*—" videlicet ille ipse quem inter ceteros publicavit Justinianus." This work, which consists of two volumes, written on thin vellum, was deposited, says Mr. Gibbon, on the authority of Brenckman (*Hist. Pandect. Florent. l.* 1. *c.* x. xi. xii. *p.* 62. 93.) as a sacred relic in a rich casket, in the ancient palace of the republic, new bound in purple, and shown to curious travellers by the monks and magistrates, bare headed and with lighted tapers.

(*a*) First printed by Antonio Miscomini at Florence, with the following singular colophon: *Impressit ex archetypo Antonius Miscominus. Familiares quidam Politiani recognovere. Politianus ipse nec Horthographian se ait, nec omnino alienam praestare culpam.* FLORENTIÆ ANNO SALUTIS M.CCCC.LXXXIX. *Decimo tertio kalendas Octobris.* In 4°. This book, like all those I have seen of the same printer, is most elegantly and correctly executed, and is a proof of the speedy proficiency made in typography at Florence.

authors, we are alſo indebted to Lorenzo de' Medici, to whom Politiano was accuſtomed, as they rode out on horſeback, to repeat the various remarks which had occurred to him in his morning ſtudies (*a*). At the requeſt of Lorenzo, he was at length induced to commit them to paper, and to arrange them in order for the preſs. On their publication he inſcribed them to his great friend and benefactor; not, as he aſſures him, merely for the purpoſe of teſtifying his gratitude, for the aſſiſtance and advice which he had in the courſe of his work received from him, but that it might obtain favor, and derive authority, from the celebrity of his name (*b*).

The publication of this work ſoon afterwards led Politiano into a controverſy, in which he conducted himſelf with firmneſs and moderation, and which terminated greatly to his honor. Lodovico Sforza, anxious to throw a veil over the guilt of his uſurpation by an attention to the promotion of letters, had prevailed upon Giorgio Merula among other learned men, to eſtabliſh his reſidence at Milan, where he enjoyed an ample penſion from the duke. The character of Merula ſtood high for his acquirements in Latin literature (*c*); but neither

(*a*) *Pol. in præf. ad Miſcel.*

(*b*) Nec erunt opinor hæc quoque noſtra, quamquam levioris operis ſtudia, ſeu ludicra verius, dedecori tibi Laurenti Medices, cui nunc adſcribuntur. Adſcribuntur autem non magis adeo ut me gratum beneficiis tuis approbent, aut reponant gratiam, quod auxiliarium te, quodque conſiliarium habuerunt, quam ut auſpicato procedant, & ut in iis tui memoria frequentetur, ex quo liber auctoritatem capiens magni celebritate nominis commendetur. *Pol. in præf. ad Miſcell.*

(*b*) To Merula we are indebted for the firſt edition of the comedies

his proficiency in learning, nor his intercourſe with the great, nor even his advanced age, had ſoftened or improved a diſpoſition naturally jealous and auſtere. He had however ſingled out Politiano as the only perſon among the ſcholars of Italy who, in his opinion, poſſeſſed any ſhare of merit, and upon an interview which they had together at Milan, had acknowledged, that the reſtoration of the language of the ancient Romans depended upon his exertions (*a*). No ſooner, however, did

of Plautus, printed at Venice, *per Johannem de Colonia & Vindelinum de Spira*, 1472. He alſo corrected and commented on the works of Juvenal, of Martial, of Quintilian, of Auſonius, the *Scriptores de re ruſtica*, and other ancient authors; ſeveral of which have been publiſhed with his remarks. Merula was the diſciple of Filelfo, and like him was frequently engaged in thoſe acrimonious conteſts which perhaps promoted, whilſt they diſgraced, the cauſe of literature. One of theſe debates was with Galeotto Marzio, who, about the year 1468, wrote his treatiſe *De homine*, in the firſt book of which he deſcribes the exterior, and in the ſecond, the interior parts of man. This work Merula attacked with great bitterneſs, and with a conſiderable diſplay of critical ſagacity. The commentary of Merula was printed without date or place, and inſcribed to Lorenzo and Giuliano de' Medici; but as the author in his dedication refers to the eſtabliſhment of the academy at Piſa as a recent tranſaction, it was probably publiſhed about the year 1472. From this edition I ſhall give the dedication, as a ſtriking memorial of the early reputation which theſe illuſtrious brothers had acquired as patrons of learning (*v. App. No.* LIII.). In the copy before me, the critique on Galeotto is followed by a comment on an epiſtle of Sappho, inſcribed to M. Ant. Maurocenus, and by ſome obſervations on Virgil, addreſſed to Lodovico Gonzago, prince of Mantua. Some account of the life and labors of Merula may be found in *Tirab. Storia della Lett. Ital. v.* vi. *part.* 1. *p.* 291. *Zeno. Diſſ. Voſſ. vol.* ii, *p.* 83.

(*a*) Meminiſti credo, quod in frequenti auditorio Venetiis, cum

the *Miſcellanea* of Politiano make their appearance, than Merula availed himſelf of an opportunity of demonſtrating his own ſuperiority by depreciating the labors of his rival; aſſerting that ſuch of the remarks of Politiano as were entitled to commendation, might be found in the critical works which he had himſelf previouſly publiſhed, or were in the memory of his pupils who had attended his public inſtructions (*a*). He even inſinuated that he had collected no inconſiderable number of groſs errors, which he might probably make public on ſome future occaſion. Politiano was ſoon apprized of this injurious treatment; and as he was not ſlow at reſenting an indignity, it it is probable that Merula would have experienced the weight of his reſentment, had no other conſiderations interpoſed. Merula ſtood high in the opinion of his patron, whilſt Politiano was known to live on terms of the cloſeſt intimacy with Lorenzo de' Medici. An open attack might therefore have compromiſed the name of Lorenzo, whoſe connexions with Lodovico were of too much importance to be endangered in a literary conteſt. Thus circumſtanced, Politiano adopted a more diſcrete and ſerious method of bringing on a diſcuſſion. He addreſſed a letter to the duke, entreating that he would exert his authority with Merula, to induce him to publiſh his criticiſms; at the ſame time tranſmitting for his peruſal a letter to Merula of ſimilar

ad me acceſſiſſes, palam dixerim, te illum eſſe, quem priſcæ & Romanæ doctrinæ inſtauratorem mihi pollicerer.

Mer. Ep. int. Ep. Pol. lib. xi. *Ep.* 5.

(*a*) *Ibid.*

import (*a*). Merula however refused either to retract the opinions which he had avowed, or to communicate to Politiano his remarks. In answer to a sarcasm, which Politiano might well have spared, he replies, " You reproach me with my grey " locks—I feel not their effects. I yet possess vigor " of mind and strength of body; celerity of thought " and tenacity of memory; of these let Politiano " beware (*b*)." Several letters on this subject appear in the epistles of Politiano, and the contest was rising to an extreme of violence, when Merula suddenly died. This event gave Politiano real concern, not only on account of the loss of a man, of whose talents he entertained a high opinion, but as tending to deprive him still more effectually of the opportunity of defending his work (*c*). Anxious however that nothing might be omitted which was necessary to the vindication of his character, he again addressed himself to the duke, with earnest entreaties to transmit to him the criticisms of Merula; but to no purpose. This formidable composition, if indeed it ever existed, was reduced to a few loose and unimportant observations. The letters of Lodovico, which are remarkable for their kindness and attention to Politiano, seem however at length to have satisfied his restless apprehensions. " You can have no reason, " Angelo," says the duke, " to fear any injury to " your reputation from the suppression of the

(*a*) *Pol. Epist. lib.* xi. *Ep.* 1, 2.
(*b*) *Merulæ Ep. inter Ep. Pol. lib.* xi. *Ep.* 5.
(*c*) *Pol. Epist. lib.* xi. *Ep.* 11.

" remarks of Merula, as this cannot be attributed " to you, who, so far from wishing to conceal " them, have used your utmost endeavours with " us to lay them before the public; of which " the present letter may serve as a testimony (*a*)."

The institution of public seminaries for promoting the knowledge of the ancient languages, the respect paid to those who undertook the task of instruction, and the ample compensation they derived, not only from the liberality of individuals, but from the public at large, powerfully co-operated with the causes before mentioned in infusing a just taste for classical literature. Of the establishment of the academy at Pisa, by the exertions of Lorenzo de' Medici, a brief account has before been given (*b*); but his attention to the cause of learning was by no means confined to this institution. The studies at Pisa were chiefly restricted to the Latin language, or to those sciences of which it was the principal vehicle; but it was at Florence only that the Greek tongue was inculcated under the sanction of a public institution, either by native Greeks, or learned Italians who were their powerful competitors, whose services were procured by the diligence of Lorenzo de' Medici, and repaid by his bounty (*c*).

(*a*) *Pol. Epist. lib.* xi. *Ep.* 21.

(*b*) *Vol.* I. *p.* 156.

(*c*) Ille animadvertens jam tum litteras circa exitum laborare, Pisis Scholas litterarum Latinarum, Florentiæ Græcarum instituit; viros doctissimos aere suo ac magno undecumque accersiit, studiosos & fovit, & juvit, nec prius in hoc elaborare destitit, quam ita restitueret, ut non facile iterum ad id precipitium pervenire possent.

Caii Silvani Germanici Ep. ad Leonem X. *v. Band. Cat. v.* ii. *p.* 117.

Hence

Hence ſucceeding ſcholars have been profuſe of their acknowledgments to their great patron, who firſt formed that eſtabliſhment, from which (to uſe their own ſcholaſtic figure) as from the Trojan horſe, ſo many illuſtrious champions have ſprung, and by means of which the knowledge of the Greek tongue was extended, not only through all Italy, but through France, Spain, Germany, and England, from all which countries numerous pupils attended at Florence, who diffuſed the learning they had there acquired throughout the reſt of Europe (*a*).

Of this inſtitution the firſt public profeſſor was the eminent Johannes Argyropylus, who, after having enjoyed for ſeveral years the favor and protection of Coſmo and Piero de' Medici, and having had a principal ſhare in the education of Lorenzo, was ſelected by him as the perſon beſt qualified to give inſtructions on the Greek tongue. Of the diſciples of Argyropylus, Politiano, if not the moſt diligent, was the moſt ſucceſsful. With the precepts which he imbibed, he acquired a predilection for the ſource from whence they

Florentiam quoque & Latinis & Græcis litteris clariſſime inſignivit, exquiſitis atque ingentibus etiam præmiis allectis utriuſque facultatis viris omnium judicio peritiſſimis.

Raph. Brandolini Ep. ad Leonem X. *v. Band. v.* ii. *p.* 371. *Plut.* xlvi. *Cod.* 2.

(*a*) Quo ſane tempore Florentiæ, veluti in celeberrimo totius orbis theatro, eruditiſſimi viri, tanquam ex equo Trojano innumerabiles proceres, ſeſe in orbem terrarum effuderunt. Quamobrem non modo Italia, ſed etiam Gallia, Hiſpania, Germania, & Britannia hujuſmodi beneficium Medicum familiæ acceptum referunt.

Petri Angelii Epiſt. ap. Band. Cat. ii. 397.

flowed; and his writings discover numerous instances of his affection and veneration for the man who first opened to him the treasures of Grecian literature. To the unlimited applause bestowed by the scholar on the master, one exception only occurs. Argyropylus had professed an open hostility to the reputation of Cicero, whom he represented as a sciolist in the Greek tongue, and as unacquainted with the tenets of the different sects of philosophy, to which so many of his writings relate. The acuteness of Argyropylus, and the influence of his authority, degraded in the estimation of his pupils the character of the Roman orator; and Politiano, in his riper years, seems to shudder at the recollection of the time when the ignorance of Tully was a matter taken for granted by him and his fellow-students (*a*). During the long residence of Argyropylus in Italy he had acquired an extensive knowledge of the Latin language—a species of praise to which few of his countrymen are entitled. His translations into Latin of various tracts of Aristotle, are, for the most part, inscribed to his successive patrons of the family of the Medici, in language expressive of his respect and gratitude (*b*). Among his auditors

(*a*) Et ut homo erat omnium (ut tum quidem videbatur) acerrimus in disputando, atque aurem (quod ait Persius) mordaci lotus aceto, praeterea verborum quoque nostrorum funditator maximus, facile id vel nobis vel ceteris, tum quidem suis sectatoribus persuaserat: ita ut, (quod pene dictu quoque nefas) pro concesso inter nos haberetur, nec philosophiam scisse M. Tullium, nec litteras Graecas.

Pol. in Miscel. cap. 1.

(*b*) *Band. Cat. Bibl. Laur. v.* iii. *p.* 3, 4. 234. 242. 359, *&c.*

we find Donato Acciajuoli, Janus Pannonius, and the German prelate Johannes Reuchlinus, who having had the singular good fortune to obtain some previous knowledge of the Greek tongue, displayed, it is said, on his first interview with Argyropylus, such an acquaintance with it, as induced the Greek to exclaim with a sigh, "*Alas,* "*Greece is already banished beyond the Alps* (*a*)."

To the industry of Argyropylus, and the excellence of his precepts, his disciple Acciajuoli has borne ample testimony; affirming, that whilst he inculcated his doctrines, the times of the ancient philosophers seemed to be again renewed (*b*). If however we may give credit to the testimony of Paulus Jovius, the precepts and the practice of Argyropylus were not entirely consistent with each other; and the obesity of his figure, which was supported by an immoderate supply of food and wine, seemed to mark him out as belonging to a different sect of philosophers (*c*). But, the bishop of Nocera had too many passions to gratify, to permit him to perform the part of a faithful his-

(*a*) *Hodius de Græc. illust. p.* 201.

(*b*) Cum post interitum quorundam doctissimorum hominum, studia Florentina magna ex parte remissa viderentur, venit in hanc urbem Argyropylus Byzantius, vir ingenio præstans summusque philosophus, ut juventutem litteris græcis ac bonis artibus erudiret: jamque plures annos doctrinam tradidit nobis tanta copia, tam multiplicibus variisque sermonibus, ut visus sit temporibus nostris veterum philosophorum memoriam renovare. *Acciaiol. ap. Hod. de Græcis,* 202.

(*c*) Vini & cibi æque avidus & capax, & multo abdomine ventricosus, immodico melopeponum esu autumnalem accersivit febrem, atque ita septuagesimo ætatis anno ereptus est. *Jovii Elog.* XXVIII.

torian, and there are few of his characters that are not discolored or distorted by the medium through which they are seen. The same authors attributes the death of Argyropylus to the intemperate use of melons, which brought on an autumnal fever, that put a period to his life in the seventieth year of his age. This event took place at Rome, where he had fixed his residence some time previous to the year 1471 (*a*).

After an interval of a few years, during which there is reason to believe that the office of public Greek professor at Florence was filled by Theodorus Gaza, and not by Politiano, as asserted by Jovius, the loss of Argyropylus was supplied by Demetrius Chalcondyles, who was invited by Lorenzo de' Medici to take upon himself that employment about the year 1479 (*b*). It is generally understood that an enmity subsisted between Politiano and Chalcondyles, in consequence of which the latter

(*a*) *Hodius de Græc. illust. p.* 198. where the author has given a translation of the Greek epigram of Politiano, expressing his earnest wishes for the return of Argyropylus to Florence.

(*b*) Demetrius Chalcondyles, diligens grammaticus, & supra græcorum mores, cum nihil in eo fallaciarum aut fuci notaretur, vir utique lenis & probus, scholam Florentiæ instauravit, desertam ab Argyropylo, & a Politiano, deficientibus græcis occupatam. *Jov. Elog.* xxix. This information, if not refuted, is rendered highly problematical by the Greek epigram written by Politiano to Chalcondyles, on his arrival at Florence, in which he considers him as the successor of Gaza, and as supplying the maternal office of nourishing the unfledged offspring of literature, deserted by their former parent. A mode of expression not likely to be used by Politiano to a man who was to supersede him in his office of public instructor. A translation of this epigram is given by Hody, *p.* 211.

was eventually under the necessity of quitting Florence, whence he retired to Milan; but for this opinion the only authority is that of Jovius, and of those who have implicitly confided in his relation (*a*). This author, always hostile to the character of Politiano, would induce us to believe, that the Italian scholar, actuated by his jealousy of the Greek, and availing himself of his superior wit and eloquence, endeavoured to injure Chalcondyles by drawing off his pupils, and engaging them in his own auditory; and that Lorenzo de' Medici, as well in order to remove the causes of their contention, as to avail himself of their mutual emulation, divided between them the task of educating his children. It may however be observed that no traces of this dissension are to be found in the narrative of any contemporary author; and that although the known irascibility of Politiano, and his acknowledged animosity to the Greeks, may seem to strengthen the credit of Jovius, yet these circumstances become, on further consideration, the most decisive evidence of his want of authenticity. The antipathies of Politiano were never concealed; and his letters, which extend nearly to the time of his death, contain many instances of that vehemence with which he attacked all those who he conceived had given him just cause

(*a*) Boissard, Baillet, Varillas, &c. The dissensions between Politiano and Chalcondyles have also engaged much of the attention of Menckenius, *Ang. Pol. vita*, p. 65. and of Bayle, *Dict. Hist. Art. Politien*, who have doubted of the veracity of the narrative of Jovius, without adducing that evidence of its improbability which a more minute examination would have supplied.

of offence; but of any dissensions with Chalcondyles no memorial is to be found. On the contrary, Chalcondyles is frequently noticed, both by the Italian scholar and his correspondents, as living with him in habits of intimacy (*a*). The rest of the information derived from Jovius is equally futile. The uninterrupted affection that subsisted between Lorenzo and Politiano, would have prevented the former from adopting a measure which the latter could only have considered as an impeachment of his talents; but independent of inferences drawn from this source, we have positive evidence, that however the children of Lorenzo might attend the incidental instructions of others, Politiano had the constant superintendence of their education, and was addressed on all occasions as the sole person honored with that important trust (*b*).

From the Florentine institution, it is not difficult to discover the progress of Grecian literature to the rest of Europe; but the traces of the channels by which it was conveyed are in no instance more conspicuous than in those which communicated

(*a*) In the year 1491, being only the year previous to the death of Lorenzo de' Medici, Pomponius Lætus writes to Politiano, "Commenda me Medicibus patri & liberis litterarum patronis. Deinde plurima salute Demetrium impertias." To which Politiano replies, "Medices nostri unice tibi favent. Demetrius autem salutem sibi à te dictam totidem verbis remuneratur. In Fesulano sexto idus Augusti, MCCCCXCI." *Pol. Ep. lib.* i. *Ep.* 17, 18.

(*b*) Thus Lod. Odaxius ad Pol. "Demetrium vero virum eruditissimum, Petrumque in primis *discipulum tuum*, elegantissimæ atque amplissimæ spei adolescentem, nomine meo salvos facito."

Pol. Ep. lib. iii. *Ep.* 3.

with this country. William Grocin (*a*), who was for ſome years profeſſor of Greek literature in the univerſity of Oxford, had made a journey to Italy and had reſided for the ſpace of two years at Florence, where he attended the inſtructions of Chalcondyles and of Politiano. Thomas Linacer (*b*), whoſe name deſervedly holds the firſt rank among the early Engliſh ſcholars, availed himſelf of a ſimilar opportunity; and, during his abode at Florence, was ſo eminently diſtinguiſhed by the elegance of his manners and his ſingular modeſty, that he is ſaid to have been ſelected by Lorenzo de' Medici as the aſſociate of his children in their ſtudies (*c*).

Such were the cauſes that in the fifteenth century concurred to promote the ſtudy of the ancient languages in Italy; but one circumſtance yet remains to be noticed, which was perhaps more efficacious than any other in giving life and energy to theſe purſuits. An acquaintance with the learned languages was, at this period, the moſt direct path, not only to riches and literary fame, but to political eminence; and the moſt accompliſhed ſcholars were, in almoſt every government of Italy, the firſt

(*a*) Nam & Grocinum memini, virum ut ſcis multifaria doctrina magno quoque & exercitato ingenio, his ipſis litteris duos continuos annos, etiam poſt prima illa rudimenta, ſolidam operam dediſſe; idque ſub ſummis doctoribus Demetrio Chalcondyla & Angelo Politiano.

Guil. Latimer. in Ep. ad Eraſm. ap. Menck. in vitâ Polit.

(*b*) Linacrum item acri ingenio virum, totidem aut etiam plures annos ſub iiſdem præceptoribus impendiſſe. *Ibid.*

(*c*) *Jovii Elog.* lxiii.

minifters of the time. This arofe in a great degree from the very general ufe of the Latin tongue, in the negotiations of different ftates, which rendered it almoft impoffible for any perfon to undertake the management of public affairs, without an habitual acquaintance with that language; but this was more particularly exemplified in Florence, where the moft permanent officers were uniformly felected on account of their learning. During a long courfe of years the place of fecretary, or chancellor of the republic, (for thefe terms feem to have been indifcriminately ufed,) was filled by fcholars of the firft diftinction. In the beginning of the fifteenth century, it was held by Coluccio Salutati, who had been the intimate friend of Petrarca and of Boccaccio, and is denominated by Poggio, "*The common father and inftructor of all* "*the learned* (*a*)." He was fucceeded by Leonardo Aretino, whofe fervices to the republic were repaid by many privileges and favors conferred on himfelf and his defcendants (*b*). After the death of Leonardo, this office was given to Carlo Marfuppini (*c*), and was afterwards fucceffively held by Poggio Bracciolini (*d*), and Benedetto Accolti (*e*). During a great part of the time that the affairs of Florence were directed by Lorenzo de' Medici, the chancellor of the Republic was Bartolomeo

(*a*) *v. ante, p.* 59. Salutati died about the year 1410.
(*b*) *v. ante, v.* I. *p.* 22.
(*c*) *Ibid.*
(*d*) *Ibid p.* 26,
(*e*) *Ibid. p.* 93,

Scala, whoſe life affords the beſt example of the honors and emoluments which were derived from the cultivation of literature. Scala deduced his origin from parents of the loweſt rank, nor did he poſſeſs from his birth even the privileges of a Florentine citizen (*a*). An early proficiency in letters recommended him to the notice of Coſmo de' Medici; and it was the pride of Scala to avow the meanneſs of his birth, and the obligations which he owed to his earlieſt patron (*b*). The loſs of Coſmo was amply compenſated to Scala by the favor of his deſcendants, through whoſe aſſiſtance he gradually roſe to honors and to affluence, and in the year 1472 was intruſted with the ſeal of the republic. In imitation of his predeceſſors in this office, Scala began a hiſtory of Florence, of which he lived to complete only four books (*c*). His apologues are highly commended by

(*a*) 'E lo Scala, figliuol d'un mulinaro,
Ovver d'un teſſitor di panni lini,
Che colle ſue virtù ſi fece chiaro,
E fu Gonfalonier de' Fiorentini,
Cavalier a Spron d'oro, e non avaro,
Tanto è, voi m'intendete cittadini,
Non s'ha queſti a chiamar nobile e degno,
Che acquiſtò roba, onor, virtute, e ingegno?

L'Altiſſimo, in Bart. Scalæ vita a Mannio. Flor. 1768.

(*b*) Veni nudus omnium rerum bonarum, egenus ad Remp. viliſſimis ortus parentibus, multa cum fide, nullis omnino divitiis, aut titulis, nullis clientelis, nullis cognationibus. Coſmus tamen Pater patriæ noſtræ me complexus eſt, recepitque in familiæ obſequia, &c.

Scalæ Ep. inter. Pol. Ep. lib. xii, *Ep.* 16.

(*c*) Hos edere Joannes Cinellius paraverat, ſed id contigit Oligero Jacobæi, ope Cl. Magliabechii, ſumptibus Nicolai Angeli Tinaſſi, anno MDCLXXVII. *Manni, vita Bart. Scalæ, p.* 47.

Landino and Ficino. Of his poetry, ſpecimens remain both in the Latin and Italian languages, and the former have obtained a place in the celebrated collection of the Latin poems of his illuſtrious countrymen (*a*). Conſidering the proverbial uncertainty of public favor, the life of Scala may be eſteemed a life of unuſual proſperity. He tranſacted the concerns of the republic with acknowledged fidelity, induſtry, and ability; arrived at the higheſt dignities of the ſtate; amaſſed wealth; ranked with men of learning; and left at his death a numerous progeny to inherit his riches and his reſpectability. In his controverſy with Politiano, he appears however as a ſcholar to manifeſt diſadvantage; but the impetuoſity of his adverſary hurried him into a conteſt which it is evident he would willingly have avoided, and in which every effort to extricate himſelf only brought down a ſeverer chaſtiſement.

From the epiſtles of Politiano it appears, that for ſome time theſe angry diſputants had ſhared the favor of Lorenzo de' Medici without diſcovering any ſymptoms of jealouſy; and had even been in the habit of ſubmitting to each other their literary works for mutual correction. Scala, however, having diſcovered, or ſuſpected, that Lorenzo had employed Politiano to reviſe the letters which he had written in the execution of his office, as chancellor of the republic, began to entertain a ſecret enmity againſt his rival, and omitted no

(*a*) *Carm. illuſt. Poet. Ital. v.* viii. *p.* 489.

opportunity of depreciating his writings (*a*). Politiano was no ſooner aware that his literary reputation was attacked, than he gave a looſe to feelings which it is probable he had before with difficulty ſuppreſſed ; and notwithſtanding the rank and reſpectability of Scala, addreſſed him in a ſtyle that ſhows the high opinion which he entertained of his own talents, and his contempt of thoſe of his adverſary. Alluding in one of his letters to the parentage of Scala, he gives him the appellation of *monſtrum furfuraceum*. In another, he honors him with a comment on this title (*b*). To the boaſting of Scala, reſpecting the approbation expreſſed of him by Lorenzo, he returns an anſwer which in theſe days (whether more poliſhed or more barbarous, the reader may determine) could only have been expiated in the blood of one of the diſputants (*c*). In this tranſaction it muſt be allowed that Politiano ſuffered himſelf to be carried beyond all reaſonable bounds, and forgot that reſpect which he owed, if not to the character of his opponent, at leaſt to his own dignity and

(*a*) Scis autem tu quoque litteras illum (Laurentium) ſæpe tuas publice ſcriptas rejeciſſe, nobiſque dediſſe formandas, quæ prima odii livoriſque in me tui cauſa extitit. *Pol. Ep. lib.* xii. *Ep.* 18.

(*b*) At ego *monſtrum* te vocavi *furfuraceum;* monſtrum quidem, quod ex colluvione monſtrorum compoſitus eſt, furfuraceum vero quod in piſtrini ſordibus natus, & quidem piſtrino digniſſimus. *Ibid.*

(*c*) " Extat," thus Scala writes to Politiano, " & illa de me " Laurentii Medicis præclariſſima vox, qua nuſquam collocatum melius " fuiſſe honorem homini novo teſtificatus eſt." *Lib.* xii. *Ep.* 16. To which Politiano laconically replies, " De Coſmo quæ jactas, deque " Laurentio Medice, *falſa omnia*." *Ibid. Ep.* 18.

repntation. It may perhaps be thought that Lorenzo de' Medici ought to have interpofed his authority to fupprefs a conteft which contributed fo little to the credit of the parties, but it was not till after the death of Lorenzo that the difpute became fo outrageous. It muft be obferved that Menckenius, the hiftorian of Politiano, has on this occafion attributed to the expreffions of Scala, an import which it is certain they were not intended to convey (*a*).

If the circumftances before related were not

(*a*) In the early part of the quarrel, Scala has the following paffage, in a letter to Politiano: "Tu certe præter ceteros, mi Politiane, " naturæ multum debes, illa tibi ingenium iftud dedit: ut corporis " modo prætermittam dotes, quæ nonnihil & ipfæ habere a quibufdam " putantur momenti ad felicitatem & fortunæ commoda: quæ profecto " juvare nativam virtutem, nifi ipfa fefe deferat, vehementer folent. " Cæcus fit funditus qui hæc non viderit." "Si quid video (fay Menckenius) " funt & hæc per ludibrium forfan & per invidiam a " Scala dicta, ut obfcœnos Politiani mores perftringeret, quafi is " nempe corporis fui copiam principi juventuti fecerit, femper ita " amantes ftudiofofque fui Medicæos habiturus. Ut adeo mirari vix " fatis poffim, non fenfiffe hos aculeos nec his quidquam repofuiffe " Politianum, &c." In fuppofing he could fee fo much clearer into the concerns of Politiano than Politiano himfelf, Menckenius is miftaken; it certainly never came into the head of either of the difputants, that this paffage contained any infinuation of the nature alluded to by Menckenius. Giuliano de' Medici had been dead many years, nor had he in his lifetime given room for fuch an imputation; and at all events there is no probability that Scala would have hazarded the moft remote infinuation of this kind, againft a family on whofe favor he exifted, to fay nothing of the inattention with which Politiano treats this paffage, which he certainly confidered only as a piece of ridicule on his *wry neck* and *hooked nofe*, and as fuch thought it below his attention.

ſufficiently characteriſtic of the ſpirit of the times we might advert to the other governments of Italy; where we ſhould find, that offices of the higheſt truſt and confidence were often filled by men who quitted the ſuperintendence of an academy, or the chair of a profeſſor, to tranſact the affairs of a nation. Alfonſo, king of Naples, and Franceſco Sforza, contended in liberality with each other, to ſecure the ſervice of Beccatelli (*a*). Pontano was the confidential adviſer, and frequently the repreſentative to other powers, of Ferdinand, the ſon of Alfonſo (*b*). The brothers of the family

(*a*) *Zeno, Diſſ. Voſſ. v.* i. *p.* 309. *& vide ante, v.* I. *p.* 53.

(*b*) Giovanni Pontano, or according to the academical appellation which he adopted, Jovianus Pontanus, was a native of Cerreto, in Umbria, but when young and friendleſs took up his reſidence at Naples. His learning recommended him to Alfonſo, and afterwards to Ferdinando; by whom he was intruſted with the higheſt offices of the ſtate. Beſides his undertaking many important embaſſies, Pontano was chief ſecretary to the king, and on one occaſion his repreſentative as vice-roy of Naples. As a ſcholar he was the only perſon of the age whoſe productions can contend for ſuperiority with thoſe of Politiano. His poems were publiſhed by Aldus in two volumes, 1513. 1518. His proſe works in three volumes, 1518, 1519. Among the latter, is a treatiſe *De ingratitudine*, in which he aſſumes the merit of having been inſtrumental in concluding peace between Ferdinand and the pope, and gives a looſe to his exultation in having rendered his king ſo important a ſervice; but alas, Pontano lived to give the fulleſt comment on his treatiſe in his own conduct. For although he enjoyed the favor of the family of Arragon for nearly half a century, yet when Charles VIII. of France, in the year 1495, ſeized upon the kingdom of Naples, and aſſumed the emblems of royalty, Pontano, in the name of the Neapolitans, made the public oration to him, and took care not to forget the defects of his royal patrons, with which he had the beſt opportunities of being acquainted. *Zeno, Diſſ. Voſſ.*

of Simoneta directed for a considerable time the affairs of Milan (*a*). Bernardo Bembo, and Francesco Barbaro, maintained the literary, no less than the political dignity of the Venetian Republic, and left each of them a son who eclipsed the reputation of his father (*b*). When eminent talents were not engaged in public services, they were rewarded by the most flattering attention, and often by the pecuniary bounty of illustrious individuals, who relaxed from the fastidiousness of rank, in the company of men of learning, or have left memorials of their regard by their epistolary correspondence.

Nor was it seldom that the characters of the scholar, and of the man of rank, were united in the same person. Of this Giovanni Pico of Mirandula, to whom we have before frequently adverted, is perhaps the most illustrious instance. This accomplished nobleman, of whom many extraordinary circumstances are related, and who certainly exhibited a wonderful example of the powers of the human mind, was born at Mirandula in the year 1463, and was one of the younger children of Giovan-Francesco Pico, prince of Mirandula and Concordia (*c*). So quick was his

v. ii. p. 172. *Guicciard. Ist. d'Italia, lib.* ii. Pontano died in 1603. at the age of 77 years.

(*a*) *vide ante, v.* I. *p.* 178.

(*b*) Ermolao Barbaro, patriarch of Aquileia, and the cardinal Pietro Bembo, both of whom will again occur to our notice in the course of the work.

(*c*) Voltaire, who erroneously gives Pico the name of Jean-François, is also mistaken in relating that he resigned the sovereignty of Mirandula

apprehension, so retentive his memory, that we are told a single recital was sufficient to fix in his mind whatever became the object of his attention. After having spent seven years in the most celebrated universities of Italy and France, he arrived at Rome in the twenty-first year of his age, with the reputation of being acquainted with twenty-two different languages (*a*). Eager to signalize himself as a disputant, Pico proposed for public debate nine hundred questions, on mathematical, theological, and scholastic subjects, including also inquiries into the most abstruse points of the Hebraic, Chaldaic, and Arabic tongues (*b*). This

to reside at Florence. *Essai, tom.* ii. *p.* 296. *Ed. Gen.* Pico neither enjoyed nor had any pretensions to the sovereignty, which, after the death of his father, devolved on his elder brother Galeotto, and afterwards on his nephew Giovan-Francesco; by whom we have a voluminous life of his uncle, written in Latin, and prefixed to his works, which, whilst it affords much information respecting this extraordinary man, displays a deplorable degree of superstition in the author. The mother of Pico was of the family of Boyardo the poet.

(*a*) " Cela," says Voltaire very justly, " n'est certainement pas " dans le cours ordinaire de la nature. Il n'y a point de langue qui " ne demande environ une année pour la bien savoir. Quiconque " dans une si grande jeunesse en sait vingt deux, peut être soupçonné " de les savoir bien mal, ou plutôt il en sait les elemens, ce qui est " ne rien savoir." *Essai, ut sup.*

(*b*) Voltaire, not satisfied with these 900 questions, has increased their number to 1400; and informs us that they may be found at the head of the works of Pico. *Essai, ut sup.* It is to be wished that he had pointed out in what edition of the works of Pico he had discovered these questions; for the existence of which he seems to have had the same authority as he had for supposing that the learning of those days consisted merely in an acquaintance with the sophisms of the schoolmen, or that the sciences were then held in contempt by

measure, which in its worst light could only be considered as an ebullition of youthful vanity, might, without any great injustice, have been suffered to evaporate in neglect; but the Romish prelates, instead of consigning these propositions to their fate, or debating them with the impartiality of philosophers, began to examine them with the suspicious eyes of churchmen, and selected thirteen of them as heretical. To vindicate himself from this dangerous imputation, Pico composed a Latin treatise of considerable extent, which he is said to have written in the space of twenty days, and which he inscribed to Lorenzo de' Medici, under whose protection he had sheltered himself from persecution at Florence (*a*). The character and acquirements of Pico afforded to his contemporaries a subject for the most unbounded panegyric. "He was a man," says Politiano, "or rather a hero, on whom nature had lavished "all the endowments both of body and mind; "erect and elegant in his person, there was some-"thing in his appearance almost divine. Of a "perspicacious mind, a wonderful memory, in-"defatigable in study, distinct and eloquent in

princes and men of eminence. Assertions unworthy of an author who professes to write *sur les mœurs & l'esprit de nations.*

(*a*) *Apologia tredecim quæstionum.* This treatise was published with the other Latin works of Pico, at Venice, *per Bernardinum Venetum,* an. MCCCCLXXXXVIII. in folio, from which edition I shall give the dedication of the *Apologia,* as it is strongly expressive of the esteem and admiration of its author, for Lorenzo de' Medici.

v. *App. No.* LIV.

"speech,

" ſpeech, it ſeems doubtful whether he was more " conſpicuous for his talents or his virtues. Intimately converſant with every department of " philoſophy, improved and invigorated by the " knowledge of various languages, and of every " honorable ſcience, it may truly be ſaid, that " no commendation is equal to his praiſe."

The inſtances before given of the critical talents of Pico, whatever may be thought of their accuracy, will at leaſt juſtify him from the reproof of Voltaire, who is of opinion that the works of Dante and Petrarca would have been a more ſuitable ſtudy for him, than the ſummary of St. Thomas, or the compilations of Albert the great *(a)*. But the literary purſuits of Pico were not confined to commentaries upon the works of others. From the ſpecimens which remain of his poetical compoſitions in his native language, there is reaſon to form a favorable judgment of thoſe which have periſhed. Creſcimbeni confeſſes, that by his early death the Tuſcan poetry ſuſtained a heavy loſs, and that his accompliſhed pen might have reſcued it from its degraded ſtate, without the intervention of ſo many other eminent men, whoſe labors had been employed to the ſame purpoſe *(b)*. The few pieces which remain of his Latin poetry induce us to regret the ſeverity of their author. Theſe poems he had arranged in five books, which he ſubmitted to the correction of Politiano, who, having performed his taſk, returned them to their author, with an elegant apology for

(*a*) *Volt. Eſſai, tom.* ii. *p.* 296.

(*b*) *Creſcimb. Iſt. della volgar poeſia, v.* ii. *p.* 336.

the freedoms which he had taken (*a*). Soon afterwards Pico committed his five books to the flames, to the great regret of Politiano, who has perpetuated this incident by a Greek epigram (*b*). If the works thus destroyed were equal in merit to his Latin elegy addressed to Girolamo Benivieni, posterity have reason to lament the loss (*c*).

Among the circumstances favorable to the promotion of letters in the fifteenth century, another yet remains to be noticed, which it would be unpardonable to omit; and which, if it did not greatly contribute towards their progress, certainly tended, not only to render the study of languages more general, but to remove the idea that the acquisition of them was attended with any extraordinary difficulty. This was the partiality shown to these studies, and the proficiency made in them, by women, illustrious by their birth, or eminent for their personal accomplishments. Among these, Alessandra, the daughter of Bartolomeo Scala was peculiarly distinguished. The extraordinary beauty of her person was surpassed by the endowments of her mind. At an early age she was a proficient, not only in the Latin, but the Greek tongue (*d*), which she had studied under Joannes

(*a*) Neque ego judicis (ita me semper ames) sed Momi personam indui, quem ferunt sandalium Veneris tandem culpasse, cum Venerem non posset. Confodi igitur versiculos aliquos, non quod eos improbarem, sed quod tanquam equestris ordinis, cedere reliquis, veluti senatoribus videbantur atque patriciis. *Pol. Ep. lib.* i. *Ep.* 4.

(*b*) *Ibid. lib.* i. *Ep.* 7.

(*c*) Opere di Benivieni, *p.* 75. *Ed. Ven.* 1524.

(*d*) Some of the Greek poems of Alessandra appear in the works

Lascar and Demetrius Chalcondyles. Such an union of excellence attracted the attention, and is supposed to have engaged the affections of Politiano; but Alessandra gave her hand to the Greek Marullus, who enjoyed at Florence the favor of Lorenzo de' Medici, and in the elegance of his Latin compositions, emulated the Italians themselves (*a*). Hence probably arose those dissen-

of Politiano. *Ed. Ald.* 1498. And Politiano is supposed to have addressed to this Lady several of his amorous verses.

(*a*) The works of Marullus were published at Florence, under the title of HYMNI ET EPIGRAMMATA. At the close we read, *Impressit Florentiæ Societas Colubris* v. *kal. Decembris*, MCCCCLXXXXVII. His epigrams are inscribed to Lorenzo, the son of Pier-Francesco de' Medici. The following lines to the father of his mistress possess no inconsiderable share of elegance:

AD BARTHOLOMEUM SCALAM.

Cum musæ tibi debeant latinæ
Tot juncto pede scripta, tot soluto
Tot sales latio lepore unctos,
Tot cultis documenta sub figuris,
Tot volumina patriæ dicata,
Quæ nulli taceant diu minores,
Tot prætoria jura, tot curules,
Tot fasces proprio labore partos:
Plus multo tamen, o beate amice est
Quod Scalam Latio pater dedisti.
Aucturam numerum novem sororum,
Casto carmine castiore vita.

The three books of Hymns of Marullus are addressed, not to the objects of Christian worship, but to the Pagan deities, or the phenomena of nature, whence, perhaps, the remark of Erasmus; "Marulli "pauca legi, tolerabilia, si minus haberent paganitatis."

ſions between Marullus and Politiano, the monuments of which yet remain in their writings (*a*).

Of yet greater celebrity is the name of Caſſandra Fidelis. Deſcended from anceſtors who had changed their reſidence from Milan to Venice, and had uniformly added to the reſpectability of their rank by their uncommon learning, ſhe began at an early age to proſecute her ſtudies with great diligence, and acquired ſuch a knowledge of the learned languages, that ſhe may with juſtice be enumerated among the firſt ſcholars of the age (*b*). The letters which occaſionally paſſed between Caſſandra and Politiano demonſtrate their mutual eſteem, if indeed ſuch expreſſion be ſufficient to characterize the feelings of Politiano, who expreſſes in language unuſually florid, his high admiration of her extraordinary acquirements, and his expectation of the benefits which the cauſe of letters would derive from her labors and example (*c*). In

(*a*) Among the epigrams of Politiano are ſeveral of the moſt outrageous kind, againſt ſome perſon whom he attacks under the name of *Mabilius;* and in the poems of Marullus are ſome pieces, little inferior in abuſe, of which *Ecnomus* is the ſubject. Under theſe masks it is ſuppoſed, and not without reaſon, that theſe rival ſcholars directed their shafts at each other.

(*b*) The letters and orations of this lady were publiſhed at *Pavia* in 1636, by Jac. Ph. Tomaſini, who has prefixed to them ſome account of her life.

(*c*) " O decus Italiæ, virgo, quas dicere grates, quaſve referre " parem, quod etiam honore me tuarum literarum non dedignaris? " mira profecto fides, tales proficiſci à femina, quid autem à femina " dico, imò verò à puella & virgine potuiſſe, &c." " Tibi verò tanta " incepta Deus optimus maximus ſecundet: & cum receſſeris à

the year 1491; the Florentine ſcholar made a viſit to Venice, where the favorable opinion which he had formed of her writings was confirmed by a perſonal interview. "Yeſterday," ſays he, writing to his great patron, "I paid a viſit to the celebrat-"ed Caſſandra, to whom I preſented your reſpects. "She is indeed, Lorenzo, a ſurpriſing woman, as "well from her acquirements in her own lan-"guage, as in the Latin; and in my opinion ſhe "may be called handſome. I left her, aſtoniſhed "at her talents. She is much devoted to your "intereſts, and ſpeaks of you with great eſteem. "She even avows her intention of viſiting you at "Florence, ſo that you may prepare yourſelf to "give her a proper reception (*a*)." From a letter of this lady, many years afterwards, to Leo X. we learn, that an epiſtolary correſpondence had ſubſiſted between her and Lorenzo de' Medici (*b*); and it is with concern we perceive that the remembrance of this intercourſe is revived, in order to induce the pontiff to beſtow upon her ſome pecuniary aſſiſtance; ſhe being then a widow, with a numerous train of dependants. She lived however to a far more advanced period, and died in the year 1558, having then completed a full

"parentibus, is autor contingat, & conſors qui ſit iſta virtute non "indignus: ut quæ nunc propemodum ſua ſponte naturalis ingenii "flamma ſemel emicuit, ita crebris deinceps aut audita flatibus, aut "enutrita ſomitibus effulgeat, ut a noſtrorum hominum præcordiis "animoque, nox omnis, geluque, penitus & languoris in litteris & "inſcitiæ diſcutiatur." *Pol. Ep. int. Caſſ. Fid. Ep.* 101.

(*a*) *v. Pol. Ep. in App. No.* LI.

(*b*) *Caſſ. Fidelis. Ep.* 123.

century. Her literary acquirements, and the reputation of her early aſſociates, threw a luſtre on her declining years; and as her memory remained unimpaired to the laſt, ſhe was reſorted to from all parts of Italy, as a living monument of thoſe happier days, which were never adverted to without regret (*a*).

That this attention to ſerious ſtudies, by which theſe celebrated women diſtinguiſhed themſelves, was the characteriſtic of the ſex in general, cannot perhaps be with truth aſſerted. The admiration beſtowed on thoſe who had ſignalized themſelves, affords indeed a ſtrong preſumption to the contrary. Yet the pretenſions of the ſex to literary eminence were not confined to theſe inſtances. The Italian hiſtorians have noticed many other women of high rank who obtained by their learning no inconſiderable ſhare of applauſe (*b*). Politiano celebrates as a tenth muſe a lady of Sienna, to whom he gives the name of Cecca (*c*); and from the numerous pieces in the learned languages, profeſſedly addreſſed to women, we may reaſonably infer, that theſe ſtudies were at that time more generally diffuſed amongſt them, than they have been at any ſubſequent period.

Having thus adverted to ſome of the principal cauſes which accelerated the progreſs of claſſical literature in the fifteenth century, and obſerved

(*a*) *Tomaſin. in vitâ Caſſandræ, p.* 42.

(*b*) *Tiraboſchi, Storia della Lett. Ital. vol.* vi. *parte* 2. *p.* 163.

(*c*) Mnemoſyne audito Senenſis carmine Ceccæ,
Quando inquit decima eſt nata puella mihi?

the active part which Lorenzo de' Medici took in every transaction that was favorable to its promotion, it may now be proper briefly to inquire what was the result of exertions so earnestly made and so long continued; and whether the tree, which had been transplanted with much difficulty, and nourished by such constant attention, brought forth fruit sufficient to repay the labor that had been bestowed upon it.

One of the first efforts of the Italian scholars was the translation of the most eminent Greek authors into Latin. Among the earliest and most assiduous of these translators is Leonardo Aretino, whose versions of various works of Plato, Xenophon, Plutarch, and other Greek authors, form a list too extensive to be recognised in the present work (*a*). The labors of Ficino, though not so numerous, are yet more voluminous. Some account of them is found in a Latin epistle from their author to Politiano: "Why, my friend," says Ficino, "have you so often desired to know "what works I have published? Is it that you "celebrate them in your verses? But approbation "is not due to number so much as to choice, "and merit is distinguished by quality rather "than quantity (*b*)." If Ficino had adhered more

(*a*) A very full catalogue of the works of Leonardo is given by Laur. Mehus, and prefixed to his edition of the Letters of this celebrated scholar. *Flor.* 1741. This catalogue comprises no less than sixty-three different productions, many of which are translations from the Greek.

(*b*) *v. App.* No. LV. Of the works there mentioned, several have been published, the early editions of which are yet held in esteem.

closely to this maxim, it would certainly have diminished nothing of his reputation, which is buried under the immense mass of his own labors. The earliest production in this department of letters, which united elegance with fidelity, is the translation of the history of Herodian, by Politiano (*a*). This work he inscribed to Innocent VIII. in a manly and judicious address, in which he briefly states the rules that he had prescribed to himself in the execution of his work, which are yet deserving of the notice of all who engage in similar undertakings (*b*).

From his early years Politiano had closely attached himself to the study of the writings of Homer; and whilst he was very young, had begun

His translation of Plato was first printed at Florence without date, and again at Venice, 1491. His version of Plotinus, printed by Miscomini, at the expense of Lorenzo de' Medici, though not published till after his death, is a fine specimen of typography; at the close we read,

Magnifico sumptu Laurentii Medicis patriæ servatoris, impressit ex archetypo Antonius Miscominus Florentiæ Anno MCCCCLXXXXII. *Nonis Maii.*

(*a*) Printed three times in the year 1493, viz. at Rome, at Bologna by *Plato de Benedictis*, and at the last-mentioned place by *Bazalerius de Bazaleriis*. Of these editions the second is the most esteemed.

Maittaire, Ann. Typ. v. i. p. 558. *De Bure. Bibl. Inst. No.* 4840.

(*b*) Quæ sane nostræ fuerunt partes, tentavimus profecto, utinamque etiam effecerimus, uti omnia ex fide responderent, ne inepta peregrinitas, ne græculæ usquam figuræ, nisi si quæ jam pro receptis habentur, latinam quasi pollucrent castitatem; ut eadem propemodum esset linguæ utriusque perspicuitas, eædemque munditiæ, idem utrobique sensus atque indoles, nulla vocum morositas, nulla anxietas.

Pol. in præfat. Ed. Ald. 1498.

to tranſlate the Iliad into Latin hexameter verſe (*a*). Whoever is acquainted with the great extent of his powers, and the peculiar energy of his Latin compoſitions, will regret that of this monument of his induſtry not a veſtige remains. That he had made a conſiderable progreſs in this work, appears from many authorities; and there is even reaſon to believe, that his perſeverance finally overcame the difficulties of his undertaking. Ficino, writing to Lorenzo de' Medici, and congratulating him on the ſucceſs of his attention to liberal ſtudies, particularly adverts to the protection afforded by him to Politiano, of whoſe tranſlation of the Grecian bard he ſpeaks in thoſe terms of florid adulation which too frequently characterize his letters (*b*),

(*a*) An epitome of the Iliad in Latin verſe, under the fictitious name of Pindar the Theban, is amongſt the MSS. of the Laurentian Lib. *Plut.* xxxviii. *Cod.* xii. 2. and has alſo been publiſhed in the Ed. of Homer by Spondanus Baſil, 1583. Another tranſlation of the Grecian bard is ſaid to have been executed in the fifteenth century, by Niccolo Valla, who died at twenty-one years of age. *P. Corteſ. de Hom. doct. p.* 46. *Valerian. de Literat. Infel. lib.* ii. A tranſlation of the Iliad into Latin proſe, by Lorenzo Valla, was publiſhed at Breſcia 1474, and Lorenzo was accuſed of having availed himſelf of a tranſlation made a century before, by Leontius Pilatus, which tranſlation has alſo been inſcribed to Petrarca. *Hod. de Græc. illuſt. p.* 10.

(*b*) "Divites alii ferme omnes miniſtros nutriant voluptatum; Tu "ſacerdotes muſarum nutris. perge precor mi Laurenti; nam illi "voluptatam ſervi evadent, tu vero muſarum delitiæ. Summus "muſarum ſacerdos, Homerus, in Italiam, te duce, venit. Et qui "hactenus circum vagus & mendicus fuit tandem apud te dulce "hoſpitium reperit. Nutris domi Homericum illum adoleſcentem, "Angelum Politianum, qui græcam Homeri perſonam latinis colori"bus exprimat. Exprimit jam, atque id quod mirum eſt in tam

Another contemporary author has however plainly indicated that Politiano completed his important task (*a*), to the progress of which he has occasionally adverted in his own works (*b*). Whether his youthful labors fell a sacrifice to the severity of his riper judgment, or perished in the general dispersion of the Medicean Library, of which he lived to be a witness, is a question which must yet remain undecided.

The early part of the fifteenth century was distinguished by a warm admiration of the writings of the ancients, and an extreme avidity to possess them. This was succeeded, as might be expected, by an attention to the accuracy of

" tenere ætati, ita exprimit ut nisi quis græcum fuisse Homerum " noverit, dubitaturus sit, e duobus uter naturalis sit & uter pictus " Homerus, &c." *Fic. Ep. lib.* i.

(*a*) Amongst the Latin poems of Alessandro Braccio, the contemporary and friend of Politiano, and well known by his translation of the works of Appian, is the following epigram:

" AD LAURENTIUM MEDICEM.

" Tempora nostra tibi multum debentia Laurens,
" Non minus hoc debent, nobile propter opus,
" Maeonium, duce te quod nuper & auspice, vatem,
" Convertit Latios Angelus in numeros,
" Cumque decore suo cum majestate legendum,
" Dat nobis qualem Græcia docta legit,
" Ut dubites *Latius* malit quam *Græcus Homerus*
" Esse, magis patrius hunc nisi vincat amor."

Band. Cat. Laur. lib. iii. 780.

(*b*) " Nam & ego is sum qui ab ineunte adolescentia, ita hujus " eminentissimi poetæ studio ardoreque flagraverim, ut non modo " cum totum legendo olfecerim, pœneque contriverim, sed juvenili " quodam, ac prope temerario ausu, vertere etiam in Latinum " tentaverim." *Pol. Orat. in Exp. Homeri in op. Ald.* 1498.

the text, and an ardent desire of transfusing their beauties into a language more generally known. Towards the latter part of the century a further progress was made; and from commenting, and translating, the Italians began to emulate these remains of ancient genius. Those who distinguished themselves during the time of Cosmo, and Piero de' Medici, have already attracted some share of our notice; but it must in general be acknowledged, that although their labors exhibit at times a tolerable knowledge of the mechanical parts of learning, and have the body and form of poetic composition, yet the animating spirit that should communicate life and motion is sought for in vain; or if it be any where discoverable, is only to be found in the licentious productions of Beccatelli (*a*). Of that kind of composition which may be called classical, modern Italy had seen no examples. The writings of Landino, of which specimens have been already given, are however entitled to some share of approbation; and if they be not marked by any powerful efforts of imagination, nor remind us strongly of the ancient authors, they possess a flow of language, and facility of diction and versification, much superior to his predecessors. A further proficiency was made by Naldo Naldio, or *Naldo de Naldis*, the friend of Ficino and Politiano, and the frequent panegyrist of the Medici (*b*). The poem of Ugolino

(*a*) *v. ante, v.* I. *p.* 55.

(*b*) The poems of Naldio are printed in the *Selecta Poemata Italorum, v.* vi. *p.* 412. of these the first is addressed, *Ad Petrum*

Verini, " *De Illuſtratione Urbis Florentiæ,*" is perhaps more eſtimable for the authenticity of the information it communicates, than for its poetical excellence, yet Verini has left other teſtimonies that entitle him to rank with the firſt Latin poets of his age (*a*). These pieces are principally devoted

Medicem in obitu magni Coſmi ejus genitoris, qui vere dum vixit optimus Parens cognominatus ſuit. An extract from this piece in the Appendix, No. LVI. will ſufficiently show, that Naldio was poſſeſſed of no inconſiderable talents for Latin poetry. Another of the poems of Naldio is addreſſed to Annalena, a nun, probably the ſiſter-in-law of Bernardo Pulci (*v. ante, vol.* i. *p.* 250.), in which the poet laments the death of Albiera Albizzi, the wife of Sigiſmundo Stuſa, on whoſe death Politiano has alſo left a beautiful Latin elegy. It is probable there were two ſucceſſive authors of this name, whoſe works are inſerted in the *Carmina illuſt.* it can ſcarcely be ſuppoſed that the ſame perſon who addreſſed himſelf to Piero on the death of his father in 1464, and had before written a poem to Coſmo on the death of his ſon John, should be the author of the pieces in this collection which are inſcribed to Leo X. who did not enter on his pontificate till 1513. Politiano has left the following commendatory epigram on the writings of Naldio:

> Dum celebrat Medicem *Naldus*, dum laudat amicam,
> Et pariter gemino raptus amore canit,
> Tam lepidum unanimes illi ornavere libellum,
> Phœbus, Amor, Pallas, Gratia, Muſa, Fides.

(*a*) The example of Landino in affixing to his poetical labors the name of his miſtreſs (*v. ante, vol.* i. *p.* 91.) was followed by Verini, who gave the title of *Flametta* to his two books of Latin elegies, which he inſcribed to Lorenzo de' Medici, and which yet remain in the Laurentian Library (*Plut.* xxxix. *cod.* 42.). Bandini ſuppoſes that Landino, as well as many other learned men of thoſe times, had a real object of his paſſion, for which he gives a very ſatisfactory reaſon. " Neque hoc nomen fictum eſſe crediderim, quum revera " mihi compertum ſit, illius ævi litteratos viros, *ut nunc quoque*

to the praiſes of the Medici, and frequently advert to the characters of Lorenzo and Giuliano, and to the circumſtances of the times (*a*).

In Michael Verini, the ſon of Ugolino, we have a ſurpriſing inſtance of early attainments in learning. He was born in 1465; and although he died at the age of ſeventeen years, yet in that ſhort ſpace of time he had obtained the admiration, and conciliated the eſteem of his learned contemporaries. His principal work is a collection of Latin *diſticha*, which exhibit great facility both of invention and expreſſion, and an acquaintance with human life and manners far beyond his years. His Latin letters, of which a large collection is preſerved in the Laurentian Library (*b*), and which are chiefly addreſſed to his father, are as honorable to the paternal kindneſs of the one, as to the filial affection of the other. His death is ſaid to have been occaſioned by his repugnance to obey the preſcription of his phyſicians, who recommended an experiment which it ſeems his modeſty did not approve, and he fell a ſacrifice to his per-

" *accidit*, puellas in deliciis habuiſſe plurimum, in earumque laudem " carmina, ad inſtar illa Ovidii quæ amatoria nuncupantur, exaraſſe."
Band. Spec. Lit. Flor. v. i. p. 120.

(*a*) In the Laurentian Library (*Plut.* xxvi. *cod.* 21.) is preſerved a poem by Ugolino, to which he has given the name of *Paradiſus*. On his imaginary excurſion to the celeſtial regions, the poet meets with Coſmo de' Medici, who converſes with him at great length on the affairs of Florence, and particularly on the ſituation of his own family.

(*b*) *Plut.* lxxxx. *cod.* 28. From theſe letters Bandini has in his valuable catalogue given copious extracts. v. iii. p. 462, *&* *ſeq.*

tinacious chaſtity (*a*). From his letters it appears that both he and his father lived on terms of intimacy and friendſhip with Landino, Bartolomeo Fontio, and Politiano, and that Lorenzo de' Medici occaſionally paſſed a leiſure hour in convivial intercourſe with this learned family (*b*).

The reputation acquired by the Florentines in the cultivation of Latin poetry ſtimulated the exertions of other Italian ſcholars. On the memorable occaſion of the conſpiracy of the Pazzi, Platinus Platus, a Milaneſe, addreſſed to Lorenzo de' Medici a copy of verſes, which obtained his

(*a*) This event has been commemorated both in verſe and proſe, in Latin and Italian, by many contemporary authors. (*v. App. No.* LVII.) Verini is not the only inſtance of the kind on record. If we may believe Ammirato, the death of the cardinal of Lisbon in 1459 was occaſioned by a ſimilar circumſtance. *Amm. Iſt. Flor. v.* iii. *p.* 89. That ſuch a remedy had been preſcribed to Verini, is apparent from the following affecting paſſage in one of his letters: "Inſuperabilis me valitudo confecit, membra ut ſint pallore macieque "deformia; nocte crucior, die non quieſco, & quod me acrius torquet, "in tanto dolore ſpes nulla ſalutis. Quamquam medici, & tota "domus, & amici, nihil pericli afferant, deprehendo tamen tacitos "in vultu timores, ſuſpiria, murmur, taciturnitatem, mæroris cuncta "ſigna proſpicio; ſed cui notior morbus quam mihi? Quidquid ac"ciderit, utinam forti animo feramus; ſcio mihi nullum de vita factum "reſtare pænitendum, niſi quod potueram valitudini conſulere ſapien"tius; verum mihi *pudor*, vel potius *ruſticitas* obfuit — vale."

(*b*) "Fingit Homerus Jovem ipſum, alioſque Deos, Olympo relicto, "apud Ethiopas divertiſſe, cœnaſſe, luſiſſe: Auguſtum etiam orbis "terrarum principem, apud privatos ſine ullo apparatu cœnitaſſe: "ſed cur vetera? Laurentius Medices urbis noſtræ facile primus, "apud patrem meum pranſus eſt nonnumquam," &c.

Mic. Ver. Ep. 15. *ad Sim. Caniſianum. ap. Band. Cat. v.* iii. *p.* 483.

warm approbation (*a*). The exertions of Lorenzo in eſtabliſhing the academy at Piſa gave riſe to a poem of greater merit and importance, by Carolus de Maximis (*b*). To the authors before mentioned we may add the names of Cantalicio, Nicodemo Folengi, Aleſſandro Braccio, and Aurelio Augurelli, all of whom have cultivated Latin poetry with different degrees of ſucceſs, and have addreſſed ſome portion of their works to Lorenzo de' Medici to which the reader may not be diſpleaſed to refer (*c*).

(*a*) Laurentius Medices, quanta voluptate adficeretur in perlegendis poeticis ejuſdem (Plati) lucubrationibus, quantoque illum in pretio haberet, teſtatus eſt in epiſtola ad ipſum ſcripta, ob acceptum ex ejus carminibus non mediocre doloris levamen in neſarie patrata fratris ſui cæde: ait enim, "vetus eſt verbum, mi Platine, *inſuavem eſſe in* " *luctu muſicam:* ego vero tuis perlectis verſiculis, re ipſa reperi " nihil tam maxime ad ſolatium facere quam muſicam." *Saxius in Hiſt. Litteraria Typogr. Mediol. ap. Band. in Cat. Bib. Laur. v.* ii. *p.* 193. Theſe verſes are published in the *Select. Poem. Ital. v.* vii. *p.* 256.

(*b*) DE STUDIO PISANAE URBIS ET EJUS SITUS MAXIMA FELICITATE AD LAURENTIUM MEDICEM. This piece is preſerved in the Laurentian Library (*Plut.* lxxxxi. *cod.* 46. *v. Band. Cat. v.* iii. *p.* 850.), and contains ſo full, and at the ſame time ſo elegant an eulogy on the character of Lorenzo, and particularly on his attention to the promotion of letters, that I have given it a place in the Appendix, No. LVIII.

(*c*) The poems of Cantalicio are published in the *Carmina Illuſt. Poet. Ital. vol.* iii. *p.* 123. and are inſcribed to Lorenzo de' Medici. Thoſe of Folengi are inſerted in the ſame work, *vol.* iv. *p.* 419. Aleſſandro Braccio was equally eminent in politics and letters. He was for ſome time ſecretary of the Florentine republic, and died on an embaſſy to pope Alexander VI. His tranſlation of Appian into Italian is yet highly eſteemed, and forms part of the *Collana*, or

Of all these authors, though some possess a considerable share of merit, not one of them can contend in point of poetical excellence with Politiano, who in his composition approaches nearer to the standard of the ancients than any man of his time; yet, whilst he emulates the dignity of

series of Italian historical works. The Latin poems of Braccio, though very numerous, have not yet been published, but are preserved in the Laurentian Library. *Plut.* lxxxxi. *cod.* 40, 41. Many of them are inscribed to Lorenzo de' Medici and other men of eminence, as Landino, Ficino, Bartolomeo Scala, Ugolini Verini, &c. I have before adduced some lines of this author to Lorenzo de' Medici, and shall hereafter avail myself of an opportunity of producing a more extensive specimen of his works. The following epigram addressed to Politiano is not inapplicable to our present subject:

v. Band. Cat. v. iii. *p.* 781.

AD ANGELUM BASSUM POLITIANENSEM.

Tanta tibi tenero quum surgat pectore virtus,
  Quanta vel annoso vix queat esse seni,
Ac tua grandisono reboent quum, *Basse*, cothurno
  Carmina, magnanimo non nisi digna duce,
Et tibi sit locuples oris facundia docti,
  Teque suis ditet Græcia litterulis,
Te precor ad longos ut servet Jupiter annos,
  Incolumemque sinat vivere posse diu.
Nam tua Mæonio multum certantia vati
  Carmina quis dubitet, Virgilioque fore?
Atque decus clarum nostræ magnumque futurum
  Quis neget ætatis te, memorande puer?
Sis igitur felix, nostri spes maxima saecli,
  Teque putes nobis charius esse nihil.

Aurelio Augurelli is more generally known. His poems have frequently been published. The first edition is that of Verona, 1491, in 4to; the most correct and elegant, that of Aldus, 1505. These poems rank in the first class of modern Latin poetry.

Virgil,

Virgil, or reminds us of the elegance of Horace, he ſuggeſts not to our minds the idea of ſervile imitation. Of the character of his writings various opinions have indeed been entertained, which have been detailed at large by Baillet, and ſtill more copiouſly by Menckenius (*a*). It may therefore be ſufficient on this occaſion to caution the reader againſt an implicit acquieſcence in the opinions of two aminent living authors who have either obliquely cenſured, or too cautiouſly approved his poetical works (*b*). In the attempt made by Politiano to reſtore a juſt taſte for the literature of the ancients, it is not to be denied that he had

(*a*) *Baillet Jugemens des Sçavans, vol.* iv. *p.* 18. *Menck. in vitâ Pol. paſſim.*

(*b*) Tiraboſchi, adopting the ſentiments of Giraldi, acknowledges that Politiano was poſſeſſed of a vivid genius, of extenſive powers, and of uncommon and diverſified erudition; but cenſures his Latin poetry as deficient in elegance and choice of expreſſion. *Tirab. Storia della Lett. Ital. vol.* vi. *par.* 2. *p.* 234. Fabroni, adverting to the Italian poetry of Politiano, inſinuates, that the Latin muſes were reſerved and coy, to one who had obtained the favor of their ſiſter at ſo early an age, by his verſes on the *Gioſtra* of Giuliano de' Medici. *Fabr. in vitâ Laur. p.* 157. To oppoſe to theſe opinions the authority of many other eminent men who have mentioned the Latin writings of Politiano with almoſt unlimited praiſe, would only be to detail the compilations of Baillet or Menckenius. But the works of Politiano are yet open to the inſpection of the inquiſitive ſcholar; and though certainly unequal in point of merit, perhaps according to the time of life at which they were produced, will be found, upon the whole, to poſſeſs a vigor of ſentiment, a copiouſneſs of imagination, and a claſſical elegance of expreſſion, which, if conſidered with reference to the age in which he lived, entitle them to the higheſt eſteem.

powerful coadjutors in Pontano and Sanazaro (*a*), whose labors have given to the delightful vicinity of Naples new pretensions to the appellation of classic ground. Nor will it diminish his reputation if we admit that the empire which he had founded was in the next century extended and secured by the exertions of Fracastoro, Vida, Naugerio, and Flaminio (*b*), in whom the great poets of the Augustan age seem once more to be revived.

(*a*) Giacopo Sanazaro, or, by his academical appellation, Actius Sincerus Sanazarius, was a Neapolitan, born in the year 1458, and equally eminent by his Italian and Latin compositions. In the former, his reputation is chiefly founded on his *Arcadia;* in the latter, on his poem in three books, *De partu Virginis,* which is allowed, however, to be greatly blemished by the introduction of the pagan deities to the mysteries of the Christian religion.

(*b*) I cannot mention these names without regretting the limits to which I am necessarily confined. The rivals of Virgil, of Ovid, and of Catullus, ought not, in a work that touches on the rise of letters, to be commemorated at the foot of a page. The *Syphilis* of Fracastoro, *sive de Morbo Gallico,* though an unpromising subject, is beyond comparison the finest Latin poem that has appeared since the times of the ancients. The writings of Vida are more generally known, and would be entitled to higher applause, if they did not frequently discover to the classical reader an imitation of the ancients that borders on servility. Naugerio was a noble Venetian, who died young on an embassy from the republic. In his last moments he destroyed all his writings then in his possession, as not being sufficiently correct for the public eye; but the few that had been previously distributed among his friends were collected and published by them after his death, and breathe the true spirit of poetry. In Flaminio we have the simplicity and tenderness of Catullus, without his licentiousness. To those who are acquainted with his writings, it will not be thought extravagant to assert, that many of them, in the species of composition to which they are confined, were never excelled. The question addressed by

Whilſt the ſtudy of polite literature was thus emerging from its ſtate of reptile torpor, the other ſciences felt the effects of the ſame invigorating beam; and the city of Florence, like a ſheltered garden in the opening of ſpring, re-echoed with the earlieſt ſounds of returning animation. The Platonic academy exiſted in full ſplendor, and ſerved as a common bond to unite, at ſtated intervals, thoſe who had ſignalized themſelves by ſcientific or literary purſuits. The abſurd pretenſions of judicial aſtrology were freely examined and openly expoſed; and obſervation and experiment were at length ſubſtituted in the place of conjecture and of fraud (*a*). Paolo Toſcanelli had already erected his celebrated Gnomon (*b*). Lorenzo da Volpaja conſtructed for Lorenzo de' Medici, a clock, or piece of mechaniſm, which not only

him to a friend, reſpecting the writings of Catullus, "Quando leggete— "non vi ſentite voi liqueſare il cuore di dolcezza?" may with confidence be repeated to all thoſe who are converſant with his works.

(*a*) Pico of Mirandula was one of the firſt who entered the liſts againſt this formidable adverſary of real knowledge, in his treatiſe in twelve books, *adverſus Aſtrologos*, which is found in the general collection of his works. *Ven.* 1498.

(*b*) This Gnomon, which has juſtly been denominated the nobleſt aſtronomical inſtrument in the world, was erected by Toſcanelli, about the year 1460, for the purpoſe of determining the ſolſtices, and thereby aſcertaining the feaſts of the Romiſh church.. It is fixed in the cupola of the church of S. Maria del fiore, at the height of 277 Pariſian feet. A ſmall orifice tranſmits from that diſtance the rays of the ſun to a marble flag, placed in the floor of the church. This inſtrument was, in the preſent century, corrected and improved at the inſtance of M. de la Condamine, who acknowledges it to be a ſtriking proof of the capacity and extended views of its author.

marked the hour of the day, but the motions of the ſun and of the planets, the eclipſes, the ſigns of the zodiac, and the whole revolutions of the heavens (*a*). A laudable attempt was made by Franceſco Berlinghieri to facilitate the ſtudy of geography, by uniting it with poetry (*b*). In metaphyſics ſeveral treatiſes made their appearance, ſome of which are inſcribed by their authors to Lorenzo de' Medici (*c*). His efforts to promote the important ſcience of medecine, and to reſcue it from the abſurdities in which it was enveloped are acknowledged by ſeveral of its moſt eminent profeſſors, who cultivated it on more rational principles, and have attributed their proficiency

(*a*) Politiano has left a very particular deſcription of this curious piece of machinery. *Ep. lib.* iv. *Ep.* 8. A ſingular ſpectacle was alſo deviſed by Lorenzo de' Medici for the amuſement of the populace, a memorial of which is preſerved in a poem by Naldio, *Carm. Illuſt. v.* vi. *p.* 436. entitled *Elegia in ſeptem Stellas errantes ſub humana ſpecie per urbem Florentinam curribus a Laurentio Medice Patriæ Patre duci juſſas, more triumphantium.* From this poem we learn that the planets were perſonified and diſtinguiſhed by their proper attributes, and that they performed their evolutions to the ſound of muſic, with verſes explanatory of their motions and ſuppoſed qualities.

Nec tantum ſignis quot erant ea ſidera certis
  Monſtraſti, Medices, qua ſpecieque forent,
Dulcibus at numeris ſuavi modulatus ab ore
  Singula quid faciant præcipis arte cani.

(*b*) The *Geografia* of Berlinghieri was publiſhed with maps at Florence in the year 1480.

(*c*) Niccolo Fulginato addreſſed to Lorenzo his treatiſe *De Ideis,* which yet remains in manuſcript in the Laurentian Library. *Plut.* lxxxii. *cod.* 22. *Band. Cat.* iii. 201. and Leonardo Nogarola a work entitled *De Immortalitate animæ. Plut.* lxxxiii. *cod.* 22. *Band. Cat.* iii. 219.

to his bounty (*a*). In the practice and theory of music, Antonio Squarcialupi excelled all his predecessors; and Lorenzo is said to have written a poem in his praise (*b*). His liberality was emulated by many other illustrious citizens, who were allied to him by affinity, or attached by the ties of friendship and of kindred studies, and the innumerable literary works of this period, the production of Florentine authors, evince the success that attended their exertions. Of these works many yet hold a high rank, not only for practical knowledge, but for purity of diction; and upon the whole they bear the stamp of industry, talents, and good sense. And as they may be preferred,

(*a*) Bernardus de Torniis, dedicating to Giovanni de' Medici, when a cardinal, his treatise *de Cibis Quadragesimalibus*, thus addresses him: "Laurentius, pater tuus, Reverendissime Domine, tanta erga "me utitur humanitate, ac tot beneficiis Tornium adstringit, ut filiis "totique domui, perpetuo me debere profitear. Degustavi nutu ejus "medicinalem scientiam, neque sui caussa defuit quidquam, quo ad "illius apicem potuerim pervenire." *Band. Cat. v. i. p.* 659. In the Laurentian Library are several medical works addressed to Lorenzo, as Joh. Calora. Compend. Febrium. *Band. Cat.* iii. 42. Joh. Aretini de Medicinæ & legum præstantia, &c. *ib.* iii. 141.

(*b*) This I mention on the authority of Mr. Tenhove. "En fait "de musique," says he, giving an account of Leo. Bat. Alberti, "il ne cédait qu'au seul Antoine Squarcialupo. J'ai sous les yeux "un poëme que Laurent de' Médicis fit en l'honneur de ce dernier; car quel est le genre de talents au quel Médicis ne faisait pas "accueil?" *Mém. Généal. de la Maison de Médicis. lib. x. p.* 99. I regret that this poem of Lorenzo has escaped my researches. Valori relates, that Lorenzo being present when the character of this celebrated musician was the subject of censure, observed to his detractors, *If you knew how difficult it is to arrive at excellence in any science, you would speak of him with more respect. Val. in vitâ Laur. p.* 45.

both in point of information and compoſition, to the productions that immediately preceded them, ſo they are perhaps more truly eſtimable than many of thoſe of the enſuing century; when, by an overſtrained attention to the beauty of language, the importance of the ſubject was frequently neglected or forgotten, and the talents of the firſt men of the age being devoted rather to words than to things, were overwhelmed in a prolixity of language, that in the form of letters, orations, and critical diſſertations, became the opprobrium of literature, and the deſtruction of true taſte.

CHAP. VIII.

DOMESTIC character of Lorenzo de' Medici—Accused of being addicted to licentious amours—Children of Lorenzo — His conduct towards them — Politiano accompanies them to Pistoia — They remove to Cassagiolo — Dissensions between Politiano and Madonna Clarice — He retires to Fiesole, and writes his poem entitled RUSTICUS *— Piero de' Medici — Giovanni de' Medici — Lorenzo discharges his debts, and quits commerce for agriculture — Villa of Poggio-Cajano—Careggi—Fiesole and other domains—Piero visits the Pope—Giovanni raised to the dignity of a cardinal—Admonitory letter of Lorenzo—Piero marries Alfonsina Orsini — Visits Milan — Learned ecclesiastics favored by Lorenzo — Mariana Gennazano — Girolamo Savonarola — Matteo Bosso — Death of Madonna Clarice—Assassination of Girolamo Riario—Tragical death of Galeotto Manfredi prince of Faenza.*

HAVING hitherto traced the conduct of Lorenzo de' Medici in public life, we may now be allowed to follow him to his domestic retreat, and observe him in the intercourse of his family, the education of his children, or the society of his friends. The mind of man varies with his local situation, and before it can be justly estimated, must be viewed in those moments when it expands in the warmth of confidence, and exhibits

its true colors in the sunshine of affection. Whether it was from the suggestions of policy, or the versatility of his natural diposition, that Lorenzo de' Medici turned with such facility from concerns of high importance to the discussion of subjects of amusement, and the levity of convivial intercourse, certain it is, that few persons have displayed this faculty in so eminent a degree. "Think not," says Politiano, writing to his friend (*a*), "that any of our learned associates, "even they who have devoted their lives to "study, are to be esteemed superior to Lorenzo "de' Medici, either for acuteness in disputation. "or for good sense in forming a just decision; or "that he yields to any of them in expressing his "thoughts with facility, variety, and elegance. "The examples of history are as familiar to him as "the attendants that surround his table; and when "the nature of his subject admits of it, his con-"versation is abundantly seasoned with the salt col-"lected from that ocean, from which Venus herself "first sprung (*b*)." His talent for irony was peculiar, and folly and absurdity seldom escaped his animad-

(*a*) *Ang. Polit. Lodovico Odaxio. Ep. lib.* iii. *Ep.* 6.

(*b*) ——— Lususque Salesque,
Sed lectus pelago, quo Venus orta sales,

Says Jacques Moisant, Sieur de Brieux. *v.* Menagiana, *tom.* i. *p.* 59. where the author has traced this sentiment from Plutarch to Politiano, and downwards to Victorius, Heinsius, and de Brieux. "Quelque belle & fine, au reste," says he, "que soit cette pensée, "usée aujourd'hui comme elle est, on n'oserait plus la répeter."

verſion (*a*). In the collections formed by the Florentines, of the *motti e burle* of celebrated men, Lorenzo bears a diſtinguiſhed part; but when expreſſions adapted to the occaſion of a moment are tranſplanted to the page of a book, and ſubmitted to the cool conſideration of the cloſet, they too often remind us of a flower cropt from its ſtalk, to be preſerved in arid deformity. Poſſibly too, thoſe who have aſſumed the taſk of ſelection may not have been accurate in their choice, and perhaps the celebrity of his name may have been an inducement to others to attribute to him witticiſms unworthy of his character. Yet the *bon-mots* of Lorenzo may rank with many of thoſe which have been publiſhed with importance, and read with avidity (*b*). Grazzini has alſo introduced this eminent man as amuſing himſelf

(*a*) "Quum jocabatur, nihil hilarius; quum mordebat nihil aſperius." *Valori, in vitâ, p.* 14.

(*b*) Several of them are related by Valori, and many others may be found in the *Facetie, Motti e Burle, di diverſi Signori, &c. Raccolte per Lod. Domenichi. Ven.* 1588. One of his kinſmen, remarkable for his avarice, having boaſted that he had at his villa a plentiful ſtream of fine water, Lorenzo replied, *If ſo, you might afford to keep cleaner hands.* Bartolommeo Soccini, of Sienna, having obſerved, in alluſion to the defect in Lorenzo's ſight, that the air of Florence was injurious to the eyes; *True,* ſaid Lorenzo, *and that of Sienna to the brain.* Being interrogated by Ugolino Martelli, why he roſe ſo late in the morning, Lorenzo in return inquired from Martelli, why he roſe ſo ſoon, and finding that it was to employ himſelf in trifles, *My morning dreams,* ſaid Lorenzo, *are better than thy morning's buſineſs.* When Soccini eloped from Florence, to evade his engagements as profeſſor of civil law there, and being taken and brought back, was committed to priſon, he complained that a man of his eminence ſhould undergo ſuch a ſhameful puniſhment. *You ſhould*

with a piece of meditated jocularity, in order to free himſelf from the importunate viſits of a phyſician, who too frequently appeared at his table; but, for the veracity of this narrative, we have only the authority of a profeſſed noveliſt (*a*). Nor is it likely that Lorenzo, though he frequently indulged in the licence allowed by the Roman ſatiriſt, would have forgotten the precaution with which it is accompanied (*b*), or would have miſemployed his time and his talents, in contriving and executing a ſtale and inſipid jeſt.

Although there is reaſon to believe that Clarice Orſini, the wife of Lorenzo, was not the object of his early paſſion, yet that he lived with her in uninterrupted affection, and treated her on all

remember, ſaid Lorenzo, *that the shame is not in the punishment, but in the crime.* *Val. p.* 14. *Dom. p.* 121, *&c.*

(*a*) Anton-Franceſco Grazzini, detto Il Laſca. *Novelle, Ed. Lond.* 1756. *La terza Cena, Nov.* x. The argument of this novel is as follows: "Lorenzo vecchio de' Medici da due traveſtiti, fa condurre "Maeſtro Manente ubbriaco una ſera dopo cena ſegretamente nel ſuo "palagio, e quivi e altrove lo tiene, ſenza ſapere egli dove ſia, lungo "tempo al bujo, facendogli portar mangiare da due immaſcherati; "dopo per via del Monaco buffone, da a credere alle perſone, lui "eſſer morto di peſte, perciocchè cavato di caſa ſua un morto, in ſuo "ſcambio lo fa diſotterrare. Il Magnifico poi con modo ſtravagante "manda via Maeſtro Manente, il quale finalmente creduto morto da "ognuno, arriva in Firenze, dove la moglie, penſando che fuſſe l' anima "ſua, lo caccia via come ſe fuſſe lo ſpirito, e dalla gente avuto la "corſa, trova ſolo Burchiello, che lo riconoſce, e piatendo prima la "moglie in Veſcovado, e poi alli Otto è rimeſſa la cauſa in Lorenzo, "il quale fatto venire Nepo da Galatrona, fa veder alle perſone, ogni "coſa eſſer intervenuta al Medico per forza d'incanti; ſicchè riavuta "la donna, Maeſtro Manente piglia per ſuo avvocato San Cipriano."

(*b*) Nec luſiſſe pudet—ſed non incidere ludum. *Hor. Ep. lib.* i.

occaſions with the reſpect due to her rank and her virtues, appears from many circumſtances. He has not however eſcaped an imputation which has ſometimes attached itſelf to names of great celebrity, and which indeed too often taints the general maſs of excellence with the leaven of human nature. "Such a combination of talents "and of virtues," ſays Machiavelli, "as appeared "in Lorenzo de' Medici, was not counterbalanced "by a ſingle fault, although he was incredibly "devoted to the indulgence of an amorous paſ-"ſion (*a*)." In aſſerting a particular defect, it is remarkable that the hiſtorian admits it not as an exception to his general approbation. Yet it is not to be denied, that if ſuch an accuſation were eſtabliſhed, it would be difficult to apologize for Lorenzo, although the manners of the age, and the vivacity of his natural diopoſition, might be urged in extenuation of his miſconduct. In juſtice however to his character, it muſt be obſerved, that the hiſtory of the times furniſhes us with no information, either as to the circumſtances attending his amours, or the particular objects of his paſſion (*b*); nor indeed does there appear, from

(*a*) *Hiſt. Flor. lib.* viii.

(*b*) On lui a encore réproché le défaut des ames héroiques & ſenſibles, trop de penchant à l'amour. Je ſçai qu'il aima prodigieuſement les femmes, & j'ignore comment cette ſource inépuiſable de faibleſſes, n'en fut point une pour lui. S'il brûlait vivement, il brulait ſenſement; jamais ſes galanteries ne firent ombrage aux citoyens, parcequ'elles n'influérent en rien ſur ſa conduite publique. Sa vie grave, & ſa vie badine, étaient tellement ſeparées, qu'on eût dit qu'il y avait deux hommes en lui.

Tenhove, Mém. Généal. de la Maiſon de Médicis, liv. xi. *p.* 143.

the teſtimony of his contemporaries, any reaſon to infer that he is juſtly charged with this deviation from the rules of virtue, and of decorum (*a*). Probably this imputation is founded only on a preſumption ariſing from the amorous tendency of ſome of his poetical writings; and certain it is that if the offspring of imagination and the effuſions of poetry be allowed to decide, his conviction will be apparent in almoſt every line. It may perhaps be obſerved that theſe pieces were chiefly the productions of his youth, before the reſtrictions of the marriage vow had ſuppreſſed the breathings of paſſion; but how ſhall we elude the inference which ariſes from the following lines?

Teco l'aveſſi il ciel donna congiunto
In matrimonio: ah che pria non veniſti
Al mondo, o' io non ſon più tardo giunto?

O that the marriage bond had join'd our fate,
Nor I been born too ſoon, nor thou too late!

Or from theſe, which are ſtill more explicit?

Ma queſto van penſiero a che ſoggiorno?
Se tu pur dianzi, ed io ſui un tempo avanti,
Dal laccio conjugal legato intorno?

(*a*) In the poem of Brandolini, *De laudibus Laur. Med.* (*App. No.* L.) the attention of Lorenzo to the dictates of morality and decorum, as well in himſelf as others, is the particular ſubject of panegyric, and that by a contemporary writer. Had the conduct of Lorenzo been notoriouſly licentious, ſuch praiſe would have been the ſevereſt ſatire.

But why these thoughts irrelevant and vain!
If I, long since in Hymen's fetters tied,
Am doom'd to hear another call thee bride?

Nor must it be denied that this elegiac fragment, though incorrect and unfinished, is distinguished by that pathos and glow of expression which genuine passion can alone inspire (*a*). If in this piece Lorenzo be amorous, in others he is licentious; and if we admit the production of a moment of levity, as the evidence of his feelings, the only regret that he experienced was from the reflection, that he had in the course of his past time imprudently neglected so many opportunities of collecting the sweets that were strown in his way (*b*). But shall we venture to infer, that because Lorenzo wrote amorous verses, and amused himself with *jeux d'esprit*, his life was dissolute, and his conduct immoral? "As poetry is the flower of science," says Menage, "so there is not a single person of "education who has not composed, or at least "wished to compose verses; and as love is a "natural passion, and poetry is the language of "love, so there is no one who has written verses "who has not felt the effects of love." If we judge with such severity, what will become of the numerous throng of poets who have thought it sufficient to alledge in their justification, that if

(*a*) v. this piece, entitled *Elegia*, in the poems of Lorenzo, published at the close of this volume.

(*b*) See the piece entitled *La Confessione*, also printed amongst his poems at the end of the present volume.

Their verse was wanton, yet their lives were chaste?

or what shall we say to the extensive catalogue of learned ecclesiastics, who have endeavoured to fill the void of celibacy, by composing verses on subjects of love (*a*)?

Whatever may be thought of the conduct or the sentiments of Lorenzo on this head, it does not appear that he left any offspring of illicit love; but by his wife Clarice he had a numerous progeny, of which three sons and four daughters arrived at the age of maturity. Piero his eldest son was born on the fifteenth day of February 1471; Giovanni, on the eleventh day of December 1475; and Giuliano, his youngest, in 1478. Of these the first was distinguished by a series of misfortunes too justly merited, the two latter by an unusual degree of prosperity; Giovanni having obtained the dignity of the Tiara, which he wore by the name of Leo X.; and Giuliano having allied himself by marriage to the royal house of France, and obtained the title of duke of Nemours.

In no point of view does the character of this extraordinary man appear more engaging than in his affection towards his children, in his care of their education, and in his solicitude for their welfare. In their society he relaxed from his important occupations, and accustomed himself to

(*a*) For this catalogue, from Heliodorus bishop of Tricca in Thessaly, to M. Du Bois doctor in Theology at Paris, the reader may consult the *Anti-Baillet* of M. Menage, written by him when upwards of seventy years of age, and the most singular instance of industry, wit, vanity, and learning that the annals of literature can produce.

ſhare their pleaſures and promote their amuſements (a). By what more certain means can a parent obtain that confidence ſo neceſſary to enable him to promote the happineſs of his children? The office of an inſtructor of youth he conſidered as of the higheſt importance. "If," ſays he, "we "eſteem thoſe who contribute to the proſperity "of the ſtate, we ought to place in the firſt rank "the tutors of our children, whoſe labors are to "influence poſterity, and on whoſe precepts and "exertions the dignity of our family, and of our "country, in a great meaſure depends (b)."

Soon after the conſpiracy of the Pazzi, when Lorenzo thought it expedient to remove his family to Piſtoia, they were accompanied by Politiano, as the inſtructor of his ſons, who gave frequent information to his patron of their ſituation, and

(a) ——— "Si dilettaſſe d'huomini faceti e mordaci, & di "giuochi puerili, più che a tanto huomo non pareva ſi conveniſſe; "in modo che molte volte fu viſto tra i ſuoi figliuoli e figliuole, tra "i loro traſtulli meſcolarſi." *Mac. Hiſt. lib.* viii. On this ſubject I muſt not omit the comment of the intereſting and elegant Tenhove: "Eſt-il un ſpectacle plus touchant, que celui de voir un tel homme "dépoſer le fardeau de la gloire au ſein de la nature? A des yeux "non viciés Laurent de' Medicis parait bien grand, & bien aimable, "lors'quil joue à croix & pile avec le petit duc de Nemours, ou "qu'il ſe roule a terre avec Leon X." *Tenh. Mém. Généal. lib.* xi. *p.* 142.

(b) Si feræ partus ſuos diligunt, qua nos in liberos noſtros indulgentia eſſe debemus? Et ſi omnes, qui civitati conſulunt, cari nobis ſunt, certe in primis liberorum inſtitutores, quorum induſtria ſempiternum tempus ſpectat, quorumque præceptis, conſiliis, & virtute, retinebimus familiæ & reipublicæ dignitatem.

Laur. Med. ad Polit. ap. Fabr. v. i. p. 166.

the progreſs made in the education of his children. Theſe conſidential letters enable us to form a more accurate idea of the diſpoſition of their author, than we can collect from any of his writings intended for publication. Reſtleſs, impatient of control, concentering all merit in the acquiſition of learning, he could brook no oppoſition to his authority. The intervention of Madonna Clarice, in the direction of her children, was in his judgment impertinent, becauſe ſhe was unlettered, and a woman. In one of his letters he earneſtly requeſts that Lorenzo will delegate to him a more extenſive power; whilſt in another, written on the ſame day, he acknowledges that this requeſt was made under the impulſe of paſſion, and ſolicits indulgence for the infirmity of his temper. The ſubſequent eminence of his pupils renders theſe letters intereſting (*a*). What friend of literature can be indifferent to the infancy of Leo the Tenth? "Piero," ſays Politiano, "attends "to his ſtudies with tolerable diligence. We "daily make excurſions through the neighbour-"hood, we viſit the gardens with which this city "abounds, and ſometimes look into the library "of Maeſtro Zambino, where I have found ſome "good pieces, both in Greek and Latin. Giovanni "rides out on horſeback, and the people follow "him in crowds." From Piſtoia the family retired in the cloſe of the year to Caſſagiolo, where they paſſed the winter; from whence Politiano continued

(*a*) They are given, from the collection of Fabroni, in the Appendix to the preſent volume, *No.* LIX.

his

his correſpondence with Lorenzo, and occaſionally addreſſed himſelf to his mother, Madonna Lucretia between whom and this eminent ſcholar there ſubſiſted a friendly and confidential intercourſe. Theſe letters afford an additional proof of the querulouſneſs of genius, and may ſerve to reconcile mediocrity to its placid inſignificance (*a*). "The only "news I can ſend you," thus he writes to this lady, "is, that we have here ſuch continual rains "that it is impoſſible to quit the houſe, and the "exerciſes of the country are changed for childiſh "ſports within doors. Here I ſtand by the fire-"ſide, in my great coat and ſlippers, that you "might take me for the very figure of melancholy. "Indeed I am the ſame at all times; for I neither "ſee, nor hear, nor do any thing that gives me "pleaſure, ſo much am I affected by the thoughts "of our calamities; ſleeping and waking they ſtill "continue to haunt me. Two days ſince we were "all rejoicing upon hearing that the plague had "ceaſed—now we are depreſſed on being informed "that ſome ſymptoms of it yet remain. Were "we at Florence we ſhould have ſome conſolation, "were it only that of ſeeing Lorenzo when he "returned to his houſe; but here we are in con-"tinual anxiety, and I, for my part, am half "dead with ſolitude and wearineſs. The plague "and the war are inceſſantly in my mind. I "lament paſt misfortunes, and anticipate future "evils; and I have no longer at my ſide my dear "Madonna Lucretia, to whom I might unboſom

(*a*) *v. App. No.* LX.

" my cares." Such is the melancholy ſtrain in which Politiano addreſſes the mother of Lorenzo; but we ſeldom complain except to thoſe we eſteem, and this letter is a better evidence of the feelings of Politiano, than a volume of well-turned compliments.

In conciliating the regard of Clarice, Politiano was not equally fortunate. Her interference with him in his office, appeared to him as an unpardonable intruſion. " As for Giovanni," ſays he, " his mother employs him in reading the pſalter, " which I by no means commend. Whilſt ſhe " declined interfering with him, it is aſtoniſhing " how rapidly he improved, inſomuch that he " read without any aſſiſtance. There is nothing," he proceeds, " which I aſk more earneſtly of " Heaven, than that I may be able to convince " you of my fidelity, my diligence, and my " patience, which I would prove even by my " death. Many things however I omit, that amidſt " your numerous avocations I may not add to " your ſolicitude." When Politiano wrote thus to his patron, it is not to be ſuppoſed that his conduct at Caſſagiolo was diſtinguiſhed by moderation or complacency. The diſſenſions between him and Madonna Clarice conſequently increaſed, till at length the intemperance or the arrogance of Politiano afforded her a juſt pretext for compelling him to quit the houſe. By a letter from Clarice to her huſband on this occaſion, we are informed of the provocation which ſhe received, and muſt confeſs that ſhe had ſufficient cauſe for the meaſures ſhe adopted; for what woman can bear with patience the ſtings of ridicule (*a*)? "I "ſhall be glad," ſays ſhe, "to eſcape being made "the ſubject of a tale of Franco's, as Luigi Pulci "was; nor do I like that Meſſer Agnolo ſhould "threaten that he would remain in the houſe in "ſpite of me. You remember I told you, that "if it was your will he ſhould ſtay, I was per-"fectly contented; and although I have ſuffered "infinite abuſe from him, yet if it be with your "aſſent, I am ſatisfied. But I do not believe it "to be ſo." On this trying occaſion, as on many others, Politiano experienced the indulgence and friendſhip of Lorenzo, who, ſeeing that a reconciliation between the contending perties was impracticable, allowed the baniſhed ſcholar a reſidence in his houſe at Fieſole. No longer fretted by female oppoſition, or wearied with the monotonous taſk of inculcating learning, his mind ſoon recovered its natural tone; and the fruits of the leiſure which he enjoyed yet appear in a beautiful Latin poem, inferior in its kind only to the Georgics of Virgil, and to which he gave the title of *Ruſticus.* In the cloſe of this poem, he thus expreſſes his gratitude to his conſtant benefactor:

Talia FESULEO lentus meditabar in antro,
Rure ſub urbano Medicum, qua mons ſacer urbem
Mæoniam, longique volumina deſpicit ARNI.
Qua bonus hoſpitium felix, placidamque quietem

(*a*) The letter of Clarice to her husband is given in the Appendix, *No.* LXI.

Indulget LAURENS, LAURENS haud ultima Phœbi
Gloria, jactatis LAURENS fida anchora musis;
Qui si certa magis permiserit otia nobis,
Afflabor majore Deo. ——

Thus flow the strains, whilst here at ease reclin'd
At length the sweets of calm repose I find;
Where FESULÉ, with high impending brow,
O'erlooks Mæonian FLORENCE stretch'd below.
Whilst ARNO, winding through the mild domain,
Leads in repeated folds his lengthen'd train;
Nor thou thy poet's grateful strain refuse,
LORENZO! sure resource of every muse;
Whose praise, so thou his leisure hour prolong,
Shall claim the tribute of a nobler song.

Were we to give implicit credit to the testimony of his tutor, Piero de' Medici united in himself all the great qualities by which his progenitors had been successively distinguished: "The talents of "his father, the virtues of his grandfather, and the "prudence of the venerable Cosmo (a)." Lorenzo himself had certainly formed a favorable opinion of his capacity; and is said to have remarked that his eldest son would be distinguished for ability, his second for probity, his third by an amiable temper (b). The fondness of a parent was gratified

(a) Scis autem quam gratus multitudini sit & civibus, Petrus noster, non minus jam sua, quam familiæ gloria; scilicet in quo Patris ingenium, Patrui virtus, Patrui magni humanitas, Avi probitas, Proavi prudentia, pietas Abavi reviviscit: omnium vero majorum suorum liberalitas, omniumque animus. *Pol. Ep. lib.* xii. *Ep.* 6.

(b) *Valori in vitâ Laur. p.* 64.

in obſerving thoſe inſtances of an extraordinary memory, which Piero diſplayed in his childhood, and in liſtening to the poetical pieces which he was accuſtomed to recite to the familiar circle of friends, who perhaps admired, and certainly applauded his efforts. Among theſe were ſome of the whimſical productions of Matteo Franco (*a*). As he advanced in years, his father was deſirous that he ſhould always participate in the converſation of thoſe eminent ſcholars who frequented the palace of the Medici; and it was with pleaſure that Lorenzo ſaw the mutual attachment that ſubſiſted between his ſon and the profeſſors of literature in general (*b*). The celebrated epiſtles of Politiano, which were

(*a*) Quin idem parens tuus, pené infantem adhuc te, quædam ex his (Franci carminibus) facetiora, ridiculi gratia docebat, quæ tu deinde inter adductus amicos balbutiebas, & eleganti quodam geſtu, qui quidem illam deceret ætatulam, commendabas. *Pol. Ep. ad Pet. Med. lib.* x. *Ep.* 12.

(*b*) Landino, in his dedication of the works of Virgil to Piero de' Medici, thus adverts to the attention of Lorenzo to the education of his children, and particularly of Piero: "Plurima ſunt quæ in illo "(Laurentio) admirer; ſed illud præ ceteris, quod in liberis educandis "indulgentioris quidem parentis numquam, optimi vero ac ſapientiſſi-"mi ſemper, ſumma ſedulitate officium compleverit. In te vero "informando, atque erudiendo, quid umquam omiſit? Nam quamvis "ipſe per ſe quotidie admoneret, præciperet, ac juberet, tamen cum "ſciret quanti eſſet, ne a Præceptoris latere umquam diſcederes, ex "omni hominum doctorum copia, Angelum Politianum elegit, virum "multa ac varia doctrina eruditum, Poetam vero egregium, egregi-"umque Oratorem, ac denique totius antiquitatis diligentem per-"ſcrutatorem cui puerilem ætatem tuam & optimis moribus fingendam, "& optimis artibus ac diſciplinis excolendam traderet." *Band. Spec. Lit. Flor.* v. i. *p.* 222. *in not.*

collected by their author at the instance of Piero, and to whom they are inscribed in terms of grateful affection, bear ample testimony to his acquirements; and the frequent mention made of his name by the learned correspondents of Politiano, is a convincing proof of his attention to their interests, and his attachment to the cause of letters. Happy if the day that opened with such promising appearances had not been so suddenly overclouded;

——— *Sed zephyri spes portavere paternas.*

and Piero, by one inconsiderate step, which his subsequent efforts could never retrieve, rendered ineffectual all the solicitude of his father, and all the lessons of his youth.

Giovanni, the second son of Lorenzo, was destined from his infancy to the church. Early brought forward into public view, and strongly impressed with a sense of the necessity of a grave deportment, he seems never to have been a child. At seven years of age he was admitted into holy orders, and received the tonsura from Gentile, bishop of Arezzo. From thenceforth he was called Messer Giovanni, and was soon afterwards declared capable of ecclesiastical preferment. Before he was eight years of age he was appointed by Louis XI. of France, abbot of Fonte Dolce, which was immediately succeeded by a presentation from the same patron, to the archbishopric of Aix in Provence; but in this instance the liberality of the king was opposed by an invincible objection, for before the investiture could be obtained from the pope, information was received at Florence that the archbiſhop was yet living. This diſappointment was however compenſated by the abbacy of the rich monaſtery of Paſignano (*a*). Of the glaring indecorum of beſtowing ſpiritual functions on a child, Lorenzo was fully ſenſible, and he accordingly endeavoured to counteract the unfavorable impreſſion which it might make on the public mind, by inculcating upon his ſon the ſtricteſt attention to his manners, his morals, and his improvement. He had too much ſagacity not to be convinced, that the ſureſt method of obtaining the rewards of merit is to deſerve them; and Meſſer Giovanni was not more diſtinguiſhed from his youthful aſſociates by the high promotions which he enjoyed, than he was by his attention to his ſtudies, his ſtrict performance of the duties enjoined him, and his inviolable regard to truth.

In providing for the expenſes of the wars in which the Florentines had been engaged, conſiderable debts had been incurred; and as they had not yet learnt the deſtructive expedient of anticipating their future revenue, or transferring their own burdens to their poſterity, it became neceſſary to provide for the payment of theſe demands. Beſides the debts contracted in the name of the republic, Lorenzo had been obliged to have recourſe to his agents in different countries to borrow large ſums of money, which had been applied to the exigencies of the ſtate; but it was

(*a*) Theſe particulars are circumſtantially related in the Ricordi of Lorenzo, who ſeems to have intereſted himſelf in the early promotion of his ſon with uncommon earneſtneſs. *v. App. No.* LXII.

no improbable conjecture, that the money which had been lavishly expended during the heat of the contest would be repaid with reluctance when the struggle was over. These considerations occasioned him great anxiety; for whilst on the one hand he dreaded the disgrace of being wanting in the performance of his pecuniary engagements, he was not perhaps less apprehensive on the other hand of diminishing his influence in Florence, by the imposition of additional taxes. From this difficulty he saw no possibility of extricating himself, but by the most rigid attention, as well to the improvement of the public revenue, as to the state of his own concerns. The increasing prosperity of the city of Florence seconded his efforts, and in a short time the creditors of the state were fully reimbursed, without any increase of the public burdens. His own engagements yet remained incomplete; but whilst he was endeavouring, from his large property and extensive concerns, to discharge the demands against him, a decree providing for the payment of his debts out of the public treasury relieved him from his difficulties, and proved that the affection of his fellow-citizens yet remained unimpaired (*a*). Lorenzo did not however receive this mark of esteem, without bitterly exclaiming against the negligence and imprudence of his factors and correspondents, who, by their inattention to his affairs, had reduced him to the necessity of accepting such a favor. From this period he determined to close his mercantile

(*a*) *Valori in vitâ Laur. p.* 38,

concerns with all possible expedition, well considering, that besides the inherent uncertainty of these transactions, the success of them depended too much on the industry and integrity of others. He therefore resolved to turn his attention to occupations more particularly under his own inspection, and to relinquish the fluctuating advantages of commerce, for the more certain revenue derived from the cultivation of his rich farms and extensive possessions in different parts of Tuscany.

His villa of Poggio-Cajano was, in his intervals of leisure, his favorite residence. Here he erected a magnificent mansion (*a*), and formed the complete establishment of a princely farmer. Of this fertile domain, and of the labors of Lorenzo in its cultivation and improvement, one of his contemporaries has left a very particular and authentic description (*b*). "The village of Cajano," says he, "is built on the easy slope of a hill, and is at the "distance of about ten miles from Florence. The "road to it from the city is very spacious, and "excellent even in winter, and is in every respect "suitable for all kinds of carriages. The river "Ombrone winds round it with a smooth deep "stream, affording great plenty of fish. The villa

(*a*) ——— Medicum quid tecta superba,
Carregi, & Trebii: Fesulana aut condita rupe
Commemorem? jutes Luculli tecta superba:
Quaque, fine exemplo *Cajana* palatia *Laurens*
Aedificat, quorum scandet fastigia, tanquam
Per planum iret eques, partesque equitabit in omnes.
Ug. Verini de illust. Urb. lib. ii.

(*b*) *Mic. Verini Ep.* xvi. *ap. Band. Cat. Bib. Laur. v.* iii. *p.* 483.

" of Lorenzo is denominated *Ambra*, either from " the name of the river, or on account of its ex- " traordinary beauty. His fields are occasionally " refreshed with streams of fine and wholesome " water, which Lorenzo, with that magnificence " which characterizes all his undertakings, has " conveyed by an aqueduct over mountains and " precipices for many miles (*a*). The house is not " yet built, but the foundations are laid. Its situ- " ation is midway between Florence and Pistoia. " Towards the north, a spacious plain extends to " the river, and is protected from the floods, " which sudden rains sometimes occasion, by an " immense embankment. From the facility with " which it is watered in summer, it is so fertile, " that three crops of hay are cut in each year; " but it is manured every other year lest the soil " should be exhausted. On an eminence about " the midle of the farm are very extensive stables, " the floors of which, for the sake of cleanliness, are " laid with stone. These buildings are surrounded " with high walls and a deep moat, and have four " towers like a castle. Here are kept a great number " of most fertile and productive cows, which afford

(*a*) This aqueduct is frequently celebrated in the poems of Politiano.

In fontem Laurentii Medicis Ambram.

" Ut lasciva suo furtim daret oscula Lauro,
" Ipsa sibi occultas reperit Ambra vias."

And again,

In eumdem.

" Traxit amatrices hæc usque ad limina Nymphas,
" Dum jactat Laurum sæpius Ambra suum."

" a quantity of cheese, equal to the supply of the " city and vicinity of Florence; so that it is now " no longer necessary to procure it as formerly " from Lombardy. A brood of hogs fed by the " whey grow to a remarkable size. The villa " abounds with quails, and other birds, particu- " larly water fowl, so that the diversion of fowling " is enjoyed here without fatigue. Lorenzo has " also furnished the woods with pheasants and " with peacocks which he procured from Sicily. " His orchards and gardens are most luxuriant, " extending along the banks of the river. His " plantation of mulberry trees is of such extent, " that we may hope ere long to have a diminution " in the price of silk. But why should I proceed " in my description? come and see the place " yourself; and you will acknowledge, like the " queen of Sheba when she visited Solomon, that " the report is not adequate to the truth."

Like the gardens of Alcinous, the farm of Lorenzo has frequently been celebrated in the language of poetry. To his own poem, on the destruction of his labors by the violence of the river, we have before adverted (*a*). Politiano thus concludes his Sylva devoted to the praises of Homer, to which, on account of its having been written at this place, he has given the name of *Ambra* (*b*):

(*a*) *Vol.* I. *p.* 287. and *v.* the poem of *Ambra* in *vol.* iv.

(*b*) Politiano addressed this poem to Lorenzo Tornabuoni, the cousin of Lorenzo de' Medici, of whom a very favorable character may be found in the letters of Politiano (*Lib.* xii. *Ep.* 6.). " Debe-

Macte opibus, macte ingenio, meo gloria LAURENS,
Gloria musarum LAURENS! montesque propinquos
Persodis, & longo suspensos excipis arcu,
Prægelidas ducturus aquas, qua prata supinum
Lata videt podium, riguis uberrima lymphis;
Aggere tuta novo, piscosisque undique septa
Limitibus, per quæ multo servante molosso
Plena Tarentinis succrescunt ubera vaccis;
Atque aliud nigris missum (quis credat) ab Indis,
Ruminat ignotas armentum discolor herbas.
At vituli tepidis clausi fœnilibus intus,
Expectant tota sugendas nocte parentes.
Interea magnis lac densum bullit ahenis,
Brachiaque exertus senior, tunicataque pubes
Comprimit, & longa siccandum ponit in umbra.
Utque piæ pascuntur oves, ita vastus obeso
Corpore, sus calaber cavea stat clausus olenti,
Atque aliam ex alia poscit grunnitibus escam.
Celtiber ecce sibi latebrosa cuniculus antra
Perforat; innumerus net serica vellera bombyx;
At vaga floriferos errant dispersa per hortos,
Multiforumque replent operosa examina suber;
Et genus omne avium captivis instrepit alis.
Dumque Antenorei volucris cristata Timavi
Parturit, & custos capitoli gramina tondet,
Multa lacu se mersat anas, subitaque volantes
Nube diem fuscant Veneris tutela columbæ.

" tur hæc silva tibi, vel argumento, vel titulo, nam & Homeri studio-
" sus es, quasique noster consectaneus, & propinquus Laurentii
" Medicis, summi præcellentisque viri, qui scilicet Ambram ipsam
" Cajanam, prædium (ut ita dixerim) omniferum, quasi pro laxamen-
" to sibi delegit civilium laborum. Tibi ergo poemation hoc quale-
" cunque est, nuncupamus, &c." Pridie nonas Nov. MCCCCLXXXV.

Go on, Lorenzo, thou the muſe's pride,
Pierce the hard rock and ſcoop the mountain's ſide;
The diſtant ſtreams ſhall hear thy potent call,
And the proud arch receive them as they fall.
Thence o'er thy fields the genial waters lead,
That with luxuriant verdure crown the mead.
There riſe thy mounds th'oppoſing flood that ward,
There thy domains thy faithful maſtives guard.
Tarentum there her horned cattle ſends,
Whoſe ſwelling teats the milky rill diſtends;
There India's breed of various colors range,
Pleas'd with the novel ſcene and paſtures ſtrange,
Whilſt nightly clos'd within their ſhelter'd ſtall,
For the due treat their lowing offspring call.
Mean time the milk in ſpacious coppers boils,
With arms upſtript the elder ruſtic toils,
The young aſſiſt the curdled maſs to ſqueeze,
And place in cooling ſhades the recent cheeſe.
Wide o'er thy downs extends thy fleecy charge;
There the Calabrian hog obeſe and large,
Loud from his ſty demands his conſtant food;
And Spain ſupplies thee with thy rabbit brood.
Where mulberry groves their length of ſhadow ſpread,
Secure the ſilk-worm ſpins his luſtrous thread;
And cull'd from every flower the plunderer meets,
The bee regales thee with her rifled ſweets.
There birds of various plume, and various note,
Flutter their captive wings; with cackling throat
The Paduan fowl betrays her future breed,
And there the geeſe, once Rome's preſervers, feed,
And ducks amuſive ſport amidſt thy floods,
And doves, the pride of Venus, throng thy woods.

When Lorenzo was prevented by his numerous avocations from enjoying his retreat at Poggio-Cajano, his other villas in the vicinity of Florence afforded him an opportunity of devoting to his own use, or the society of his friends, those shorter intervals of time which he could withdraw from the service of the public. His residence at Careggi was in every respect suitable to his rank. The house, which was erected by his grandfather, and enlarged by his father, was sufficiently commodious. The adjacent grounds, which possessed every natural advantage that wood and water could afford, were improved and planted under his own directions (*a*), and his gardens were provided with every vegetable, either for ornament or use, which the most diligent research could supply (*b*). But Fiesole seems to

(*a*) These particulars are adverted to in the following lines of Francesco Camerlini:

Allusio in Villam Caregium Laurentii Medices.

Caregium gratæ charites habitare feruntur,
  Gratus ager, chari gratior umbra loci,
Cosmus honos, patriæque pater construxerat aedes,
  Disposuitque emptos ordine primus agros.
Degener haud tanto natus Petrus inde parenti,
  Curavit partes amplificare suas.
Vixque tibi, Laurens, in tanta mole reliquit
  Quod peragas, nisi quod maxima semper agis,
Tu dignos Faunis lucos, fontesque Napæis
  Struxisti, & deceant quæ modo rura Deos.

Band. Cat. Bib. Laur. v. iii. *p.* 545.

(*b*) This was perhaps one of the earliest collections of plants in Europe, which deserves the name of a Botanical Garden; the authority of Sabbati, who dates the commencement of that at Rome in

have been the general resort of his literary friends, to many of whom he allotted habitations in the neighbourhood, during the amenity of the summer months. Of these Politiano and Pico were the most constant, and perhaps the most welcome guests. Landino, Scala, and Ficino were also frequent in their visits; and Crinitus, the pupil of Politiano, and Marullus, his rival in letters and in love, were occasionally admitted to this select society (*a*). " Superior perhaps," says Voltaire (substituting however Lascar and Chalcondyles, for Scala and Crinitus), " to that of the boasted " sages of Greece." Of the beauties of this place

the pontificate of Nicholas V. about the year 1450, being rejected by our eminent botanist Dr. Smith; who gives the priority to that of Padua in 1533. *v. Sabb. Hort. Rom. v.* i. *p.* 1. *Dr. Smith's Introduct. Discourse to the Transact. of the Linn. Soc. p.* 8. Of the garden of Lorenzo a very particular account is given by Alessandro Braccio in a Latin poem addressed to Bernardo Bembo, and preserved in the Laurentian Library, *Plut.* lxxxxi. *sup. cod.* 41. *Band. Cat. v.* iii. *p.* 787.; from which catalogue I shall insert it in the Appendix, *No.* LXIII.

(*a*) Petrus Crinitus (or Piero de' Ricci) thus addresses Marullus:

Nuper Fæsuleis (ut soleo) jugis,
Mentem Lesbiaco carmine molliter
Solari libuit: mox teneram chelyn,
Myrto sub virido deposui, & gradum,
Placuit ad urbem flectere,
Qua noster *Medices* pieridum Parens
Marulle, hospitium dulce tibi exhibet,
Ac te perpetuis muneribus fovens,
Phœbum non patitur tela resumere.
Laurens Camœnarum decus.

Crin. op. Lugd. 1554. *p.* 553.

and of the friendly intercourſe that ſubſiſted among theſe eminent men, Politiano, in a letter to Ficino, gives us ſome idea (*a*). "When you "are incommoded," ſays he, "with the heat of "the ſeaſon in your retreat at Careggi, you will "perhaps think the ſhelter of Fieſole not unde-"ſerving your notice. Seated between the ſloping "ſides of the mountain, we have here water in "abundance, and being conſtantly refreſhed with "moderate winds, find little inconvenience from "the glare of the ſun. As you approach the houſe "it ſeems emboſomed in the wood, but when "you reach it, you find it commands a full "proſpect of the city. Populous as the vicinity "is, yet I can here enjoy that ſolitude ſo grati-"fying to my diſpoſition. But I ſhall tempt you "with other allurements. Wandering beyond the "limits of his own plantation, Pico ſometimes "ſteals unexpectedly on my retirement, and draws "me from my ſhades to partake of his ſupper. "What kind of ſupper that is you well know; "ſparing indeed, but neat, and rendered grate-"ful by the charms of his converſation. Be you "however my gueſt. Your ſupper here ſhall be "as good, and your wine perhaps better, for in "the quality of my wine I ſhall contend for "ſuperiority even with Pico himſelf."

Beſides his places of reſidence before noticed, Lorenzo had large poſſeſſions in different parts of Tuſcany. His houſe at Caſſagiolo, near the village of that name among the romantic ſcenes of the

(*a*) *Pol. Ep. lib. x. Ep.* 14.

Appenines,

Appenines, had been the favorite residence of his grandfather Cosmo'; who, on being asked why he preferred this place to his more convenient habitation at Fiesole, is said to have assigned as a reason, that Caffagiolo seemed pleasanter, because all the country he could see from his windows was his own. At Agnana, in the territory of Pisa, Lorenzo had a fertile domain, which he improved by draining and bringing into cultivation the extensive marshes that lay in its neighbourhood, the completion of which was only prevented by his death (*a*). Another estate in the district of Volterra was rendered extremely fruitful by his labors, and yielded him an ample revenue. Valori relates, that Lorenzo was highly gratified with the amusement of horse-racing, and that he kept many horses for this purpose, amongst which was a roan, that on every occasion bore away the prize. The same author professes to have heard from Politiano, that as often as this horse happened to be sick, or was wearied with the course, he refused any nourishment except from the hands of Lorenzo, at whose approach he testified his pleasure by neighing and by motions of his body, even whilst lying on the ground; so that it is not to be wondered at, says this author, by a kind of commendation rather more striking than just, that Lorenzo should be the delight of mankind, when even the brute creation expressed an affection for him (*b*).

(*a*) *Valor. in vitâ Laur. p.* 39.

(*b*) Delectabatur maxime equorum cursu. Quare equos plurimos habuit in delitiis, in quibus ille fuit, quem de colore morellum appel-

In the year 1484, at which time Piero de' Medici, the eldeſt ſon of Lorenzo, was about fourteen years of age, his father judged it expedient to ſend him to Rome on a viſit to the pope, and appointed Scala and Politiano as his companions. He did not however implicitly confide in their diſcretion, but drew up himſelf very full and explicit directions for the conduct of his ſon during his abſence. Theſe inſtructions yet remain, and may ſerve, as much as any circumſtance whatever, to give us an idea of the ſagacity and penetration of Lorenzo, and of his attention, not only to the regulation of the manners of his ſon, but to the promotion of his own views (*a*). He adviſes him to ſpeak naturally, without affectation, not to be anxious to diſplay his learning, to uſe expreſſions of civility, and to addreſs himſelf with ſeriouſneſs, and yet with eaſe to all. On his arrival at Rome, he cautions him not to take precedence of his countrymen who are his ſuperiors in age; "for though you are my ſon," ſays he, "you will remember that you are only a "citizen of Florence like themſelves." He ſuggeſts

labant, tantae pernicitatis, ut ex omnibus certaminibus victoriam ſemper reportaverit. De hoc equo ipſe a Politiano audivi, quod mirum legentibus videatur, non tamen novum, eum, quoties vel ægrotaret, vel defeſſus eſſet, niſi a Laurentio oblatum cibum omnem faſtidire ſolitum, & quotieſcumque ille accederet, motu corporis, & hinnitu, quamvis humi proſtratum, animi lætitiam fuiſſe teſtatum, ut non jam mirum ſit tantopere hominibus gratum, quem etiam feræ dilexerint. *Valor. in vitâ, p.* 49.

(*a*) This curious paper of private inſtructions from Lorenzo to his ſon yet remains, and is given in the Appendix, from the collection of Fabroni (*No.* LXIV.).

to him what topics it will be proper for him to dwell upon in his interview with the pope; and directs him to expreſs, in the moſt explicit manner, the devotion of his father to the holy ſee. He then proceeds to the eſſential object of his miſſion. "After having thus recommended me to his holineſs, "you will inform him, that your affection for your "brother induces you to ſpeak a word in his favor. "You can here mention that I have educated him "for the prieſthood, and ſhall cloſely attend to his "learning and his manners, ſo that he may not diſ-"grace his profeſſion. That in this reſpect I repoſe "all my hopes on his holineſs; who, having already "given us proofs of his kindneſs and affection, "will add to our obligations by any promotion "which he may think proper to beſtow upon him. "Endeavouring by theſe and ſimilar expreſſions to "recommend your brother to his favor as much as "lies in your power."

In whatever manner Piero acquitted himſelf on his youthful embaſſy, it is probable that this interview accompliſhed the object on which the future fortunes of his houſe were ſo materially to depend, and Giovanni de' Medici, when only thirteen years of age, ranked with the prime ſupporters of the Roman church. It ſeems, however, that although the pope had complied with the preſſing inſtances of Lorenzo, in beſtowing on his ſon the dignity of a cardinal, he was not inſenſible of the indecorum of ſuch a meaſure, for he expreſsly prohibited him from aſſuming the inſignia of his rank for three years, requeſting that he would apply that interval to the diligent profecution of his ftudies. He accordingly went to Pifa, where the regularity of his conduct, and his attention to his improvement, juftified in fome degree the extraordinary indulgence which he had experienced; in confequence of which his father made the moft preffing inftances to the pope to fhorten the term of his probation. " Truft " the management of this bufinefs to me," faid Innocent, " I have heard of his good conduct, and " of the honors which he has obtained in his col- " lege difputes. I confider him as my own fon, " and fhall, when it is leaft expected, order his " promotion to be made public; befides which, it " is my intention to do much more for his advance- " ment than is at prefent fuppofed." The three years were, however, fuffered to elapfe, and the young cardinal was then admitted to all the honors of his rank, the inveftiture having been performed by Matteo Boffo, prior of the monaftery at Fiefole, who has left, in one of his letters, a particular narrative of the ceremony (*a*). After paffing a few days with his father at Florence, Giovanni haftened to Rome to pay his refpects to the pope. On his approach to that city he was met and congratulated by feveral other cardinals, who made no hefitation in receiving into their number fo young an affociate. By the ferioufnefs and propriety of his demeanor, he obviated as much as poffible the unfavorable impreffion which a promotion fo unprecedented had made on the public mind. Soon after his arrival

(*a*) *Recuperationes Fefulanæ. Ep.* cx. As the work does not frequently occur, I shall give this letter in the Appendix, No. LXV.

at Rome, his father addreſſed to him an admonitory letter, as conſpicuous for ſound ſenſe as for paternal affection; but which diſcovers the deep policy of Lorenzo, and the great extent of his views. This letter may, without any unreaſonable aſſumption, be conſidered as the guide of the future life and fortunes of a ſon, who afterwards attained the higheſt rank in Chriſtendom, and ſupported it with a dignity which gave it new luſtre (*a*).

Lorenzo de' Medici,

To Giovanni de' Medici, Cardinal.

"You, and all of us who are intereſted in your "welfare, ought to eſteem ourſelves highly favored "by providence, not only for the many honors "and benefits beſtowed on our houſe, but more "particularly for having conferred upon us, in "your perſon, the greateſt dignity we have ever "enjoyed. This favor, in itſelf ſo important, is "rendered ſtill more ſo by the circumſtances with "which it is accompanied, and eſpecially by the "conſideration of your youth, and of our ſituation "in the world. The firſt thing that I would there-"fore ſuggeſt to you is, that you ought to be "grateful to God, and continually to recollect that "it is not through your merits, your prudence, "or your ſolicitude, that this event has taken

(*a*) The original will be found in the Appendix, No. LXVI. "Hæc epiſtola," ſays Fabroni, "tanquam Cycnea fuit prudentiſſimi "hominis vox & orationis; paulo enim poſt ille mortem obivit." *Fabr. in vitâ*, ii. 313.

" place, but through his favor, which you can " only repay by a pious, chaste, and exemplary " life; and that your obligations to the performance of these duties are so much the greater, " as in your early years you have given some reasonable expectation that your riper age may " produce such fruits. It would indeed be highly " disgraceful, and as countrary to your duty as " to my hopes, if at a time when others display " a greater share of reason, and adopt a better mode " of life, you should forget the precepts of your " youth, and forsake the path in which you have " hitherto trodden. Endeavour therefore to alleviate the burden of your early dignity, by " the regularity of your life, and by your perseverance in those studies which are suitable to " your profession. It gave me great satisfaction " to learn, that, in the course of the past year, " you had frequently, of your own accord, gone " to communion and confession; nor do I conceive that there is any better way of obtaining " the favor of heaven, than by habituating yourself to a performance of these and similar duties. " This appears to me to be the most suitable and " useful advice which, in the first instance, I can " possibly give you.

" I well know, that as you are now to reside at " Rome, that sink of all iniquity, the difficulty of " conducting yourself by these admonitions will " be increased. The influence of example is itself prevalent; but you will probably meet with " those who will particularly endeavour to corrupt

" and incite you to vice; becauſe, as you may " yourſelf perceive, your early attainment to ſo " great a dignity is not obſerved without envy, " and thoſe who could not prevent your receiving " that honor, will ſecretly endeavour to diminiſh " it, by inducing you to forfeit the good eſtimation " of the public; thereby precipitating you into " that gulf into which they have themſelves fallen; " in which attempt the conſideration of your " youth will give them a confidence of ſucceſs. " To theſe difficulties you ought to oppoſe your- " ſelf with the greater firmneſs, as there is at preſent " leſs virtue amongſt your brethren of the college. " I acknowledge indeed that ſeveral of them are " good and learned men, whoſe lives are exem- " plary, and whom I would recommend to you " as patterns of your conduct. By emulating them " you will be ſo much the more known and " eſteemed, in proportion as your age, and the " peculiarity of your ſituation, will diſtinguiſh " you from your colleagues. Avoid however, as " you would Scylla or Charibdis, the imputation " of hypocriſy; guard againſt all oſtentation, either " in your conduct or your diſcourſe; affect not " auſterity, nor even appear too ſerious. This " advice you will, I hope, in time underſtand and " practiſe better than I can expreſs it.

" You are not unacquainted with the great im- " portance of the character which you have to " ſuſtain, for you well know that all the Chriſtian " world would proſper if the cardinals were what " they ought to be; becauſe in ſuch a caſe there

" would always be a good pope, upon which the " tranquillity of Christendom so materially de- " pends. Endeavour then to render yourself such, " that if all the rest resembled you, we might ex- " pect this universal blessing. To give you par- " ticular directions as to your behaviour and " conversation, would be a matter of no small " difficulty. I shall therefore only recommend, " that in your intercourse with the cardinals, and " other men of rank, your language be unassuming " and respectful, guiding yourself however by your " own reason, and not submitting to be impelled " by the passions of others, who, actuated by " improper motives, may pervert the use of their " reason. Let it satisfy your conscience that your " conversation is without intentional offence; and " if, through impetuosity of temper, any one " should be offended, as his enmity is without " just cause, so it will not be very lasting. On this " your first visit to Rome, it will however be more " advisable for you to listen to others than to speak " much yourself.

" You are now devoted to God and the church; " on which account you ought to aim at being a " good ecclesiastic, and to show that you prefer the " honor and state of the church, and of the apostolic " see, to every other consideration. Nor, while " you keep this in view, will it be difficult for " you to favor your family and your native place. " On the contrary, you should be the link to bind " this city closer to the church, and our family " with the city; and although it be impossible to

" foresee what accidents may happen, yet I doubt " not but this may be done with equal advantage " to all; observing, however, that you are always " to prefer the interests of the church.

" You are not only the youngest cardinal in the " college, but the youngest person that ever was " raised to that rank; and you ought therefore to " be the most vigilant and unassuming, not giving " others occasion to wait for you either in the chapel, " the consistory, or upon deputations. You will " soon get a sufficient insight into the manners of " your brethren. With those of less respectable " character, converse not with too much intimacy; " not merely on account of the circumstance in " itself, but for the sake of public opinion. Con- " verse on general topics with all. On public " occasions let your equipage and dress be rather " below than above mediocrity. A handsome house " and a well-ordered family will be preferable to a " great retinue and a splendid residence. Endeavour " to live with regularity, and gradually to bring " your expenses within those bounds which in a " new establishment cannot perhaps be expected. " Silk and jewels are not suitable for persons in " your station. Your taste will be better shown in " the acquisition of a few elegant remains of anti- " quity, or in the collecting of handsome books, " and by your attendants being learned and well- " bred rather than numerous. Invite others to your " house oftener than you receive invitations. Prac- " tise neither too frequently. Let your own food " be plain, and take sufficient exercise, for those

" who wear your habit are ſoon liable; without " great caution, to contract infirmities. The ſtation " of a cardinal is not leſs ſecure than elevated; on " which account thoſe who arrive at it too frequently " become negligent, conceiving that their object is " attained and that they can preſerve it with little " trouble. This idea is often injurious to the life " and character of thoſe who entertain it. Be atten- " tive therefore to your conduct, and confide in " others too little rather than too much. There is " one rule which I would recommend to your at- " tention in preference to all others: Riſe early in " the morning. This will not only contribute to " your health, but will enable you to arrange and " expedite the buſineſs of the day; and as there " are various duties incident to your ſtation, ſuch " as the performance of divine ſervice, ſtudying, " giving audience, &c. you will find the obſervance " of this admonition productive of the greateſt " utility. Another very neceſſary precaution, par- " ticularly on your entrance into public life, is to " deliberate every evening on what you have to " perform the following day, that you may not be " unprepared for whatever may happen. With " reſpect to your ſpeaking in the conſiſtory, it will " be moſt becoming for you at preſent to refer " the matters in debate to the judgment of his " holineſs, alledging as a reaſon your own youth " and inexperience. You will probably be deſired " to intercede for the favors of the pope on par- " ticular occaſions. Be cautious however that you " trouble him not too often; for his temper leads

" him to be most liberal to those who weary him " least with their solicitations. This you must ob- " serve, lest you should give him offence, remem- " bering also at times to converse with him on " more agreeable topics; and if you should be " obliged to request some kindness from him, let " it be done with that modesty and humility which " are so pleasing to his disposition. Farewel."

As the policy of Lorenzo led him to support a powerful influence at Rome, and as he had frequently experienced the good effects of the connexion which subsisted between him and the family of the Orsini, he thought it advisable to strengthen it; and accordingly proposed a marriage between his son Piero, and Alfonsina, the daughter of Roberto Orsini, count of Tagliacozzo and Albi. This proposal was eagerly listened to by Virginio Orsini, who was then considered as the head of that powerful family, the chiefs of which, though subordinate to the pope, scarcely considered themselves as subjects, and frequently acted with the independence of sovereign princes. In the month of March 1487, these nuptials were celebrated at Naples, in the presence of the king and his court with extraordinary pomp (*a*). Lorenzo, on his marriage with Clarice Orsini, had received no portion; but the reputation which he had now acquired was more than an equivalent for the pride

(*a*) Si fece lo sposalitio in Castello, nella Sala grande, presente il Re e tutta la Corte, con gran cena, e festa. Il Re non poeta fare maggiori dimostrazioni verso il Sig. Virginio. *Bern. Oricellarii Ep. ap. Fabr. v. ii. p.* 316.

of anceſtry, and Virginio agréed to pay 12,000 Neapolitan ducats as a portion with his daughter (*a*). On this occaſion Piero was accompanied by Bernardo Rucellai, who had married Nannina, one of the ſiſters of Lorenzo, and who has not only ſignalized himſelf as a protector of learned men, but was himſelf one of the moſt accompliſhed ſcholars of his time (*b*).

(*b*) *Extant in Filz.* 1. I capitoli di matrimonio tra l'Alfonſina de Urſinis figlia del quondam Roberto de Urſinis conte di Tagliacozzo e d'Albi, e Piero de' Medici, comparente Virginio de Urſinis fratel conſobrino. Dos fuit Ducatorum Neapolitanorum 12,000 *Fabr. ut ſup.*

(*c*) The talents and acquirements of Rucellai juſtly entitled him to the honor of ſo near an alliance with the family of the Medici. His public life has indeed incurred the cenſure of the Florentine hiſtorians of the ſucceeding century, who wrote under the preſſure of a deſpotic government; but it is not difficult to perceive that his crime was an ardent love of liberty, which he preferred to the claims of kindred, and the expectations of perſonal aggrandizement. *Ammir. Opuſc. vol.* ii. *Elog.* ii. 161. *Comment. di Nerli. p.* 64. His Latin hiſtorical works, "*De Bello Italico,*" and "*De Bello Piſano,*" have merited the approbation of the diſcriminating Eraſmus. "Novi Venetiæ," ſays he, "Bernardum Ocricularium (Oricellarium) cujus Hiſtorias ſi "legiſſes, dixiſſes alterum *Salluſtium,* aut certe Salluſtii temporibus ſcriptas." *Apotheg. lib.* viii. The former of theſe works was firſt publiſhed at London by Brindley in 1724, and again by William Bowyer, with the treatiſe *de Bello Piſano,* in 1733. Bernardo was alſo a poet, and appears in the *Canti Carnaſcialeſchi* as the author of the *Trionſo della Calunnia. Cant. Carnas. p.* 125. But the poetical reputation of Bernardo is eclipſed by that of his ſon Giovanni Rucellai, author of the tragedy of *Roſmunda.* and of that beautiful didactic poem *Le Api,* which will remain a laſting monument that the Italian language requires not the ſhackles of rhime to render it harmonious. "Homme de Goût (ſays Tenhove) dans vos promenades ſolitaires "prenez quelquefois ſon poême.

The marriage of Pier de'Medici was soon afterwards followed by that of his sister Maddalena with Francesco Cibò, the son of the pope, and who then bore the title of count of Anguillara (*a*). Of the three other daughters of Lorenzo, Lucretia intermarried with Giacopo Salviati (*b*), Contessina with Piero Ridolfi, and Louisa, his youngest, after having been betrothed to Giovanni de' Medici, of a collateral branch of the same family, died before the time appointed for the nuptials (*c*).

"Ed odi quel che sopra un verde prato,
"Cinto d'abeti e d'onorati allori,
"Che bagna or un muscoso e chiaro fonte,
"Canta de l'api del suo florid' orto."

(*a*) These nuptials were celebrated at Rome in the year 1488. Maddalena, who was very young, was accompanied by Matteo Franco, the facetious correspondent of Pulci, (*vol.* I. *p.* 256.) the vivacity of whose character did not prevent Lorenzo from selecting him for this important trust, in the execution of which he conciliated in a high degree the favor of the pope, and his courtiers.

Pol. Ep. lib. x. *Ep.* 12.

(*b*) *Vide vol.* I. *p.* 211.

(*c*) Besides his three sons and four daughters before enumerated, Lorenzo had other children, all of whom died in their infancy, as appears by a letter from him to Politiano; who having occasion to acquaint him with the indisposition of some part of his family, and being fearful of alarming him, addressed his letter to Michellozzi, the secretary of Lorenzo. In his answer, Lorenzo reproves, with some degree of seriousness, the ill-timed distrust of Politiano, and with true stoical dignity, declares that it gave him more uneasiness than the intelligence that accompanied it. "Can you then conceive," says he, "that my temper is so infirm, as to be disturbed by such an event? "If my disposition had been by nature weak, and liable to be impelled "by every gust, yet experience has taught me how to brave the "storm. I have not only known what it is to bear the sickness, but "even the death of some of my children. The untimely loss of my

In the year 1488, Piero de' Medici took a journey to Milan, to be preſent at the celebration of the nuptials of the young duke Galeazzo Sforza, with Iſabella, grand daughter of Ferdinand, king of Naples. The whole expenſe of this journey was defrayed by Lodovico Sforza, who paid a marked reſpect to Piero, and directed that he ſhould always appear in public at the ſide of the duke. By a letter yet exiſting from the Florentine legate to Lorenzo de' Medici, it appears that theſe nuptials were celebrated with great magnificence (*a*); but amidſt the ſplendor of diamonds and the glitter of brocade, were entwined the ſerpents of treachery and of guilt. Even in giving the hand of Iſabella to a nephew, whom he regarded rather as an implement of his ambition than as his lawful ſovereign, Lodovico burnt with a criminal paſſion for her himſelf; and the graveſt of the Italian hiſtorians aſſures us, that it was the public opinion that he had by means of magic and incantations prevented the conſummation of a marriage, which while it promoted his political views, deprived him of the object of his love (*b*). The prejudices of the age, and the wickedneſs of Lodovico, ſufficiently countenance the probability of ſuch an attempt; but that the means employed were ſo

" father when I was in my twenty-firſt year, left me ſo much expoſed
" to the attacks of fortune, that life became a burden to me. You
" ought therefore to have known, that if nature denied me firmneſs,
" experience has ſupplied the defect."

Laur. Ep. in. Ep. Pol. lib. x. Ep. 5.

(*a*) *v. App. No.* LXVII.

(*b*) *Guicciard. Hiſt. d'Italia, lib. i.*

far ſucceſsful, as to prevent that circumſtance taking place for ſeveral months, is an aſſertion, of the veracity of which poſterity may be allowed to doubt.

Of this princeſs an incident is recorded which does equal honor to her conjugal affection and her filial piety (*a*). When Charles VIII. of France, at the inſtigation of Lodovico Sforza, entered Italy, a few years after her marriage, for the avowed purpoſe of depriving her father of the throne of Naples, he paſſed through Pavia, where the young duke then lay on his death-bed, not without giving riſe to ſuſpicions that he had been poiſoned. Touched with his misfortunes, and mindful of the relationſhip between Galeazzo and himſelf, who were ſiſters children, Charles reſolved to ſee him. The preſence of Lodovico, who did not chuſe to riſque the conſequences of a private and confidential interview, whilſt it reſtricted the converſation of the king to formal inquiries about the health of the duke, and wiſhes for his recovery, excited both in him and in all preſent a deeper compaſſion for the unhappy prince. Iſabella perceived the general ſympathy; and throwing herſelf at the feet of the monarch, recommended to his protection her unfortunate huſband and her infant ſon; at the ſame time, by tears and entreaties, earneſtly endeavouring to turn his reſentment from her father and the houſe of Aragon. Attracted by her beauty, and moved by her ſolicitations, Charles appeared for a

(*a*) *Guicciard. Hiſt. d'Italia, lib.i.*

moment to relent, and the fate of Italy was ſuſpended in the balance; but the king recollecting the importance of his preparations, and the expectations which his enterpriſe had excited, ſoon ſteeled his feelings againſt this feminine attack, and reſolved, in ſpite of the ſuggeſtions of pity and the claims of humanity, to perſevere in his deſign.

Having now ſecured the tranquillity of Italy and the proſperity of his family by every means that prudence could dictate, Lorenzo began to enjoy the fruits of his labors. Theſe he found in the affection and good-will of his fellow-citizens; in obſerving the rapid progreſs of the fine arts, towards the promotion of which he had ſo amply contributed; in the ſociety and converſation of men of genius and learning; and in the inexhauſtible ſtores of knowledge with which he had enriched his own diſcriminating and comprehenſive mind.

As his natural diſpoſition, or the effects of his education, frequently led him to meditate with great ſeriouſneſs on moral and religious ſubjects, ſo there were no perſons for whom he entertained a greater eſteem than thoſe who adorned their character as teachers of religion by a correſponding rectitude of life and propriety of manners. Amongſt theſe he particularly diſtinguiſhed Mariano da Genazano, an Auguſtin monk and ſuperior of his order, for whoſe uſe, and that of his aſſociates, he erected in the ſuburbs of Florence an extenſive building, which he endowed as a monaſtery, and to which he was himſelf accuſtomed occaſionally to retire, with a few ſelect friends, to enjoy the converſation

of

of this learned ecclesiastic. Politiano, in the preface to his *Miscellanea*, inveighing against those who affected to consider the study of polite letters as inconsistent with the performance of sacred functions, adduces Mariano as an illustrious instance of their union. "On this account," says he to Lorenzo, "I cannot sufficiently admire your highly "esteemed friend Mariano, whose proficiency in "theological studies, and whose eloquence and "address in his public discourses, leave him with-"out a rival. The lessons which he inculcates "derive additional authority from his acknowled-"ged disinterestedness, and from the severity of his "private life; yet there is nothing morose in his "temper, nothing unpleasingly austere; nor does "he think the charms of poetry, or the amuse-"ments and pursuits of elegant literature, below "his attention." In one of his letters, the same author has left a very explicit account of the talents of Mariano, as a preacher (*a*). "I was lately "induced," says he, "to attend one of his lectures, "rather to say the truth through curiosity, than "with the hope of being entertained. His ap-"pearance however interested me in his favor. "His address was striking, and his eye marked "intelligence. My expectations were raised. He "began—I was attentive; a clear voice—select ex-"pression—elevated sentiment. He divides his "subject—I perceive his distinctions. Nothing per-"plexed; nothing insipid; nothing languid. He "unfolds the web of his argument—I am enthralled.

(*a*) *Pol. Ep. lib.* iv. *Ep.* 6.

" He refutes the ſophiſm—I am freed. He intro-
" duces a pertinent narrative—I am intereſted. He
" modulates his voice—I am charmed. He is
" jocular—I ſmile. He preſſes me with ſerious
" truths—I yield to their force. He addreſſes the
" paſſions—the tears glide down my cheeks. He
" raiſes his voice in anger—I tremble and wiſh
" myſelf away."

Of the particular ſubjects of diſcuſſion which engaged the attention of Lorenzo and his aſſociates in their interviews at the convent of San Gallo, Valori has left ſome account which he derived from the information of Mariano himſelf. The exiſtence and attributes of the Deity, the inſufficiency of temporal enjoyments to fill the mind, and the probability and moral neceſſity of a future ſtate, were to Lorenzo the favorite objects of his diſcourſe. His own opinion was pointedly expreſſed. " He is dead even to this life," ſaid Lorenzo, " who " has no hopes of another (*a*)."

Although the citizens of Florence admired the talents, and reſpected the virtues of Mariano, their attention was much more forcibly excited by a preacher of a very different character, who poſſeſſed himſelf of their confidence, and entitled himſelf to their homage, by foretelling their deſtruction. This was the famous Girolamo Savonarola, who afterwards acted ſo conſpicuous a part in the popular commotions at Florence, and contributed ſo eſſentially to the accompliſhment of his own predictions. Savonarola was a native of Ferrara, but the reputation

(*a*) *Valor. in vitâ, p.* 48.

which he had acquired as a preacher, induced Lorenzo de' Medici to invite him to Florence, where he took up his refidence in the year 1488 (*a*), and was appointed prior of the monaftery of S. Marco. By pretenfions to fuperior fanctity, and by a fervid and overpowering elocution, he foon acquired an aftonifhing afcendency over the minds of the people; and in proportion as his popularity increafed, his difregard of his patron became more apparent, and was foon converted into the moft vindictive animofity. It had been the cuftom of thofe who had preceded Savonarola in this office, to pay particular refpect to Lorenzo de' Medici, as the fupporter of the inftitution. Savonarola however not only rejected this ceremony, as founded in adulation, but as often as Lorenzo frequented the gardens of the monaftery, retired from his prefence, pretending that his intercourfe was with God and not with man. At the fame time, in his public difcourfes, he omitted no opportunity of attacking the reputation and diminifhing the credit of Lorenzo, by prognofticating the fpeedy termination of his authority, and his banifhment from his native place. The divine word, from the lips of Savonarola, defcended not amongft his audience like the dews of heaven; it was the piercing hail, the deftroying fword, the

(*a*) In 1489, according to Tirabofchi, *Storia della Lett. Ital.* v. vi. *par.* 2. *p.* 377.; but Savonarola himfelf, in his *Trattato delle Rivelationi della reformatione della Chiefa*, *Ven.* 1536, (if indeed the work be his,) affigns an earlier period. In this work the fanatic affumes the credit of having foretold the death of Innocent VIII. of Lorenzo de' Medici, the irruption of the French into Italy, &c.

herald of deſtruction. The friends of Lorenzo frequently remonſtrated with him, on his ſuffering the monk to proceed to ſuch an extreme of arrogance; but Lorenzo had either more indulgence or more diſcretion than to adopt hoſtile meaſures againſt a man, who, though moroſe and inſolent, he probably conſidered as ſincere. On the contrary, he diſplayed his uſual prudence and moderation, by declaring that whilſt the preacher exerted himſelf to reform the citizens of Florence, he ſhould readily excuſe his incivility to himſelf. This extraordinary degree of lenity, if it had no influence on the mind of the fanatic, prevented in a great degree the ill effects of his harangues; and it was not till after the death of Lorenzo, that Savonarola excited thoſe diſturbances in Florence, which led to his own deſtruction, and terminated in the ruin of the republic.

Another eccleſiaſtic, whoſe worth and talents had conciliated the favor of Lorenzo, was Matteo Boſſo, ſuperior of the convent of regular canons at Fieſole. Not leſs converſant with the writings of the ancient philoſophers, than with the theological ſtudies of his own times, Boſſo was a profound ſcholar, a cloſe reaſoner, and a convincing orator; but to theſe he united much higher qualifications—a candid mind, an inflexible integrity, and an intereſting ſimplicity of life and manners. To his treatiſe *De veris animi gaudiis* is prefixed a recommendatory epiſtle from Politiano to Lorenzo de' Medici, highly favorable to the temper and character of the author (*a*). On the publication

(*a*) This treatiſe was firſt published in octavo, at Florence. by Ser Franciſco Bonacurſi. Anno Salutis MCCCCLXXXXI. Sexto Idus

of this piece, Boſſo tranſmitted a copy to Lorenzo, with a latin letter, preſerved in the *Recuperationes Feſulanæ*, another work of the ſame anthor, highly deſerving the attention of the ſcholar (*a*). In this letter Boſſo bears teſtimony to the virtues and to the piety of Lorenzo ; but whether this teſtimony ought to be received with greater confidence, becauſe Boſſo was the confeſſor of Lorenzo, the reader will decide for himſelf.

Of theſe his graver aſſociates, as well as of the companions of his lighter hours, Lorenzo was accuſtomed to ſtimulate the talents by every means in his power. His own intimate acquaintance with the tenets of the ancient philoſophers, and his acute and verſatile genius, enabled him to propoſe to their diſcuſſion, ſubjects of the moſt intereſting nature, and either to take a chief part in the converſation, or to avail himſelf of ſuch obſervations as it might occaſion. It appears alſo, that at ſome times he amuſed himſelf with offering to their conſideration ſuch topics as he well knew would elude

Februarii. From this edition I ſhall give the introductory letter of Politiano. *v. App. No.* LXVIII.

(*a*) This book is eſtimable not only for its contents, but as being one of the fineſt ſpecimens of typography of the fifteenth century. Inſtead of a title, we read, QUÆ HOC VOLUMINE HABENTUR VARIA DIVERSAQUE ET LONGA EX DISPERSIONE COLLECTA QUO BREVI SUB TITULO SUBJICIANTUR AC NOMINE RECUPERATIONES FESULANAS LECTOR AGNOSCITO. And at the cloſe, RECUPERATIONES FESULANAS *has elegantiſſimas, opus quidem aureum & penitus divinum quam caſtigatiſſime Impreſſit omni ſolertia* PLATO DE BENEDICTIS *Bononienſis in alma civitate Bononiæ. Anno Salutis* MCCCCLXXXXIII. *decimo tertio* KALENDAS AUGUSTAS. *Folio.* The letter from Boſſo to Lorenzo de' Medici is given in the Appendix, *No.* LXIX.

their researches, although they might exercise their powers; as men try their strength by shooting arrows towards the sky. Of this we have an instance in the sonnet addressed by him to Salviati (*a*). "When the mind," says he, "escapes from the "storms of life, to the calm haven of reflection, "doubts arise which require solution. If no one "can effectually exert himself to obtain eternal "happiness, without the special favor of God. "and if that favor be only granted to those who "are well disposed towards its reception, I wish "to know whether the grace of God, or the good "disposition, first commences?" The learned theologian to whom this captious question was addressed, took it into his serious consideration, and after dividing it into seven parts, attempted its solution in a Latin treatise of considerable extent, which is yet preserved in the Laurentian Library (*b*).

Lorenzo was not however destined long to enjoy

(*a*) Lo spirito talora a se ridutto,
E dal mar tempestoso e travagliato
Fuggito in porto tranquillo e pacato,
Pensando ha dubbio e vuolne trar costrutto,
S'egli è ver, che da Dio proceda tutto,
E senza lui nulla è, cioè il peccato;
Per sua grazia se ci è concesso e dato
Seminar qui per corre eterno frutto;
Tal grazia in quel sol fa operazione
Ch' a riceverla è volto e ben disposto,
Dunque che cosa è quella ne dispone?
Qual prima sia, vorrei mi fosse esposto,
O tal grazia, o la buona inclinazione:
Rispondi or tu al dubbio, ch' è proposto.

(*b*) *Georgii Benigni Salviati, in Rhythmum acutissimum magni Laurentii Medicis Quaestiones septem, &c.* PLUT. lxxxiii. *Cod.* 18.

that tranquillity which he had so assiduously labored to secure. His life had scarcely reached its meridian, when the prospect was overhung with dark and lowering clouds. The death of his wife Clarice, which happened in the month of August 1488, was a severe shock to his domestic happiness. He was then absent from Florence, and did not arrive in time to see her before she died, which it seems gave rise to insinuations that his conjugal affection was not very ardent (*a*); but the infirm state of his own health at this time had rendered it necessary for him to visit the warm baths, where he received an account of her death before he was apprized of the danger of her situation. From his youth he had been afflicted with a disorder which occasioned extreme pain in his stomach and limbs. This complaint was probably of a gouty tendency, but the then defective state of medicine rendered it impossible for him to obtain any just information respecting it. The most eminent physicians in Italy were consulted, and numerous remedies were prescribed, without producing any beneficial effect (*b*). By frequenting the tepid baths

(*a*) Piero de Bibbiena, the secretary of Lorenzo, writes thus to the Florentine ambassador at Rome; *Prid. Kal. Sextil.* 1488: A hore 14 mori la Clarice. Se voi sentiste che Lorenzo fosse biasimato di costà per non essersi trovato alla morte delle moglie, scusatelo. Parve al Leoni necessario, che andasse a prender l'acque della Villa, e poi non si credeva che morisse si presto. *Fabr. v.* ii. *p.* 384.

(*b*) Some of these remedies are of a singular nature. Pietro Bono Avogradi, in a letter dated the eleventh of February 1488, advises Lorenzo, as a sure method of preventing a return of the *dolore di zonture*, or arthritic pains, with which he was afflicted, to make use of a stone called an heliotrope, which being set in gold, and worn on

of Italy, he obtained a temporary alleviation of his sufferings: but, notwithstanding all the assistance he could procure, his complaints rather increased than diminished, and for some time before his death, he had reconciled his mind to an event which he knew could not be far distant. When his son Giovanni took his departure for Rome, to appear in the character of cardinal, Lorenzo with great affection recommended him to the care of Filippo Valori and Andrea Cambino, who were appointed to accompany him on his journey; at the same time expressing his apprehensions, which the event but too well justified, that he should see them no more (*a*).

In the year 1488, Girolamo Riario, whose machinations had deprived Lorenzo of a brother, and had nearly involved Lorenzo himself in the same destruction, fell a victim to his accumulated crimes. By the assistance of Sixtus IV. he had possessed himself of a considerable territory in the vicinity of the papal state, and particularly of the cities of Imola and Forli, at the latter of which he had fixed his residence, and supported the rank of an independent prince. In order to strengthen his interest in Italy, he had connected himself with the powerful family of the Sforza, by a marriage with Caterina, sister of Galeazzo Sforza, duke of Milan, whose un-

the finger so as to touch the skin, would produce the desired effect. "This," says he, "is a certain preservative against both gout and "rheumatism; I have tried it myself, and found that its properties "are divine and miraculous." With the same letter he transmits to Lorenzo his *prognostics* for the year 1488. *App. No.* LXX.

(*a*) *Valor. in vitâ Laur. p.* 65.

happy fate has already been related (*a*). The general tenor of the life of Riario feems to have correfponded with the fpecimen before exhibited. By a long courfe of oppreffion he had drawn upon himfelf the hatred and refentment of his fubjects, whom he had reduced to the utmoft extreme of indigence and diftrefs. Stimulated by repeated acts of barbarity, three of them refolved to affaffinate him, and to truft for their fafety, after the perpetration of the deed, to the opinion and fupport of their fellow-citizens. Although Riario was conftantly attended by a band of foldiers, thefe men found means to enter his chamber in the palace at the hour when he had juft concluded his fupper. One of them having cut him acrofs the face with a fabre, he took fhelter under the table, whence he was dragged out by Lodovico Orfo, another of the confpirators, who ftabbed him through the body. Some of his attendants having by this time entered the room, Riario made an effort to efcape at the door, but there received from the third confpirator a mortal wound. It is highly probable that he was betrayed by the guard, for thefe three men were even permitted to ftrip the dead body, and throw it through the window, when the populace immediately rofe and facked the palace. The infurgents, having fecured the widow and children of Riario, were only oppofed by the troops in the fortrefs of the town, who refufed to furrender it either to their entreaties or their threats. Being required, under pain of death, to exert her influence in obtaining

(*a*) *Vol.* I. *p.* 177.

for the populace poſſeſſion of the fortreſs, the princeſs requeſted that they would permit her to enter it; but no ſooner was ſhe ſecure within the walls than ſhe exhorted the ſoldiers to its defence, and raiſing the ſtandard of the duke of Milan, threatened the town with deſtruction. The inhabitants attempted to intimidate her by preparing to execute her children in her ſight, for which purpoſe they erected a ſcaffold before the walls of the fortreſs; but this unmanly proceeding, inſtead of awakening her affections, only excited her contempt, which ſhe is ſaid to have expreſſed in a very emphatic and extraordinary manner (*a*). By her courage the inhabitants were however reſiſted, until Giovanni Bentivoglio, with a body of two thouſand foot and eight hundred cavalry, from Bologna, gave her effectual aſſiſtance, and being joined by a ſtrong reinforcement from Milan, compelled the inhabitants to acknowledge as their ſovereign Ottavio Riario, the eldeſt ſon of Girolamo (*b*).

Lorenzo de' Medici has not eſcaped the imputation of having been privy to the aſſaſſination of his old and implacable adverſary; but neither the relations of contemporary hiſtorians, nor the general tenor of his life, afford a preſumption on which to ground ſuch an accuſation (*c*); although

(*a*) Riſpoſe loro quella forte femmina, che ſe aveſſero fatti perir que' figliuoli, reſtavano a lei le forme per farne degli altri; e vi ha che dice (queſta giunta forſe fu immaginata e non vera) aver' ella anche alzata la gonna per chiarirli, che dicea la verità.

Murat. Ann. vol. ix. *p.* 556.

(*b*) *Chronica Boſſiana. an.* 1488. *Ed.* 1492.

(*c*) " Indignum ſane facinus fuit, quod in Hieronymum Riarium " Comitem admiſſum eſt; cujus participem Laurentium fuiſſe *multi*

it is certain, that ſome years previous to this event, he had been in treaty with the pope to deprive Riario of his uſurpations, and to reſtore the territories occupied by him to the family of Ordolaffi, their former lords, which treaty was fruſtrated by the pope having inſiſted on annexing them to the ſtates of the church (*a*). The conſpirators however, ſoon after the death of Riario, apprized Lorenzo of the event, and requeſted his aſſiſtance; in conſequence of which he diſpatched one of his envoys to Forli, with a view of obtaining authentic in-

" *contendunt*, & ab eo ad ulciſcendas præteritorum temporum injurias " comparatum." *Fabr. in vitâ, vol.* i. *p.* 175. There is however great reaſon to ſuſpect that the modern biographer of Lorenzo has inadvertently given weight and credit to an accuſation, which, if eſtabliſhed, would degrade his character to that of a treacherous aſſaſſin. In vindication of him againſt this charge, I muſt therefore obſerve, that of the many accuſers to whom Fabroni adverts, I have not met with one of the early hiſtorians who has even glanced at Lorenzo as having been aſſociated with the conſpirators, or privy to the prepetration of the deed. Neither Machiavelli nor Ammirato, although they all relate the particulars of the tranſaction, have implicated in it the name of Lorenzo. Muratori, whoſe annals are compiled from contemporary and authentic documents, and who may therefore be conſidered as an original writer, is equally ſilent on this head. The ancient chronicle of Donato Boſſo, printed only four years after the event, gives a yet more particular account, but alludes not to any interpoſition on the part of Lorenzo; and even Raffaello Maffei, his acknowledged adverſary, though he adverts to the death of Riario, attributes it only to the interference of his own ſubjects. It is indeed a ſtrong indication of the dignity of the character of Lorenzo, that a charge ſo natural, and ſo conſiſtent with the ſpirit of the times, ſhould not have been alledged againſt him; and having been exculpated in the eyes of his contemporaries, it is ſurely not for poſterity to criminate him.

(*a*) *Fabron. Adnot. & Monum. v.* iii. *p.* 316.

formation as to the disposition of the inhabitants, and the views of the insurgents (*a*), when finding that it was their intention to place themselves under the dominion of the pope, he declined any interference on their behalf, but availed himself of the opportunity of their dissensions, to restore to the Florentines the fortress of Piancaldoli, which had been wrested from them by Riario (*b*). That the assassins of Riario were suffered

(*a*) The letter from Lodovico and Clecco d' Orsi, two of the conspirators, to Lorenzo de' Medici, written only a few days after the event, is inserted in the Appendix, and indisputably shows, that although they supposed Lorenzo would be gratified by the death of his adversary, he had no previous knowledge of such an attempt. To this I shall also subjoin the letter to Lorenzo from his envoy, which gives a minute account of the whole transaction, and by which it appears, that although the pope had incited the conspirators to the enterprise, by expressing his abhorrence of the character of Riario, yet that no other person was privy to their purpose. *App. No.* LXXI.

(*b*) In the attack of this place, the Florentines lost their eminent citizen, Cecca, the engineer, whose skill had facilitated the success of their enterprise. In the *Exhortatio* of Philippus Reditus, addressed to Piero de' Medici, *in Magnanimi sui parentis imitationem*, the MS. of which is preserved in the Laurentian Library, this incident is particularly related; and as the passage has not hitherto been published, having been omitted, with many others, in the edition of Lami, *Delic. Erudit. vol.* xii. printed from a copy in the Riccardi Library, I shall here insert it: "Piancaldolii arx strenue nostris recuperatur. Ad iv. vero Kalendas Maias, nuntiata nece Hieronymi "Riarii, Imolæ Forliviique Tyranni, Piancaldolis oppidum nostrum, "olim ab eo per summum nefas nobis ereptum, admirabili quadam "nostrorum celeritate, tuo magnanimo Genitore procurante, strenuo "recuperatur. In cujus arcis obsidione, Franciscus, cognomine "Ciccha, Fabrum magister, vir vel in expugnandis vel in defendendis "urbibus tam nostra, quam nostrorum patrum memoria perillustris, "sagitta ictus capite, pro patria feliciter occubuit." The death of Cecca is related with some variation by Vassari, *Vita del Cecca.*

to escape with impunity, is perhaps the best justification of their conduct, as it affords a striking proof that he had deserved his fate.

Another event soon afterwards took place at Faenza, which occasioned great anxiety to Lorenzo, and called for the exertion of all his conciliatory powers. If the list of crimes and assassinations which we have before had occasion to notice, may be thought to have disgraced the age, that which we have now to relate exhibits an instance of female ferocity, which renewed in the fifteenth century the examples of Gothic barbarity (*a*). By the me-

" Costui, quando i Florentini avevano l' esercito intorno a' Piancaldoli, " con l' ingegno suo fece si, che i soldati vi entrarono dentro per via " di mine senza colpo di spada. Dopo seguitando più oltre il medesimo " esercito a certe altre castella, come volle la mala sorte, volendo " egli misurare alcune altezze in un luogo difficile, fu ucciso; per" ciocchè, avendo messo il capo fuor del muro per mandar un filo " abasso, un prete, che era fra gli avversarii, i quali più temevano " l' ingegno del Cecca, che le forze di tutto il campo, scaricatogli " una balestra a panca, gli conficcò di sorte un verettone nella testa, " che il poverello di subito se ne morì."

(*a*) There is a striking coincidence between this event, and the narrative of Paulus Diaconus, upon which Giovanni Ruccellai has founded his tragedy of *Rosmunda.* Alboin, king of the Huns, having conquered and slain in battle Comundus, king of the Geppidi, compels his daughter *Rosmunda* to accept of him in marriage, with a view of uniting their dominions under his sole authority; but not satisfied with the accession of power, he gratifies a brutal spirit of revenge, by compelling her, at a public feast, to drink from the skull of her slaughtered father, which he had formed into a cup. This insult the princess avenges, by seducing to her purpose two of the king's intimate friends, who, in order to entitle themselves to her favor, assassinate him in the hour of intoxication. Ruccellai has however preserved his heroine from the crimes of prostitution and assassination, and has introduced a disinterested lover in the person of *Almachilde,*

diation of Lorenzo, who was equally the friend of the Manfredi and the Bentivoli, a marriage had taken place between Galeotto Manfredi, prince of Faenza, and Francefca, daughter of Giovanni Bentivoglio, which for fome time feemed to be productive of that happinefs to the parties, and thofe advantages to their refpective families, which Lorenzo had in view. It was not long however before Francefca difcovered, or fufpected, that her hufband was engaged in an illicit amour, the information of which fhe thought proper to communicate both to her father and to Lorenzo. Ever on the watch to obtain further proofs of his infidelity, fhe found an opportunity of liftening to a private interview between Galeotto, and fome pretender to aftrological knowledge, in whom it feems he was credulous enough to place his confidence. Inftead, however, of gaining any intelligence as to the object of her curiofity, fhe heard predictions and denunciations, which, as fhe thought, affected the fafety of her father, and being unable to conceal her indignation, fhe broke in upon their deliberations, and reproached her hufband with his treachery. Irritated by the intrufion and the pertinacity of his wife, Galeotto retorted with great bitternefs; but findiug himfelf unequal to a conteft of this nature, he had recourfe to more violent methods, and by menaces and blows reduced her to obedience. Bentivoglio was no fooner apprized of the ignomi-

who executes vengeance on the king from generous and patriotic motives. In juftice to the author, it muft alfo be obferved, that the horrid incident upon which the tragedy is founded, is narrated only, and not reprefented before the audience.

nious treatment which his daughter had received, and of the circumſtances which had given riſe to it, than he reſolved to carry her off from her huſband by force. Taking with him a choſen body of ſoldiers, he approached Faenza by night, and ſeizing on Franceſca and her infant ſon, brought them in ſafety to Bologna. This ſtep he followed up, by preparing for an attack on the dominions of his ſon-in-law; but Galeotto having reſorted to Lorenzo for his mediation, a reconciliation took place, and Franceſca ſhortly afterwards returned to Faenza. Whether ſhe ſtill harboured in her boſom the lurking paſſions of jealouſy and revenge, or whether ſome freſh inſult on the part of her huſband had rouſed her fury, is not known; but ſhe formed and executed a deliberate plan for his aſſaſſination. To this end ſhe feigned herſelf ſick, and requeſted to ſee him in her chamber. Galeotto obeyed the ſummons, and on entering his wife's apartments, was inſtantly attacked by four hired aſſaſſins, three of whom ſhe had concealed under her bed. Though totally unarmed, he defended himſelf courageouſly; and as he had the advantages of great perſonal ſtrength and activity, would probably have effected his eſcape; but when Franceſca ſaw the conteſt doubtful, ſhe ſprung from the bed, and graſping a ſword, plunged it into his body, and accompliſhed his deſtruction with her own hand. Conſcious of her guilt, ſhe immediately took refuge with her children in the caſtle, until her father once more came to her relief. On his approach to Faenza, Bentivoglio was joined by the Milaneſe troops, who had been engaged in reinſtating the family of Riario at Forli. The citizens of

Faenza, conceiving that it was his intention to deprive them of Aftorgio, the infant fon of Galeotto, or rather perhaps under that pretext to poffefs himfelf of the city, refufed to furrender to him his daughter and her family. He immediately attacked the place, which was not only fuccefsfully defended by the citizens, but in an engagement which took place under the walls. Borgomini, the commander of the Milanefe troops, loft his life, and Bentivoglio was made a prifoner. During this difpute Lorenzo de' Medici had warmly efpoufed the caufe of the citizens, and had encouraged them with promifes of fupport, in cafe they fhould find it neceffary in preferving their independence. The fuccefs of their exertions, and the difafter of Bentivoglio, changed the object of his folicitude, and no fooner did he receive intelligence of this event, than he difpatched a meffenger to Faenza, to interfere on the behalf of Bentivoglio, and if poffible to obtain his releafe. This was with fome difficulty accomplifhed, and Bentivoglio immediately reforted to Florence, to return his thanks to his benefactor. Some time afterwards Lorenzo, at the requeft of Bentivoglio, folicited the liberation of his daughter, which was alfo complied with; and he was at length prevailed upon to intercede with the pope, to relieve her from the ecclefiaftical cenfures which fhe had incurred by her crime. The reafon given by Bentivoglio to Lorenzo, for requefting his affiftance in this laft refpect, will perhaps be thought extraordinary—*He had an intention of providing her with another hufband!*

CHAP. IX.

PROGRESS of the arts — State of them in the middle ages — Revival in Italy — Guido da Sienna — Cimabue — Giotto — Character of his works — The Medici encourage the arts — Masaccio — Paolo Uccello — Fra Filippo — Antonio Pollajuolo — Baldovinetti — Andrea da Castagna — Filippo Lippi — Luca Signorelli — Progress of Sculpture — Niccolo and Andrea Pisani — Ghiberti — Donatello — Imperfect state of the arts — Causes of their improvement — Numerous works of Sculpture collected by the ancient Romans — Researches after the remains of antiquity — Petrarca — Lorenzo de' Medici brother of Cosmo — Niccolo Niccoli — Poggio Bracciolini — Collection of antiques formed by Cosmo — Assiduity of Lorenzo in augmenting it — Lorenzo establishes a school for the study of the antique — Michelagnolo Buonarroti — Resides with Lorenzo — Forms an intimacy with Politiano — Advantages over his predecessors — His sculptures — Rapid improvement of taste — Raffaelle d'Urbino — Michelagnolo unjustly censured — Other artists favored by Lorenzo — Gian-Francesco Rustici — Francesco Granacci — Andrea Contucci — Lorenzo encourages the study of Architecture — Giuliano da San Gallo — Attempts to renew the practice of Mosaic — Invention of engraving on copper — Revival of engraving on gems and stones.

THOSE periods of time which have been most favorable to the progress of letters and science, have generally been distinguished by an equal proficiency in the arts. The productions of Roman sculpture, in its best ages, bear nearly the same proportion to those of the Greeks, as the imitative labors of the Roman authors bear to the original works of their great prototypes. During the long ages of ignorance that succeeded the fall of the Western empire, letters and the fine arts underwent an equal degradation; and it would be as difficult to point out a literary work of those times which is entitled to approbation, as it would be to produce a statue or a picture. When these studies began to revive, a Guido da Sienna, a Cimabue, rivalled a Guittone d' Arezzo, or a Piero delle Vigne. The crude buds that had escaped the severity of so long a winter soon began to swell, and Giotto, Buffalmacco, and Gaddi were the contemporaries of Dante, of Boccaccio, and of Petrarca (*a*).

It is not however to be presumed, that, even in the darkest intervals of the middle ages, these arts were entirely extinguished. Some traces of them are found in the rudest state of society; and the efforts of the Europeans, the South Americans, and the Chinese, without rivalship and without participation, are nearly on an equality with each other. Among the manuscripts of the Laurentian Library are preserved some specimens of miniature paint-

(*a*) Videmus picturas ducentorum annorum nulla prorsus arte politas; scripta illius ætatis rudia sunt, inepta, incompta: post Petrarcham emerserunt litteræ; post Joctum surrexere pictorum manus; utraque ad summam jam videmus artem pervenisse. *Æn. Silvii (Pii* ii.) *Epist.* 119. *ap. Baldinuc. Notiz. Dec.* 1. Such was the opinion of this pontiff, who had great learning and some taste. He was only mistaken in supposing that he had seen the perfection of the art.

ings which are unqueſtionably to be referred to the tenth century, but they bear deciſive evidence of the barbariſm of the times ; and although they certainly aim at pictureſque repreſentation, yet they may with juſtice be conſidered rather as perverſe diſtortions of nature, than as the commencement of an elegant art (*a*).

Antecedent, however, to Cimabue, to whom Vaſari attributes the honor of having been the reſtorer of painting, Guido da Sienna had demonſtrated to his countrymen the poſſibility of improvement. His picture of the virgin, which yet remains tolerably entire in the church of S. Domenico, in his native place, and which bears the date of 1221, is preſumed, with reaſon, to be the earlieſt work now extant of any Italian painter (*b*). The Florentine made a bolder effort, and attracted more general admiration. Every new Production of his pencil was regarded as a prodigy, and riches and honors were liberally beſtowed on the fortunate artiſt. His picture of the Madonna, after having

(*a*) Theſe pieces have lately been engraved and publiſhed in the *Etruria Pittrice*, a work which appears periodically at Florence, and contains ſpecimens of the manner of the Tuſcan artiſts from the earlieſt times, executed ſo as to give ſome idea of the original pictures. To this work, which would have been much more valuable if greater attention had been paid to the engravings, I ſhall, in ſketching the progreſs of the art, have frequent occaſion to refer.

(*b*) Engraved in the *Etruria Pittrice*, No. iii. Under this picture is inſcribed, in Gothic characters, the following verſe:

" Me Guido de Senis diebus depinxit amenis
" Quem Chriſtus lenis nullis velit agere penis
A. D. MCCXXI."

excited the wonder of a Monarch, and given the name of *Borgo Allegro* to that diſtrict of the city whither his countrymen reſorted to gratify themſelves with a ſight of it, was removed to its deſtined ſituation in the church of *S. Maria Novella*, to the ſound of muſic, in a ſolemn proceſſion of the citizens (*a*). The modern artiſt who obſerves this picture may find it difficult to account for ſuch a degree of enthuſiaſm (*b*); but excellence is merely relative, and it is a ſufficient cauſe of approbation, if the merit of the performance exceed the ſtandard of the age. Thoſe productions which, compared with the works of a Raffaello, or a Titian, may be of little eſteem, when conſidered with reference to the times that gave them birth, may juſtly be entitled to no ſmall ſhare of applauſe.

The glory of Cimabue was obſcured by that of his diſciple Giotto (c), who from figuring the ſheep which it was his buſineſs to tend, became the beſt painter that Italy had produced (*d*). It affords no

(*a*) *Vaſari, vita di Cimabue.*

(*b*) Engraved in the *Etruria Pittrice, No.* viii. The virgin is ſeated with the infant on her knee, in a rich chair, which is ſupported by ſix angels, repreſented as adults, though leſs than the child. The head of the virgin is ſomewhat inclined, the countenance melancholy, not without ſome pretenſions to grace; the reſt of the picture is in the true ſtyle of Gothic formality.

(*c*) Credette Cimabue nella pintura,
Tener lo campo; ed ora ha Giotto il grido,
Si che la fama di colui oſcura.

Dante, Purg. Cant. xi.

(*d*) *Manni*, in his *Illuſtr. del Boccaccio, p.* 414. deduces the name of Giotto from Angiolotto, but M. Tenhove with more probability derives it from Ambrogio. *Ambrogio, Ambrogiotto, Giotto;* " Quel

inadequate proof of his high reputation, when we find him indulging his humor in an imitation of the celebrated artiſt of Cos, and ſending to the pope, who had deſired to ſee one of his drawings, a circle, ſtruck with ſuch freedom, as to ſhow the hand of a maſter, yet with ſuch truth, as to have given riſe to a proverb (*a*). Inferior artiſts hazard not ſuch freedoms with the great. Giotto ſeems however to have delighted in the eccentricities of the art. One of his firſt eſſays when he began to ſtudy under Cimabue was to paint a fly on the noſe of one of his maſter's portraits, which the deluded artiſt attempted to bruſh off with his hand (*b*); a tale that may rank with the horſe of Apelles, the curtain of Parrhaſius, or the grapes of Zeuxis. Boccaccio has introduced this celebrated painter with great approbation in one of his novels (*c*); a ſin-

" étranger," ſays this lively author, " aperçoit d'abord ſous les bizarres " déguiſemens de *Biſla*, *Betto*, *Bambo*, *Bindo*, *Bacci*, *Tani*, *Cece*, " *Giomo*, *Nigi*, *Meo*, *Nanni*, *Vanni*, *Mazo*, *Lippo*, *Lippozzo*, " *Pipo*. *Guccio*, *Mico*, *Caca*, *Toto*, *&c*. les noms de batême les plus " vulgaires & les plus communs? Les autres Italiens ſe ſont toujours " moqués de cet uſage Florentin, qui en effet n'eſt pas moins riſible " que ſi M. Hume, dans ſa belle hiſtoire d'Angleterre, nous entretenait " de *Billy le conquérant*, de *Tom Becket*, de *Jackey le grand-terrien*, " appellé *Sans-Terre*, des grands Rois *Ned*. I. & III. *du nom*, de " la bigotte *Reine Molly*, de la grand *Reine Beſs*, & de ſon cher " amant *Bobby Devereux*, envoyé par elle au ſupplice," &c.

Mém. Gén. &c. liv. i. *p.* 37.

(*a*) Divolgataſi poi queſta coſa, ne nacque il proverbio, che ancora è in uſo dirſi agli uomini di groſſa paſta: *Tu ſei più tondo che l'O di Giotto. Vaſar. vita di Giotto.*

(*b*) *Vaſari vita di Giotto.*

(*c*) Giotto ebbe un ingegno di tanta eccellenza, che niuna coſa da la natura, madre di tutte le coſe, ed operatrice, col continuo girar de'

gular conversation is said to have occurred between him and Dante (*a*); and Petrarca held his works in such high esteem, that one of his pictures is the subject of a legacy to a particular friend in his will (*b*). Upwards of a century after his death, Lorenzo de' Medici, well aware that the most efficacious method of exciting the talents of the living is to confer due honor on departed merit, raised a bust to his memory in the church of *S. Maria del Fiore*, the inscription for which was furnished by Politiano (*c*).

cieli, che egli con lo stile, e con la penna, e col pennello non dipignesse, sì simile a quella, che non simile, anzi più tosto dessa paresse.

Decam. Gior. vi. *Nov.* 5.

(*a*) Benvenuto da Imola, one of the commentators of Dante, relates, that whilst Giotto resided at Padua, Dante paid him a visit, and was received by him with great attention. Observing however that the children of Giotto bore a great resemblance to their father, whose features and appearance were not very prepossessing, he inquired how it came to pass that his pictures and his children were so very unlike to each other, the former being so beautiful, the latter so coarse. *Quia pingo de die, sed fingo de nocte*, said the painter.

Manni, Illust. del Bocc. p. 417.

(*b*) Transeo ad dispositionem aliarum rerum; predicto igitur domino meo Paduano, quia & ipse per Dei gratiam non eget, & ego nihil aliud habeo dignum se, mitto Tabulam meam sive historiam Beatæ virginis Mariæ, operis Jocti pictoris egregii, quæ mihi ab amico meo Michaele Vannis de Florentia missa est, in cujus pulchritudinem ignorantes non intelligunt, magistri autem artis stupent.

Vasari, vita di Giotto.

(*c*) Ille ego sum per quem Pictura extincta revixit,
Cui quam recta manus tam fuit & facilis,
Naturæ deerat nostræ quod defuit arti;
Plus licuit nulli pingere nec melius.

The merits of Giotto and his ſchool are appreciated with great judgment by Vaſari, who attributes to him and his predeceſſor Cimabue the credit of having baniſhed the inſipid and ſpiritleſs manner introduced by the Greek artiſts, and given riſe to a new and more natural ſtyle of compoſition. This the hiſtorian denominates the *maniera di Giotto* (*a*). " Inſtead of the harſh outline, circumſcribing the " whole figure, the glaring eyes, the pointed feet " and hands, and all the defects ariſing from a total

> Miraris turrim egregiam ſacro ære ſonantem?
> Hæc quoque de modulo crevit ad aſtra meo.
> Denique ſum JOTTUS, quid opus fuit illa referre?
> Hoc nomen longi carminis inſtar erit.

(*a*) *Proemio di Giorgio Vaſari* to the ſecond part of his work, written, like all his other prefaces, with great judgment, candor, and hiſtorical knowledge of his art. *Tractant fabrilia fabri*—The early painters are fortunate in poſſeſſing an hiſtorian, who without envy, ſpleen, or arrogance, and with as little prejudice or partiality as the imperfection of human nature will allow, has diſtributed to each of his characters, his due portion of applauſe. If he has on any occaſion shown too apparent a bias in favor of an individual, it leans towards Michelagnolo Buonarroti, in whoſe friendship he gloried, and whoſe works he diligently ſtudied; but an exceſs of admiration for this great man will ſcarcely be imputed to him as a fault. As a painter and an architect, Vaſari holds a reſpectable rank. In the former department, his productions are extremely numerous. One of his principal labors is his hiſtorical ſuite of pictures of the Medici family, with their portraits, painted for the great duke Coſmo I. in the *Palazzo Vecchio* at Florence, of which Vaſari himſelf has given a particular account, published by Filippo Giunti, in 1588, and entitled *Ragionamenti del Sig. Cav. Giorgio Vaſari ſopra le invenzioni da lui dipinte in Firenze, &c.* Reprinted in Arezzo, 1762. In this ſeries of pictures are repreſented the principal incidents in the life of Lorenzo. This work has been engraved, but not in ſuch a manner as to do juſtice to the painter.

" want of ſhadow, the figures of Giotto exhibit a " better attitude, the heads have an air of life and " freedom, the drapery is more natural, and there " are even ſome attempts at fore-ſhortening the " limbs." " Beſides theſe improvements, " continues this author, " Giotto was the firſt who repre- " ſented in his pictures, the effect of the paſſions " on the human countenance. That he did not " proceed further muſt be attributed to the difficul- " ties which attend the progreſs of the art, and to " the want of better examples. In many of the " eſſential requiſites of his profeſſion, he was indeed " equalled, if not ſurpaſſed, by ſome of his con- " temporaries. The coloring of Gaddi had more " force and harmony, and the attitudes of his figures " more vivacity. Simone da Sienna is to be preferred " to him in the compoſition of his ſubjects, and " other painters excelled him in other branches of " the art; but Giotto had laid the ſolid foundation " of their improvements. It is true, all that was " effected by theſe maſters may be conſidered only " as the firſt rude ſketch of a ſculptor towards com- " pleting an elegant ſtatue, and if no further pro- " greſs had been made, there would not, upon the " whole, have been much to commend; but who- " ever conſiders the difficulties under which their " works were executed, the ignorance of the times, " the rarity of good models, and the impoſſibility " of obtaining inſtruction, will eſteem them not only " as commendable, but wonderful productions, " and will perceive with pleaſure theſe firſt ſparks " of improvement which afterwards fanned into " ſo bright a flame."

The patronage of the family of the Medici is almoſt contemporary with the commencement of the art. Giovanni de' Medici, the father of Coſmo, had employed his fellow-citizen, Lorenzo de' Bicci, to ornament with portraits a chamber in one of his houſes in Florence, which afterwards became the reſidence of Lorenzo, the brother of Coſmo (*a*). The liberality of Coſmo led the way to further improvement. Under Maſaccio, the ſtudy of nature and actual obſervation were ſubſtituted to cold and ſervile imitation. By this maſter, his competitors, and his ſcholars, every component branch of the art was carried to ſome degree of perfection. Paolo Uccello was the firſt who boldly ſurmounted the difficulty which Giotto, though ſenſible of its importance, had ineffectually attempted to overcome, and gave that ideal depth to his labors, which is the eſſence of picture ſque repreſentation (*b*). This he accompliſhed by his ſuperior knowledge of perſpective, which he ſtudied in conjunction with the celebrated Giannozzo Manetti, and in the attainment of which the painter and the ſcholar were mutually ſerviceable to each other (*c*). The rules which he thence acquired he applied to practice, not only in

(*a*) *Vaſar. vita di Lor. de' Bicci.*

(*b*) E da oſſervare che non ſi trova prima di lui neſſuno ſcorto di figure, perciò a ragione può dirſi aver quello valent' uomo fatto un gran progreſſo nell arte. *Etruria Pittrice, No.* xiv.

(*c*) E fu il primo che poneſſe ſtudio grande nella proſpettiva, introducendo il modo di mettere le figure ſu' piani, dove eſſe poſar devono, diminuendole a proporzione; il che, da maeſtri avanti a lui, ſi faceva a caſo, e ſenz' alcuna conſiderazione.

Baldinuc. Dec. ii. *del. par.* i. *ſec.* iv.

the back-grounds of his pictures, but in his representation of the human figure, of which he expressed the *Scorci*, or fore-shortenings, with accuracy and effect (*a*). The merit of having been the first to apply mathematical rules to the improvement of works of art, and the proficiency which he made in so necessary and so laborious a study, if it had not obtained from Vasari a greater share of praise, ought at least to have secured the artist from that ridicule with which he seems inclined to treat him (*b*). The elder Filippo Lippi gave to his figures a boldness and grandeur before unknown. He attended also to the effect of his back-grounds, which were however in general too minutely finished. About two years after his death, which happened in the year 1469, Lorenzo de' Medici, who was then absent from Florence on a journey, to congratulate Sixtus IV. on his accession to the pontificate, took the opportunity of passing through Spoletto, where he requested permission from the magistrates to remove the ashes of the artist to the church of *S. Maria del Fiore* at Florence. The community of that place were however unwilling to relinquish so honorable a deposit; and Lorenzo was therefore content to

(*a*) In his picture of the inebriety of Noah, in the church of S. Maria Novella, is a figure of the patriarch stretched on the ground, with his feet towards the front of the picture; yet, even in this difficult attitude, the painter has succeeded in giving an explicit idea of his subject. *Etrur. Pittr. No.* xiv.

(*b*) La moglie soleva dire che tutta la notte Paolo stava nello scrittoio, per trovar i termini della prospettiva, e che quando ella lo chiamava a dormire, egli le diceva, *O che dolce cosa è questa prospettiva!*
Vasar Vita di Paolo.

testify his respect for the memory of the painter, by engaging his son, the younger Filippo, to erect in the church of Spoletto a monument of marble, the inscription upon which, written by Politiano, has led his historian Menckenius into a mistake almost too apparent to admit of an excuse (*a*).

In the anatomy of the human figure, which now began to engage the more minute attention of the painter, Antonio Pollajuolo took the lead of all his competitors. By accurate observation, as well on the dead as on the living, he acquired a competent knowledge of the form and action of the muscles (*a*), which he exemplified in a striking manner in his picture of Hercules and Antæus,

(*a*) *In Philippum Fratrem Pictorem.*

Conditus hic ego sum picturæ fama PHILIPPUS;
 Nulli ignota meæ est gratia mira manus.
Artifices potui digitis animare colores,
 Sperataque animos fallere voce diu.
Ipsa meis stupuit natura expressa figuris,
 Meque suis fassa est artibus esse parem.
Marmoreo tumulo MEDICES LAURENTIUS hic me
 Condidit: ante humili pulvere tectus eram.

From the appellation of *Frater*, given to Lippi by Politiano, Menckenius conjectures, that he was his brother. "Is enim quis sit, "cujus hic frater dicitur Philippus, si Politianus non est, hariolari non possum." *Menck. in vitâ Pol. p.* 31. Filippo had entered into holy orders, whence he was called *Fra Filippo;* a circumstance which Menckenius might easily have discovered, though he professes not to have been able to obtain any information respecting it. "Nihil enim "eâ de re scriptores alii, cùm non desint, qui maxime excelluisse hunc "*Philippum* nobilissima pingendi arte suo confirment testimonio." *Ibid. p.* 637.

(*b*) Egli s'intese degl'ignudi più modernamente, che fatto non avevano gli altri maestri innanzi a lui; e scorticò molti uomini, per vedere

painted for Lorenzo de' Medici, in which he is ſaid not only to have expreſſed the ſtrength of the conqueror, but the languor and inanimation of the conquered (*a*); but his moſt celebrated work is the death of S. Sebaſtian, yet preſerved in the chapel of the Pucci family at Florence, and of which Vaſari has given a particular account (*b*). In this picture, the figure of the dying ſaint was painted from nature after Gino Capponi. In the figures of the two aſſaſſins, who are bending their croſs-bows, he has ſhown great knowledge of muſcular action. Baldovinetti excelled in portraits, which he frequently introduced in his hiſtorical ſubjects. In a picture of the queen of Sheba on a viſit to Solomon, he painted the likeneſs of Lorenzo de' Medici, and of the celebrated mechanic, Lorenzo da Volpaia (*c*); and in another picture, intended as its companion, thoſe of Giuliano de' Medici, Luca Pitti, and other Florentine citizens. The reſemblance of Lorenzo

la notomia lor ſotto; e fu primo a moſtrare il modo di cercare i muſcoli, che aveſſero forma, ed ordine nelle figure.

Vaſari vita di Pollajuolo.

(*a*) *Vaſari, ut ſupra.*

(*b*) *Vaſari, ut ſupra.* This picture is engraved and published in the *Etruria Pittrice, No.* xxiv.

(*c*) Ritraſſe coſtui aſſai di naturale, e dove nella detta cappella fece la ſtoria della Reina Saba, che va a udire la ſapienza di Salomone, ritraſſe il magnifico Lorenzo de' Medici, che fu padre di papa Leone decimo, Lorenzo dalla Volpaja eccellentiſſimo maeſtro d'oriuoli, ed ottimo aſtrologo, il quale fu quello, che fece per il detto Lor. de' Medici il belliſſimo oriuolo che ha oggi il Sig. Duca Coſimo in Palazzo; nel quale oriuolo tutte le ruote de' pianeti camminano di continuo; il che è coſa rara, e la prima che fuſſe mai fatta di queſta maniera.

Vaſar. vita di Baldov. v. ante, p. 115.

was alſo introduced by Domenico Ghirlandajo, in a picture of S. Franceſco taking the habit, painted by him in the chapel of the Trinity at Florence, Until this time the pictures of the Tuſcan artiſts had been executed in diſtemper, or with colors rendered coheſive by glutinous ſubſtances. The practice of painting in oil, ſo eſſentially neceſſary to the duration of a picture, was now firſt introduced amongſt his countrymen by Andrea da Caſtagna (*a*). The younger Filippo Lippi attempted, and not without effect, to give a greater ſhare of energy and animation to his productions. His attitudes are frequently bold and diverſified; and his figures have expreſſion, vivacity, and motion (*b*). It is deſerving

(*a*) Era nel ſuo tempo in Firenze un tal Domenico da Venezia, pittore di buon nome, col quale egli (Andrea) aveva fintamente legata grande amicizia, affine di cavargli dalla mano la maeſtría di colorire a olio, che allora in Toſcana non era da alcun altro praticata, nè meno ſaputa, fuori che da Domenico, come gli riuſci da fare. *Baldin. Dec.* iii. *ſec.* v. The invention of painting in oil, though introduced ſo late into Italy, is probably more ancient than has generally been ſuppoſed. It is commonly attributed to the Flemish artiſts, Hubert and John Van Eyck, who flouriſhed about the year 1400; but profeſſor Leſſing, in a ſmall treatiſe "*ſur l'ancienneté de la peinture à l'huile,*" printed at Brunſwick in 1774, has endeavoured to show that this art is of much greater antiquity. His ſuggeſtions have ſince been confirmed by the reſearches of M. de Mechel of Baſle, who, in arranging the immenſe collection of pictures of the imperial gallery of Vienna, has diſcovered ſeveral pieces painted in oil, as early as the thirteenth and fourteenth centuries. Of theſe the earlieſt is a picture by Thomas de Mutina, a Bohemian gentleman; the others are by Theodoric, of Prague, and Nic. Wurmſer, of Straſbourg; both artiſts at the court of the emperor Charles IV.

v. Mechel, Catal. des Tabl. de Vienne, &c. in preſ.

(*b*) His celebrated picture of S. Filippo and the ſerpent, painted

of remark, that he prepared the way to the ſtudy of the antique, by introducing into his pictures, the vaſes, utenſils, arms, and dreſſes of the ancients (*a*). But of all the maſters of this period, perhaps Luca Signorelli united the moſt important excellencies; his compoſition was good; in drawing the naked figure he particularly excelled (*b*); in his picture of the inſtitution of the euchariſt, yet exiſting in the choir of the cathedral at Cortona (*c*), the figure of Chriſt might be miſtaken for the production of one of the Caracci. In the variety and expreſſion of countenance, in the diſpoſition of the drapery, even in the juſt diſtribution of light, this picture has great merit; and if ſome remnants of the manner of the times prevent us from giving it unlimited approba-

in the chapel of the Strozzi at Florence, and engraved in the *Etruria Pittrice, No.* xxvii. is a ſufficient proof of the truth of this remark. Filippo Lippi was the ſon of the former painter of the ſame name, uſually called Fra Filippo. Lorenzo employed him to ornament his palace at Poggio Cajano, where he painted a ſacrifice in Freſco, but the work was left unfiniſhed.

(*a*) Non lavorò mai opera alcuna, nelle quale delle coſe antiche di Roma con gran ſtudio non ſi ſerviſſe, in vaſi, calzari, trofei, bandiere, cimieri, ornamenti di tempi, abbigliamenti di portature da capo, ſtrane fogge da doſſo, armature, ſcimitarre, ſpade, toghe, manti, ed altre coſe diverſe e belle, che grandiſſimo e ſempiterno obbligo ſe gli debbe.

Vaſar. vita di Filip.

(*b*) Col fondamento del diſegno, e degli ignudi particolarmente, e con la grazia della invenzione, e diſpoſizione delle hiſtorie, aperſe alla maggior parte degli artefici la via alla ultima perfezzione dell' arte, alla quale poi poterono dar cima quelli che ſeguirono. *Vaſar. vita di Luca Signorelli.* It muſt however be obſerved, that Luca lived till 1521, before which time an important reformation had taken place in the arts.

(*c*) Engraved in the *Etruria Pittrice*, No. xxvii.

tion, it may certainly be considered as the harbinger of a better taste.

The art of sculpture, dependent on the same principles, and susceptible of improvement from the same causes as that of painting, made a proportionable progress. The inventive genius of the Italian artists had very early applied it to almost every variety of material; and figures in wood, in clay, in metals, and in marble, were fashioned by Giovanni and Niccolo Pisano, by Agostino and Agnolo Sanese, which, though rude and incorrect, excited the admiration of the times in which they were produced. Their successor Andrea Pisano, the contemporary of Giotto, supported the credit of the art, which was then endangered by the sudden progress of its powerful rival; and in the early part of the fifteenth century the talents of Ghiberti and Donatello carried it to a degree of eminence which challenged the utmost exertions, and perhaps even excited the jealousy, of the first painters of the age. It must indeed be acknowledged, that the advantages which sculpture possesses are neither few nor unimportant. The severe and simple mode of its execution, the veracity of which it is susceptible, and the durability of its productions, place it in a favorable point of view, when opposed to an art whose success is founded on illusion, which not only admits, but courts meretricious ornament, and whose monuments are fugitive and perishable (*a*).

(*a*) I am aware that much is to be said on the opposite side of the question, but I mean not to discuss a subject upon which almost every writer on the history of the arts has either directly or incidentally exer-

These arts, so distinct in their operations, approach each other in works in *rilievo*, which unite the substantial form that characterizes sculpture, with the ideal depth of picturesque composition. In this province Donatello particularly excelled; and in Cosmo de' Medici he found a patron who had judgment to perceive, and liberality to reward his merits. But the genius of Donatello was not confined to one department. His group of Judith and Holofernes, executed in bronze for the community of Florence, his statue of S. George, his Annunciation, and his Zuccone, in one of the niches of the Campanile at Florence, all of which yet remain, have met with the uniform approbation of succeeding times, and are perhaps as perfect as the narrow principles upon which the art was then conducted would allow.

Notwithstanding the exertions of these masters, which were regarded with astonishment by their contemporaries, and are yet entitled to attention and respect, it does not appear that they had raised their views to the true end of the profession (*a*). Their characters rarely excelled the daily

cised his ingenuity. Among others, I may refer the reader to the *Proemi* of Vasari, the *Lezzione* of Benedetto Varchi, *della maggioranza dell' arti*, the works of Baldinucci, Richardson, and Mengs, and to the posthumous works of Dr. Adam Smith, lately published, in which the reader will find many acute observations on this subject.

(*a*) È necessario il confessare, che non poteva la pittura, benchè fatta viva dalle mani di que' maestri, far gran pompa di se stessa, perchè molto le mancava di disegno, di morbidezza, di colorito, di scorti, di movenze, di attitudini, di rilievo, e di altre finezze e vivacità, onde ella potesse in tutto e per tutto assomigliarsi al vero. *Baldin. Dec.* iii. *sec.* v.

prototypes

prototypes of common life; and their forms, although at times sufficiently accurate, were mostly vulgar and heavy. In the pictures which remain of this period, the limbs are not marked with that precision which characterizes a well-informed artist. The hands and feet, in particular, appear soft, enervated, and delicate, without distinction of sex or character. Many practices yet remained that evince the imperfect state of the art. Ghirlandajo and Baldovinetti continued to introduce the portraits of their employers in historic composition, forgetful of that *simplex duntaxat & unum* with which a just taste can never dispense. Cosimo Roselli, a painter of no inconsiderable reputation, attempted by the assistance of gold and ultramarine, to give a factitious splendor to his performances. To every thing great and elevated, the art was yet a stranger; even the celebrated picture of Pollajuolo exhibits only a group of half naked and vulgar wretches, discharging their arrows at a miserable fellow-creature, who by changing places with one of his murderers, might with equal propriety become a murderer himself (*a*). Nor was it till the time of

(*a*) Objects of horror and disgust, the cold detail of deliberate barbarity, can never be proper subjects of art, because they exclude the efforts of genius. Even the powers of Shakspeare are annihilated in the butcheries of Titus Andronicus. Yet the reputation of some of the most celebrated Italian painters has been principally founded on this kind of representation. "Ici," says M. Tenhove, "c'est S. "Etienne qu'on lapide, & dont je crains que la cervelle ne rejaillisse "sur moi; plus loin c'est S. Barthélémi tout sanglant, tout écorché; "je compte ses muscles & ses nerfs. Vingt flèches ont criblé Sebastien. "L'horrible tête du Baptiste est dans ce plat. Le gril de S. Laurent

Michelagnolo that painting and ſculpture roſe to their true object, and inſtead of exciting the wonder, began to rouſe the paſſions and intereſt the feelings of mankind.

By what fortunate concurrence of circumſtances the exquiſite taſte evinced by the ancients in works of art was revived in modern times, deſerves inquiry. It has generally been ſuppoſed that theſe arts, having left in Greece ſome traces of their former ſplendor, were tranſplanted into Italy by Greek artiſts, who, either led by hopes of emolument, or impelled by the diſaſtrous ſtate of their own country, ſought, among the ruins of the weſtern empire, a ſhelter from the impending deſtruction of the eaſt. Of the labors of theſe maſters, ſpecimens indeed remain in different parts of Italy; but, in point of merit, they exceed not thoſe of the native Italians, and ſome of them even bear the marks of deeper barbariſm (*a*). In fact, theſe arts were equally debaſed in Greece and in Italy, and it was not

" ſert de pendant a la chaudière de S. Jean — Je recule d'horreur." *Mém. Gén. lib.* x. May it not well be doubted, whether ſpectacles of this kind, ſo frequent in places devoted to religious purpoſes, may not have had a tendency rather to keep alive a ſpirit of ferocity and reſentement, than to inculcate thoſe mild and benevolent principles in which the eſſence of religion conſiſts?

(*a*) Veniſe, & quelques villes de la Romagne, ou de l'ancien Exarchat de Ravenne, montrent encore des traces de ces barbouillages Grecs. Le caractère d'un aſſez profonde barbarie s'y fait ſentir. La peinture qui repréſente les obſèques de St. Ephraim, qu'on voit dans le *Muſeo Sacro*, partie de la Bibliothéque du Vatican, paſſe pour le triſte chef d'œuvre de ces fils bâtards de Zeuxis.

Tenh. Mém. Gén. lib. vii.

therefore by an intercourse of this nature that they were likely to receive improvement. Happily, however, the same favorable circumstances which contributed to the revival of letters took place also with respect to the arts; and if the writings of the ancient authors excited the admiration and called forth the exertions of the scholar, the remains of ancient skill in marble, gems, and other durable materials, at length caught the attention of the artist, and were converted from objects of wonder, into models of imitation. To facilitate the progress of these studies, other fortunate circumstances concurred. The freedom of the Italian governments, and particularly that of Florence, gave to the human faculties their full energies (*a*). The labors of the painter were early associated with the mysteries of the prevailing religion, whilst the wealth and ostentation of individuals and of states held out rewards, sufficient to excite the endeavours even of the phlegmatic and the indolent.

From the time of the consul Mummius, who, whilst he plundered the city of Corinth of its beautiful productions of art, regarded them rather as household furniture, than as pieces of exquisite skill (*b*), the avidity of the Romans for the works

(*a*) L'uomo libero, con volontà, fa tutto quel che può, più, o meno, secondo la sua capacità; ma lo schiavo fa al più quello, che gli si comanda, e guasta la sua propria volontà, colla violenza, che gli si fa, per ubbidire. L'abito di farlo opprime finalmente la sua capacità, e la sua razza peggiora, fino, a non più desiderare quello, che dispera ottenere. *Opere di Mengs. v. i. p.* 228.

(*b*) Mummius tam rudis fuit, ut capta Corintho, cum maximorum

of the Greciam artists had been progressively increasing, till at length they became the first objects of proconsular rapacity, and the highest gratification of patrician luxury. The astonishing number which Verres had acquired during his government of Sicily, forms one of the most striking features of the invectives of Cicero; who asserts, that throughout that whole province, so distinguished by the riches and taste of its inhabitants, there was not a single statue or figure, either of bronze, marble, or ivory, not a picture or a piece of tapestry, not a gem or a precious stone, not even a gold or silver utensil, of the workmanship of Corinth or Delos, which Verres during his prætorship had not sought out and examined, and if he approved of it, brought it away with him; insomuch that Syracuse, under his government, lost more statues than it had lost soldiers in the victory of Marcellus (*a*). Such however was

artificum perfectas manibus tabulas ac statuas in Italiam portandas locaret, juberet prædici conducentibus, si eas perdidissent, novas eos reddituros. *Vel. Paterc. lib.* I. *c.* 13.

(*a*) The very minute account given by the Roman orator, in his fourth accusation against Verres, of the pieces of Grecian sculpture which he obtained from Sicily, has enabled the Abbé Fraguier to draw up a dissertation which he has entitled the *Gallery of Verres. Mém. de litt. v.* ix. *p.* 260. *Winkel. Storia delle art. del Disegno, lib.* x. *c.* 3. *Ed. Milan,* 1779. *in not.* Amongst those particularly enumerated by Cicero, is a marble statue of Cupid by Praxiteles, a Hercules in bronze by Myron, two Canephoræ, or female figures, representing Athenian virgins, bearing on their heads implements of sacrifice, the work of Polycletes; a celebrated statue of Diana, which, after having been carried off from the citizens of Segesta by the Carthaginians, was restored to them by Scipio Africanus, another of Mercury, which had been given them by the same liberal benefactor, the statues of Ceres,

the desolation which took place in Italy during the middle ages, occasioned not only by natural calamities, but by the yet more destructive operation of moral causes, the rage of superstition and the ferocity of barbarian conquerors, that of the innumerable specimens of art, which, till the times of the later emperors, had decorated the palaces and villas of the Roman nobility, scarcely a specimen or a vestige was, in the beginning of the fifteenth century, to be discovered. Even the city of Rome could only display six statues, five of marble and one of brass, the remains of its former splendor (*a*); and the complaint of Petrarca was not therefore without reason, that Rome was in no place less known than in Rome itself (*b*).

In tracing the vicissitudes which the arts have

of Æsculapius, of Bacchus, and lastly that of Jupiter himself, of which the sacrilegious *amateur* scrupled not to plunder his temple at Syracuse. *Cic. in Verrem. lib.* iv.

(*a*) Hoc videbitur levius fortasse, sed me maximè movet, quod his subjiciam; ex inumeris ferme colossis, statuisque tum marmoreis, tum æneis (nam argenteas atque aureas minimè miror fuisse conflatas) viris illustribus ob virtutem positis, ut omittam varia signa, voluptatis atque artis causa publicè ad spectaculum collocata, marmoreas quinque tantùm, quatuor in Constantini thermis; duas stantes ponè equos, Phidiæ & Praxitelis opus; duas recubantes; quintam in foro martis, statuam quæ hodie Martis fori nomen tenet; atque æneam solam equestrem deauratam, quæ est ad Basilicam Lateranensem, Septimio Severo dicatam, tantùm videmus superesse. *Pog. de varietate Fortunæ, p.* 20. The equestrian statue to which Poggio adverts, as that of Sep. Severus, is now recognized as the statue of Marcus Aurelius.

(*b*) Qui enim hodie magis ignari rerum Romanorum sunt quam Romani cives? Invitus dico, nusquam minus Roma cognoscitur quam Romæ. *Epist. Fam. lib.* vi. *Ep.* 2.

experienced, we obſerve with pleaſure, that the ſame perſons who ſignalized themſelves by their attention to preſerve the writings of the ancient authors, were thoſe to whom poſterity is indebted for the reſtoration of a better taſte in the arts. Petrarca himſelf is one of the firſt who diſplayed a marked attention to the remains of antiquity (*a*). On his interview with the emperor Charles IV. at Mantua, he preſented to that monarch a conſiderable number of coins, which he had himſelf collected; at the ſame time aſſuring him, that he would not have beſtowed them on any other perſon, and, with a degree of freedom which does him honor, recommending to the emperor, whilſt he ſtudied the hiſtory, to imitate the virtues of the perſons there repreſented (*b*). Lorenzo de' Medici, the brother

(*a*) The famous Cola di Rienzi, who called himſelf Tribune of Rome, and attempted in the fourteenth century to eſtabliſh the ancient republic, was, as well as his friend and panegyriſt Petrarca, a great admirer of the remains of antiquity. It is not indeed improbable, as Tiraboſchi conjectures, that the indulgence of this taſte firſt incited him to his romantic project. The character of Rienzi is given by a contemporary author in the following terms, which may ſerve as a curious ſpecimen of the Italian language: "*Fo da ſoa joventutine*
"*nutricato de latte de eloquentia, bono Grammatico, megliore Ret-*
"*torico, Autoriſta bravo. Deh como e quanto era veloce leitore!*
"*Molto uſava Tito Livio, Seneca, e Tullio, e Balerio Maſſimo:*
"*molto li dilettava le magnificentie de Julio Ceſare raccontare.*
"*Tutto lo die ſe ſpeculava negl' intagli de marmo, li quali jaccio*
"*intorno a Roma. Non era aitri che eſſe che ſapeſſe lejere li antichi*
"*pataffij. Tutte ſcritture antiche volgarizzava; queſte fiure de*
"*marmo juſtamente interpretava.*"

Tirab. Storia della Let. Ital. v. v. *p.* 314. *Mém. pour la vie de Petr. v.* ii. *p.* 335.

(*b*) Ecce (inquit) Cæſar, quibus ſucceſſiſti; ecce quos imitari ſtudeas.

of Cofmo, diftinguifhed himfelf not only by his affiduity in collecting the remains of ancient authors, but alfo by a decided predilection for works of tafte, in the acquifition of which he emulated the celebrity of his brother (*a*). From the funeral oration pronounced by Poggio on the death of Niccolo Niccoli, to whom the caufe of literature is perhaps more indebted than to any individual who held merely a private ftation, we learn, that he was highly delighted with paintings and pieces of fculpture, of which he had collected a greater number, and of more exquifite workmanfhip, than any perfon of his time; and that vifitors thronged to fee them, not as to a private houfe, but as to a public exhibition (*b*). Nor was Poggio himfelf lefs attentive to the difcovery and acquifition of thefe precious remains (*c*). "My chamber," fays he, "is furrounded

& mirari, ad quorum formulam, atque imaginem, te componas, quos præter te unum nulli hominum daturus eram. *Epift. Fam. lib.* x.

(*a*) Erat enim (Laurentius) ditiffimus agri, ditiffimufque auri, atque pretiofæ veftis, & univerfæ fupellectilis, fignis, tabulis pictis, vafis cælatis, margaritis, libris, mirum in modum affluit, &c.

Ant. Tudertani Orat. in Ep. Amb. Trav.

(*b*) Delectabatur admodum tabulis & fignis ac variis colaturis, prifcorum more. Plura enim prope folus atque exquifitiora habebat quam ceteri fere omnes. Ad quæ vifenda multi alliciebantur, ut non privato aliquo in loco, fed in Theatro quodam collocata ac expofita effe affirmares. *Poggii Op. p.* 276.

(*c*) "Effectus fum," fays he, in his jocular ftyle, "admodum "capitofus. Id quale fit, fcire cupis? Habeo cubiculum refertum "capitibus marmoreis, inter quæ unum eft elegans, integrum: alia "truncis naribus, fed quæ vel bonum artificem delectent. His & "nonnullis fignis que procuro, ornare volo Academiam meam Val-"darninam, quo in loco quiefcere eft animus," &c.

Poggii Epift. ad Nic. Nicol.

" with bufts in marble, one of which is whole and " elegant. The others are indeed mutilated, and " fome of them are even nofelefs, yet they are fuch " as may pleafe a good artift. With thefe, and " fome other pieces which I poffefs, I intend to " ornament my country feat." In a letter from Poggio to Francefco da Piftoia, a monk who had travelled to Greece in fearch of antiquities, we have a much more explicit inftance of the ardor with which he purfued this object (a) " By your letters from " Chios," fays Poggio, I learn " that you have " procured for me three bufts in marble, one of " Minerva, another of Jupiter, a third of Bacchus. " Thefe letters afforded me great fatisfaction, for I " am delighted beyond expreffion with pieces of " fculpture. I am charmed with the fkill of the " artift, when I fee marble fo wrought as to imitate " Nature herfelf. You alfo inform me that you " have obtained a head of Apollo, and you add " from Virgil,

" Miros ducent de marmore vultus."

" Believe me, my friend, you cannot confer a " greater favor on me than by returning laden " with fuch works, by which you will abundantly " gratify my wifhes. Different perfons labor under " different diforders; that which principally affects " me is an admiration of thefe productions of emi- " nent fculptors, to which I am perhaps more " devoted than becomes a man who may pretend " to fome fhare of learning. Nature herfelf, it is

(a) *App. No.* LXXII.

"true, muſt always excel theſe her copies; yet I "muſt be allowed to admire that art, which can "give ſuch expreſſion to inert materials, that "nothing but breath ſeems to be wanting. Exert "yourſelf therefore I beſeech you to collect, either "by entreaties or rewards, whatever you can find "that poſſeſſes any merit. If you can procure a "complete figure, *triumphatum eſt.*" Being informed by Franceſco, that a Rhodian named Suffretus had in his poſſeſſion a conſiderable number of antique ſculptures, Poggio addreſſed a letter to him, earneſtly requeſting to be favored with ſuch ſpecimens from his valuable collection as he might think proper to ſpare, and aſſuring him, that his kindneſs ſhould be remunerated by the earlieſt opportunity (*a*). In the ſame earneſt ſtyle, and for the ſame purpoſe, he addreſſed himſelf to Andreolo Giuſtiniano, a Venetian, then reſiding in Greece. Induced by his preſſing entreaties, both Suffretus and Giuſtiniano intruſted to the monk ſome valuable works; but, to the great diſappointment of Poggio, he betrayed the confidence repoſed in him, and under the pretext that he had been robbed of them in his voyage, defrauded Poggio of the chief part of his treaſures, which, as it afterwards appeared, he preſented to Coſmo de' Medici. The indignation of Poggio on this occaſion is poured forth in a letter to Giuſtiniano, whoſe liberality he again ſolicits and which he profeſſes to have in ſome degree repaid, by obtaining for him from the pope a diſpenſation

(*a*) *App. No.* LXXIII.

to enable his daughter to marry (*a*). Thus ſacrilegiouſly, though almoſt excuſably, bartering the favors of the church, for the objects of his favorite ſtudy, and the gratification of his taſte.

The riches of Coſmo de' Medici, and the induſtry of Donatello (*b*), united to give riſe to the celebrated collection of antiquities, which, with conſiderable additions, was tranſmitted by Piero to his ſon Lorenzo, and is now denominated the *Muſeum Florentinum.* By an eſtimate or account taken by Piero on the death of his father, it appears that theſe pieces amounted in value to more than 28,000 florins (*c*). But it was reſerved for Lorenzo to enrich this collection with its moſt valuable articles, and to render it ſubſervient to its true purpoſe, that of inſpiring in his countrymen a correct and genuine taſte for the arts.

Of the earneſtneſs with which Lorenzo engaged in this purſuit, ſome inſtances have already been adduced (*d*). " Such an admirer was he," ſays Valori (*e*), " of all the remains of antiquity, that " there was not any thing with which he was more " delighted. Thoſe who wiſhed to oblige him were

(*a*) *App. No.* LXXIV.

(*b*) Egli (Donato) fu potiſſima cagione che a Coſimo de' Medici ſi deſtaſſe la volontà dell' introdurre a Fiorenza le antichità, che ſono ed erano in caſa Medici, le quali tutte di ſua mano acconciò.

Vaſar. vita di Donato.

(*c*) *Fabr. in vità Coſm. Adnot. & Monum. p.* 231. *v. App. No.* LXXV.

(*d*) *Vol.* I. *p.* 152. See alſo the letter from Politiano to Lorenzo. *App. No.* LI.

(*e*) *Valor. in vità Laur. p.* 18.

" accuſtomed to collect, from every part of the
" world, medals and coins, eſtimable for their age
" or their workmanſhip, ſtatues, buſts, and whatever
" elſe bore the ſtamp of antiquity. On my return
" from Naples," adds he, " I preſented him with
" figures of Fauſtina and Africanus in marble, and
" ſeveral other ſpecimens of ancient art; nor can
" I eaſily expreſs with what pleaſure he received
" them." Having long deſired to poſſeſs the reſemblance of Plato, he was rejoiced beyond meaſure, when Girolamo Roſcio of Piſtoia preſented to him a figure in marble of his favorite philoſopher, which was ſaid to have been found amongſt the ruins of the academy (*a*). By his conſtant attention to this purſuit, and by the expenditure of conſiderable ſums, he collected under his roof all the remains of antiquity that fell in his way, whether they tended to illuſtrate the hiſtory of letters or of arts (*b*). His acknowledged acquaintance with theſe productions induced the celebrated Fra Giocondo, of Verona, the moſt induſtrious antiquarian of his time, to inſcribe to him his collection of ancient inſcriptions, of which Politiano, who was a competent judge of the ſubject, ſpeaks with high approbation (*c*).

(*a*) In the diligent reſearches made at the inſtance of Lorenzo for the diſcovery of ancient manuſcripts, his agents frequently met with curious ſpecimens of art. The inventory of the books purchaſed by Giovanni Laſcar, from one Nicolo di Jacopo da Siena, concludes with particularizing a marble ſtatue. This contract and inventory are yet preſerved in MS. in the archives of the *Palazzo Vecchio* at Florence. *Filz.* lxxxi. *No.* 26.

(*b*) *Valor. in vitâ Laur. p.* 18.

(*c*) *Polit. Miſcell. c.* 77.

But it is not the induſtry, the liberality, or the judgment ſhown by Lorenzo in forming his magnificent collection, ſo much as the important purpoſe to which he deſtined it, that entitles him to the eſteem of the profeſſors and admirers of the arts. Converſant from his youth with the fineſt forms of antiquity, he perceived and lamented the inferiority of his contemporary artiſts, and the impoſſibility of their improvement upon the principles then adopted. He determined therefore to excite among them, if poſſible, a better taſte, and by propoſing to their imitation the remains of the ancient maſters, to elevate their views beyond the forms of common life, to the contemplation of that ideal beauty which alone diſtinguiſhes works of art from mere mechanical productions. With this view he appropriated his gardens, adjacent to the monaſtery of S. Marco, to the eſtabliſhment of a ſchool or academy for the ſtudy of the antique, and furniſhed the different buildings and avenues with ſtatues, buſts, and other pieces of ancient workmanſhip. Of theſe he appointed the ſculptor Bertoldo, the favorite pupil of Donatello, but who was then far advanced in years, ſuperintendant. The attention of the higher rank of his fellow-citizens was incited to theſe purſuits by the example of Lorenzo; that of the lower claſs, by his liberality. To the latter he not only allowed competent ſtipends, whilſt they attended to their ſtudies, but appointed conſiderable premiums as the rewards of their proficiency (*a*).

(*a*) *Vaſari, vita di Torrigiano, e di Michelagnolo, &c.*

To this inſtitution, more than to any other circumſtance, we may, without heſitation, aſcribe the ſudden and aſtoniſhing proficiency which, towards the cloſe of the fifteenth century, took place in the arts, and which commencing at Florence, extended itſelf in concentric circles to the reſt of Europe. The gardens of Lorenzo de' Medici are frequently celebrated by the hiſtorian of the painters, as the nurſery of men of genius (*a*); but if they had produced no other artiſt than Michelagnolo Buonarroti, they would ſufficiently have anſwered the purpoſes of their founder. It was here that this great man began to imbibe that ſpirit, which was deſtined to effect a reformation in the arts, and which he could perhaps have derived from no other ſource (*b*). Of a noble,

(*a*) Vaſari adverts alſo to this eſtablishment in his *Ragionamenti.* " Lorenzo aveva fatto ſare il Giardino, ch'è ora in ſu la piazza di " San Marco, ſolamente perchè lo teneva pieno di figure antiche di " marmo, e pitture aſſai, e tutte eccellenti, ſolo per condurre una " ſcuola di giovani, i quali alla ſcultura, pittura, e architettura " attendeſſino a imparare, ſotto la cuſtodia di Bertoldo ſcultore, già " diſcepolo di Donatello, i quali giovani, tutti o la maggior parte " furno eccellenti; fra quali fu uno il noſtro Michelagnolo Buonarroti, " che è ſtato lo ſplendore, la vita, e la grandezza della ſcultura, " pittura, e architettura, avendo voluto moſtrare il cielo, che non " poteva, nè doveva naſcere, ſe non ſotto queſto magnifico e illuſtre " uomo, per laſſar la ſua patria ereditaria, e il mondo di tante onorate " opere, quante ſi veggono di lui oggi, e di molti altri che io ho " viſte, di coteſta ſcuola onorata." *Vaſar. Ragionamenti, p.* 75.

(*b*) Mengs, on ſeveral occaſions, attributes the ſuperior excellence of Michelagnolo to the ſame favorable circumſtance. " Michelagnolo, " approfittandoſi delle ſtatue raccolte dai Medici, aprì gli occhi, e " conobbe che gli antichi avean tenuta una certa arte nell' imitare la " verità, con cui ſi faceva la imitazione più intelligibile, e più bella, " che nello ſteſſo originale," and again, after giving an hiſtorical

but reduced family, he had been placed by his father, when young, under the tuition of the painter Ghirlandajo, from whom Lorenzo, desirous of promoting his new establishment, requested that he would permit two of his pupils to pursue their studies in his gardens; at the same time expressing his hopes, that they would there obtain such instruction, as would not only reflect honor on the institution, but also on themselves and on their country. The students who had the good fortune to be thus selected were Michelagnolo and Francesco Granacci (*a*). On the first visit of Michelagnolo, he found in the gardens his future adversary, Torrigiano, who, under the directions of Bertoldo, was modelling figures in clay. Michelagnolo applied himself to the same occupation, and his work soon afterwards attracted the attention of Lorenzo, who, from these early specimens, formed great expectations of his

" account of the progress of the arts, he adds, In quello stato di cose " scappò un raggio di quella stessa luce, che illuminò l'antica Grecia, " quando Michelagnolo, il quale col suo gran talento avea già superato " il Ghirlandajo, vide le cose degli antichi Greci nella collezione " del magnifico Lorenzo de' Medici."

Op. di Mengs, vol. ii. *p.* 99. 109.

(*a*) Dolendosi adunque Lorenzo, che amor grandissimo portava alla pittura, e alla scultura, che ne' suoi tempi non si trovassero scultori celebrati, e nobili, come si trovavano molti pittori di grandissimo pregio, e fama, deliberò di fare una scuola; e per questo chiese a Domenico Ghirlandajo, che se in bottega sua avesse de' suoi giovani, che inclinati fossero a ciò, gli inviasse al giardino, dove egli desiderava di essercitarli e creargli in una maniera, che onorasse se, e lui, e la città sua. Laonde da Domenico gli furono per ottimi giovani dati fra gli altri Michelagnolo, e Francesco Granacci.

Vasar. vita di Michelagn.

talents. Encouraged by ſuch approbation, be began to cut in marble the head of a faun, after an antique ſculpture (*a*), which, though unaccuſtomed to the chiſel, he executed with ſuch ſkill as to aſtoniſh Lorenzo; who, obſerving that he had made ſome intentional deviations from the original, and that in particular he had repreſented the lips ſmoother and had ſhown the tongue and teeth, remarked to him, with his accuſtomed jocularity, that he ſhould have remembered that old men ſeldom exhibit a complete range of teeth. The docile artiſt, who paid no leſs reſpect to the judgment, than to the rank of Lorenzo, was no ſooner left to himſelf, than he ſtruck out one of the teeth, giving to the part the appearance of its having been loſt by age (*b*). On his next viſit, Lorenzo was equally delighted with the diſpoſition and the genius of his young pupil, and ſending for his father, not only took the ſon under his particular protection, but made ſuch a proviſion for the old man, as his age and the circumſtances of his numerous family required (*c*).

(*a*) This early ſpecimen of the genius of Michelagnolo is yet preſerved in the Medicean gallery at Florence, in the keeper's room, and is equal, ſays Bottari, to a piece of Grecian workmanship; it has been engraved and published by Gori, in Condivi's life of Michelagnolo; but as Bottari obſerves, "poco felicemente, e con gran pregiu-" dizio dell' originale." *v. Bottari, not. ut ſup.*

(*b*) *Condivi, vita di Michelagnolo, p. 5. &c.*

(*c*) We learn from the narrative of Condivi, who relates theſe circumſtances with inſufferable minuteneſs, that when Lodovico, the father of Michelagnolo, encouraged by the kindneſs of Lorenzo, requeſted an office in the *Dogana* or cuſtom houſe, *in the place of Marco Pucci*, Lorenzo, who intended to provide him with a much better eſtabliſhment, replied, laying his hand on his shoulder, *Tu ſarai*

From this time till the death of Lorenzo, which included an interval of four years, Michelagnolo constantly resided in the palace of the Medici, and sat at the table of Lorenzo, among his most honored guests; where, by a commendable regulation, the troublesome distinctions of rank were abolished, and every person took his place in the order of his arrival. Hence the young artist found himself at once associated, on terms of equality, with all that was illustrious and learned in Florence, and formed those connexions and friendships which, if they do not create, are at least necessary to promote and reward superior talents (*a*). His leisure hours were passed in contemplating the intaglios, gems, and medals, of which Lorenzo had collected an astonishing number, whence he imbibed that taste for antiquarian researches, which was of essential service to him in his more immediate studies, and which he retained to the close of his life (*b*).

Whilst Michelagnolo was thus laying the sure

sempre povero. He gave him however the office for which he applied, which was worth eight scudi per month, *poco più o meno,* says the accurate historian. *Condiv. ut sup.*

(*a*) Lorenzo fece dare a Michelagnolo una bonna camera in casa, dandogli tutte quelle comodità, ch' egli desiderava, nè altrimenti trattandolo si in altro, si nella sua mensa, che da figliuolo: alla quale, come d'un tal' uomo, sedeano ogni giorno personaggi nobilissimi e di grande affare. Ed essendovi questa usanza, che quei, che da principio si trovavano presenti, ciascheduno appresso il magnifico secondo il suo grado sedesse, non si movendo di luogo, per qualunque dipoi sopraggiunto fosse; avenne bene spesso, che Michelagnolo sedette sopra i figliuoli di Lorenzo, ed altre persone pregiate, di che tal casa di continuo fioriva ed abbondava, &c. *Cond. ut supr.*

(*b*) *Condiv. ut supra.*

foundation

foundation of his future fame, and giving daily proofs of his rapid improvement, he formed an intimacy with Politiano, who reſided under the ſame roof, and who ſoon became warmly attached to his intereſts. At his recommendation, Michelagnolo executed a *baſſo-rilievo* in marble, the ſubject of which is the battle of the Centaurs. This piece yet ornaments the dwelling of one of his deſcendants; and, although not wholly finiſhed, diſplays rather the hand of an experienced maſter, than that of a pupil. But its higheſt commendation is, that it ſtood approved even in the riper judgement of the artiſt himſelf; who, although not indulgent to his own productions, did not heſitate, on ſeeing it ſome years afterwards, to expreſs his regret that he had not entirely devoted himſelf to this branch of art (*a*). The death of Lorenzo too ſoon deprived him of his protector. Piero, the ſon of Lorenzo, continued indeed to ſhow to him the ſame marks of kindneſs which his father had uniformly done; but that prodigality, which ſo ſpeedily diſſipated his authority, his fortune, and his fame, was extended even to his amuſements; and the talents of Michelagnolo, under the patronage of Piero, inſtead of impreſſing on braſs or on marble the forms of immortality, were condemned to raiſe a ſtatue of ſnow (*b*)! Nor was this intercourſe of long

(*a*) Così la impreſa gli ſuccedette, che mi rammenta udirlo dire, che quando la rivede, cognoſſe quanto torto egli abbia fatto alla natura, a non ſeguitar prontamente l'arte della ſcultura, facendo giudizio per quell' opera, quanto poteſſe riuſcire. *Cond. vita di M. A.*

(*b*) Eſſendo in Firenze venuta dimolta neve, Pier de' Medici,

continuance, for Piero, inſtead of affording ſupport to others, was ſoon obliged to ſeek, in foreign countries, a ſhelter for himſelf.

The hiſtory of Michelagnolo forms that of all the arts which he profeſſed. In him ſculpture, painting and architecture ſeem to have been perſonified. Born with talents ſuperior to his predeceſſors, he had alſo a better fate. Ghilberti, Donatello, Verocchio, were all men of genius, but they lived during the gentile ſtate of the art (*a*). The light had now riſen, and his young and ardent mind, converſant with the fineſt forms of antiquity, imbibed, as its genuine ſource, a reliſh for their excellence. With the ſpecimens of ancient art, the depoſitaries of ancient learning were unlocked to him, and of theſe alſo he made no inconſiderable uſe. As a poet he is entitled to rank high amongſt his countrymen; and the triple wreaths of painting, ſculpture, and architecture, with which his diſciples decorated his tomb, might, without exaggeration, have been interwoven with a fourth (*b*).

figliuol maggiore di Lorenzo, che nel medeſimo luogo del padre era reſtato, ma non nella medeſima grazia, volendo, come giovane, far fare nel mezzo della ſua corte una ſtatua di neve ſi ricordò di Michelagnolo, e fattolo cercare, gli fece far la ſtatua, &c. *Condiv. p.* 8. This ſtatue was a juſt emblem of the fortunes of its founder.

(*a*) Michelagnolo, ch'ebbe sì grande ingegno, non traſſe dal ſuo proprio fondo la ſua arte, nè con quello ſolo avrebbe trovata la ſtrada di uſcir da' limiti di quello ſtile ſecco, e ſervile, che fin allora regnava in Italia; e ſenza un grande ſtudio, nè ſenza l'oſſervazione delle ſtatue antiche, non ſarebbe ſtato forſe che uguale a un Donatello, e a un Ghiberti. *Opere di Mengs, v.* ii. *p.* 183.

(*b*) The poems of Michelagnolo were publiſhed by his great-nephew Michelagnolo, Buonarroti il Giovane, at Florence, in 1623, and are

Of the ſculptures of Michelagnolo, ſome yet remain in an unfiniſhed ſtate, which ſtrikingly diſplay the comprehenſion of his ideas and the rapidity of his execution. Such are the buſt of Brutus, and the ſtatue of a female figure, in the gallery at Florence. In the latter the chiſel has been handled with ſuch boldneſs, as to induce a connoiſſeur of our own country to conjecture that it would be neceſſary, in the finiſhing, to reſtore the cavities (*a*). Perhaps a more involuntary homage was never paid to genius, than that which was extorted from the ſculptor Falconet, who having preſumed upon all occaſions to cenſure the ſtyle of Michelagnolo, without having had an opportunity of inſpecting any of his works, at length obtained a ſight of two of his ſtatues, which were brought into France by cardinal Richelieu. *I have ſeen Michelagnolo*, exclaimed the French artiſt, *he is terrific* (*b*).

The labors of the painter are neceſſarily tranſitory for ſo are the materials that compoſe them. In a few years Michelagnolo will be known, like an

ranked with the *Teſti di Lingua* of Italian literature. They were again reprinted at Florence in 1726, with the *Lezzioni* of Benedetto Varchi, and Mario Guiducci, on ſome of his ſonnets. Tenhove has juſtly appreciated their merits. "Les ſonnets & les *Canzoni* de Michelange "ne ſont point chargés d'ornemens ambitieux; ils ſe reſſentent de "l'auſtère ſimplicité de ſon génie: cependant rien ne les fait autant "valoir, que la main dont ils ſont partis." *Mém. Gén. liv.* xix. *p.* 317.

(*a*) *Richardſon, Deſcription des Tabl. &c. vol.* iii. *p.* 87.

(*b*) "J'ai vu Michelange; *Il eſt effrayant.*" *Falcon. ap. Tenh.* The pieces which occaſioned this exclamation were two of the ſtatues intended to compoſe a part of the monument of Julius II.

ancient artiſt, only by his works in marble Already it is difficult to determine, whether his reputation be enhanced or diminiſhed by the ſombre repreſentations of his pencil in the Pauline and Sixtine chapels, or by the few ſpecimens of his cabinet pictures, now rarely to be met with, and exhibiting only a ſhadow of their original excellence. But the chief merit of this great man is not to be ſought for in the remains of his pencil, nor even in his ſculptures, but in the general improvement of the public taſte which followed his aſtoniſhing productions. If his labors had periſhed with himſelf, the change which they effected in the opinions and the works of his contemporaries would ſtill have entitled him to the firſt honors of the art. Thoſe who from ignorance, or from envy, have endeavoured to depreciate his productions, have repreſented them as exceeding in their forms and attitudes the limits and the poſſibilities of nature, as a race of beings, the mere creatures of his own imagination; but ſuch critics would do well to conſider, whether the great reform to which we have alluded could have been effected by the moſt accurate repreſentations of common life, and whether any thing ſhort of that ideal excellence which he only knew to embody, could have accompliſhed ſo important a purpoſe. The genius of Michelagnolo was a leaven which was to operate on an immenſe and heterogeneous maſs, the ſalt intended to give a reliſh to inſipidity itſelf; it was therefore active, penetrating, energetic, ſo as not only effectually to reſiſt the contagious effects of a depraved taste, but to communicate a portion of its spirit to all around.

Of the contemporary artists of Michelagnolo, such only are entitled to high commendation as accompanied his studies, or availed themselves of his example. Among these appears the divine Raffaello; second to his great model only in that grandeur of design which elevates the mind, superior to him in that grace which interests the heart. Endowed, if not with vigor sufficient alone to effect a reform, with talents the best calculated to promote its progress (*a*). It is well known that the works of this exquisite master form two distinct classes, those which he painted before, and those which he painted after he had caught from the new Prometheus a portion of the ethereal fire—those of the scholar of Perugino and of the competitor of Michelagnolo. "Happy "age," exclaims, with more than common animation, the historian of the painters, "and happy "artists, for so I may well denominate you who, "have had the opportunity of purifying your eyes "at so clear a fountain; who have found your "difficulties removed, your crooked paths made "straight by so wonderful an artist: know then, "and honor the man who has enabled you to "distinguish between truth and falshood, and let "your gratitude be shown in returning your thanks

(*a*) Raffaello stesso ci ha lasciate nelle sue opere le tracce de' suoi studj; e senza le lezioni di Fra Bartolommeo, e la vista delle opere di Michelagnolo, e delle cose antiche, non goderemmo oggi le sue maravigliose pitture. *Op. di Mengs*, *v.* ii. *p.* 189.

" to heaven, and in imitating Michelagnolo in all " things (*a*).

Genius is ever obnoxious to that criticism which mediocrity escapes, nor has this test been wanting to the merits of Michelagnolo. The parasites of a vicious court, and a corrupt age, have not hesitated to charge him with indecency, in introducing naked figures in his celebrated picture of the last judgment. This accusation was made even in his lifetime, by one who called himself his friend, and

(*a*) *Vasari, vita di Michelagnolo.* Gianfrancesco Grazzini, called *Il Lasca*, also celebrates his countryman in the true Florentine idiom:

Giotto fu il primo, ch' alla dipintura,
Già lungo tempo morta, desse vita.
E Donatello messe la scultura
Nel suo dritto sentier, ch' era smarrita:
Così l'architettura
Storpiata, e guasta, dalle man' de' Tedeschi,
Anzi quasi basita,
Da Pippo Brunelleschi,
Solenne Architettor, fu messa in vita;
Onde gloria infinita
Meritar questi tre spirti divini,
Nati in Firenze e nostri cittadini.
E di queste tre arti, i Fiorentini
Han sempre poi tenuto il vanto e'l pregio.
Dopo questo, l'egregio
Michelagnol divin, dal cielo eletto,
Pittor, scultore, architettor perfetto,
Che dove i primi tre maestri eccellenti
Gittaro i fondamenti,
Alle tre nobil' arti ha posto il tetto.
Onde meritamente,
Chiamato è dalla gente
Vero maestro, e padre del disegno, &c.

Il Lasca, sop. la dipintura della Cupola.

who ſaw no impropriety in repreſenting it as proceeding from the obſcene lips of Pietro Aretino (*a*). It ſoon however became ſo prevalent, that in the pontificate of Paul IV. it was in contemplation to deſtroy this aſtoniſhing picture, which was at laſt only preſerved by the expedient of covering thoſe parts which were ſuppoſed to be likely to excite in the minds of the depraved ſpectators ideas unſuitable to the ſolemnity of the place. The painter who undertook this office was ever afterwards diſtinguiſhed by the name of *Il Braghettone.* Theſe inculpations were renewed in the ſucceeding century, by a man of talents and celebrity, who united like Michelagnolo, the character of a painter and a poet, without having one idea in common with him (*b*). But what ſhall we ſay of an artiſt who

(*a*) In the dialogue of Lodovico Dolce on painting, entitled *L'Aretino* — Aretino, who is ſuppoſed to ſpeak the ſentiments of the author, obſerves, "Chi ardirà di affermar, che ſtia bene, che nella "chieſa di San Pietro, prencipe degli apoſtoli, in una Roma, ove "concurre tutto il mondo, nella cappella del Pontefice, il quale, "come ben dice il Bembo, in terra ne aſſembra Dio, ſi veggano "dipinti tanti ignudi, che dimoſtrano diſoneſtamente dritti e reverſi: "coſa nel vero, (favellando con ogni ſommeſſione,) di quel ſantiſ- "ſimo luogo indegna." Fabrini, the other colloquialiſt, juſtifies Michelagnolo by alledging the example of Raffaello, who is ſaid to have deſigned the laſcivious prints engraved by Marcantonio Raimondi, under which the ſame Aretino wrote his infamous verſes; but it is eaſy to ſee that ſuch a juſtification is an admiſſion of the charge. *Dolce, Dialog. p.* 236. *Ed. Flor.* 1735.

(*b*) Salvator Roſa, in his ſatire entitled *La Pittura*, relating inſtances of the arrogance and pride of his predeceſſors, introduces the well-known ſtory of the critic *Biagio*, who, having cenſured the famous picture of the laſt judgment, was, in return, repreſented by Michel-

could mingle with the contemplation of a ſubject ſo intereſting to all mankind, which unites every thing terrible and ſublime, and abſorbs all other paſſions, an idea that can only have a relation to the decorums of modern life, and to that factitious decency which, by affecting concealment, acknowledges a pruriency of imagination, to which true taſte, as well as true modeſty, is a ſtranger?

The favors of Lorenzo de' Medici were not however excluſively beſtowed. Although he well knew how to appreciate and to reward extraordinary excellence, he was not inattentive to the juſt claims

agnolo in a group of the damned. According to Salvator, Biagio thus addreſſed the painter:

> Michel Agnolo mio, non parlo in gioco,
> Queſto che dipingete è un gran giudizio,
> Ma del giudicio voi n'avete poco.
> Io non vi tallo intorno all' artifizio,
> Ma parlo del coſtume, in cui mi pare
> Che il voſtro gran ſaper ſi cangi in vizio.
> Sapevi pur che il figlio di Noè,
> Perchè ſcoperſe le vergogne al padre,
> Tirò l'ira di Dio ſovra di ſe;
> E voi, ſenza temer Chriſto e la Madre
> Fate, che moſtrin le vergogne parte,
> Infin de' Santi qui l'intiere ſquadre.

And that it may not be imagined that Salvator did not himſelf approve the ſentiments of the critic, he adds,

> In udire il pittor queſte propoſte,
> Divenuto di rabbia roſſo, e nero,
> Non potè proferir le ſue riſpoſte;
> Nè potendo di lui l'orgoglio altero
> Sfogare il ſuo furor per altre bande.
> Dipinſe nell' inferno il Cavaliero.

Satir. di Salv. Roſa. Ed. Lond. 1791.

of thoſe who made a proficiency in any branch of the arts. Where the indication of talents appeared he was ſolicitous to call them into action, to accelerate their progreſs, and to repay their ſucceſs. "It is highly deſerving of notice," ſays Vaſari, "that all thoſe who ſtudied in the gardens of the "Medici, and were favored by Lorenzo, became "moſt excellent artiſts, which can only be attributed "to the exquiſite judgment of this great patron of "their ſtudies, who could not only diſtinguiſh men "of genius, but had both the will and the power "to reward them (*a*)." By his kindneſs the eminent ſculptor Ruſtici was placed under the care of Andrea Verocchio (*b*), where he formed an intimacy with the celebrated Lionardo da Vinci; but although he availed himſelf of the friendſhip and the inſtructions of this wonderful man, he acknowledged Lorenzo as the parent of his ſtudies (*c*). Franceſco Granacci, the fellow-ſtudent of Michelagnolo, partook alſo of

(*a*) È gran coſa ad ogni modo, che tutti coloro, i quali furono nella ſcuola del Giardino de' Medici, e favoriti dal Mag. Lorenzo vecchio, furono tutti eccellentiſſimi; la qual coſa d'altronde non può eſſere avvenuta, ſe non dal molto, anzi infinito giudizio di quel nobiliſſimo ſignore, vero Mecenate degli uomini virtuoſi; il quale come ſapeva conoſcere gl' ingegni, e ſpirti elevati, così poteva e ſapeva riconoſcergli e premiargli. *Vaſari, vita del Ruſtici.*

(*b*) Portandoſi dunque beniſſimo Giovanfranceſco Ruſtici, cittadin Fiorentino, nel diſegnare, e fare di terra, mentre era giovinetto, fu da eſſo magnifico Lorenzo, il quale lo conobbe ſpiritoſo, e di bello e buon ingegno, meſſo a ſtare, perchè imparaſſe, con Andrea del Verocchio, &c. *Vaſari, vita del Ruſtici.*

(*c*) Eſſendo poi tornata in Fiorenza la Famiglia de' Medici, Il Ruſtico ſi fece conoſcere al Cardinale Giovanni, per creatura di Lorenzo ſuo padre, e fu ricevuto con molte carezze. *Ibid.*

the favor of Lorenzo, and was occasionally employed by him in preparing, the splendid pageants with which he frequently amused the citizens of Florence; in the decoration of which Granacci displayed uncommon taste (*a*). The reputation acquired by the pupils of S. Marco soon extended beyond the limits of Italy. At the request of the king of Portugal, Lorenzo sent into that country Andrea Contucci, where he left various monuments of his talents in sculpture and architecture (*b*). The encouragement afforded by him to the professors of every branch of the arts, may be estimated in some degree by the numerous pieces executed at his expense by the first masters of the time, accounts of which are occasionally dispersed through the voluminous work of Vasari. Like his ancestor Cosmo, Lorenzo often forgot the superiority of the patron in the familiarity of the friend, and not only excused but delighted in the capriciousness which frequently distinguishes men of talents. In this number was Niccolo Grosso, a Florentine citizen, who wrought

(*a*) Francesco Granacci---fu uno di quelli, che dal Magnifico Lorenzo de' Medici fu messo a imparare nel suo giardino, &c. E perchè era molto gentile, e valeva assai in certe galanterie, che per feste di carnovale si facevano nella città, fu sempre in molte cose simili dal Magnifico Lorenzo de' Medici adoperato.

Vasari, vita di Fr. Granac.

(*b*) Per queste, e per l'altre opere d'Andrea, divulgatosi il nome suo, fu chiesto al magnifico Lorenzo vecchio de' Medici, nel cui giardino avea, come si è detto, atteso agli studj del disegno, dal re di Portagallo, perchè mandatogli da Lorenzo, lavorò per quel re molte opere di scultura, e d'architettura, e particolarmente un bellissimo palazzo, &c. *Vasar. vita di Contucci.*

ornaments in iron with extraordinary ſkill. Conſcious of his merits Niccolo reſolved to labor only for thoſe who paid him ready money, referring his employers to the ſign ſuſpended at his door, which repreſented books of account deſtroyed in the flame. Lorenzo, deſirous of preſenting to ſome of his powerful friends abroad a ſpecimen of Florentine ingenuity, called upon Niccolo to engage him to execute for him a piece of his workmanſhip; but the ſurly artiſan, who was buſy at his anvil, inſtead of acknowledging the honor intended him, bluntly told Lorenzo that he had other cuſtomers who, having firſt applied, muſt be firſt ſerved. The invincible pertinacity of Niccolo, in refuſing to work till he had received his uſual depoſit, occaſioned Lorenzo to give him the name of *Il Caparra* (*a*), by which he was ever afterwards generally known (*b*).

The ſtudy of architecture, as revived by Brunelleſchi, received additional ſupport from the encouragement afforded by Lorenzo de' Medici, who, to the munificence of his grandfather, ſuperadded a knowledge of this ſcience equal to that of a practical artiſt. At his inſtance, and often at his individual expenſe, the city of Florence was ornamented with a profuſion of elegant buildings, as well for private reſidence, as public purpoſes. Convinced that the art was founded on fixed and determined principles, which were only to be diſcovered in the labors of the ancients, he juſtly reprobated thoſe profeſſors who, neglecting the

(*a*) From *Arrha*, *Arrhabo*, a pledge, or earneſt.

(*b*) *Vaſari, vita di Simone detto il Cronaca.*

rules of Vitruvius, followed only the variable suggestions of their own fancy. Nor was he less severe on those who, without any previous knowledge of the art, conceived themselves equal to the task of conducting a building on an extensive scale, and, in the erection of their dwellings, chose to become their own architects. "Such people," said Lorenzo "buy repentance at too dear a rate (*a*)." Of this description was his relation, Francesco de' Medici, who having erected a large house at Majano, and made several alterations in its progress, complained to Lorenzo of the great expense with which it had been attended: "That is not to be wondered at," replied Lorenzo, "when, instead of erecting your "building from a model, you draw your model "from your building (*b*)." His superior judgment in works of this kind was acknowledged on many occasions. Ferdinand, king of Naples, intending to build a palace, conceived no one more competent to direct him in the choice of a plan than Lorenzo. His assistance was also sought for on a similar occasion by the duke of Milan; and Filippo Strozzi, in the erection of a mansion, which in grandeur of design and richness of execution is not inferior to a royal residence, availed himself greatly of his advice and directions (*c*). It does not however appear, that

(*a*) Illos vel maxime reprehendere solebat quicumque in diem temeré ædificarent, eos dicens *caro admodum emere pœnitentiam.*

Valor. in vitâ, p. 63.

(*b*) *Valor. ut supra.*

(*c*) Multi enim, multa regia ædificia de Laurentii consilio extruxere. In quibus Philippi Strociæ insulares ædes, quæ amplitudine sua, &

Lorenzo on any occasion thought proper to dispense with the aid of those who had made this art their more immediate study. Having formed the intention of erecting his place at Poggio-Cajano, he obtained designs from several of the best architects of the time, and amongst the rest from Giuliano the son of Paolo Giamberto, whose model was preferred by Lorenzo, and under whose directions the building was carried on; but in the construction of the picturesque and singular flight of steps, which communicated to every part with such convenience, that a person might ascend or descend even on horseback, Lorenzo availed himself of a design of Stefano d'Ugolino, a painter of Siena, who died about the year 1350 (*a*). Lorenzo was desirous that the ceiling of the great hall should be formed by a single arch, but was appprehensive that it would not be practicable, on account of its extent. Giuliano was at that time erecting a residence for himself in Florence, where he took an opportunity of executing one in the manner suggested by Lorenzo, and succeeded so effectually as to remove his doubts on this head. The ceiling at Poggio-Cajano was accordingly completed, and is acknowledged to be the

grata membrorum dispositione, totiusque ædificii venustate & magnificentia superant, sine ulla controversia, non solum privatas domos, sed principales & regias. Magno area constitit in urbe media: impendium ad centum aureorum millia accessurum putatur. De modulo Philippus Laurentium consuluit, qui quidem aderat omnibus super hac re operam suam cupientibus, nec civilibus solum, sed etiam externis. *Valor. in vitâ, p.* 63. For a particolar account of this splendid residence, *v. Vasari, vita di Simone detto il Cronaca.*

(*a*) *Vasar. vita di Giuliano da San Gallo, v.* ii. *p.* 78.

largeſt vaulted roof of modern workmanſhip that had then been ſeen (*a*). The talents of this artiſt induced Lorenzo to recommend him to Ferdinand king of Naples, to whom he preſented, on the part of Lorenzo, the model of an intended palace. His reception was highly honorable. On his departure Ferdinand ſupplied him with horſes, apparel, and other valuable articles, amongſt which was a ſilver cup containing ſeveral hundred ducats. Giuliano, whilſt he declined accepting it, expreſſed a deſire that the king would gratify him with ſome ſpecimen of ancient art, from his extenſive collection, which might be a proof of his approbation. Ferdinand accordingly preſented him with a buſt of the emperor Adrian, a ſtatue of a female figure larger than life, and a ſleeping Cupid; all of which Giuliano immediately ſent to Lorenzo, who was no leſs pleaſed with the liberality of the artiſt, than with the acquiſition of ſo valuable a treaſure (*b*). At the requeſt of the celebrated Mariano Genazano, Lorenzo had promiſed to erect, without the gate of San Gallo at Florènce, a monaſtery capable of containining one hundred monks. On the return

(*a*) Giuliano had before been employed by Lorenzo in fortifying the town of Caſtellana, when that place was attacked by the duke of Calabria, in which he rendered eſſential ſervices to his patron. The Florentines were at that time very defective in the uſe of their artillery, which they ſcarcely ventured to approach, and which frequently occaſioned fatal accidents to thoſe who directed it; but the ingenuity of the young architect remedied this defect; in conſequence of which the army of the duke was ſo ſeverely cannonaded as to be obliged to raiſe the ſiege. *Vaſar. ut ſupra.*

(*b*) *Vaſar. vita di Giuliano da San Gallo.*

of Giuliano to Florence, he engaged him in this work, whence he obtained the name of *San Gallo*, by which he was always afterwards diſtinguiſhed (*a*). Whilſt this building was carrying forwards, Giuliano was alſo employed by Lorenzo in deſigning and erecting the extenſive fortifications of Poggio Imperiale, preparatory to the founding a city on that ſpot, as was his intention (*b*). To this artiſt, who arrived at great eminence in the enſuing century, and to his brother Antonio, architecture is indebted for the completion of the Tuſcan order, as now eſtabliſhed; and for conſiderable improvements in the Doric.

Beſides the many magnificent works begun under the immediate directions of Lorenzo, he ſedulouſly attended to the completion of ſuch buildings as had been left imperfect by his anceſtors. On the church of S. Lorenzo, the building of which was begun by his great grandfather Giovanni, and continued by his Grandfather Coſmo, he expended a large ſum. At the requeſt of Matteo Boſſo he alſo completed the monaſtery begun by Brunelleſchi at Fieſole (*c*),

(*b*) Giuliano remonſtrated with Lorenzo on this alteration.—" By " your calling me *San Gallo*," ſaid he, " I ſhall loſe my name, and " inſtead of becoming reſpectable by the antiquity of my family, I " ſhall have to found it anew. Surely," ſaid Lorenzo, " it is more " honorable to be the founder of a new family by your own talents, " than to reſt your reputation on the merits of others." *Vaſar. ut ſupra.*

(c) *Vaſar. ut ſupra.*

(*a*) The letter of Boſſo, which was addreſſed to Lorenzo in the height of his proſperity, and touches upon many circumſtances of his life and character, is given from the *Recuperationes Feſulanæ*, in the Appendix, *No.* LXXVI.

at the ſame time expreſſing his regret that he ſhould have rendered it neceſſary to ſolicit him to do that which he conceived to be an indiſpenſible duty (*a*).

Amongſt the various kinds of pictureſque repreſentation practiſed by the Greeks and Romans, and tranſmitted by them to after-times, is that of Moſaic; a mode of execution, which, in its durability of form, and permanency of color, poſſeſſes diſtinguiſhed advantages, being unaffected by drought or moiſture, heat or cold, and periſhing only with the building to which it has been originally attached. This art, during the middle ages, had experienced the ſame viciſſitudes as attended all thoſe with which it is ſo nearly connected. Some attempts had, however, been made to reſtore it by Andrea Tafi, the contemporary of Giotto (*b*); and even Giotto himſelf had cultivated it, not without ſucceſs, although the celebrated picture over the great door of St. Peter at Rome, called the *Navicella di Giotto*, is ſaid to be a more modern work, copied from a former one of that artiſt (*c*). Lorenzo was deſirous of introducing this mode of execution into more general practice. On expreſſing to Graſſione, a Florentine painter, his intention of ornamenting with work of this kind the vault of a large cupola, the painter ventured to obſerve to him that he had not artiſts equal to the taſk: "We have money enough "to make them," replied Lorenzo; and although

(*a*) *Fabr. in vitâ, v. i. p.* 148.

(*b*) *Vaſar. vita di Andrea.*

(*c*) *Tenh. Mém. Généal. liv. vii. p.* 131.

Graſſione

Graffione ftill continued incredulous (*a*), Lorenzo foon afterwards met with a perfon who fuited his purpofe in the painter Gherardo, who had generally applied himfelf to works in miniature. The fpecimen produced by Gherardo for the infpection of Lorenzo was a head of S. Zenobio, with which he was fo well pleafed, that he refolved to enlarge the chapel of that faint at Florence, in order to give the artift an opportunity of exhibiting his talents in a wider field. With Gherardo he affociated Domenico Ghirlandajo, as a more complete mafter of defign, and the work was commenced with great fpirit. Vafari affures us, that if death had not interpofed there was reafon to believe from the part that was executed, that thefe artifts would have performed wonderful things (*b*).

But if the attempts made by Lorenzo to reftore the practice of Mofaic were thus in a great degree fruftrated, a difcovery was made about the fame period which proved an ample fubftitute for it, and which has given to the works of the painter that

(*a*) Graffione, with that familiarity which the artifts appear to have ufed towards Lorenzo, replied, " Eh Lorenzo, i danari non fanni i " maeftri, ma i maeftri fanno i danari."

(*b*) By whofe death the further progrefs of this work was interrupted, may be doubted. The words of Vafari are, "Per lo che Gherardo, " affottigliando l'ingegno, harebbe fatto con Domenico mirabiliffime " cofe, fe la morte non vi fi fuffe interpofta; come fi può giudicare " dal principio della detta capella, che rimafe imperfetta." But, by a fubfequent paffage in the life of Ghirlandajo, it feems it was the death of Lorenzo that prevented the completion of the work, " —— " come, per la morte del predetto Magnifico Lorenzo, rimafe imperfetta " in Fiorenza la Capella di S. Zanobi, comminciata a lavorare di " Mufaico Domenico in compagnia di Gherardo miniatore."

permanency which even the durability of Mosaic might not perhaps have supplied. This was the art of transferring to paper impressions from engravings on copper, or other metals; an invention which has tended more than any other circumstance to diffuse throughout Europe a just and general taste for the arts.

This discovery is attributed by the Italians to Maso, or Tomaso Finiguerra, a goldsmith of Florence, who being accustomed to engrave on different metals for the purpose of inlaying them, occasionally tried the effects of his work by taking off impressions, first on sulphur, and afterwards on paper, by means of a roller, in such a manner that the figures seemed to have been traced with a pen. It does not appear that Finiguerra ever applied this invention to any other purpose than that of ascertaining the progress of his work; nor have the researches of the most diligent inquirers discovered a single print that can with any degree of probability be attributed to him; but Baccio Baldini, another goldsmith, conceiving that this discovery might be applied to more important purposes, began to engrave on metals, solely with a view of transmitting impressions to paper. Possessing, however, no great skill in design, he prevailed on Sandro Botticello to furnish him with drawings suitable for his purpose. The concurrence of Antonio Pollajuoli, and Andrea Mantegna, carried the art to greater perfection. Of the works of the last-mentioned master many specimens yet remain, which do credit to his talents. The beginning of the ensuing century produced a much superior artist in Marcantonio Raimondi, by whose industry the numerous productions of Raffaello, the transcripts of his rich and creative mind, were committed to paper with an accuracy which he himself approved, and may serve as a standard to mark in future times the progress or the decline of the arts (*a*).

(*a*) The credit of having given rise to this elegant and useful art has been contended for by different countries, and their various pretensions have been weighed and considered by many authors. It is however generally agreed, that it begun with the goldsmiths, and was afterwards adopted by the painters. The union of these two professions has thus produced a third, which has risen to considerable importance. The Germans, who have disputed with the Italians the honor of the invention with the greatest degree of plausibility, have not in point of fact controverted the narrative given by the Italians of the rise of the art, nor brought forwards any account of their own, but have simply endeavoured to show that it was practised in Germany at an earlier period. Mr. Heincken asserts, that the earliest prints engraved in Italy that bear a date, are the maps to the edition of Ptolemy, printed at Rome in 1478; the earliest picturesque representations, those prefixed to some of the cantos of Dante in 1482; whilst he adduces instances of German execution that bear the date of 1466, by comparing the manner of which with other pieces, apparently of earlier workmanship, he conjectures that the art had its rise in Germany about the year 1440. *Idée Générale, p.* 232. *Non nostrum tantas componere lites.* I shall only observe, that little dependance is to be placed on conjectures from prints without a date, particularly those of German workmanship, as the artists of that country continued to produce them in the most rude and Gothic style, both as to design and execution, long after the beginning of the sixteenth century, when Albert Durer, and Luca van Leyden had set them a better example. On the other hand, impartiality obliges me to remark, that Thiraboschi, who strenuously claims for his countrymen the merit of the discovery, has not discussed this subject with his usual accuracy. First, he is mistaken in asserting that Baldinucci fixes the commencement of the art in the beginning of the fifteenth century, *Storia della Lett. Ital. v.* ii. *p.* 2. *p.* 399. Baldinucci only says in

Whilst the art of transferring to paper impressions from copper was thus first practised, that of engraving in gems and stones was again successfully revived. The predilection of Lorenzo de' Medici for the beautiful specimens of skill which the ancients have left in materials of this nature, has frequently been noticed (*a*). Of those which once formed a part of his immense collection, some occasionally occur that seem to have been the objects of his more particular

general, that the art had its beginning in the fifteenth century. "*Quest'* "*arte ebbe suo principio nel secolo del* 1400." Secondly, on the authority of a document produced by Manni, he supposes that Tomaso Finiguerra, the inventor of the art, died prior to the year 1424; but both Vasari and Baldinucci inform us, that the Finiguerra in question was contemporary with Pollajuolo, who was only born in 1426. It is singular that this judicious author did not reflect how slight that evidence must be which rests merely on a similarity of name, particularly in Florence, where, for the sake of distinction, it was often necessary to resort to the patronymics for several generations. *v. Vasari, vite de' Pittori, passim. Baldinucci comminciamento e progresso dell' arte dell' intagliare in Rame. Fir.* 1686. *Heineken Idée générale d'une Collection complette d'Estampes, &c.*

(*a*) The collection of antiques formed by Lorenzo is thus celebrated by a contemporary author:

> Cælatum argento, vel fulvo quidquid in auro est
> Ædibus hoc, LAURENS, vidimus esse tuis,
> Praxitelis, Phœnicis, Aristonis, atque Myronis
> Fingere tam doctæ quod potuere manus
> Cunachus, aut Mentor, Pythias, vel uterque Polycles
> Lysippus quidquid, Callimachusque dedit.
> Quæ collegisti miro virtutis amore
> Magnanimum reddunt nomen ubique tuum.
> Artificum monumenta foves, referuntur in auro
> Argento, tabulis, & lapide ora Deûm.
>
> *F. Camerlini, ap. Band. Cat. Bibl. Laur. v.* iii. *p.* 545.

admiration, and bear upon ſome conſpicuous part the name of their former proprietor, thus expreſſed LAVR. MED. (*a*). Nor is it improbable that Michel-

(*a*) Theſe letters appear on a cameo in onyx of different colors, repreſenting the entry of Noah and his family into the ark, of which an engraving is given by Gori in his edition of the life of Michelagnolo by Condivi. Among the gems or cameos of this deſcription, of which I have met with impreſſions, or *geſſi*, are thoſe of Diomed with the palladium, or a large oval cameo, in which the letters LAUR. MED. are engraved on the ſide of the rock or ſtone on which he ſits — A centaur, with the letters engraved on the exergue — Dædalus fixing on the wings of Icarus; the inſcription is on the pedeſtal upon which Icarus ſtands, extending his wings over the upper part of the piece; and laſtly, the celebrated gem repreſenting Apollo and Marſyas, of which I ſhall tranſcribe a more particular account from the excellent work of Mr. Tenhove. " La gravure antique qui ſervait de cachet " à Laurent, & qui appartient encore au Grand-Duc de Toſcane, eſt " un morceau accompli. Les ſuffrages qu'elle a mérités dans tous les " tems, ſont ſuffiſamment atteſtés par cette foule de copies qui en " ont été faites dans les tems anciens & modernes. Apollon dans " une attitude noble tient ſa lyre, & regarde avec dédain Marſyas, " qui, les mains liées derrière le dos, & attaché à un arbre, attend " la juſte punition de ſa témérité. Le jeune Scythe qui doit exécuter " la ſentence, eſt à genoux aux pieds d'Apollon, & ſemble implorer " ſa clémence. Le carquois & les flèches du Dieu ſont ſuſpendus " à une des branches de l'arbre, & ſur la terraſſe ſont les flûtes qui " ont ſi mal ſervi le Satyre. Cette même pierre montée en bague avait " autrefois décoré la main parricide de Néron; ce monſtre était dans " l'uſage d'en ſceller ſes ſanguinaires reſcrits. On ſçait qu'il eut la " folie de s'eſtimer le premier muſicien de ſon tems, & par le choix " qu'il fit de ce ſujet il voulut ſans doute écarter les concurrens, & " intimider ceux qui oſeraient entrer en lice avec lui. Peut-être même " regarda-t'il ſa main gauche & prit-il Apollon pour modèle, lorſqu'il " fit fouetter juſqu'au ſang & écorcher, pour ainſi dire, ce chanteur " Menedème dont il était jaloux, & dont les hurlemens mêmes lui " parurent ſi mélodieux, qu'il ne pût s'empêcher d'y applaudir avec

agnolo, who paſſed among theſe treaſures a conſiderable portion of his time, was indebted to the liberality of Lorenzo for the beautiful Intaglio which he is ſuppoſed to have worn as his ſeal (*a*).

The protection and encouragement afforded by Lorenzo to every other branch of art, was not with-held from this his favorite department. From the early part of the fifteenth century, ſome ſpecimens of the aſtoniſhing proficiency of the ancients in works of this nature had occaſionally been diſcovered; and as the public taſte improved, they were ſought for with avidity, and only to be purchaſed at conſiderable prices. In the pontificate of Martin V. and again in that of Paul II. ſome attempts had been made to rival, or at leaſt to imitate, theſe productions, but the firſt artiſt whoſe name ſtands recorded in modern times, is Giovanni delle Corniuole, ſo called from his having generally exerciſed his ſkill upon the ſtone called a Cornelian. The muſeum of Lorenzo de' Medici was the ſchool in which he ſtudied. The proficiency he made correſponded to the

" tranſport.——Les vûes de Laurent étaient un peu plus raiſonnables, " ſans doute il ne choiſit cette pierre qu' à cauſe de la beauté merveil-" leuſe du travail."

(*a*) Chiaro documento ſi ha, che uno degli eſtimatori è raccoglitori intelligenti de' più prezioſi avanzi dell' erudita antichità, e di gioie intagliate da eccellenti Maeſtri greci, e di medaglie, e di altre ſimili rarità, fu il Mag. Lorenzo, per tale celebrato, e riconoſciuto dall' inſigno Ezec. Spanemio nella Diſs. i. *De præſtan & uſu Numiſm. antiquor.* Nè è maraviglia ſe Michelagnolo potè acquiſtare la ſtupendiſſima gemma annulare, la quale paſſò poi nelle mani e nel teſoro del re Criſtianiſſimo; e forſe ch' anch' eſſo altre si fatte rarità averà acquiſtate de' più eccellenti artefici greci.

Gori, Notiz. Storic. ſopra la vita di Michelagn. di Condivi, p. 101.

advantages which he poſſeſſed, and anſwered the purpoſes which his liberal patron had in view. The numerous pieces of his workmanſhip in various ſizes, and on various materials, were the admiration of all Italy. One of his moſt celebrated productions was the portrait of Savonarola, who was then in the meridian of his popularity at Florence. Giovanni immediately met with a formidable competitor in a Milaneſe, who alſo loſt the name of his family in that of his art, and was called Domenico de' Camei. The likeneſs of Lodovico Sforza, engraved by Domenico in a large onyx, was conſidered as the moſt extraordinary ſpecimen of modern ſkill. By theſe maſters, and their ſcholars, this elegant, but unobtruſive branch of the fine arts kept pace with its more oſtentatious competitors; and even in the moſt flouriſhing period of their elevation, under the pontificate of Leo X. the eye that had contemplated the divine ſculptures of Michelagnolo, or had dwelt with delight on the paintings of Raffaello, or of Titian, might have turned with pleaſure to the labors of Valerio Vicentino, or of Giovanni Bologneſe, which compreſſed into the narroweſt bounds the accurate repreſentations of beauty, ſtrength, or grace, and gave to the moſt ineſtimable productions of nature the higheſt perfection of art.

CHAP. X.

LORENZO de' MEDICI intends to retire from public life—Is taken sick and removes to Careggi—His conduct in his last sickness—Interview with Pico and Politiano—Savonarola visits him--Death of Lorenzo—His character—Review of his conduct as a statesman—Attachment of the Florentines to him—Circumstances attending his death—Testimonies of respect to his memory—Death of Innocent VIII. and accession of Alexander VI.—Irruption of the French into Italy—Expulsion of the Medici from Florence—Death of Ermolao Barbaro—Of Pico of Mirandula—Of Agnolo Politiano—Absurd accounts respecting the death of Politiano—His monody on Lorenzo—Politiano celebrated by Cardinal Bembo—Authentic account of his death—Disturbances excited by Savonorola—Adherents of the Medici decapitated--Disgrace and execution of Savonarola—Death of Piero de' Medici—His character--Sonnet of Piero de' Medici-Cardinal Giovanni de' Medici—Restoration of the family to Florence—Elevation of Leo X.—Leo promotes his relations—Restores his dominions to peace—Rise of the reformation—Age of Leo X.—The Laurentian Library restored—Giuliano de' Medici duke of Nemours—Ippolito de' Medici—Lorenzo de' Medici duke of Urbino—Alessandro de' Medici—Descendants of Lorenzo de' Medici the brother of Cosmo—Giovanni de' Medici—Lorenzo de' Medici—Alessandro assumes the sovereignty of Florence—Is assassinated by Lorenzino—Motives and consequences of the attempt—Cosmo de' Medici first grand duke—Death of Filippo Strozzi, and final extinction of the republic—Conclusion.

THAT love of leifure which is infeparable from a mind confcious of its own refources, and the confideration of his declinining ftate of health, were probably the motives that induced Lorenzo de' Medici to aim at introducing his two elder fons into public life at fo early and almoft premature an age. The infirmities under which he labored not only difqualified him at times from attending with his accuftomed vigilance to the affairs of the republic, but rendered it alfo neceffary for him often to abfent himfelf from Florence, and to pafs fome portion of his time at the warm baths in various parts of Italy, of which thofe of Siena and Porrettana, afforded him the moft effectual relief. At thofe feafons which were not embittered by ficknefs, he appears to have flattered himfelf with the expectation of enjoying the reward of his public labors, and partaking of the general happinefs which he had fo effentially contributed to promote, in a peaceful and dignified retirement, enlivened by focial amufements, by philofophic ftudies, and literary purfuits. Thefe expectations were built upon the moft fubftantial foundation, the confcioufnefs that he had difcharged his more immediate duties and engagements; but his feelings on this occafion are beft expreffed in his own words (*a*): "What," fays he, "can be more defirable to a well-regulated mind, "than the enjoyment of leifure with dignity? This

(*a*) *Ap. Fabr. in vitâ Laur. v.* I. *p.* 196.

" is what all good men wish to obtain, but which " great men alone accomplish. In the midst of public " affairs we may indeed be allowed to look forwards " to a day of rest; but no rest should totally seclude " us from an attention to the concerns of our country. " I cannot deny that the path which it has been my " lot to tread has been arduous and rugged, full of " dangers, and beset with treachery; but I console " myself in having contributed to the welfare of my " country, the prosperity of which may now rival " that of any other state, however flourishing. Nor " have I been inattentive to the interests and advance- " ment of my own family, having always proposed " to my imitation the example of my grandfather " Cosmo, who watched over his public and private " concerns with equal vigilance. Having now obtain- " ed the object of my cares, I trust I may be allowed " to enjoy the sweets of leisure, to share the reputa- " tion of my fellow-citizens, and to exult in the glory " of my native place." His intentions were more explicitly made known to his faithful companion Politiano, who relates, that sitting with him in his chamber a few days before his death, conversing on subjects of letters and philosophy, he then told him that he meant to withdraw himself as much as possible from the tumult of the city, and to devote the remainder of his days to the society of his learned friends; at the same time expressing his confidence in the abilities of his son Piero, on whom it was his intention that the conduct of the affairs of the republic should principally devolve (*a*).

(*a*) *Polit. Ep. lib.* iv. *Ep.* 2. But Guicciardini informs us that

The profpect of relaxation and happinefs he was not however deftined to realize. Early in the year 1492, the complaint under which he labored attacked him with additional violence, and whilft the attention of his phyficians was employed in adminiftering relief, he contracted a flow fever which efcaped their obfervation, or eluded their fkill, until it was too late effectually to oppofe its progrefs. The laft illnefs of Lorenzo de' Medici, like that of moft other great men, is reprefented as being extraordinary in its nature. Politiano defcribes his diforder as a fever, of all others the moft infidious, proceeding by infenfible degrees, not like other fevers, by the veins or arteries, but attacking the limbs, the inteftines, the nerves, and deftroying the very principle of life. On the firft approach of this dangerous complaint he had removed from Florence to his houfe at Careggi, where his moments were enlivened by the fociety of his friends, and the refpectful attentions of his fellow-citizens. For medical advice, his chief reliance was upon the celebrated Pier Leoni of Spoleto, whom he had frequently confulted on the ftate of his health; but as the diforder increafed, further affiftance was fought for, and Lazaro da Ticino, another phyfician, arrived at Careggi. It feems to have been the opinion of Politiano that the advice of Lazaro was too late reforted to; but if we may judge from the nature of

Lorenzo was well aware of the real character of his fon, "e fi era "fpeffo lamentato, con li amici più intimi, che l'imprudenza ed "arroganza del figliuolo, partorirebbe la rovina della fua cafa."

Guic. Hift. lib. i.

the medicines employed by him, he rather contributed to accelerate than to avert the fatal moment. The mixture of amalgamated pearls and jewels, with the most expensive potions, might indeed serve to astonish the attendants, and to screen the ignorance of the physician, but were not likely to be attended with any beneficial effect on the patient. Whether it was in consequence of this treatment, or from the nature of the disorder itself, a sudden and unexpected alteration soon took place; and whilst his friends relied with confidence on the exertions made in his behalf, he sunk at once into such a state of debility as totally precluded all hopes of his recovery, and left him only the care of preparing to meet his doom in a manner consistent with the eminence of his character, and the general tenor of his life.

Notwithstanding the diversity of occupations which had successively engaged his attention, and the levity, not to say licentiousness, of some of his writings, the mind of Lorenzo had always been deeply susceptible of religious impressions. This appears not only from his attention to the establishment and reform of monastic houses (*a*), but from his *laudi*, or hymns, many of which breathe a spirit of devotion nearly bordering on enthusiasm. During his last sickness, this feature of his character became more prominent; nor did he judge it expedient, or perhaps think it excusable, to separate the essential from the ceremonial part of religion. Having therefore performed the offices of the church with peculiar fervor, and adjusted with sincerity and decorum his spiritual

(*a*) Of this several instances are given by his historian Valori, *p.* 58, *&c.*

concerns, he requested a private interview with his son Piero, with whom he held a long and interesting conversation on the state of the republic, the situation of his family, and the conduct which it would be expedient for Piero to pursue. Of the precepts which he thought it necessary to inculcate on his successor, we derive some information from Politiano, which was probably obtained from the relation of his pupil (*a*). "I doubt not," said Lorenzo, "that you "will hereafter possess the same weight and authority "in the state which I have hitherto enjoyed; but as "the republic, although it form but one body, has "many heads, you must not expect that it will be "possible for you on all occasions so to conduct your-"self as to obtain the approbation of every individu-"al. Remember, therefore, in every situation to pur-"sue that course of conduct which strict integrity "prescribes, and consult the interests of the whole

(*b*) The circumstances preceding and attending the death of Lorenzo are minutely related by Politiano in a letter to Jacopo Antiquario, *lib.* iv. *Ep.* 2. upon the authority of which I have principally relied, as will be seen, without troubling the reader with continual references, by adverting to the letter in the Appendix, *No.* LXXVII. Fabroni has incorporated this letter in the body of his work, as both the narrative and the evidence of the facts it relates; but as Politiano has mingled with much authentic information many instances of that superstition which infested the age, and has, perhaps, shown too unlimited a partiality to the family of his patrons, I have thought it incumbent on me to separate, according to the best of my judgment, the documents of history from the dreams of the nursery, and the representations of truth from the encomiums of the friend, leaving my reader to consult the original, and to adopt as much more of the account as he may think fit.

"community, rather than the gratification of a part." These admonitions, if attended to, might have preserved Piero from the ruin which the neglect of them soon brought down, and may yet serve as a lesson to those whose authority rests, as all authority must finally rest, on public opinion. The dutiful and patient attendance of Piero on his father during his sickness was however a pledge to Lorenzo that his last instructions would not be forgotten, and, by confirming the favorable sentiments which he appears to have entertained of the talents and the disposition of his son, served at least to alleviate the anxiety which he must have felt on resigning, thus prematurely, the direction of such a vast and rapid machine into young and in experienced hands.

At this interesting period, when the mind of Lorenzo, relieved from the weight of its important concerns, became more sensibly alive to the emotions of friendship, Politiano entered his chamber. Lorenzo no sooner heard his voice than he called on him to approach, and, raising his languid arms, clasped the hands of Politiano in his own, at the same time stedfastly regarding him with a placid, and even a cheerful countenance. Deeply affected at this silent but unequivocal proof of esteem, Politiano could not suppress his feelings, but, turning his head aside, attempted as much as possible to conceal his sobs and his tears. Perceiving his agitation, Lorenzo still continued to grasp his hand, as if intending to speak to him when his passion had subsided, but finding him unable to resist its impulse, he slowly, and as it were unintentionally relaxed his hold, and Politiano, hastening into an inner apartment, flung himself on a bed, and gave way to his grief. Having at length composed himself, he returned into the chamber, when Lorenzo again called to him, and inquired with great kindness why Pico of Mirandula had not once paid him a visit during his sickness. Politiano apologized for his friend, by assuring Lorenzo that he had only been deterred by the apprehension that his presence might be troublesome. "On the con-"trary," replied Lorenzo, "if his journey from the "city be not troublesome to him, I shall rejoice to "see him before I take my final leave of you." Pico accordingly came, and seated himself at the side of Lorenzo, whilst Politiano, reclining on the bed, near the knees of his revered benefactor, as if to prevent any extraordinary exertion of his declining voice, prepared for the last time to share in the pleasures of his conversation. After excusing himself to Pico for the task he had imposed upon him, Lorenzo expressed his esteem for him in the most affectionate terms, professing that he should meet his death with more cheerfulness after this last interview. He then changed the subject to more familiar and lively topics, and it was on this occasion that he expressed, not without some degree of jocularity, his wishes that he could have obtained a reprieve, until he could have completed the library destined to the use of his auditors. This interview was scarcely terminated when a visitor of a very different character arrived. This was the haughty and enthusiastic Savonarola, who probably thought, that in the last moments of agitation and of suffering, he might be enabled to collect materials for his factious purposes.

With apparent charity and kindness, the priest exhorted Lorenzo to remain firm in the catholic faith; to which Lorenzo professed his strict adherence. He then required an avowal of his intention, in case of his recovery, to live a virtuous and well-regulated life; to this he also signified his sincere assent. Lastly he reminded him, that, if needful, he ought to bear his death with fortitude. "With cheerfulness," replied Lorenzo, "if such be the will of God." On his quitting the room, Lorenzo called him back, and as an unequivocal mark that he harboured in his bosom no resentment against him for the injuries which he had received, requested the priest would bestow upon him his benediction; with which he instantly complied, Lorenzo making the usual responses with a firm and collected voice (*a*).

(*a*) In the life of Savonarola, written in Latin, at considerable length, by Giovanfrancesco Pico prince of Mirandula, nephew of the celebrated Pico whom we have had occasion so frequently to mention, an account is given of this interview, which differs in its most essential particulars from that which is above related. If we may credit this narrative, Lorenzo, when at the point of death, sent to request the attendance of Savonarola, to whom he was desirous of making his confession. Savonarola accordingly came, but, before he would consent to receive him as a penitent, required that he should declare his adherence to the true faith; to which Lorenzo assented. He then insisted on a promise from Lorenzo, that if he had unjustly obtained the property of others, he would return it. Lorenzo, after a short hesitation, replied, "Doubtless, father, I "shall do this, or, if it be not in my power, I shall enjoin it as a duty upon "my heirs." Thirdly, Savonarola required that he should restore the republic to liberty, and establish it in its former state of independence; to which Lorenzo not chusing to make any reply, the priest left him without giving him his absolution. *Savonar. vita, inter vit. select. viror. ap. Bates. Lond.* 1704. A story that exhibits evident symptoms of

No

No ſpecies of reputation is ſo cheaply acquired as that derived from death-bed fortitude. When it is fruitleſs to contend, and impoſſible to fly, little applauſe is due to that reſignation which patiently awaits its doom. It is not therefore to be conſidered as enhancing that dignity of character which Lorenzo had ſo frequently diſplayed, that he ſuſtained the laſt conflict with equanimity. "To judge from "his conduct, and of his ſervants," ſays Politiano, "you would have thought that it was they who "momentarily expected that fate, from which he "alone appeared to be exempt." Even to the laſt the ſcintillations of his former vivacity were perceptible. Being aſked, on taking a morſel of food how he reliſhed it, "As a dying man always does," was his reply. Having affectionately embraced his ſurrounding friends, and ſubmitted to the laſt ceremonies of the church, he became abſorbed in meditation, occaſionally repeating portions of ſcripture, and accompanying his ejaculations with elevated eyes, and ſolemn geſtures of his hands, till the energies of life gradually declining, and preſſing to his lips a magnificent crucifix, he calmly expired.

In the height of his reputation, and at a premature period of life, thus died Lorenzo de' Medici; a man who may be ſelected from all the characters of ancient and modern hiſtory, as exhibiting the moſt remarkable inſtance of depth of penetration, ver-

that party-ſpirit which did not ariſe in Florence until after the death of Lorenzo, and which, being contradictory to the account left by Politiano, written before the motives for miſrepreſentation exiſted, is only rendered deſerving of notice by the neceſſity of its refutation.

ſatility of talent, and comprehenſion of mind (*a*). Whether genius be a predominating impulſe, directing the mind to ſome particular object, or whether it be an energy of intellect that arrives at excellence in any department in which it may be employed, it is certain that there are few inſtances in which, a ſucceſsful exertion in any human purſuit has not occaſioned a dereliction of many other objects, the attainment of which might have conferred immortality. If the powers of the mind are to bear down all obſtacles that oppoſe their progreſs, it ſeems neceſſary that they ſhould ſweep along in ſome certain courſe, and in one collected maſs. What then ſhall we think of that rich fountain which, whilſt it was poured out by ſo many different channels, flowed through each with a full and equal ſtream? To be abſorbed in one purſuit, however important, is not the characteriſtic of the higher claſs of genius, which, piercing through the various combinations, and relations of ſurrounding circumſtances, ſees all things in their juſt dimenſions and attributes to each its due. Of the various occupations in which Lorenzo engaged, there is not one in which he was not eminently ſucceſsful; but he was moſt particularly diſtinguiſhed in thoſe which juſtly hold the firſt rank in human eſtima-

(*a*) " Soyons avares," ſays M. Tenhove, " du titre ſacré de grand " homme, prodigué ſi ſouvent & ſi ridiculement aux plus minces per- " ſonnages, mais ne le refuſons point à Laurent de Medicis. Malheur " à l'ame froide & mal organiſée, qui ne ſentirait pas ſon extrême " mérite! On peut en toute ſûreté s'eſtimer de ſon admiration pour " lui." *Mém. Gén. liv.* xi. *p.* 146.

tion. The facility with which he turned from subjects of the highest importance to those of amusement and levity, suggested to his countrymen the idea that he had two distinct souls combined in one body. Even his moral character seems to have partaken in some degree of the same diversity, and his devotional poems are as ardent as his lighter pieces are licentious. On all sides he touched the extremes of human character, and the powers of his mind were only bounded by that impenetrable circle which prescribes the limits of human nature.

As a statesman, Lorenzo de' Medici appears to peculiar advantage. Uniformly employed in securing the peace and promoting the happiness of his country by just regulations at home, and wise precautions abroad, and teaching to the surrounding governments those important lessons of political science, on which the civilization and tranquillity of nations have since been found to depend. Though possessed of undoubted talents for military exploits, and of sagacity to avail himself of the imbecility of neighbouring powers, he was superior to that avarice of dominion which, without improving what is already acquired, blindly aims at more extensive possessions. The wars in which he engaged were for security, not for territory; and the riches produced by the fertility of the soil, and the industry and ingenuity of the inhabitants of the Florentine republic, instead of being dissipated in imposing projects and ruinous expeditions, circulated in their natural channels, giving happiness to the individual, and respectability to the state. If he was not insensible to the charms of ambition, it was the ambition to deſerve rather than to enjoy; and he was always cautious not to exact from the public favor more than it might be voluntarily willing to beſtow. The approximating ſuppreſſion of the liberties of Florence, under the influence of his deſcendants, may induce ſuſpicions unfavorable to his patriotiſm; but it will be difficult, not to ſay impoſſible, to diſcover, either in his conduct or his precepts, any thing that ought to ſtigmatize him as an enemy to the freedom of his country. The authority which he exerciſed was the ſame as that which his anceſtors had enjoyed, without injury to the republic, for nearly a century, and had deſcended to him as inſeparable from the wealth, the reſpectability, and the powerful foreign connexions of his family. The ſuperiority of his talents enabled him to avail himſelf of theſe advantages with irreſiſtible effect; but hiſtory ſuggeſts not an inſtance in which they were devoted to any other purpoſe than that of promoting the honor and the independence of the Tuſcan ſtate. It was not by the continuance, but by the dereliction of the ſyſtem that he had eſtabliſhed, and to which he adhered to the cloſe of his life, that the Florentine republic ſunk under the degrading yoke of deſpotic power; and to his premature death we may unqueſtionably attribute, not only the deſtruction of the commonwealth, but all the calamities that Italy ſoon afterwards ſuſtained.

The ſympathies of mind, like the laws of chemical affinity, are uniform. Great talents attract admiration, the offering of the underſtanding; but the qualities of the heart can alone excite affection, the offering of the heart. If we may judge of Lorenzo de' Medici by the ardor with which his friends and contemporaries have expreſſed their attachment, we ſhall form concluſions highly favorable to his ſenſibility and his ſocial virtues. The exaction of thoſe attentions uſually paid to rank and to power, he left to ſuch as had no other claims to reſpect; he rather choſe to be conſidered as the friend and the equal, than as the dictator of his fellow-citizens. His urbanity extended to the loweſt ranks of ſociety; and while he enlivened the city of Florence by magnificent ſpectacles and amuſing repreſentations, he partook of them himſelf with a reliſh that ſet the example of feſtivity. It was the general opinion in Florence, that whoever was favored by Lorenzo could not fail of ſucceſs. Valori relates, that in the repreſentation of an engagement on horſeback, one of the combatants, who was ſuppoſed to contend under the patronage of Lorenzo, being overpowered and wounded, avowed his reſolution to die rather than ſubmit to his adverſary, and it was not without difficulty that he was reſcued from the danger, to receive from the bounty of Lorenzo the reward of his well-meant though miſtaken fidelity.

The death of Lorenzo, which happened on the eighth day of April 1492, was no ſooner known at Florence than a general alarm and conſternation ſpread throughout he city, and the inhabitants gave way to the moſt unbounded expreſſions of grief. Even thoſe who were not friendly to the Medici lamented in this misfortune the proſpect of the evils to come. The agitation of the public mind was increased by a singular coincidence of calamitous events, which the superstition of the people considered as portentous of approaching commotions. The physician, Pier Leoni, whose prescriptions had failed of success, being apprized of the result, left Careggi in a state of distraction, and precipitated himself into a well in the suburbs of the city (*a*). Two days preceding the death of Lorenzo, the great dome of the *Reparata* was struck with lightning, and on the side which approached towards the chapel of the Medici, a part of the building fell. It was

(*a*) Whether Leoni died a voluntary death has been doubted. The enemies of the Medici, who upon the death of Lorenzo began to meditate the ruin of his family, have accused Piero his son with the perpetration of the deed, and this opinion is openly avowed by Giacopo Sanazaro in an Italian poem in *terza Rima*, in which he has imitated Dante with great success, *v. App. No.* LXXVIII. But I must observe, that this poem bears internal evidence of its having been written after the Medici were driven from Florence, when their enemies were laboring by every possible means to render them odious. On the other hand, besides the testimony of Politiano that Leoni accelerated his own death, we have that of Petrus Crinitus (Piero Ricci), a contemporary author, who, in his treatise *De honesta Disciplina*, has a chapter *De hominibus qui se ipsos in puteum jaciant*, in which he thus adverts to the death of Leoni: " Sed enim quod nuper accidit in Petro Leonio, " mirificum certe visum est; quando is, & in philosophia vir excellens, " ac prudentia propé egregia, in puteum se Florentino suburbano " immersit." *Lib.* iii. *cap.* 9. This circumstance is also related by Valerianus. *De infel. literatorum, lib.* i. It appears, however, from an account of the death of Lorenzo, published by Fabroni, from a MS. diary of an anonymous Florentine author yet preserved in the Magliabechi library, *Cod.* xvii. *Class.* 25. that Leoni entertained apprehensions for his safety from the attendants of Lorenzo, who, without just cause, suspected that he had occasioned his death by poison. I shall give the extract from this diary in the Appendix, *No.* LXXIX,

alſo obſerved that one of the golden *palle* or balls, in the emblazonment of the Medicean arms, was at the ſame time ſtruck out. For three nights, gleams of light were ſaid to have been perceived proceeding from the hill of Fieſole, and hovering above the church of S. Lorenzo, where the remains of the family were depoſited. Beſides theſe incidents, founded perhaps on ſome caſual occurrence, and only rendered extraordinary by the workings of a heated imagination, many others of a ſimilar kind are related by contemporary authors, which, whilſt they exemplify that credulity which characterizes the human race in every age, may at laſt ſerve to ſhow that the event to which they were ſuppoſed to allude was conceived to be of ſuch magnitude as to occaſion a deviation from the ordinary courſe of nature (*a*). From Careggi the body of Lorenzo was conveyed to the church of his patron ſaint, amidſt the tears and lamentations of all ranks of people, who bewailed the loſs of their faithful protector, the glory of their city, the companion of their amuſements, their common father and friend. His obſequies were without oſtentation, he having a ſhort time before his death given expreſs directions to

(*a*) *Ficinus in fine Plotini. Flor.* 1492. *Ammir. lib.* xxvi. *v.* iii. *p.* 186. Even Machiavelli, an author ſeldom accuſed of ſuperſtition, ſeems on this occaſion to concede his incredulity to the general opinion. " Nè morì mai alcuno, non ſolamente in Firenze, ma in Italia, con " tanta fama di prudenza, nè che tanto alla ſua patria doleſſe. E come " dalla ſua morte ne doveſſe naſcere grandiſſime rovine, ne moſtrò il " cielo molti evidentiſſimi ſegni, &c." *Hiſt. lib.* viii. This author concludes his celebrated hiſtory, as Guicciardini begins, with the higheſt eulogium on the character of Lorenzo.

that effect. Not a tomb or an inscription marks the place that received his ashes; but the stranger, who, smitten with the love of letters and of arts, wanders amidst the splendid monuments erected to the chiefs of this illustrious family, the work of Michelagnolo and of his powerful competitors, whilst he looks in vain for that inscribed with the name of Lorenzo, will be reminded of his glory by them all.

Throughout the rest of Italy the death of Lorenzo was regarded as a public calamity of the most alarming kind. Of the arch which supported the political fabric of that country he had long been considered as the centre, and his loss seemed to threaten the whole with immediate destruction. When Ferdinand, king of Naples, was informed of this event, he exclaimed, "this man has lived long enough for "his own glory, but too short a time for Italy (*a*)." Such of the Italian potentates as were more nearly connected with the Medici sent ambassadors to Florence on this occasion. Letters of condolance were transmitted to Piero from almost all the sovereigns of Europe. Many distinguished individuals also paid this last tribute to the memory of their friend and benefactor (*b*). Among these communications, dictated by flattery, by friendship, and by political motives, there is one of a more interesting nature.

(*a*) "Satis sibi vir immortalitate dignissimus vixit, sed parum Italiæ. "Utinam ne quis eo sublato, moliatur, quæ vivo, tentare ausus non fuisset." In which Ferdinand was supposed to allude to Lod. Sforza.

Fabr. vita Laur. v. i. *p.* 219.

(*b*) These letters, forming a collection in two volumes, are yet preserved in *MS.* in the *Palazzo Vecchio* at Florence, *Filz.* xxv. *No.* xv.

This is a letter from the young cardinal Giovanni de' Medici to his elder brother, written four days after the death of their father, which evinces that the cardinal was not without apprehensions from the temper and disposition of Piero, and does equal honor to his prudence and to his filial piety.

The Cardinal Giovanni de' Medici, at Rome, to Piero de' Medici, at Florence.

" My dearest brother, now the only support of " our family; what I have to communicate to thee, " except my tears, I know not; for when I reflect " on the loss we have sustained in the death of our " father, I am more inclined to weep than to relate " my sorrow. What a father have we lost! How " indulgent to his children! Wonder not then that " I grieve, that I lament, that I find no rest. Yet, " my brother, I have some consolation in reflecting " that I have thee, whom I shall always regard in " the place of a father. Do thou command — I shall " cheerfully obey. Thy injunctions will give me " more pleasure than I can express — order me — " put me to the test, there is nothing that shall pre- " vent my compliance. Allow me however, my " Piero, to express my hopes, that in thy conduct " to all, and particularly to those around thee, I " may find thee as I could wish — beneficent, liberal, " affable, humane; by which qualities there is " nothing but may be obtained, nothing but may " be preserved. Think not that I mention this from " any doubt that I entertain of thee, but because " I esteem it to be my duty. Many things strengthen

" and console me; the concourse of people that " surround our house with lamentations, the sad " and sorrowful appearance of the whole city, the " public mourning, and other similar circum- " stances, these in a great degree alleviate my grief; " but that which relieves me more than all the rest, " is, that I have thee, my brother, in whom I place " a confidence that no words can describe, &c. *Ex* " *urbe, die 12th Ap.* 1492 (*a*)."

The common mediator of Italy being now no more, the same interested and unenlightened motives which had so often rendered that country the seat of treachery and of bloodshed again began to operate, and the ambitious views of the different sovereigns became the more dangerous as they were the more concealed. Such was the confidence which they had placed in Lorenzo, that not a measure of importance was determined on by any of them without its being previously communicated to him, when, if he thought it likely to prove hostile to the general tranquillity, he was enabled either to prevent its execution, or at least to obviate its ill effects; but upon his death a general suspicion of each other took place, and laid the foundation of the unhappy consequences that soon afterwards ensued. The impending evils of Italy were accelerated by the death of Innocent VIII. who survived Lorenzo only a few months, and still more by the elevation to the pontificate of Roderigo Borgia, the scourge of Christendom, and the opprobrium of the human race (*b*).

(*a*) For the original, *v. App. No.* LXXX.

(*b*) A striking instance of the influence which Lorenzo had obtained

Piero de' Medici, on whom the eyes and expectations of the public were turned, gave early indications that he was unable to sustain the weight that had devolved upon him. Elated with the authority derived from his father, but forgetting the admonitions by which it was accompanied, he relaxed the reins that controlled all Italy, to grasp at the supreme dominion of his native place. For this purpose he secretly formed a more intimate connexion with the king of Naples and the pope, which being discovered by the penetrating eye of Lodovico Sforza, raised in him a spirit of jealousy, which the professions and assurances of Piero could never allay. An interval of dissatisfaction, negotiation, and distrust took place, till at length the solicitations of Lodovico and the ambition of Charles VIII. brought into Italy a more formidable and warlike race, whose arrival spread a general terror and alarm, and convinced, too late, the states and sovereigns of that country of the folly of their

over the mind of Innocent VIII. appears from one of his unpublished letters preserved in the *Palazzo Vecchio* at Florence (*Filz.* lix. *No.* xiv), dated the 16th day of June 1488, from which we collect, that the pope had transmitted to him the list of an intended promotion of cardinals, which Lorenzo returns, informing him that he approves of the nomination of such of them whose names he has marked with a pen, and exhorting him to carry his intentions with respect to them into execution, concluding his letter with reminding the pope *chè si può consolare ancor lui, se ne ricordi.* In fact, the assumption of Giovanni de' Medici to the purple took place early in the following year; and as Innocent VIII. only made one promotion of cardinals during his pontificate, it appears that Lorenzo had sufficient address to procure the name of his son, who was then only thirteen years of age, to be included in the list.

mutual diſſenſions. Even Lodovico himſelf, who in the expectation of weakening his rivals, and of veſting in himſelf the government of Milan, had inceſſantly labored to accompliſh this object, no ſooner ſaw its approach than he ſhrunk from it in terror; and whilſt he was obliged, for the ſake of conſiſtency, to perſevere in exhorting Charles to proceed in his enterpriſe againſt the kingdom of Naples, he endeavoured by ſecret emiſſaries to excite againſt him the moſt formidable oppoſition of the Italian powers. Lodovico having for this purpoſe diſpatched an envoy to Florence, Piero conceived that he had obtained a favorable opportunity of convincing the king of France of the inſincerity of his pretended ally, and thereby of deterring him from the further proſecution of his undertaking; but however laudable his purpoſe might be, the means which he adopted for its accompliſhment reflect but little credit on his talents. In the palace of the Medici was an apartment which communicated with the gardens by a ſecret door, conſtructed by Lorenzo de' Medici for the purpoſe of convenience and retirement. In this room, Piero, pretending to be ſick, contrived an interview with the agent of Lodovico, whilſt the envoy of Charles VIII. ſecreted behind the door, was privy to their converſation (*a*). Whether Piero had not the addreſs to engage the Milaneſe ſufficiently to develope the views of his maſter, or whether the French envoy found the Italian politicians equally undeſerving of confidence, reſts only on conjecture;

(*a*) *Oricell. de bello Ital. p.* 24.

but the communication of this incident to Charles tended not in the ſlighteſt degree to avert the impending calamity. On the contrary, the conduct of Piero being made known to Lodovico, rendered any further communication between them impoſſible, and by preventing that union of the Italian ſtates, which alone could have oppoſed with effect the further progreſs of the French arms, facilitated an enterpriſe that could owe its ſucceſs only to the miſconduct of its opponents (*a*).

This unfortunate event led the way to another incident more immediately deſtructive to the credit and authority of Piero de' Medici. Charles, at the head of his troops, had, without reſiſtance, reached the confines of the Florentine ſtate, and had attacked the town of Sarzana, which Lorenzo, after having recovered it from the Genoeſe, had ſtrongly fortified. The approach of ſuch a formidable body of men, the reputation they had acquired, and the atrocities they had committed in their progreſs, could not fail of exciting great conſternation in Florence, where the citizens began freely to expreſs their diſſatisfaction with Piero de' Medici, who they aſſerted had, by his raſh and intemperate meaſures, provoked the reſentment of a powerful ſovereign, and endangered the very exiſtence of the republic. This criſis ſuggeſted to Piero the ſituation in which his father ſtood, when, in order to terminate a war which threatened him with deſtruction, he had haſtened to Naples, and, placing himſelf in the power of an avowed enemy, had returned to Florence with the credentials

(*a*) *Guicciard. Hiſt. d'Italia, lib.* i.

of peace (*a*). The preſent ſeaſon appeared to him favorable for a ſimilar attempt; but, as Guicciardini judiciouſly obſerves, it is dangerous to guide ourſelves by precedent, unleſs the caſes be exactly alike; unleſs the attempt be conducted with equal prudence, and, above all, unleſs it be attended with the ſame good fortune (*b*). The impetuoſity of Piero prevented him from obſerving theſe diſtinctions — haſtening to the French camp, he threw himſelf at the feet of Charles, who received his ſubmiſſion with coldneſs and diſdain (*c*). Finding his entreaties ineffectual, he became laviſh in his offers to promote the intereſts of the king, and, as a pledge of his fidelity, propoſed to deliver up to him not only the important fortreſs of Sarzana, which had till then ſucceſsfully reſiſted his attacks, but alſo the town of Pietra Santa, and the cities of Piſa and Leghorn, Charles at the ſame time undertaking to reſtore them, when he had accompliſhed his conqueſt of the kingdom of Naples (*d*). The temerity of Piero in

(*a*) *v. ante, Vol.* I. *p.* 224.

(*b*) *Guicciard. Hiſt. d'Italia, lib.* i.

(*c*) *Oricell. de bello Ital. p.* 39.

(*d*) The French were themſelves aſtoniſhed at the prodigality of Piero, and the facility with which he delivered into their hands places of ſo much importance. " Ceux qui traitoyent avec Pierre," ſays P. " de Commines, m'ont compté, & à pluſieurs autres l'ont dit, en ſe " raillant & moquant de lui, qu'ils étoient ébahis comme ſi tot accordia " ſi grand choſe, & à quoi ils ne s'attendoient point." *Mém. de Commines, liv.* vii. *p.* 198. The day after Piero had entered into his unfortunate treaty, Lodovico Sforza arrived at the French camp, when Piero, who was not at open enmity with him, excuſed himſelf for not having met him on the road, becauſe Lodovico had miſſed his

provoking the resentment of Charles, added to his inability to ward off, and his pusillanimity in resisting the blow, completed what his ambition and his arrogance had begun, and for ever deprived him of the respect and confidence of his fellow-citizens. On his return to Florence, after this disgraceful compromise, he was refused admittance into the palace of the magistrates, and, finding that the people at large were so highly exasperated against him as to endanger his personal safety, he hastily withdrew himself from his native place, and retreated to Venice (*a*).

way. "It is true enough," said Lodovico, "that one of us has lost "his way, but perhaps it may prove to be yourself." *Guic. lib.* i.

(*a*) Condivi relates an extraordinary story respecting Piero de' Medici, communicated to him by Michelagnolo, who had it seems formed an intimacy with one Cardiere, an improvvisatore, that frequented the house of Lorenzo, and amused his evenings with singing to the lute. Soon after the death of Lorenzo, Cardiere informed Michelagnolo, that Lorenzo had appeared to him, habited only in a black and ragged mantle thrown over his naked limbs, and had ordered him to acquaint Piero de' Medici, that he would in a short time be banished from Florence. Cardiere, who seems judiciously to have feared the resentment of the living more than that of the dead, declined the office; but soon afterwards Lorenzo entering his chamber at midnight, awoke him, and reproaching him with his inattention, gave him a violent blow on the cheek. Having communicated this second visit to his friend, who advised him no longer to delay his errand, he set out for Carreggi, where Piero then resided, but meeting him with his attendants about midway between that place and Florence, he there delivered his message, to the great amusement of Piero and his followers; one of whom, Bernardo Divizio, afterwards Cardinal da Bibbiena, sarcastically asked him, *Whether, if Lorenzo had been desirous of giving information to his son, it was likely he would have preferred such a messenger to a personal communication?* The biographer adds, with great solemnity, "La vision del Cardiere, o delusion diabolica, o

The diſtreſs and devaſtation which the inhabitants of Italy experienced for a ſeries of years after this event, have afforded a ſubject upon which their hiſtorians have dwelt with melancholy accuracy. Amidſt theſe diſaſters, there is perhaps no circumſtance that ſo forcibly excites the regret of the friends of letters, as the plundering of the palace of the Medici, and the diſperſion of that invaluable library, whoſe origin and progreſs have before been traced. The French troops that had entered the city of Florence without oppoſition, led the way to this ſacrilegious deed, in the perpetration of which they were joined by the Florentines themſelves, who openly carried off, or ſecretly purloined, whatever they could diſcover that was intereſting, rare, or valuable. Beſides the numerous manuſcripts in almoſt every language, the depredators ſeized, with contentious avidity, the many ineſtimable ſpecimens of the arts with which the houſe of the Medici abounded, and which had long rendered it the admiration of ſtrangers, and the chief ornament of the city. Exquiſite pieces of ancient ſculpture, vaſes, cameos, and gems of various kinds, more eſtimable for their workmanſhip than for their native value, ſhared in the general ruin; and all that the aſſiduity and the riches

"predizion divina, o forte immaginazione, ch' ella ſi foſſe, ſi verificò."—But the awful ſpectre is now before me—I ſee the terrified muſician ſtart from his ſlumbers; his left hand graſps his beloved lyre, whilſt, with his right thrown over his head, he attempts to ſhroud himſelf from the looks of Lorenzo, who, with a countenance more in ſorrow than in anger, points out to him his deſtined miſſion. To realize this ſcene ſo as to give it intereſt and effect, required the glowing imagination and the animated pencil of a Fuseli.

of

of Lorenzo and his anceſtors had been able to accumulate in half a century, was diſſipated or demoliſhed in a day (*a*).

The ſame reverſe of fortune that overwhelmed the political labors of Lorenzo, that rendered his deſcendants fugitives, and diſperſed his effects, ſeemed to extend to his friends and aſſociates, almoſt all of whom unhappily periſhed within a ſhort interval after his death, although in the common courſe of

(*a*) The deſtruction of this invaluable collection is pathetically related by Bernardo Ruccellai. "Hic me ſtudium charitaſque litterarum "antiquitatis admonet, ut non poſſim non deplorare inter ſubitas "fundatiſſimæ familiæ ruinas, Mediceam bibliothecam, inſigneſque "theſauros, quorum pars a Gallis, pars a paucis e noſtris, rem turpiſſimam honeſta ſpecie prætendentibus, furaciſſime ſubrepta ſunt. "Nam cum jam pridem gens Medicea floreret omnibus copiis, terra, "marique cuncta exquirere, dum ſibi Græcarum, Latinarumque litterarum monumenta, toreumata, gemmas, margaritas, aliaque "hujuſcemodi opera, natura ſimul & antiquo artificio conſpicua compararent," &c. "Teſtimonio ſunt litteræ gemmis ipſis inciſæ, Laurentii nomen præferentes, quas ille ſibi familiæque ſuæ proſpiciens "ſcalpendas curavit, futurum ad poſteros regii ſplendoris monumentum," &c. "Hæc omnia magno conquiſita ſtudio, ſummiſque parta "opibus, & ad multum ævi in deliciis habita, quibus nihil nobilius, "nihil Florentiæ quod magis viſendum putaretur, uno puncto temporis "in prædam ceſſere; tanta Gallorum avaritia, perfidiaque noſtrorum "fuit." *De bello Ital. p.* 52, *&c.* This event is alſo commemorated by P. de Commines, who, with true Gothic ſimplicity, relates the number, weight, and ſaleable value of the articles of which the palace of the Medici was plundered. The antique vaſes he denominates, "beaux pots d'agate --- & tant de beaux camayeux, bien taillés que "merveilles (qu' autrefois j'avois veus) & bien trois mille medales "d'or & d'argent, bien la peſanteur de quarante livres; & croi qu'il "n'y avoit point autant de belles medales en Italie. Ce qu'il perdit "ce jour en la cité valoit cent mille ecus & plus."

Mém. de Com. liv. vii. *c.* 9.

nature they might have expected a longer life. The first of these eminent men was Ermolao Barbaro, of whose friendly intercourse with Lorenzo many testimonies remain, and who died of the plague in the year 1493, when only thirty-nine years of age (*a*).

(*a*) The life and learned labors of Ermolao have afforded a subject of much discussion to Vossius, Bayle, and others, and have been considered with particular accuracy by Apostolo Zeno, *Dissert. Voss. v.* ii. *p.* 348. *& seq.* His first work was a treatise *De Cælibatu*, which he wrote at eighteen years of age. His *Castigationes Plinianæ* entitle him to rank with the most successful restorers of learning. Politiano denominates him, *Hermolaus Barbarus barbariæ hostis acerrimus. Miscel. cap.* xc. Being on an embassy to Rome in the year 1491, Innocent VIII. conferred on him the high dignity of Patriarch of Aquileja, which he accepted without regarding the decree of the Venetian government, which directed that none of their ministers at the court of Rome should receive any ecclesiastical preferment without the consent of the council. His father, who held the second office in the state, is said to have died of chagrin, because he could not prevail upon his countrymen to approve the preferment of his son. But Ermolao availed himself of his dismission from public business, to return with greater earnestness to this studies, and in two years wrote more than he had done for twenty years preceding. In his last sickness at Rome, Pico of Mirandula sent him a remedy for the cure of the plague, composed of the oil of scorpions, the tongues of asps, &c. "Ut "nihil fieri posset contra pestilentem morbum commodius aut presen-"tius." *Crin. de honest. discip. lib.* i. *c.* 7. But this grand panacea arrived too late. "Egli non è da tacersi," says Apostolo Zeno, "un "gran fregio di questo valente uomo, ed è, che visse, e morì *vergine*." Which information is confirmed by the authority of Piero Dolfini, who, in a letter to Ugolino Verini, asserts, QUOD ABSQUE ULLA CARNIS CONTAGIONE VIXERIT. *Diss. Voss.* ii. *p.* 365. A very particular account of the manners and person of Ermolao is given in a letter from Piero de' Medici to his father Lorenzo, then absent at the baths of Vignone, from which it appears, that he had paid a visit to Florence, and was received there with great honor as the friend of Lorenzo.

App. No. LXXXI.

This event was ſucceeded by the death of Pico of Mirandula, who in his thirty-ſecond year fell a victim to his avidity for ſcience, and has left poſterity to regret that he turned his aſtoniſhing acquiſitions to ſo little account. Nor did Politiano long ſurvive his great patron. He died at Florence on the twenty-fourth day of September 1494, when he had juſt completed his fortieth year.

It is painful to reflect on the propenſity which has appeared in all ages to ſully the moſt illuſtrious characters by the imputation of the moſt degrading crimes. Jovius, with apparent gravity, informs us, that Politiano, having entertained a criminal paſſion for one of his pupils, died in the paroxyſm of an amorous fever, whilſt he was ſinging his praiſes on the lute (*a*); and this prepoſterous tale has been repeated, with ſingular variations, by many ſubſequent writers. To attempt a ſerious refutation of ſo abſurd a charge would be an uſeleſs undertaking; but it may not be unintereſting to inquire by what circumſtances it was firſt ſuggeſted; as it may ſerve to ſhow on how ſlight a foundation detraction can erect her ſuperſtructure. On the death of Lorenzo de' Medici, Politiano attempted to pour forth his grief in the following monody to his memory, which,

(*a*) Ferunt eum ingenui adoleſcentis inſano amore percitum, facile in letalem morbum incidiſſe. Correpta enim citharâ, quum eo incendio, & rapida febre torreretur, ſupremi furoris carmina decantavit; ita, ut mox delirantem, vox ipſa & digitorum nervi, & vitalis denique ſpiritus, inverecunda urgente morte, deſererent: quum maturando judicio integræ ſtatæque ætatis anni, non ſine gravi Muſarum injuria, doloreque ſeculi, feſtinante fato eriperentur. *Jovii. Elog. cap.* xxxviii.

although left in an unfinished state, and not to be ranked in point of composition with many of his other writings, is strongly expressive of the anguish and agitation of his mind:

Monodia in Laurentium Medicem.

Quis dabit capiti meo
Aquam? quis oculis meis
Fontem lachrymarum dabit?
Ut nocte fleam,
Ut luce fleam.
Sic turtur viduus solet;
Sic cygnus moriens solet;
Sic luscinia conqueri.
Heu miser, miser;
O dolor, dolor.
— LAURUS impetu fulminis
Illa illa jacet subito;
LAURUS omnium celebris
Musarum choris,
Nympharum choris,
Sub cujus patula coma,
Et Phœbi lyra blandius
Et vox dulcius insonat.
Nunc muta omnia,
Nunc surda omnia.
— Quis dabit capiti meo
Aquam? quis oculis meis
Fontem lachrymarum dabit?
Ut nocte fleam,
Ut luce fleam.
Sic turtur viduus solet;

Sic cygnus moriens ſolet;
Sic luſcinia conqueri.
Heu miſer, miſer;
O dolor, dolor.

Who from perennial ſtreams ſhall bring
Of guſhing floods a ceaſeleſs ſpring?
That through the day in hopeleſs woe,
That through the night my tears may flow.
As the reft turtle mourns his mate,
As ſings the ſwan his coming fate,
As the ſad nightingale complains,
I pour my anguiſh and my ſtrains.
Ah wretched, wretched paſt relief,
O grief, beyond all other grief.

—Through heaven the gleamy lightning flies,
And prone on earth my LAUREL lies:
That laurel, boaſt of many a tongue,
Whoſes praiſes every muſe has ſung,
Which every dryad of the grove,
And all the tuneful ſiſters love.
That laurel, that erewhile diſplayed
Its ample honors; in whoſe ſhade
To louder notes was ſtrung the lyre,
And ſweeter ſang th' Aonian quire,
Now ſilent, ſilent all around,
And deaf the ear that drank the ſound.

—Who from perennial ſtreams ſhall bring,
Of guſhing floods a ceaſeleſs ſpring?
That through the day in hopeleſs woe,
That through the night my tears may flow.

As the reft turtle mourns his mate,
As fings the fwan his coming fate,
As the fad nightingale complains,
I pour my anguifh aud my ftrains.
Ah wretched, wretched paft relief,
O grief, beyond all other grief,

Such was the object of the affections of Politiano, and fuch the amorous effufion, in the midft of which he was intercepted by the hand of death; yet if we advert to the charges which have been brought againft him we fhall find that they are chiefly, if not wholly, to be attributed to a mifreprefentation, or perverfion, of thefe lines. Of thofe who, after Jovius have repeated the accufation, one author informs us, that the verfes which Politiano addreffed to the object of his love were fo tender and impaffioned, that he expired juft as he had finifhed the fecond couplet (*a*). Another relates that in the frenzy of a fever he had eluded the vigilance of his guard, and efcaping from his bed, feized his lute, and began to play upon it under the window of a young Greek of whom he was enamoured, whence he was brought back by his friends, half dead, and expired in his

(*a*) *Varillas, Anecdotes de Florence, lib.* iv. *p.* 196. "La paffion "criminelle qu'il avoit pour un de fes écoliers de haute qualité, ne "pouvant être affouvie, lui donna la fièvre chaude. Dans la violence "de l'accès, il fit une chanfon pour l'objet dont il étoit charmé, fe "leva du lit, prit un luth, & fe mit à la chanter fur un air fi tendre, "& fi pitoyable, qu'il expira en achevant *le fecond couplet;* le même "jour que Charles VIII. paffa les Alpes pour aller à la conquête de "Naples." This author feems equally mifinformed as to the manner and the time of the death of Politiano.

bed ſoon afterwards (*a*). We are next informed, that in a fit of amorous impatience, he occaſioned his own death, by ſtriking his head againſt the wall (*b*): whilſt a fourth author aſſures us, that he was killed by a fall from the ſtairs, as he was ſinging to his lute an elegy which he had compoſed on the death of Lorenzo de' Medici (*c*). The contrariety of theſe relations, not one of which is ſupported by the ſlighteſt pretence to ſerious or authentic teſtimony, is itſelf a ſufficient proof of their futility. Some years after the death of Politiano, the celebrated cardinal Bembo, touched with the untimely fate of a man whom he was induced by a ſimilarity of taſte and character to love and admire, paid a tribute of gratitude and reſpect to his memory in a few elegiac verſes, in which, alluding to the unfiniſhed monody of Politiano, he repreſents him as ſinking under the ſtroke of fate, at the moment when, frantic with

(*a*) " Politien, ce bel eſprit, qui parloit ſi bien Latin, s'appeloit " Ange; mais il s'en falloit beaucoup qu'il en eut la pureté. La " paſſion honteuſe & l'abominable amour dont il brûloit pour un jeune " garçon, qui étoit Grec de naiſſance, à flétri à perpétuité ſa mémoire, " & cauſa ſa mort. Car étant tombé dans un ſiévre chaude, il ſe leva " bruſquement de ſon lit, la nuit, que ſa garde étoit endormie, prit le " luth à la main, & en alla jouer ſous la fenêtre du petit Grec. On " l'en retira à demi mort, & on le remporta dans ſon lit, où il expira " bientôt après," &c. *Ab. Faydit, Remarques ſur Virgile & ſur Homere, &c. Menck, in vitâ Pol. p.* 472.

(*b*) " Vulgo fertur," ſays Voſſius, *De Hiſt. Lat. lib.* iii. *c.* 8. " obiiſſe " Politianum fœdi amoris impatientia capite in parietem illiſo."

Ap. Menck. 470.

(*c*) *Bullart, Acad. des Hommes illuſtres, tom.* i. *p.* 278. " Politien— " tomba d'un eſcalier comme il chantoit ſur ſon luth une élégie, qu'il " avoit compoſée ſur la mort de Laurent de' Medicis."

excefs of grief, he was attempting, by the power of mufic, to revoke the fatal decree which had deprived him of his friend.

Politiani Tumulus.

Duceret extincto cum mors LAURENTE triumphum,
  Lætaque pullatis inveheretur equis,
Refpicit infano ferientem pollice chordas,
  Vifcera fingultu concutiente, virum.
Mirata eft, tenuitque jugum: furit ipfe, pioque
  LAURENTEM cunctos flagitat ore Deos.
Mifcebat precibus lachrymas, lachrymifque dolorem;
  Verba miniftrabat liberiora dolor.
Rifit, & antiquæ non immemor illa querelæ,
  Orphei Tartariæ cum patuere viæ,
Hic etiam infernas tentat refcindere leges,
  Fertque fuas, dixit, in mea jura manus.
Protinus & flentem percuffit dura poetam;
  Rupit & in medio pectora docta fono.
—Heu fic tu raptus, fic te mala fata tulerunt,
  Arbiter Aufoniæ, POLITIANE, lyræ.

Whilft borne in fable ftate, LORENZO'S bier
  The tyrant death, his proudeft triumph, brings,
He mark'd a bard in agony fevere,
  Smite with delirious hand the founding ftrings.
He ftop'd—he gaz'd—the ftorm of paffion raged,
  And prayers with tears were mingled, tears with grief;
For loft LORENZO, war with fate he waged,
  And every god was call'd to bring relief.
The tyrant fmil'd—and mindful of the hour
  When from the fhades his confort Orpheus led,

"Rebellious too wouldſt thou uſurp my power,
"And burſt the chain that binds the captive dead?"
He ſpoke—and ſpeaking launch'd the ſhaft of fate,
And clos'd the lips that glow'd with ſacred fire.
His timeleſs doom 'twas thus POLITIAN met—
POLITIAN, maſter of th'Auſonian lyre.

The fiction of the poet, that Politiano had incurred the reſentment of death by his affection for the object of his paſſion, ſuggeſts nothing more than that his death was occaſioned by ſorrow for the loſs of his friend; but the verſes of Bembo ſeem to have given a further pretext to the enemies of Politiano, who appear to have miſtaken the friend whom he has celebrated, for the object of an amorous paſſion, and to have interpreted theſe lines, ſo honorable to Politiano, in a manner, not only the moſt unfavorable to his character, but the moſt oppoſite to their real purport, and to the occaſion which gave them birth (a).

(a) "Nous ſavons maintenant la véritable mort de Politien, que "le Cardinal Bembe a déguiſée dans l'épitaphe qu'il lui a dreſſée. "Comme il chantoit ſur le luth au deſſus d'un eſcalier une chanſon "qu'il avoit faite autrefois pour une fille qu'il aimoit, lorſqu'il vint "à certains vers fort pathétiques, ſon luth lui tomba des mains, & lui "tomba auſſi de l'eſcalier en bas, & ſe rompit le col." *Pier. de S. Romuald, Abrégé du Tréſor Chronol. tom.* iii. *p.* 262. *ap. Menck. p.* 476. Theſe imputations on the moral character of Politiano have alſo been frequently adverted to by other authors: thus J. C. Scaliger,

"Obſcæno moreris ſed Politiane, furore,"

And in yet groſſer terms by Andrea Dati:

"Et ne te teneam diutius, quot
"Pædicat pueros Politianus."

v. Menagiana. v. iv. *p.* 122.

From much more authentic documents which yet remain reſpecting the death of this eminent ſcholar, there is reaſon to conclude, that it was occaſioned by his grief for the loſs of his great patron, and by the ſubſequent misfortunes of a family with which he was connected by ſo many endearing ties. That he had incurred the public odium in a high degree, on account of his attachment to that family is alſo certain; and the mortification and anxiety which he on this account experienced, might contribute to accelerate the fatal event. It may alſo be obſerved, that his property was plundered during the commotions at Florence, and many of his works deſtroyed or loſt in the general devaſtation of the Laurentian Library; which incident made a deep impreſſion on his mind (*a*). In ſhort, ſuch was the ſudden tide of misfortune that burſt in upon him from all quarters, that it is probable his fortitude was unable to ſupport the ſhock; and, notwithſtanding his induſtry, his accompliſhments, and his unwearied exertions in promoting the progreſs of learning, to ſuch an extreme of miſery was he reduced, that he is too juſtly enumerated by Valerianus amongſt the unhappy children of ſcience, who have afforded examples for his ſingular work, *De infelicitate Literatorum.* But whatever was the immediate occaſion of his death, indiſputable evidence remains, that his misfortunes were not ſo much to

(*a*) This is ſufficiently apparent from the beautiful lines addreſſed to him by Tito Veſpaſiano Strozzi, published in the collection of the poems of the two Strozzi, father and ſon. by Aldo, 1513.

v. Appendix, No. LXXXII.

be attributed to his misconduct or his immorality, as to his steady adherence to the family of the Medici, at a time when the public resentment against them was excited to the highest pitch, and that he breathed his last in the midst of his relatives and friends, having first expressed his desire to be buried in the church of S. Marco, in the habit of the Domenican order. This request was complied with by the piety of his pupil Roberto Ubaldini, one of the monks of the convent of S. Marco, who has left a memorial in his own hand-writing of the circumstances attending his death (*a*). His remains were accordingly deposited in the church of S. Marco, where his memory is preserved in an epitaph very unworthy of his character and genius (*b*).

The various and discordant relations respecting the death of Politiano are happily adverted to by one of his countrymen in the following lines:

(*a*) The indefatigable Abate Mehus, in his life of Ambrogio Traversari, first produced these documents, which the reader will find in the Appendix, *No.* LXXXIII.

(*b*) POLITIANUS.

IN. HOC. TUMULO. JACET.
ANGELUS. UNUM.
QUI. CAPUT. ET. LINGUAS.
RES. NOVA. TRES. HABUIT.
OBIIT. AN. MCCCCLXXXXIV.
SEP. XXIV. ÆTATIS.
XL.

Pamphili Saxi,

De morte Angeli Politiani.

Quo cecidit ſato noſtri decus ANGELUS ævi,
  Gentis & Etruſcæ gloria, ſcire cupis?
Icterici non hunc labes triſtiſſima morbi.
  Febris ad Elyſias vel tulit atra domos;
Non inflans humor pectus, non horrida bilis;
  Mortiferæ peſtis denique nulla lues:
Sed, quoniam rigidas ducebat montibus ornos,
  Frangebat ſcopulos, decipiebat aves,
Mulcebat tigres, ſiſtebat flumina cantu,
  Plectra movens plectro dulcius Iſmario.
Non plus Threicium laudabunt Orphea gentes,
  Calliope dixit dixit: Apollo, Linum;
Jamque tacet noſtrum rupes Heliconia nomen—
  Et ſimul hunc gladio ſuppoſuere necis.
Mors tamen hæc illi vita eſt, nam gloria magna
  Invidiâ Phœbi Calliopeſque mori.

Aſk'ſt thou what cauſe conſign'd to early fate
POLITIAN, glory of the Tuſcan ſtate?
—Not loathſome jaundice tainting all the frame,
Not rapid fever's keen conſuming flame,
Not viſcous rheum that chokes the ſtruggling breath,
Nor any vulgar miniſter of death;
—'Twas that his ſong to liſe and motion charm'd
The mountain oaks, the rock's cold boſom warm'd,
Stay'd the prone flood, the tyger's rage control'd,
With ſweeter ſtrains than Orpheus knew of old.—
" Dimmed is the luſtre of my Grecian fame,"
Exclaim'd Calliope—" No more my name

"Meets even in Helicon its due regard,"
Apollo cry'd, and pierc'd the tuneful bard—
—Yet lives the bard in lasting fame approv'd,
Who Phœbus and the muse to envy mov'd.

The expulsion of Piero de' Medici from Florence, neither contributed to establish the tranquillity, nor to preserve the liberty of the republic. The inhabitants exulted for a time in the notion that they were freed from the tyranny of a family which had held them so long in subjection; but they soon discovered that it was necessary to supply its absence, by increasing the executive power of the state. Twenty citizens were accordingly chosen by the appellation of *Accopiatori*, who were invested, not only with the power of raising money, but also of electing the chief magistrates. This form of government met however with an early and formidable opposition; and to the violence of political dissensions, was soon superadded the madness of religious enthusiasm. The fanatic, Savonarola, having, by pretensions to immediate inspiration from God, and by harangues well calculated to impress the minds of the credulous, formed a powerful party, began to aim at political importance. Adopting the popular side of the question, he directed the whole torrent of his eloquence against the new mode of government; affirming, that he was divinely authorized to declare, that the legislative power ought to be extended to the citizens at large, that he had himself been the ambassador of the Florentines to heaven, and that Christ had condescended to be their peculiar monarch (*a*). The exertions of Savonarola were successful. The newly elected magistrates voluntarily abdicated their offices; and an effort was made to establish the government on a more popular basis, by vesting the legislative power of the state in the *Consiglio Maggiore*, or Council of the Citizens, and in a select body, called the *Consiglio degli Scelti*, or Select Council (*b*). The first of these was to be composed of at least one thousand citizens, who could derive their citizenship by descent, and were upwards of thirty years of age; the latter consisted of eighty members, who were elected half-yearly from the great council, and were upwards of forty years of age (*c*). These regulations, instead of uniting the citizens in one common interest, gave rise to new distinctions. The *Frateschi*, or adherents of Savonarola, who were in general favorable to the liberty of the lower classes of the inhabitants, regarded the friar as the messenger of heaven, as the guide of their temporal and eternal happiness; whilst the *Compagnacci*, or adherents to a more aristocratical government, represented him as a factious impostor; and Alexander VI. seconded their cause by fulminating against him the anathemas of the church. Thus impelled by the most powerful

(*a*) *Nerli, Commentarj de' Fatti civili di Firenze, lib.* iv. *p.* 65. *Aug.* 1728.

(*b*) To this government Machiavelli alludes in his second Decennale:

" E dopo qualche disparer trovaste,
" Nuov' ordine al governo, e furon tante,
" Che il vostro stato popolar fondaste."

(*c*) *Nerli, Comment. lib.* iv. *p.* 66, 67.

motives that can actuate the human mind, the citizens of Florence were seized with a temporary insanity. In the midst of their devotions, they frequently rushed in crowds from the church, to assemble in the public squares, crying *Viva Cristo*, singing hymns, and dancing in circles formed by a citizen and a friar, placed alternately (*a*). The hymns sung on these occasions were chiefly composed by Girolamo Benivieni, who appears to have held a distinguished rank amongst these disciples of fanaticism (*b*). The enemies of Savonarola were as immoderate in their opposition as his partisans were in their attachment. Even the children of the city were trained in opposite factions, and saluted each other with showers of pebbles; in which contests the gravest citizens were sometimes unable to resist the inclination of taking a part (*c*).

(*a*) *Nerli, Comment. lib.* iv. *p.* 75.

(*b*) Some of these compositions are preserved in the general collection of his poems. The following lines, which seem peculiarly adapted for such an occasion, may serve as a specimen:

"Non fu mai'l più bel solazzo,
"Più giocondo nè maggiore,
"Che per zelo, e per amore
"Di Jesu, diventar pazzo.
"Ognun gridi com' io grido,
"Sempre pazzo, pazzo, pazzo."

Op. di Beniv. p. 143.

(*c*) Era talvolta, predicando il frate, in sul bello della predica suonato tamburi, e fatti altri rumori per impedirlo; e molte volte gli fu nel venir da S. Marco a S. Liparata giù per la via del Cocomero, da' fanciulli de' suoi avversarj fatto baie fanciullesche, e da' fanciulli della sua parte era voluto defendere, dimanierachè, secondo il costume de' fanciulli Fiorentini, facevano a' sassi, e così combattendo facevano

Such was the ſtate of Florence in the year 1497, when Piero de' Medici, who had long waited for an opportunity of regaining his authority, entered into a negotiation with ſeveral of his adherents, who undertook, at an appointed hour, to admit him within the walls of the city, with the troops which he had obtained from the Venetian republic, and from his relations of the Orſini family. Piero did not however make his appearance till the opportunity of aſſiſting him was paſt. His abettors were diſcovered; five of them, of the chief families of Florence, were decapitated; the reſt were impriſoned or ſent into baniſhment. The perſons accuſed would have appealed from their judges to the *Conſiglio Grande*, according to a law which had lately been obtained by the influence of the *Frateſchi*; but that party, with Savonarola at their head, were clamorous for the execution of the delinquents, and in ſpite of the law which they had themſelves introduced, effected their purpoſe. Amongſt the five ſufferers was Lorenzo Tornabuoni, the maternal couſin of

infanciullire degli uomini gravi; perchè occorſe a M. Luca Corſini, benchè Dottore aſſai riputato, per favorire la parte del Frate meſcolarſi co' fanciulli a fare a' ſaſſi; e Giovanbatiſta Ridolfi, uno de' più riputati e ſavj cittadini che fuſſero a tempj ſuoi, poſta da canto la gravità, e quel grado che a un tale, e si onorato cittadino ſi conveniva, preſe un giorno l'armi, e in ſu certa occaſione, per eſſere impedita al frate la predica intorno a S. Liparata, uſci dalla caſa de' Lorini vicina a quel tempio, quaſi infuriato, ſenza ſeguito alcuno, con una roncola in iſpalla, gridando, *Viva Criſto;* com' anche gridavano i fanciulli del Frate; e di queſte cosi fatte coſe ne ſeguivano ſpeſſo.

Nerli, Comment. lib. iv. p. 74.

Lorenzo

Lorenzo de' Medici, of whose accomplishments Politiano has left a very favorable account, and to whom he has inscribed his beautiful poem entitled *Ambra* (*a*).

The authority of Savonarola was now at its highest pitch. Instead of a republic, Florence assumed the appearance of a theocracy, of which Savonarola was the prophet, the legislator, and the judge (*b*). He perceived not however that he had arrived at the edge of the precipice, and that by one step further he might incur his destruction. Amongst the methods resorted to by the opponents of Savonarola to weaken his authority, and to counteract his pretensions, they had attacked him with his own weapons, and had excited two Franciscan monks to declaim against him from the pulpit. Savonarola found it necessary to call in the aid of an assistant, for which purpose he selected Fra Domenico da Pescia, a friar of his own convent of S. Marco. The contest was kept up by each of the contending parties with equal fury, till Domenico, transported with zeal for the interests of his master, proposed to confirm the truth of his doctrines by walking through the flames, provided any of his adversaries

(*a*) *v. ante, p.* 140.

(*b*) This fanatical party proceeded so far as even to strike a coin on the occasion, a specimen of which in silver is preserved in the collection of the Earl of Orford, to whose kind communications, since the first edition of this work, I have been greatly indebted. On one side is the Florentine device, or *fleur de lys*, with the motto, SENATUS POPULUSQUE FLORENTINUS; on the other, a cross, with the motto, JESUS CHRISTUS REX NOSTER.

would ſubmit to a ſimilar teſt. By a ſingular coincidence, which is alone ſufficient to demonſtrate to what a degree the paſſions of the people were excited, a Franciſcan friar accepted the challenge, and profeſſed himſelf ready to proceed to the proof. The mode of trial became the ſubject of ſerious deliberation among the chief officers of the republic. Two deputies were elected on behalf of each of the parties, to arrange and ſuperintend this extraordinary conteſt. The combuſtibles were prepared, and over them was erected a ſcaffold, which afforded a commodious paſſage into the midſt of the flames. On the morning of the day appointed, being the ſeventeenth of April 1498, Savonarola and his champion made their appearance, with a numerous proceſſion of eccleſiaſtics, Savonarola himſelf intonating with a tremendous voice, the pſalm, *Exurgat Deus & diſſipentur inimici ejus.* His opponent, Fra Giuliano Rondinelli, attended by a few Franciſcan monks, came ſedately and ſilently to the place of trial; the flames were kindled, and the agitated ſpectators waited with impatience for the moment that ſhould renew the miracle of the Chaldean furnace. Savonarola finding that the Franciſcan was not to be deterred from the enterpriſe either by his vociferations, or by the ſight of the flames, was obliged to have recourſe to another expedient, and inſiſted that his champion Domenico, when he entered the fire, ſhould bear the hoſt along with him. This ſacrilegious propoſal ſhocked the whole aſſembly. The prelates who, together with the ſtate deputies, attended the trial, exclaimed againſt an experiment which might ſubject the catholic faith to too severe a test, and bring a scandal upon their holy religion. Domenico however clung fast to the twig which his patron had thrown out, and positively refused to encounter the flames without this sacred talisman. This expedient, whilst it saved the life of the friar, ruined the credit of Savonarola. On his return to the convent of S. Marco, he was insulted by the populace, who bitterly reproached him, that after having encouraged them to cry *Viva Cristo*, he should impiously propose to commit him to the flames. Savonarola attempted to regain his authority by addressing them from the pulpit, but his enemies were too vigilant; seizing the opportunity of his disgrace, they first attacked the house of Francesco Valori, one of his most powerful partisans, who, together with his wife, was sacrificed to their fury. They then secured Savonarola, with his associate Domenico, and another friar of the same convent, and dragged them to prison. An assembly of ecclesiastics and seculars, directed by an emissary of Alexander VI. sat in judgment upon them. The resolution and eloquence of Savonarola, on his first interview, intimidated his judges, and it was not till recourse was had to the implements of torture—the *ultima theologorum ratio*, that Savonarola betrayed his weakness, and acknowledged the fallacy of his pretensions to supernatural powers. His condemnation instantly followed, and the unhappy priest, with his two attendants, were led to execution in the same place, and with the same apparatus, as had been prepared for the contest; where, being first strangled, their bodies were committed to the flames, and lest the city should be polluted by their remains, their ashes were carefully gathered and thrown into the Arno (*a*).

From the time that Piero de' Medici quitted the city of Florence, he experienced a continual succession of mortifications and disappointments. Flattered, deserted, encouraged, and betrayed, by the different potentates to whom he successively applied for assistance, his prospects became daily more unfavorable, and his return to Florence more improbable. In the mean time a new war had arisen in Italy. Louis XII. the successor of Charles VIII. after having, in conjunction with Ferdinand, king of Spain, accomplished the conquest of Naples, disagreed with him in the partition of the spoil, and Italy became the theatre of their struggle. On this occasion Piero entered into the service of the French, and was present at an engagement that took place between them and the Spaniards, on the banks of the Garigliano, in which they were defeated with great loss. In effecting his escape, Piero attempted to pass the river, but the boat in which he with several other men of rank had embarked, being laden with heavy cannon, sunk in the midst of the current and Piero miserably perished, after having supported an exile of ten years. By his wife Alfonsina, he left a son named Lorenzo, and a daughter Clarice.

Few men have derived from nature greater

(*a*) *Nerli, Comment. lib.* iv. *p.* 78. *Savonarolæ vita, tom.* ii. *sect. additiones. Par.* 1674, *passim.*

advantages, and perhaps never any one enjoyed a better opportunity of improving them, than Piero de' Medici. A robuſt form, a vigorous conſtitution, great perſonal ſtrength and activity, and a ſhare of talents beyond the common lot, were the endowments of his birth. To theſe was added a happy combination of external affairs, reſulting from the opulence and reſpectability of his family, the powerful alliances by which it was ſtrengthened, and the high reputation which his father had ſo deſervedly acquired. But theſe circumſtances, apparently ſo favorable to his ſucceſs, were preciſely the cauſes of his early ruin. Preſuming on his ſecurity, he ſuppoſed that his authority could not be ſhaken, nor his purpoſes defeated. Forgetting the advice ſo often repeated to him by his father, *to remember that he was only a citizen of Florence*, he neglected or diſdained to conciliate the affections of the people. His conduct was the exact reverſe of that which his anceſtors had ſo long and uniformly adopted, and was attended with the effects which might reaſonably be expected from a dereliction of thoſe maxims that had raiſed them to the honorable diſtinction which they had ſo long enjoyed.

A few poetical compoſitions of Piero de' Medici, preſerved in the Laurentian Library, though not hitherto printed, place his character in a more favorable point of view, and exhibit his filial affection and his attachment to his native place in a very intereſting light (*a*). Of this the following ſonnet may be a ſufficient proof:

(*a*) They conſiſt of twenty one ſonnets, which are found at the cloſe

SONETTO.

'Sendo io national, e di te nato,
Muovati patria un poco il tuo figliuolo;
Fingiti almen pietosa del suo duolo,
Essendo in te nudrito ed allevato.
Ha ciaschedun del nascimento il fato,
Come l'uccello il suo garrire e volo;
Scusemi almen in ciò non esser solo,
Benchè solo al mio male io pur sia stato.
E se può nulla in te mio antico affetto,
Per quella pietà ch'in te pur regna
Non mi sia questo dono da te disdetto:
—Ch' almen in cener nella patria io vegna,
A riposar col padre mio diletto.
Che già ti fe sì gloriosa e degna.

SONNET.

Thy offspring, FLORENCE, nurtur'd at thy breast,
Ah let me yet thy kind indulgence prove;
Or if thou own no more a parent's love,
Thy pity sure may sooth my woes to rest.
Fate marks to each his lot: the same behest
That taught the bird through fields of air to rove,
And tunes his song, my vital tissue wove
Of grief and care, with darkest hues imprest.
But if, my fondness scorn'd, my prayer denied,
Death only bring the period of my woes,

of a manuscript volume of the poems of his father Lorenzo, *Plut.* xli. *Cod.* xxxviii. *No.* 3. Besides which Valerianus informs us, that he translated from Plutarch, a treatise on conjugal love; *Valer. de Lit. infel. lib.* ii.; but this performance has probably perished, there being no copy of it now to be found in the Laurentian Library.

Yet one dear hope ſhall mitigate my doom.
—If then my father's name was once thy pride,
Let my cold aſhes find at laſt repoſe,
Safe in the ſhelter of his honored tomb.

Of the many ties by which Lorenzo had endeavoured to ſecure the proſperity of his family amidſt the ſtorms of fortune, and the ebbs and flows of popular opinion, one only now remained—that by which he had connected it with the church; but this alone proved ſufficient for the purpoſe, and ſhows that in this, as in every other inſtance, his conduct was directed by motives of the ſoundeſt policy. After the expulſion of the family from Florence, the cardinal Giovanni de' Medici, finding that the endeavours of himſelf and his brothers to effect their reſtoration were more likely to exaſperate the Florentines than to promote that deſirable event, deſiſted from any further attempts, and determined to wait with patience for a more favorable opportunity. He therefore quitted Italy, and, whilſt that country was the theatre of treachery and war, viſited many parts of France and Germany. His diſlike to Alexander VI. who had entered into an alliance with the Florentines, and was conſequently adverſe to the views of the exiles, was an additional motive for his abſence. After the death of Alexander in the year 1503, he returned to Rome, and found in Julius II. a pontiff more juſt to his talents, and more favorable to his hopes. From this time he began to take an important part in the public affairs of Italy, and was appointed legate in the war carried on by the pope, the Venetians, and the king of Spain, againſt Louis XII. Whilſt inveſted with this dignity, he was taken priſoner by the French, in the famous battle of Ravenna, but ſoon afterwards found an opportunity of effecting his eſcape, not however without great danger and difficulty. In the mean time new diſſenſions had ſprung up at Florence, where the inhabitants, wearied with the fluctuations of a government, whoſe maxims and conduct were changed in the ſame rapid ſucceſſion as its chief magiſtrates, were at length obliged to ſeek for a greater degree of ſtability, by electing a *Gonfaloniere* for life. This authority was intruſted to Piero Soderini, who, with more integrity than ability, exerciſed it for nearly ten years. His contracted views ſuited not with the circumſtances of the times. The principal governments of Italy, with Julius at their head, had leagued together to free that country from the depredations of the French. Fearful of exciting the reſtleſs diſpoſitions of the Florentines, and perhaps of endangering the continuance of his power, the *Gonfaloniere* kept aloof from a cauſe, on the ſucceſs of which depended the tranquillity and independence of Italy. His reluctance to take an active part in the war was conſtrued into a ſecret partiality to the intereſts of the French; and, whilſt it rendered him odious to a great part of the citizens of Florence, drew upon him the reſentment of the allied powers. The victory obtained by the French at Ravenna, dearly purchaſed with the death of the gallant Gaſton de Foix, and the loſs of near ten thouſand men, proved the deſtruction of their enterpriſe; and as the cause of the French declined, that of the Medici gained ground, as well in Florence, as in the rest of Italy. The prudence and moderation of the cardinal enabled him to avail himself of these favorable dispositions without prematurely anticipating the consequences. During his residence at Rome he had paid a marked attention to the citizens of Florence who occasionally resorted there, without making any apparent distinction between those who had espoused and those who had been adverse to the cause of his family; and by his affability and hospitality, as well as by his attention to the interests of those who stood in need of his services, had acquired the good opinion of his fellow-citizens. Having thus prepared the way for his success, he took the earliest opportunity of turning the arms of the allied powers against Florence, for the avowed purpose of removing Piero Soderini from his office, and restoring the Medici to their rights as citizens. On the part of Soderini little resistance was made. The allies having succeeded in an attack upon the town of Prato, and the friends of the Medici having openly opposed the authority of Soderini, the tide of popular favor once more turned; and whilst the *Gonfaloniere* with difficulty effected his escape, the cardinal made his entrance into his native place, accompanied by his younger brother Giuliano, his nephew Lorenzo, and his cousin Giulio de' Medici, the latter of whom had been his constant attendant during all the events of his public life (a).

(a) *Guicciar. Storia d'Italia, lib.* x. *Razzi, vita di Piero Soderini. Padova,* 1737, *p.* 70, *&c.*

The reſtoration of the Medici, although effected by an armed force, was not diſgraced by the bloodſhed of any of the citizens, and a few only of their avowed enemies were ordered to abſent themſelves from Florence. Scarcely was the tranquillity of the place reſtored when intelligence was received of the death of Julius II. The cardinal loſt no time in repairing to Rome, where, on the eleventh day of March 1513, being then only thirty-ſeven years of age, he was elected ſupreme head of the church, and aſſumed the name of Leo X. The high reputation which he had acquired not only counterbalanced any objections ariſing from his youth, but rendered his election a ſubject of general ſatisfaction; and the inhabitants of Florence, without adverting to the conſequences, exulted in an event which ſeemed likely to contribute not leſs to the ſecurity than to the honor of their country. The commencement of his pontificate was diſtinguiſhed by an act of clemency which ſeemed to realize the high expectations that had been formed of it. A general amneſty was publiſhed at Florence, and the baniſhed citizens reſtored to their country. Piero Soderini, who had taken refuge in Turkey, was invited by the pope to Rome, where he reſided many years under his protection, and enjoyed the ſociety and reſpect of the prelates and other men of eminence who frequented the court, being diſtinguiſhed during the remainder of his life by the honorable title of the *Gonfaloniere* (a).

(a) *Razzi, vita di Piero Soderini, p.* 85.

The elevation of Leo X. to the pontificate eſtabliſhed the fortunes of the Medici on a permanent foundation. Naturally munificent to all, Leo was laviſh in beſtowing upon the different branches of his own family the higheſt honors and moſt lucrative preferments of the church. Giulio de' Medici was created archbiſhop of Florence, and was ſoon afterwards admitted into the ſacred college, where he acquired ſuch influence, as to ſecure the pontifical chair, in which he ſucceeded Adrian VI. who filled it only ten months after the death of Leo. The daughters of Lorenzo, Maddalena, the wife of Franceſco Cibo, Conteſſina, the wife of Piero Ridolfi, and Lucrezia, the wife of Giacopo Salviati, gave no leſs than four cardinals to the Romiſh church; there being two of the family of Salviati, and one of each of the others. Profiting by the examples of his predeceſſors, Leo loſt no opportunity of aggrandizing his relations, well knowing that, in order, to ſecure to them any laſting benefit, it was neceſſary that they ſhould be powerful enough to defend themſelves, after his death, from the rapacious aims of ſucceeding pontiffs, who, he was well aware, would probably pay as little regard to his family, as he had himſelf, in ſome inſtances, paid to the friends and families of his predeceſſors (*a*).

(*a*) Notwithſtanding his precautions, Leo could not, on all occaſions, preſerve his ſurviving relations from the inſults and injuries of his ſucceſſors. Paul III. Aleſſandro Farneſe, had in his youth been particularly favored by Lorenzo de' Medici, who, in a letter which yet remains from him to Lanfredini, his envoy at Rome, thus expreſſes

The pontificate of Leo X. is celebrated as one of the most prosperous in the annals of the Romish church. At the time when he assumed the chair, the calamities of Italy were at their highest pitch; that country being the theatre of a war, in which not only all its governments were engaged, but which was rendered yet more sanguinary by the introduction of the French, Helvetian, and Spanish troops. A council, which had long established itself at Pisa, under the influence and protection of the king of France, thwarted the measures, and at times overawed the authority of the holy see; and, in addition to all her other distresses, Italy labored under great apprehensions from the Turks, who constantly threatened a descent on that unhappy country. The address and perseverance of Leo surmounted the difficulties which he had to encounter; and during his pontificate the papal dominions enjoyed a degree of tranquillity superior to any other state in Italy. In his relations with foreign powers, his conduct is no less entitled to approbation. During the contests that took place between those powerful monarchs Charles V. and Francis I. he distinguished himself by his moderation, his

himself respecting him: "Vi lo raccommandiate quanto farei Pietro "mio figlio; e vi prego lo introduciate e lo raccommandiate caldissi-"mamente a N. S. (il papa) che non potreste farmi maggior piacere," &c. Yet, when the same Alessandro had arrived at the pontificate, he so far forgot or disregarded his early obligations, as forcibly to dispossess Lucrezia, the daughter of his benefactor, then in a very advanced age, of her residence in Rome, to make way for one of his nephews. This incident is related by Varchi with proper indignation.

Storia Fiorentina, lib. xvi. *p.* 666.

vigilance, and his political addrefs; on which account he is juftly celebrated by an eminent hiftorian of our own country, as "the only prince of the age "who obferved the motions of the two contending "monarchs with a prudent attention, or who dif- "covered a proper folicitude for the public "fafety (*a*).

Leo was not however aware, that whilft he was compofing the troubles which the ambition of his neighbours, or the mifconduct of his predeceffors, had occafioned, he was exciting a ftill more formidable adverfary, that was deftined, by a flow but certain progrefs, to fap the foundations of the papal power, and to alienate that fpiritual allegiance which the Chriftian world had kept inviolate for fo many centuries. Under the control of Leo, the riches that flowed from every part of Europe to Rome, as to the heart of the ecclefiaftical fyftem, were again poured out through a thoufand channels, till the fources became inadequate to the expenditure. To fupply this deficiency, he availed himfelf of various expedients, which, whilft they effected for a time the intended purpofe, roufed the attention of the people to the enormities and abufes of the church, and in fome meafure drew afide that facred veil, which, in fhrouding her from the prying eyes of the vulgar, has always been her fafeft prefervative. The open fale of difpenfations and indulgences for the moft enormous and difgraceful crimes was too flagrant not to attract general notice. Encouraged by the diffatisfaction which was thus excited,

(*a*) *Robertfon. Hift. of Cha.* V. *book* i.

a daring reformer arofe, and, equally regardlefs of the threats of fecular power, and the denunciations of the Roman fee, ventured to oppofe the opinion of an individual to the infallible determinations of the church. At this critical juncture, Luther found that fupport which he might in vain have fought at any other period, and an inroad was made into the fanctuary, which has ever fince been widening, and will probably continue to widen, till the mighty fabric, the work of fo many ages, fhall be laid in ruins (*a*). It is not however fo much for the tenets of their religious creed, as for the principles upon which they founded their diffent, that the reformers are entitled to the thanks of pofterity. That right of private judgment which they claimed for themfelves, they could not refufe to others; and by a mode of reafoning as fimple as it was decifive, mankind arrived at the knowledge of one of thofe great truths which form the bafis of human happinefs. It appeared that the denunciations of the church were as ineffectual to condemn, as its abfolution was to exculpate; and, inftead of an intercourfe between the man and his prieft, an

(*a*) The caufes and progrefs of the reformation are traced by Dr. Robertfon, in his Hiftory of Charles the V. book ii. in a manner that would difpenfe with any further elucidation, even if it were more intimately connected with my fubject. This celebrated hiftorian has taken occafion to refute an affertion made by Guicciardini, and, after him, by Fr. Paolo, that Leo X. beftowed the profits arifing from the fale of indulgences in Saxony, upon his fifter Maddalena, the wife of Francefco Cibo. *Guicciar. lib.* iii. *Sarpi, Storia del Concil. Trident. cap.* i. *Robertfon, Hift. Cha.* V. *book* ii. *in note.*

intercourſe took place between his conſcience and his God.

But turning from the advantages which the world has derived from the errors of Leo X. we may be allowed for a moment to inquire what it owes to his talents and to his virtues. No ſooner was he raiſed to the papal chair, than Rome aſſumed once more its ancient character, and became the ſeat of genius, magnificence, letters, and arts. One of the firſts acts of his pontificate was to invite to his court two of the moſt elegant Latin ſcholars that modern times have produced, Piero Bembo and Giacopo Sadoleti; on each of whom he conferred the rank of cardinal. The moſt celebrated profeſſors of literature from every part of Europe were induced by liberal penſions to fix their reſidence at Rome, where a permanent eſtabliſhment was formed for the ſtudy of the Greek tongue, under the direction of Giovanni Laſcar. The affability, the munificence the judgment, and the taſte of this ſplendid pontiff are celebrated by a conſiderable number of learned men, who witneſſed his accompliſhments, or partook of his bounty. Succeeding times have been equally diſpoſed to do juſtice to ſo eminent a patron of letters and have conſidered the age of Leo X. as rivalling that of Auguſtus. Leo has not however eſcaped the reproach of having been too laviſh of his favors to authors of inferior talents, and of having expended in pompous ſpectacles and theatrical repreſentations that wealth which ought to have been devoted to better purpoſes (*a*). But ſhall we condemn his con-

(*a*) *Tirab. Storia della Let. Ital.* v. viii. *par.* i. *p.* 19. *Andres, orig. e progreſſi d'ogni Letteratura,* v. i. *p.* 380.

duct, if those who had no claims on his justice, were the objects of his bounty? or may it not be doubted whether this disposition was not more favorable to the promotion of letters, than a course of conduct more discriminating and severe? Whatever kindness he might show to those who endeavoured to amuse his leisure by their levity, their singularity, or their buffoonery, no instances can be produced of his having rewarded them by such distinguished favors as he constantly bestowed on real merit; and whilst we discover amongst those who shared his friendship and partook of his highest bounty, the names of Bembo, Vida, Ariosto, Sadoleti, Casa and Flaminio, we may readily excuse the effects of that superabundant kindness which rather marked the excess of his liberality than the imperfection of his judgment.

In the attention paid by Leo X. to the collecting and preserving ancient manuscripts, and other memorials of literature, he emulated the example of his father, and by his perseverance and liberality at length succeeded in restoring to its former splendor the celebrated library, which, on the expulsion of Piero de' Medici, had become a prey to the fury or the cupidity of the populace. Such of these valuable articles as had escaped the sacrilegious hands of the plunderers, had been seized upon for the use of the Florentine state; but in the year 1496, the public treasury being exhausted, and the city reduced to great extremity, the magistrates were under the necessity of selling them to the monks of the fraternity of S. Marco, for the sum of three thousand

ducats

ducats (*a*). Whilst these valuable works were deposited at the convent, they experienced a less public, but perhaps a more destructive calamity, many of them having been distributed as presents by Savonarola, the principal of the monastery, to the cardinals, and other eminent men, by whose favor he sought to shelter himself from the resentment of the pope (*b*). When the Florentines destroyed their golden calf, and the wretched priest expiated by his death his folly and his crimes, apprehensions were entertained that the library of the Medici would once more be exposed to the rapacity of the people; but some of the youth of the noblest families of Florence, with a laudable zeal for the preservation of this monument of their national glory, associated themselves together, and undertook to guard it till the frenzy of the populace had again subsided (*c*). After the death of Savonarola, the fraternity having fallen into discredit, and being in their turn obliged to sell the library, it was purchased from them by Leo X. then cardinal de' Medici, and in the year 1508

(*a*) Eodem anno libri heredem olim Petri Medicis a conventu nostro trium millium Ducatorum pretio comparati, quos supra memoravimus in horrendo casu nostro, ex jusso dominationis Florentinæ in palatium comportatos, & per inventarium resignatos, mense Octobri, in conventum hunc S. Marci revecti sunt, novis stipulationibus factis, &c. *Maricani annal. part.* i. *ap. Mehus. Ambr. Travers. vita. p.* 72, *in praef.*

(*b*) Etiam de' libri di Piero de' Medici, i quali nella Libreria di S. Marco in buona parte si ridussono, fece parte a cardinali, per cui mezzo delle scomuniche e altri processi contragli si difendeva. Tanta forza avevano in Firenze le sue arti. *MS. di Piero Parenti. cit. da Tirab. Storia della Let. Ital. v.* vi. *part.* i. *p.* 106.

(*c*) *Tirab. ut sup.*

was removed by him to Rome, where it continued during his life, and received conſtant additions of the moſt rare and valuable manuſcripts. From Leo it devolved to his couſin Clement VII. who, upon his elevation to the pontificate, again transferred it to Florence, and by a bull, which bears date the fifteenth day of December 1532, provided for its future ſecurity. Not ſatisfied however with this precaution, he meditated a more ſubſtantial defence, and, with a munificence which confers honor on his pontificate, engaged Michelagnolo to form the deſign of the ſplendid edifice in which this library is now depoſited, which was afterwards finiſhed under the directions of the ſame artiſt, by his friend and ſcholar Vaſari.

Giuliano de' Medici, the third ſon of Lorenzo, was more diſtinguiſhed by his attention to the cauſe of literature, and by his mild and affable diſpoſition, than by his talents for political affairs. On the return of the family to Florence, he had been intruſted by his brother, then the cardinal de' Medici, with the direction of the Florentine ſtate; but it ſoon appeared that he had not ſufficient energy to control the jarring diſpoſitions of the Florentines. He therefore reſigned his authority to Lorenzo, the ſon of his brother Piero de' Medici, and on the elevation of Leo X. took up his reſidence at Rome; where under the title of captain general of the church, he held the chief command of the papal troops. By the favor of the pope he ſoon afterwards obtained extenſive poſſeſſions in Lombardy, and having intermarried with Filiberta, ſiſter of Charles duke of Savoy, and a defcendant of the houfe of Bourbon, was honored by Francis I. with the title of duke of Nemours. Of his gratitude, an inftance is recorded which it would be unjuft to his memory to omit. During his exile from Florence, he had found an hofpitable afylum with Guid' ubaldo di Montefeltro duke of Urbino, who on his death left his dominions to his adopted fon, Francefco Maria delle Rovere. Incited by the entreaties of his nephew Lorenzo, Leo X. formed the defign of depriving Rovere of his poffeffions, under the ufual pretext of their having efcheated to the church for want of legitimate heirs, and of vefting them in Lorenzo, with the title of duke of Urbino; but the reprefentations of Giuliano prevented for a time the execution of his purpofe; and it was not till after his death that Leo difgraced his pontificate by this fignal inftance of ecclefiaftical rapacity. If we may give credit to Ammirato, Giuliano at one time entertained the ambitious hope of obtaining the crown of Naples (*a*); but if fuch a defign was in contemplation, it is probable that he was incited by his more enterprifing and ambitious brother, who perhaps fought to revive the claims of the papal fee upon a kingdom, to the government of which Giuliano could, in his own right, advance no pretenfions. As a patron of learning, he fupported the ancient dignity of his family. He is introduced to great advantage in the celebrated dialogue of Bembo on the Italian tongue (*b*), and in the yet more diftinguifhed work

(*a*) *Ammir. Ift. Fior. lib.* xxix. *vol.* iii. *p.* 315.

(*b*) PROSE DI M. PIETRO BEMBO, NELLE QUALI SI RACIONA DELLA

of Castiglione, entitled *Il libro dell Cortegiano* (*a*). In the Laurentian Library several of his sonnets are yet preserved (*b*); and some specimens of his composition are adduced by Crescimbeni, which, if they display not any extraordinary spirit of poetry, sufficiently prove, that, to a correct judgment, he united an elegant taste (*c*).

Naturally of an infirm constitution, Giuliano did not long enjoy his honors. Finding his health on the decline, he removed to the monastery at Fiesole,

VOLGAR LINGUA; dedicated to the cardinal Giulio de' Medici, afterwards Clement VII. first printed at Venice by *Giovan Tacuino, nel mese di Settembre del* MDXXV. *cum privilegio di Papa Clemente, &c.*

(*a*) *In Venetia nelle case d'Aldo Romano, e d'Andrea d'Asola suo suocero, nell' anno* MDXXVIII. *del mese d'Aprile, in fol.* This work has frequently been reprinted under the more concise title of *Il Cortegiano*, by which it is also cited in the *Biblioteca Italiana* of Fontanini; but Apostolo Zeno, pleased with every opportunity of reproving the author whom he has undertaken to comment upon, shrewdly observes, in his notes on that work, "Altro è il dire semplicemente, "*il Cortegiano*, come il Fontanini vorrebbe; e altro, *Il libro del Cortegiano*, come il Castiglione ha voluto dire, e lo ha detto: la prima "maniera indicherebbe vi voler descrivere *il Cortegiano* per quello "che è; e la seconda dinota di volergli insegnare qual esser deve."

Zeno, in not. alla Bib. Ital. di. Fontan. v. ii. *p.* 353.

(*b*) PLUT. xlvi. *Cod.* xxv. *No.* 3. Another copy of his poems remains in MS. in the Strozzi Library at Florence.

(*c*) *Crescimb. Comment. v.* iii. *p.* 338. Where the author confounds Giuliano, the son of Lorenzo de' Medici, with Giuliano his brother, who lost his life in the conspiracy of the Pazzi: and even cites the authority of Politiano, "Che i versi volgari di lui erano a maraviglia "gravi, e pieni di nobili sentimenti," as referring to the writings of the younger Giuliano, although such opinion was expressed by Politiano respecting the works of Giuliano the brother of Lorenzo, before Giuliano his son was born.

in the expectation of deriving advantage from his native air; but his hopes were frustrated, and he died there in the month of March 1516, not having then fully completed his thirty-seventh year. His death was sincerely lamented by a great majority of the citizens of Florence, whose favor he had conciliated in a high degree by his affability, moderation, and inviolable regard to his promises (*a*). His tomb, in the sacristy of the church of S. Lorenzo at Florence, one of the most successful efforts of the genius of Michelagnolo, may compensate him for the want

(*a*) Ariosto has addressed a beautiful canzone to Filiberta of Savoy, the widow of Giuliano, commencing, *Anima eletta, che nel mondo folle*, in which the shade of the departed husband apostrophizes his surviving wife. The following lines, referring to Lorenzo the Magnificent, may serve to show the high veneration in which the poet held his memory:

" Questo sopra ogni lume in te risplende,
" Se ben quel tempo che si ratto corse,
" Tenesti di *Nemorse*
" Meco scettro ducal di là da' monti;
" Se ben tua bella mano freno torse,
" Al paese gentil che Appenin fende,
" E l'alpe e il mar difende:
" Nè tanto val, che a questo pregio monti,
" Che'l sacro onor de l'erudite fronti,
" Quel Tosco e'n terra e'n cielo amato LAURO,
" Socer ti fu, le cui mediche fronde
" Spesso a le piaghe, donde
" Italia morì poi, furo ristauro:
" Che fece all' Indo e al Mauro,
" Sentir l'odor de' suoi rami soavi;
" Onde pendean le chiavi
" Che tenean chiuso il tempio delle guerre,
" Che poi fu aperto, E NON È PIU CHI'L SERRE."

of that higher degree of reputation which he might have acquired in a longer life. His ſtatue, ſeated, and in a Roman military habit, may be conſidered rather as characteriſtic of his office, as general of the church, than of his exploits. The figures which recline on each ſide of the ſarcophagus, and are intended to repreſent day and night, have been the admiration of ſucceeding artiſts; but their allegorical purport may admit of a latitude of interpretation. Had the conqueſts of Giuliano rivalled thoſe of Alexander the Great, we might have conjectured, with Vaſari, that the artiſt meant to expreſs the extent of his glory, limited only by the confines of the earth (*a*); but the hyperbole would be too extravagant; and the judicious ſpectator will perhaps rather regard them as emblematical of the conſtant change of ſublunary affairs, and the brevity of human life.

By his wife Filiberta of Savoy, Giuliano de' Medici left no children; but, before his marriage, he had a natural ſon, who became an acknowledged branch of the family of the Medici, and, like the reſt of his kindred, acquired, within the limits of a ſhort life, a conſiderable ſhare of reputation. This was the celebrated Ippolito de' Medici, who, dignified with the rank of cardinal, and poſſeſſed, by the partiality of Clement VII. of an immenſe revenue, was at once the patron, the companion, and the rival of all the poets, the muſicians, and the wits of his time. Without territories, and without ſubjects, Ippolito maintained at Bologna a court far more ſplendid

(*a*) *Vaſari, vita di M. A. Buonarroti.*

than that of any Italian potentate. His aſſociates and attendants, all of whom could boaſt of ſome peculiar merit or diſtinction which had entitled them to his notice, generally formed a body of about three hundred perſons. Shocked at his profuſion, which only the revenues of the church were competent to ſupply, Clement VII. is ſaid to have engaged the *maeſtro di caſa* of Ippolito to remonſtrate with him on his conduct, and to requeſt that he would diſmiſs ſome of his attendants as unneceſſary to him. " No," replied Ippolito, " I do not retain " them in my court becauſe I have occaſion for " their ſervices, but becauſe they have occaſion for " mine (*a*)." His tranſlation of the ſecond book of the Æneid into Italian blank verſe is conſidered as one of the happieſt efforts of the language, and has frequently been reprinted (*b*). Amongſt the collections of Italian poetry may alſo be found ſome pieces of his own compoſition, which do credit to his talents (*c*).

(*a*) *Tirab. Storia della Let. Ital. v.* vii. *par.* i. *p.* 23.

(*b*) The firſt edition is that of Rome, *apud Antonium Bladum*, 1538, without the name of the author, who, at the foot of his dedication to a lady, whom he deſignates only by the appellation of *Illuſtriſſima Signora*, aſſumes the title of *Il cavaliero Errante*. The ſecond edition, now before me, is entitled, IL SECONDO DI VERGILIO *in lingua volgare volto da* HIPPOLITO DE' MEDICI *cardinale*. At the cloſe we read, *In citta di Caſtello per Antonio Mazochi Cremoneſe, & Nicolo de Guccii da Corna, ad inſtantia di M. Giovan Gallo, Dottor de leggi da Caſtello nel giorno* 20 *de Luglio* 1539. Several ſubſequent editions have appeared, as well ſeparately, as united with the other books of the Æneid, tranſlated by different perſons.

(*c*) Some of them are cited by Creſcimbeni, *della volgar poesia, lib.* ii. *vol.* ii. *p.* 368.

On the voluntary resignation of Giuliano de Medici of the direction of the Florentine state, that important trust had been confided by Leo X. to his nephew Lorenzo, who, with the assistance of the cardinal Giulio de' Medici, directed the helm of government according to the will of the pope; but the honor of holding the chief rank in the republic, although it had gratified the just ambition of his illustrious grandfather, was inadequate to the pretensions of Lorenzo; and the family of Rovere, after a vigorons defence, in which Lorenzo received a wound which had nearly proved mortal, was obliged to relinquish to him the sovereignty of Urbino, of which he received from the pope the ducal investiture in the year 1516 (*a*). After the death of his uncle Giuliano, he was appointed captain general of the papal troops, but his reputation for military skill scarcely stands higher than that of his predecessor. In the year 1518, he married Magdeleine de Boulogne, of the royal house of France, and the sole fruit of this union was Catherine de' Medici, afterwards the queen of Henry II. (*b*). The birth of the daughter cost the mother her life, and Lorenzo survived her only a few days, having, if we may credit Ammirato, fallen a victim to that loathsome disorder, the peculiar scourge of licentiousness, which had then recently commenced its ravages in

(*a*) *Nerli, Comment. lib.* vi. *p.* 130.

(*b*) Si, comme les poëtes l'ont dit, l'ancienne Hecube, avant de mettre Paris au monde, était troublée par des songes effrayans; quels noirs fantômes devaient agiter les nuits de Magdeleine de la Tour, enceinte de Catherine de Medicis? *Tenh. Mém. Gén. liv.* xx. *p.* 5.

Europe (*a*). His tomb, of the ſculpture of Michel-agnolo, is found amongſt the ſplendid monuments

(*a*) *Ammir. Iſt. Fior. lib.* xxix. *v.* ii. *p.* 335. This diſorder, which was firſt known in Italy about the year 1495, was not in its commencement ſuppoſed to be the reſult of ſexual intercourſe, but was attributed to the impure ſtate of the air, to the ſimple touch or breath of a diſordered perſon, or even to the uſe of an infected knife. Hence for a conſiderable time no diſcredit attached to the patient; and the authors of that period attribute without heſitation the death of many eminent perſons, as well eccleſiaſtical as ſecular, to this complaint. In the Laurentian Library (*Plut.* lxxii. *cod.* 38.) is a MS. entitled *Saphati Phyſici de morbo Gallico liber*, dedicated by the author Giuliano Tanio, of Prato, to Leo. X. in which he thus adverts to a learned profeſſor who was probably one of the firſt victims of this diſeaſe: "Nos anno "MCCCCXCV. extrema æſtate, egregium utriuſque juris doctorem Domi-"num Philippum Decium, Papienſem, in Florentino Gymnaſio Prati, "Piſis tunc rebellibus, publice legentem, hac labe affectum ipſi con-"ſpeximus." From the ſame author we learn that the diſorder was ſuppoſed to have originated in a long continuance of hot and moiſt weather, which occurred in the ſame year: "Ex magna pluvia ſimilis "labes apparuit, ex quibus arguunt hunc noſtræ ætatis morbum ex ſimili "cauſa ortum eſſe, ex calida ſcilicet, humidaque intemperie, quia ex "pluvia ſcilicet anni MCCCCLXXXXV. nonis Decembris emiſſa, (qua "Roma facta eſt navigabilis, ac tota fere Italia inundationes paſſa eſt." &c. Theſe authorities are greatly ſtrengthened by that of the illuſtrious Fracaſtoro, who was not only the beſt Latin poet, but the moſt eminent phyſician of his age, and who, in his *Syphilis*, accounts for the diſorder from ſimilar cauſes. After adverting to the opinion that it had been brought into Europe from the weſtern world, then lately diſcovered, he adds,

"At vero, ſi rite fidem obſervata merentur
"Non ita cenſendum: nec certe credere par eſt
"Eſſe peregrinam nobis, tranſque æquora vectam
"Contagem: quoniam in primis oſtendere multos
"Poſſumus, attactu qui nullius, hanc tamen ipſam
"Sponte ſua ſenſere luem, primique tulere.
"Præterea, & tantum terrarum tempore parvo,
"Contages non una ſimul potuiſſet obire."

of his family in the church of S. Lorenzo at Florence. He appears seated, in the attitude of deep meditation. At his feet recline two emblematical figures, the rivals of those which adorn the tomb of Giuliano,

It is remarkable also, that throughout the whole poem he has not considered this disease as the peculiar result of licentious intercourse, on which account it is perfectly unexceptionable in point of decorum. Even the shepherd *Syphilus*, introduced as an instance of its effects, is represented as having derived it from the resentment, not of Venus, but of Phœbus, excited by the adoration paid by the shepherds to Alcithous, and the neglect of his own altars; or, in other words, to the too fervid state of the atmosphere. Had the disorder in its origin been accompanied by the idea of disgrace or criminality, which attends it in modern times, the author of this poem would scarcely have denominated it,

" Infanda lues, quam nostra videtis
" Corpora depasci, quam nulli aut denique pauci
" Vitamus."

The poem of Fracastoro was first published in the year 1530; but an Italian poem on the same subject, by Niccolo Campana of Siena, was printed at that place in 1519, and again at Venice in 1537, entitled *Lamento di quel Tribulato di Strascino Campana Senese sopra el male incognito el quale tratta de la patientia & impatientia.* The style of this poem is extremely gross and ludicrous; and the author in the supposed excess of his sufferings, indulges himself in the most extravagant and profane ideas, as to the nature and origin of the complaint. At one time he supposes it to be the same disorder as that which God permitted Satan to inflict upon Job:

" Allor Sathan con tal mal pien di vitio,
" Diede a Jobbe amarissimo supplitio."

Again he asserts it to be the complaint of Simon the leper:

" Quando Cristo guari Simon lebbroso,
" Era di questo mal pessimo iniquo."

But on no occasion does he ascribe the rise of the disorder to the cause which, from the nature of his poem, might have been expected. I shall only observe, that the use of the grand mineral specific is expressly pointed out, in both these poems, as the only certain remedy.

and which are intended to reprefent morning and evening. Ariofto has alfo celebrated his memory in fome of his moft beautiful verfes (*a*). Like the Egyptians, who embalm a putrid carcafe with the richeft odors, the artift and the poet too often lavifh their divine incenfe on the moft undeferving of mankind.

Prior to his marriage with Magdeleine of Boulogne, the duke of Urbino had an illegitimate fon, named Aleffandro, in whofe perfon was confummated the deftruction of the liberties of Florence. It was commonly fuppofed that Aleffandro was the offspring of the duke by an African flave, at the time when he, with the reft of the family, were reftored to Florence; and this opinion received confirmation from his thick lips, crifped hair, and dark complexion. But it is yet more probable that he was the fon of Clement VII. Such at leaft was the information given to the hiftorian Ammirato by the grand duke Cofmo I. at the time when he read to him the memoirs which he had prepared refpecting his family; and the predilection of the pontiff for this equivocal defcendant of the houfe of Medici adds probability to the report (*b*). But whatever was his origin, the circumftances of the times, and the ambition of thofe who protected his infancy, equally

(*a*) Such at leaft I conjecture to be the purport of his poem, which commences,

"Nella ftagion che'l bel tempo rimena,
"Di mia man pofi un ramufcel di Lauro."

Rime dell' Ariofto, p. 25. *ap. Giolito,* 1557.

(*b*) *Ammir. Ift. Fior. lib.* xxx. *v.* iii. *p.* 335.

dispensed with the disadvantages of his birth, and his want of inherent merit. On failure of the legitimate branch of Cosmo de' Medici, usually styled the father of his country, derived through Lorenzo the Magnificent, Alessandro and Ippolito became necessary implements in the hands of Clement VII. to prevent the credit and authority of the family from passing to the collateral branch derived from Lorenzo the brother of Cosmo, which had gradually risen to great distinction in the state, and of which it will now be necessary to give a brief account.

Pierfrancesco de' Medici, the son of the elder Lorenzo, to whom we have before had occasion to advert (*a*), died in the year 1459, having bequeathed his immense possessions, obtained from his share in the profits acquired by the extensive traffic of the family, to his two sons, Lorenzo and Giovanni. Following the example of their father, and emulous rather of wealth than of honors, the sons of Pierfrancesco had for several years confined themselves to the limits of a private condition, although they had occasionally filled the chief offices of the republic, in common with other respectable citizens. On the expulsion of Piero, the son of Lorenzo the Magnificent, from Florence, in the year 1494, they endeavoured to avail themselves of his misconduct, and of the importance which they had gradually acquired, to aspire to the chief direction of the republic, and divesting themselves of the invidious name of Medici, assumed that of *Popolani*. The restoration of the descendants of Lorenzo the

(*a*) *v. ante, vol.* I. *p.* 138.

Magnificent to Florence, the elevation of his second ſon to the pontificate, and the ſeries of proſperity enjoyed by the family under his auſpices, and under thoſe of Clement VII. had repreſſed their ambition or fruſtrated their hopes; and Lorenzo and Giovanni, the ſons of Pierfranceſco, paſſed through life in a ſubordinate rank, the former of them leaving at his death a ſon, named Pierfranceſco, and the latter a ſon Giovanni, to inherit their immenſe wealth, and perpetuate the hereditary rivalſhip of the two families (a). But whilſt the deſcendants of Coſmo, the father of his country, exiſted only in females, or in a ſpurious offspring, thoſe of his brother Lorenzo continued in a legitimate ſucceſſion of males, and were invigorated with talents the moſt formidable to their rivals, and the moſt flattering to their own hopes. Adopting from his youth a military life, Giovanni de' Medici became one of the moſt celebrated commanders that Italy had ever produced. By the appellation of captain of the *bande nere*, his name carried terror amongſt his enemies. His courage was of the moſt ferocious kind. Equally inſenſible to pity and to danger, his opponents denominated him *Il gran Diavolo* (a). As the fervor of youth ſubſided, the talents of the commander began to

(*a*) Furono i due fratelli richiſſimi—di meglio che centocinquanta mila ſcudi, e poſſedevano di beni ſtabili, fra gli altri la caſa grande di Firenze, il palazzo di Fieſole, di Trebbio, di Caffagiolo, e di Caſtello. *Ald. Manucc. vita di Coſmo, v. i. p.* 72.

(*b*) *Varchi, Storia Fior. lib.* ii. *p.* 25. *Ed. Leyden.* The mother of Giovanni was Caterina Sforza, the widow of Girolamo Riario, who, after the death of her husband, had married the elder Giovanni de' Medici, *v. ante, p.* 168.

be developed; but in the midſt of his honors his career was terminated by a cannon ball, in the twenty-eighth year of his age. By his wife Maria Salviati, the offspring of Lucrezia, one of the daughters of Lorenzo the Magnificent, he left a ſon, Coſmo de' Medici, who, after the death of Aleſſandro, obtained the permanent ſovereignty of Tuſcany, and was the firſt who aſſumed the title of Grand Duke.

The younger Pierfranceſco left alſo a ſon, named Lorenzo, who, as well on account of his diminutive perſon, as to diſtinguiſh him from others of his kindred of the ſame name, was uſually denominated *Lorenzino*, and who was deſtined with his own hand to terminate the conteſt between the two families. Though ſmall of ſtature, Lorenzino was active and well proportioned. His complexion was dark, his countenance ſerious: when he ſmiled it ſeemed to be by conſtraint. His mother, who was of the powerful family of Soderini, had carefully attended to his education; and as his capacity was uncommonly quick, he made an early proficiency in polite letters. His elegant comedy entitled *Aridoſio*, ſtill ranks with thoſe works which are ſelected as models of the Italian language (*a*). Enterpriſing, reſtleſs,

(*a*) Creſcimbeni informs us, that this comedy was written by Lorenzino in *verſi volgari*, and printed at Bologna in 1548; and that it is alſo found in proſe, printed at Lucca in the ſame year, and reprinted at Florence in 1595. *Della volgar Poesia, vol.* v. *p.* 141. Creſcimbeni is however miſtaken; the edition of Bologna 1548 is now before me, and is wholly written in proſe. That of Florence, 1595, is enumerated by the academicians *Della Cruſca*, as one of the *Teſti di Lingua*.

fond of commotions, and full of the examples of antiquity, he had addicted himself when young to the society of Filippo Strozzi, who to an ardent love of liberty united an avowed contempt for all the political and religious institutions of his time. The talents and accomplishments of Lorenzino recommended him to Clement VII. under whose countenance he resided for some time at the Roman court; but an extravagant adventure deprived him of the favor of the pope, and compelled him to quit the city. It appeared one morning, that, during the preceding night, the statues in the arch of Constantine, and in other parts of the city, had been broken and defaced, a circumstance which so exasperated the pope, that he issued positive orders that whoever had committed the outrage, except it should appear to be the cardinal Ippolito de' Medici, should be immediately hanged (*a*). This exception indeed strongly implies that the cardinal was not free from suspicion; but whoever was the delinquent, Lorenzino bore the whole odium of the affair, and it required all the influence that Ippolito possessed with the pope to rescue his kinsman from the denunciations issued against the offender. Lorenzino gladly took the earliest opportunity of quitting the city, and retreated to his native place, where, transferring his resentment from the dead to the living,

(*a*) It has been suggested to me by very respectable authority that the heads of these statues and bas-rilievos were more probably stolen by Lorenzino for the sake of their beauty. They are even said to be yet extant in the museum at Florence.

he ſoon afterwards acted a principal part in a much more important tranſaction (*a*).

To the energy and activity of Lorenzino, and the courage of Giovanni de' Medici, Clément VII. could only oppoſe the diſſipation and inexperience of Ippolito and Aleſſandro; but the turbulent diſpoſition of the Florentines ſeconded his views, and the premature death of Giovanni, whilſt it expoſed his dominions to the ravages of the German troops, relieved him from his apprehenſions of his moſt dangerous rival (*b*). Having prevailed on the emperor and the king of France to concur in his deſign, he ſeized the opportunity afforded him by the civil diſſenſions of the Florentines, and, in the year 1532, compelled them to place at the head of the government Aleſſandro de' Medici, with the title of *Doge* of the Florentine republic (*c*). The authority of

(*a*) *Varchi, Storia Fior. lib.* xv. *p.* 618.

(*b*) The authority of the ſenator Nerli leaves no room for doubt on this head. "Non poteva quella morte ſeguire in tempo, ch' ella deſſe "più univerſale diſpiacere, nè anco in tempo, che il papa più la "ſtimaſſe, perchè s'ella ſeguiva in altri tempi, che ſua Santità non "aveſſe avuto si urgente pericolo ſopra il capo, non gli arrecava per "avventura diſpiacere alcuno, rimanendo ſicuro, e libero della geloſia "grande, ch' egli aveva del nome ſolamente del Sig. Giovanni, riſpetto "agl' intereſſi, e alla proprietà d'Aleſſandro, e d'Ippolito, i quali de- "ſiderava che fuſſero quelli, che poſſedeſſero lo ſtato, le facultà, e la "grandezza di caſa Medici."

Nerli, Comment. lib. vii. *p.* 145.

(*c*) Aleſſandro is generally ſtyled by the Italian authors the *firſt duke of Florence*, but in this they are not ſtrictly accurate. His title of *duke* was derived from Città, or Cività di Penna, and had been aſſumed by him ſeveral years before he obtained the direction of the Florentine ſtate. It muſt alſo be obſerved, that Aleſſandro did not

Aleſſandro

Aleſſandro was ſoon afterwards ſtrengthened by his marriage with Margaretta of Auſtria, a natural daughter of the emperor Charles V. The cardinal Ippolito, jealous of his ſucceſs, had attempted to pre-occupy the government; diſappointed in his hopes, and diſguſted with his eccleſiaſtical trappings, which ill ſuited the rapidity of his motions, and the vivacity of his character, he united his efforts with thoſe of Filippo Strozzi, who had married Clarice, the ſiſter of Lorenzo duke of Urbino, to deprive Aleſſandro of his new dignity; but before the arrangement could be made for the meditated attack, Ippolito ſuddenly died of poiſon, adminiſtered to him by one of his domeſtics (*b*), leaving his competitor in the undiſturbed poſſeſſion of his newly acquired power.

The period however now approached which was to transfer the dominion of Florence from the

as Robertſon conceives, " enjoy the ſame abſolute dominion as his " family have retained to the preſent times," *Hiſt. Cha.* V. *book* v. he being only declared chief or prince of the republic, and his authority being in ſome meaſure counteracted or reſtrained by two councils choſen from the citizens, for life, one of which conſiſted of forty-eight, and the other of two hundred members. *Varchi, Storia Fior. p.* 497. *Nerli, Com. lib.* xi. *p.* 257. 264. Theſe diſtinctions are deſerving of notice, as they ſerve to show the gradual progreſs by which a free country is deprived of its liberties.

(*a*) The perſon who adminiſtered the poiſon was ſaid to be Giovan-Andrea di Borgo San Sepolcro, the ſteward or bailiff of Ippolito, who was ſuppoſed to have effected this treachery at the inſtance of Aleſſandro; and this ſuſpicion received confirmation by his having eſcaped puniſhment, although he confeſſed the crime; and by his having afterwards been received at the court of Aleſſandro at Florence.

Varchi, Storia Fior. p. 566.

descendants of Lorenzo the Magnificent, to the kindred stock. In the secure possession of power, Alessandro knew no restraint. Devoted to the indulgence of an amorous passion, he sought its gratification among women of all descriptions, married and unmarried, religious and secular; insomuch that neither rank nor virtue could secure the favorite object from his licentious rapacity (*a*). The spirit

(*a*) Notwithstanding the dissolute character of Alessandro, it appears that he was possessed of strong natural sagacity, and, on some occasions, administered justice not only with impartiality, but with ability. On this head, Ammirato relates an anecdote which is worth repeating: A rich old citizen of Bergamo had lent to one of his countrymen at Florence 400 crowns, which he advanced without any person being present, and without requiring a written acknowledgment. When the stipulated time had elapsed, the creditor required his money—but the borrower, well apprized that no proof could be brought against him, positively denied that he had ever received it. After many fruitless attempts to recover it, the lender was advised to resort to the duke, who would find some method of doing him justice. Alessandro accordingly ordered both the parties before him, and after hearing the assertions of the one and the positive denial of the other, he turned to the creditor, saying, "Is it possible then, friend, that you can have lent your money "when no one was present?"—"There was no one indeed," replied the creditor, "I counted out the money to him on a post."—"Go, "bring the post then this instant," said the duke, "and I will make it "confess the truth." The creditor, though astonished on receiving such an order, hastened to obey, having first received a secret caution from the duke not to be very speedy in his return. In the mean time the duke employed himself in transacting the affairs of his other suitors, till at length turning again towards the borrower, "This man," says he, "stays "a long time with his post."—"It is so heavy, sir," replied the other, "that he could not yet have brought it." Again Alessandro left him, and returning some time afterwards, carelessly exclaimed, "What kind "of men are they that lend their money without evidence—was there "no one present but the post?"—"No indeed, sir," replied the knave.

of the Florentines, though ſinking under the yoke of deſpotiſm, began to revolt at this more opprobrious ſpecies of tyranny, and the abſentees and malecontents became daily more numerous and more reſpectable. But whilſt the ſtorm was gathering in a remote quarter, a blow from a kindred hand unexpectedly freed the Florentines from their oppreſſor, and afforded them once more an opportunity of aſſerting that liberty to which their anceſtors had been ſo long devoted. Lorenzino de' Medici was the ſecond Brutus who burſt the bonds of conſanguinity in the expectation of being the deliverer of his country. But the principle of political virtue was now extinct, and it was no longer a ſubject of doubt whether the Florentines ſhould be enſlaved; it only remained to be determined who ſhould be the tyrant. On his return from Rome to Florence, Lorenzino had frequented the court of Aleſſandro, and, by his unwearied aſſiduity and ſingular accompliſhments, had ingratiated himſelf with the duke to ſuch a degree, as to become his chief confidant, and the aſſociate of his licentious amours. But whilſt Lorenzino accompanied him amidſt theſe ſcenes of diſſipation, he had formed the firm reſolution of accompliſhing his deſtruction, and ſought only for a favorable opportunity of effecting his purpoſe. This idea ſeems to have occupied his whole ſoul, and influenced all his conduct. Even in the warmth of familiarity

" The poſt is a good witneſs then," ſaid the duke, " and ſhall make " thee pay the man his money."

Ammir. Stor. Fior. lib. xxxi. *v.* iii. *p.* 434.

which apparently subsisted between them, he could not refrain from adverting to the design of which his mind was full, and by jests and insinuations gave earnest of his intention. Cellini relates, that on his attending the duke Alessandro with his portrait executed as a medal, he found him indisposed and reclined on his bed, with Lorenzino as his companion. After boasting, as was his custom, of the wonders which he could perform in his profession, the artist concluded with expressing his hopes; that Lorenzino would favor him with a subject for an apposite reverse. "That is exactly what I am think-"ing of," replied Lorenzino, with great vivacity; "I hope ere long to furnish such a reverse as will "be worthy of the duke, and will astonish the "world (*a*)." The blind confidence of Alessandro prevented his suspicions, and he turned on his bed with a contemptuous smile at the folly or the arrogance of his relation. But whilst Lorenzino thus hazarded the destruction of his enterprise by the levity of his discourse, he prepared for its execution with the most scrupulous caution (*b*). The duke having selected as the object of his passion the wife of Lionardo Ginori, then on a public embassy at Naples, Lorenzino, to whom she was nearly related, undertook with his usual assiduity to promote the suit. Pretending that his representations had been successful, he prevailed upon the duke to pass the

(*a*) *Vita di Benvenuto Cellini, p.* 222.

(*b*) The particulars of this transaction are related at great length by Varchi, who had his information from Lorenzino himself, after the perpetration of the deed. *Storia Fior. lib.* xv.

night with him at his own houſe, where he promiſed him the completion of his wiſhes. In the mean time he prepared a chamber for his reception; and having engaged as his aſſiſtant a man of deſperate fortunes and character, called Scoroncocolo, waited with impatience for his arrival. At the appointed hour, the duke having left the palace in a maſk, according to his cuſtom when he was engaged in nocturnal adventures, came unobſerved to the houſe of Lorenzino, and was received by him in the fatal chamber. After ſome familiar converſation, Lorenzino left him to repoſe on the bed, with promiſes of a ſpeedy return. On his quitting the chamber, he ſtationed his coadjutor where he might be in readineſs to aſſiſt him, in caſe he ſhould fail in his firſt attempt, and gently opening the door, approached the bed, and inquired from the duke if he was aſleep, at the ſame inſtant paſſing his ſword through his body. On receiving the wound the duke ſprang up and attempted to eſcape at the door; but, on a ſignal given by Lorenzino, he was attacked there by Scoroncocolo, who wounded him deeply in the face. Lorenzino then grappled with the duke, and throwing him on the bed, endeavoured to prevent his cries. In the ſtruggle the duke ſeized the finger of Lorenzino in his mouth, and retained it with ſuch violence, that Scoroncocolo, finding it impoſſible to ſeparate them ſo as to diſpatch the duke without danger of wounding Lorenzino, deliberately took a knife from his pocket, and cut him acroſs the throat. The completion of their purpoſe was however only the commencement of their difficulties. Scoroncocolo, who probably knew not that the person he had assassinated was the duke, until the transaction was over, was so terrified as to be wholly unable to judge for himself of the measures to be adopted for his own safety. To the active mind of Lorenzino various expedients presented themselves, and he hesitated for some time whether he should openly avow the deed, and call upon his countrymen to assert their liberties, or should endeavour to make his escape to the absentees, to whom the information which he had to communicate would give new energy, and a fair opportunity of success. Of these measures the last seemed on many accounts to be the most advisable. Having therefore locked the door of the chamber, in which he left the dead body of the duke, he proceeded secretly to Bologna, expecting there to meet with Filippo Strozzi, but finding that he had quitted that place, he followed him to Venice, where he related to him his achievements. Filippo, well acquainted with the eccentricity of his character, refused for some time to credit his story, till Lorenzino, producing the key of the chamber, and exhibiting his hand which had been mutilated in the contest, at length convinced him of its truth. The applause bestowed by Filippo and his adherents on Lorenzino, was in proportion to the incredulity which they had before expressed. He was saluted as another Brutus, as the deliverer of his country; and Filippo immediately began to assemble his adherents, in order to avail himself of so favorable an opportunity of reſtoring to the citizens of Florence their ancient rights (*a*).

The Italian hiſtorians have endeavoured to develope the motives that led Lorenzino to the perpetration of this deed, and have ſought for them in the natural malignity of his diſpoſition; as a proof of which he is ſaid to have acknowledged, that during his reſidence at Rome, notwithſtanding the kindneſs ſhown to him by Clement VII. he often felt a ſtrong inclination to murder him. They have alſo attributed them to a deſire of immortalizing his name by being conſidered as the deliverer of his country; to a principle of revenge for the inſult which he received from the pope, in being baniſhed from Rome, which he meant to repay in the perſon of Aleſſandro, his reputed ſon; and, laſtly, to his enmity to the collateral branch of the Medici family, by which he was excluded from the chief dignity of the ſtate. How far any of theſe conjectures may be well founded, it is not eaſy to determine. Human conduct is often the reſult of impulſes, which, whilſt they ariſe in various directions, determine the mind towards the ſame object, and poſſibly all, or moſt of the cauſes before ſtated, might have concurred in producing ſo ſignal an effect. Aware of the miſconſtruction to which his principles were liable, Lorenzino wrote an apologetical diſcourſe, which

(*a*) On this occaſion a medal was ſtruck, bearing on one ſide the head of Lorenzino, and on the other the cap of liberty between two daggers; being the ſame device as that which had before been adopted by, or applied to, the younger Brutus. *v. Palin. Famil. Rom. p.* 142. This medal is in the collection of the earl of Orford.

has been preſerved to the preſent times, and throws conſiderable light on this ſingular tranſaction. In this piece he firſt attempts to demonſtrate that Aleſſandro was an execrable tyrant, who, during the ſix years that he held the chief authority, had exceeded the enormities of Nero, of Caligula, and of Phalaris. He accuſes him of having occaſioned by poiſon the death, not only of the cardinal Ippolito, but of his own mother, who reſided in an humble ſtation at *Collevecchio*, and whoſe poverty he conceived was a reproach to the dignity of his rank; and denies that the blood of any branch of the Medici family flowed in his veins. He then juſtifies, with great plauſibility, the conduct adopted by him after the death of the duke, in quitting the city to join the abſentees; and after vindicating himſelf from the imputation of having been induced by any other motive than an earneſt deſire to liberate his country from a ſtate of intolerable ſervitude, he concludes with lamenting, that the want of energy and virtue in his fellow-citizens prevented them from availing themſelves of the opportunity which he had afforded them of re-eſtabliſhing their ancient government (*a*). But whatever were the motives of this deed, the conſequences of it were ſuch as have generally been the reſult of ſimilar attempts —the riveting of thoſe chains which it was intended to break. The natural abhorrence of treachery, and the ſentiment of pity excited for the devoted object, counteract the intended purpoſe, and throw an odium even on the cauſe of liberty itſelf. No end

(*a*) For the *Apologia* of Lorenzino, *v. App. No.* LXXXIV.

can justify the sacrifice of a principle, nor was a crime ever necessary in the course of human affairs. The sudden burst of vindictive passion may sometimes operate important changes on the fate of nations, but the event is seldom within the limits of human calculation. It is only the calm energy of reason, constantly bearing up against the encroachments of power, that can with certainty perpetuate the freedom, or promote the happiness of the human race.

After the perpetration of this deed, Lorenzino, not conceiving himself in safety within the limits of Italy, continued his route till he arrived at Constantinople, from whence, after a short residence, he returned again to Venice. Having passed eleven years of exile and anxiety, he was himself assassinated by two Florentine soldiers, who, under the pretext of avenging the death of Alessandro, probably sought to ingratiate themselves with his successor, by removing a person who derived from his birth undoubted pretensions to the credit and authority which had for ages been attached to the chief of the house of Medici.

The adherents of the ruling family, at the head of whom was the cardinal Cibò, who had been the chief minister of Alessandro, conducted themselves with great prudence on the death of the duke; and before they permitted the event to be made public, not only secured the soldiery within the city, but summoned to their assistance all their allies in the vicinity of the Florentine state. They then assembled the inhabitants, avowedly to deliberate on the state of the republic, but in fact rather to receive than to dictate a form of government. If Lorenzino was the Brutus of his age, an Octavius was found in his cousin, Cosmo de' Medici, the son of Giovanni, general of the *bande nere*, and then about eighteen years of age. Being informed of the unexpected disposition of the citizens in his favor, Cosmo hastened from his seat at Mugello to Florence, where, on the ninth day of January 1536, he was invested with the sovereignty by the more modest title of chief of the republic. Despotism generally proceeds with cautious steps, and Augustus and Cosmo affected the name of citizen, whilst they governed with absolute authority.

To the election of Cosmo little opposition had been made within the city. The proposition of Palias Rucellai, to admit the party of the Strozzi to their deliberations, and that of Giovanni Canigiani, to place the supreme command in an illegitimate and infant son of Alessandro, had met with few supporters (*a*). But the numerous exiles, who by compulsion, or in disgust, had quitted their native country during the government of Alessandro, had already begun to convene together from all parts of Italy, in hopes of effecting their restoration and of establishing a form of government more consistent with their views. The cardinals Ridolfi and

(*a*) Besides an illegitimate son named Giulio, Alessandro left two illegitimate daughters, Porcia and Juliet. The son entered into the church, and became grand prior of the order of S. Stefano. Porcia took the veil, and founded the convent of S. Clement at Florence. Juliet married Francesco Cantelmo, son of the duke di Popoli, a Neapolitan nobleman. *Tenh. Mém. Gén. liv.* xxii. *p.* 92.

Salviati, both grandſons of Lorenzo the Magnificent, Bartolomeo Valori, and other citizens of high rank, uniting with Filippo Strozzi, raiſed a conſiderable body of troops, and approached towards the city; but more powerful parties had already interpoſed, and the fate of Florence no longer depended on the virtue or the courage of its inhabitants, but on the will of the emperor, or on the precarious aid of the French. Senſible of the advantages which he had already obtained by holding at his devotion the Florentine ſtate, and that ſuch influence was inconſiſtent with a republican government, Charles V. openly approved of the election of Coſmo, and directed his troops, then in Italy, to ſupport his cauſe. The exiles having poſſeſſed themſelves of the fortreſs of *Montemurlo*, in the vicinity of Florence, were unexpectedly attacked there by the Florentine troops under the command of Aleſſandro Vitelli, in the night of the firſt of Auguſt 1538, and their defeat fixed the deſtiny of their country. Bartolomeo Valori, with his two ſons, and Filippo his nephew, were made priſoners, and conducted to Florence, where he, with one of his ſons, and his nephew, was decapitated. Many other of the inſurgents experienced a ſimilar fate. The reſt were conſigned to the dungeons in different parts of Tuſcany. Filippo Strozzi, the magnanimous aſſertor of the liberties of his county, languiſhed upwards of twelve months in the priſons of Caſtello, and his ſituation became more hopeleſs in proportion as the authority of Coſmo became more eſtabliſhed. After an interval of time which ought to have obliterated the remembrance of his offence, he was cruelly ſubjected to torture, under the pretext of diſcovering the accomplices of his unfortunate enterpriſe. Finding that the remonſtrances of his friends with the emperor and the duke were not only ineffectual, but that the latter had reſolved to expoſe his fortitude to a ſecond trial, he called to his mind the example of Cato of Utica, and fell by his own hand, a devoted victim to the cauſe of freedom (*a*).

Thus terminated the Florentine republic, which had ſubſiſted amidſt the agitations of civil commotions, and the ſhock of external attacks, for upwards of three centuries, and had produced from its circumſcribed territory a greater number of eminent men than any other country in Europe. This ſingular pre-eminence is chiefly to be attributed to the nature of its government, which called forth the talents of every rank of citizens, and admitted them without diſtinction to the chief offices of the ſtate. But the ſplendor which the Florentines derived from examples of public virtue, and efforts of ſuperlative genius, was frequently tarniſhed by the ſanguinary conteſts of rival parties. The benevolent genius of Lorenzo de' Medici for a time removed this reproach, and combined a ſtate of high intellectual improvement with the tranquillity of well-ordered government. The various purſuits in which he himſelf engaged appear indeed to have been ſubſervient only

(*a*) The life of Filippo Strozzi was written by his brother Lorenzo, with great candor and impartiality, and is publiſhed at the cloſe of the Florentine hiſtory of Benedetto Varchi. *Ed. Leyd. ſine an.* After the death of Filippo, a paper in his own hand-writing was found in his boſom, which is given in the Appendix, *No.* LXXXV.

to the great purpose of humanizing and improving his countrymen. His premature death left the common wealth without a pilot, and after a long series of agitation, the hapless wreck became a rich unexpected prize to Cosmo de' Medici. With Cosmo, who afterwards assumed the title of grand duke, commences a dynasty of sovereigns, which continued in an uninterrupted succession until the early part of the present century, when the sceptre of Tuscany passed from the imbecile hands of Gaston de' Medici, into the stronger grasp of the family of Austria. During the government of Cosmo, the talents of the Florentines, habituated to great exertions, but suddenly debarred from further interference with the direction of the state, sought out new channels, and displayed themselves in works of genius and of art, which threw a lustre on the sovereign, and gave additional credit to the new establishment; but as those who were born under the republic retired in the course of nature, the energies of the Florentines gradually declined. Under the equalizing hand of despotism, whilst the diffusion of literature was promoted, the exertions of original genius were suppressed. The numerous and illustrious families, whose names had for ages been the glory of the republic, the Soderini, the Strozzi, the Ridolfi, the Ruccellai, the Valori, and the Capponi, who had negotiated with monarchs, and operated by their personal characters on the politics of Europe, sunk at once to the uniform level of subjects, and became the subordinate and domestic officers of the ruling family. From this time the history of

Florence is the hiſtory of the alliances, the negotiations, the virtues, or the vices, of its reigning prince; and even towards theſe the annals of the times furniſh but ſcanty documents. The Florentine hiſtorians, as if unwilling to perpetuate the records of their ſubjugation, have almoſt invariably cloſed their labors with the fall of the republic, and the deſire of information fortunately terminates where the want of it begins.

INDEX.

N. B. *The Roman Numerals refer to the Volume, and the Figures to the Page.*

A.

B.

INDEX.

Dante,

D.

E.

F.

G.

INDEX.

N.

O.

P.

T.

U.

V.

Z.

END OF THE SECOND VOLUME.

www.ingramcontent.com/pod-product-compliance
Lightning Source LLC
Chambersburg PA
CBHW060513030726
47498CB00004B/930

* 9 7 8 3 7 4 2 8 9 5 2 4 0 *